Praise for *An Honourable Thief*

'Fast, furious and with a hint of gallows humour. This is high-octane historical fiction'
  Daily Mail

'I loved this book. Swashbuckling action against a vivid historical backdrop. Heroic heroes and venomous villains'
  Ian Rankin

'A pacy and thoroughly engrossing thriller packed with intrigue, action and character'
  The Herald

'An absolute triumph. Five stars from me'
  James Oswald

'A tremendous entry into the world of historical fiction, a swash-buckling adventure of Jacobites and Hanoverians that takes us from the dens and alleyways of London, to the wynds and closes of Edinburgh in the company of the charismatic Jonas Flynt and a host of engaging friends and ne'er-do-wells'
  S.G. MacLean, author of *The Seeker*

'Gritty and gripping, this bold new novel evokes the best of Robert Louis Stevenson. High adventure meets espionage thriller as Jonas Flynt battles the tide of history, a dangerous femme fatale and the deadly secrets of his own past...'
  D. V. Bishop, author of *City of Vengeance*

'Reads like a genuine eighteenth century spy novel. Reeks of authenticity. I see a long future for Jonas Flynt'

Ambrose Parry, author of *The Way of All Flesh*

'*An Honourable Thief* uniquely combines a page-turning thriller with a perfectly evoked sense of time and place. Powerful stuff from a master of his craft'

Craig Russell, author of *Hyde*

'The richness of Douglas Skelton's prose brings the 18th century vividly to life in this tale of intrigue and inheritance. Historical crime fiction at its absolute best. I loved it!'

Marion Todd, author of *Old Bones Lie*

'Hugely enjoyable. Skelton's mastery of time and place inhabited with richly drawn characters is a delight. It held me to the last tantalising page'

David Gilman, author of *The Englishman*

'Jonas Flynt is one of those characters you'll be rooting for from the very first chapter – he may be a rogue, but he lives by his own strict code of honour. The twists and turns of the plot are played out against a stunning and authentic evocation of 18th century Edinburgh, with plenty of well-researched period details – it looks like Skelton has found a new home writing first-class historical fiction'

Alison Belsham, author of *The Tattoo Thief*

'Join Jonas Flynt and be transported to the 18th century. It's pitch-perfect stuff. Like all great historical novels you'll feel you're there! This is a departure for Skelton, who seems born to write high-end historical fiction'

Denzil Meyrick, author of the D. C. I. Daley Thrillers

'This is a fascinating, totally engrossing historical novel. Flynt is a most attractive, three-dimensional character and the same is true of the world he moves through. A brilliant, most enjoyable read'
    Paul Doherty, author of *The Nightingale Gallery*

'A cracking historical drama with breathless pacing and knuckle-chewing tension, all shot through with Skelton's deft characterisation and flashes of pitch-black humour. The perfect read to lose yourself in'
    Neil Broadfoot, author of *Falling Fast*

'In Jonas Flynt – the bastard son of Blackbeard and James Bond – we have an engaging and complex hero strong enough to carry any tale. *An Honourable Thief* is a real old school page-turner.'
    Michael J Malone, author of *After He Died*

'*An Honourable Thief* is brilliantly imagined and impressively written, with a faultless grasp of period and place – a gripping read from first page to last'
    R. N. Morris, author of *Summon Up the Blood*

'A compelling tale of justice and vengeance, of intrigue and plotting, all centred around a flawed eighteenth-century Jack Reacher'
    Morgan Cry, author of *Thirty-One Bones*

'A charismatic hero tangles with Jacobite intrigue and his own troubled memories in this fast-paced and multi-layered historical thriller set in London and Edinburgh'
    Maggie Craig, author of *The River Flows On*

An Honourable Thief

Douglas Skelton has published twelve non fiction books and ten crime thrillers. He has been a bank clerk, tax officer, shelf stacker, meat porter, taxi driver (for two days), wine waiter (for two hours), reporter, investigator and local newspaper editor. *Thunder Bay*, a dark and atmospheric tale of secrets, lies and murder on a Scottish island, was published to great acclaim in 2019, and was longlisted for the McIlvanney Prize. Douglas contributes to true crime shows on TV and radio and is a regular on the crime writing festival circuit.

Also by Douglas Skelton

A Company of Rogues

An Honourable Thief
A Thief's Justice

DOUGLAS SKELTON

An Honourable Thief

CANELO

First published in the United Kingdom in 2022 by Canelo

This edition published in the United Kingdom in 2023 by

Canelo
Unit 9, 5th Floor
Cargo Works, 1-2 Hatfields
London SE1 9PG
United Kingdom

A CIP catalogue record for this book is available from the British Library.

Ebook ISBN 978 1 80436 014 9
Royal Hardback ISBN 978 1 80436 015 6
B Format MMP ISBN 978 1 80436 302 7

This book is a work of fiction. Names, characters, businesses, organizations, places and events are either the product of the author's imagination or are used fictitiously. Any resemblance to actual persons, living or dead, events or locales is entirely coincidental.

Cover design by Henry Steadman

Cover images © Alamy

Look for more great books at www.canelo.co

Printed and bound in Great Britain by Clays Ltd, Elcograf S.p.A.

Prologue

The sound of breathing seemed to fill rooms, escape into corridors, tumble down staircases, echo from wainscotting and mouldings. Colonel Nathaniel Charters felt he could not escape its harshness. It was as if each rasping intake of air, each groaning exhalation, had permeated his brain until he found himself unconsciously matching his own breath to it. He stood in the doorway of the darkened receiving room adjoining the bedchamber from which the sounds emanated, staring at the man illuminated by the dying glow of the coals in the fireplace. He rested in a comfortable chair, his head against its high back, his wig slightly askew, a glass bearing the vestige of what had once been a large brandy in danger of slipping from his loose grip. His eyes were closed, his brow furrowed, his free hand cupping one ear as if he was trying to somehow block the noise, but it would be as etched in the mind of Charles Talbot, Duke of Shrewsbury, as indelibly as it was in Charters' own. He wagered they would hear it even after she had breathed her last.

A servant entered and swept the heavy curtains aside to allow a burst of daylight into the room. Charters moved to the window and stared at the new-born day. In the gardens, birds sang and plants and trees awoke to the warmth of the summer sun. Life began again after the long sleep of night, but not in these rooms. Here death croaked and coughed with every breath from the chamber beyond.

He turned away from the window to find that Shrewsbury had fixed his one good eye on him. It was said that he saw more with that single orb than many did with two.

'Colonel Charters,' he said, his voice low.

Charters gave him a slight bow. 'My apologies, Lord High Treasurer, I did not mean to disturb you.'

The duke waved the apology away, then reached up to scratch at his scalp before straightening his wig. 'I was merely taking what ease I could.' His gaze drifted towards the bedchamber door then back again as he repeated Charters' words. 'Lord High Treasurer. I have not yet become used to the title. Politics, Colonel, has been my curse. If I had a son I would sooner bind him to a cobbler than a courtier, and a hangman than a statesman.'

Charters understood the exhaustion in Shrewsbury's voice, for he had been appointed to the highest office in the land a scant two days before. Her Majesty Queen Anne had bowed to pressure from her ministers to place the realm in a steady hand before she sank into the darkness in which she now lay. His Grace had held many offices in the tumultuous years since the Glorious Revolution and had done his best to antagonise neither Tory nor Whig. Despite switching from one party to the other, he had always adhered to his own sense of honour. In politics, though, even an honourable man can have enemies, and they had often spoken against him. Yet, in these dark times, it was he to whom they turned.

Shrewsbury returned his attention to Charters. 'You have news?'

'I regret no, Your Grace. We have read through every paper, rifled every drawer, turned out every closet in the palace but there is no sign of it.'

Shrewsbury did not look surprised but his weariness seemed to deepen.

Charters asked, 'Your Grace, how certain are we of the document's existence?'

'We are not, that's the damnation of it all. We have those who say they have seen it, writ by the queen's own hand, and assert that she kept it with a bundle she had about her person at all times, but that is all.'

'And yet it was not among that bundle of papers found under her pillow.'

'No,' said the duke with a heavy sigh. 'But, Colonel Charters, we will continue in our pursuit of it, for we must leave nothing to chance. The future of the nation might well depend upon it.'

Shrewsbury stood and arched his back, stretching his arms, then drained what was left of the brandy from the glass. Charters assumed it had been drawn from Her Majesty's own bottle, one of many, for it was not for nothing they called her Brandy Nan. Charters had seldom been in the company of Queen Anne. His shadowy trade was not something a monarch would wish to be a part of, even though many dark deeds were done in her name, but he knew Shrewsbury would not have presumed to sample the liquor had she been conscious. It was known her tongue could flay and her gaze incinerate. Her Majesty was beyond such cares, though, for she was now little more than a mountain under bedclothes in that room, all but dead apart from the guttural gasp of her breath, unaware she was attended by her ladies-in-waiting, doctors and a murmur of clergy.

The sound of distant hooves reached his ears. Another messenger. There had been many of them throughout the night, taking despatches hither and yon, alerting the country to the impending death of their monarch. It was not a question of *if*, but *when*. Inevitable, Charters had overheard one of the doctors state. But whether the monarch was alive or dead, his responsibility was the security of the nation and he would be as diligent in performing that duty as he would be if she were healthy, perhaps more so, for there were indeed many dangers threatening England.

Shrewsbury's head turned to the window at the sound of the horse. 'To Edinburgh,' he said. 'They must prepare for any insurrection from the Jacobites.'

He spoke without rancour, for in his political career he had striven to remain as neutral, as even-handed, as possible. His contemporaries had seen it as a weakness, something to mock, but here he was, still standing – and in possession of the white staff of high office – while many of them languished in the political wilderness. That said, there had been those enemies who suggested he was Jacobite at heart.

Shrewsbury laid the empty glass on a table then peered through the open door into the gloom beyond. Charters could hear voices from within, doctors consulting, ladies whispering, divines praying. And over it all that stentorian breathing, the calloused, discordant sound of a life ebbing away.

In. Out.

In. Out.

'They shaved her head, did you know that?'

'I did not, Your Grace.'

'Yes,' Shrewsbury said, sadness heavy in his voice. 'God knows the poor woman has suffered enough over the years without that. I'm sure you heard the rumours about her death two years ago.'

'I did, Your Grace, and I was grateful they were unfounded.'

'Aye, as we all were. She had been ill, some kind of brain seizure, and it resulted in a twisting and discolouration of her face somehow. 'Twas deemed expedient to use paint to disguise the changes to her features.'

'I did not know that.'

'Few did, for it was never so much as whispered let alone commented upon. But in these few hours she has suffered further ignominy. They applied hot irons to her flesh to make it blister, can you imagine that?'

'For what purpose?'

The ringlets of Shrewsbury's wig shook. 'I know not. A doctor's ways are mysterious. They wrapped her feet in garlic and bled her and forced her to vomit. They gave her laudanum and brandy for the pain.' He paused, listening for a moment.

In. Out.

In. Out.

4

Shrewsbury took a deep breath of his own. 'I sometimes believe that our learned medical men are but a short step away from witches and warlocks weaving spells.'

'We are all but an inch from eternity, Your Grace.'

Shrewsbury turned away from the bedchamber door. 'Some of us engineer to avoid moving closer,' he said, nodding towards Charters' empty sleeve. 'You lost your arm at Malplaquet?'

Charters nodded, recalling for a moment the agony of the surgeon's blade slicing into flesh, sawing through bone. 'I was fortunate to be dragged from the field in time to save my life, if not my limb. Many men were not so fortunate.'

Shrewsbury pursed his lips. 'Succession can be a bloody business. You lost an arm, you lost men, to protect Spain from French influence. We, at this moment, endeavour to prevent further bloodshed here at home.' He glanced again at the open doorway. 'Would that barren plain had borne a healthy crop. Had there been a rightful heir we would not now be in this position.'

His tone was neither bitter nor reproving but gentle. He wished a different life for the queen, for her many pregnancies had resulted in only three children, with just one surviving infancy.

'Had there been an heir we would not now be destined to have a German as King,' said Charters. 'And one for whom Her Majesty herself had little time.'

The words forced Shrewsbury to face him once more, a wry smile playing on his lips. 'You disapprove of a German ruling England, Colonel Charters?'

'It is not my place to disapprove, sir.'

'You would rather a Stuart return to the throne?'

'A Stuart is on the throne, Your Grace.'

'But not a Roman Catholic. And not for much longer, I fear.'

'No, Your Grace.'

'And so we must continue our search.'

'And if we find it?'

Shrewsbury's one good eye was unwavering. 'If it is found then it must be destroyed, for its mere existence throws the entire stability of our nation into peril.'

'And if it has already been smuggled from the palace?'

'Then I fear it will be on the first tide for the Continent and thence to the Pretender.'

'If it exists.'

'Yes, *if* it exists.'

And at that moment the breathing stopped.

It did not soften. It did not fade. One second it was there, and then it was not. The two men regarded each other in the sudden silence. Nothing was said, for to speak might be in some way disrespectful.

The door to the bedchamber swung open and the angular figure of Dr Arbuthnot appeared, his face drawn, his wig in his hand as he used a cloth to wipe at his scalp. He looked first at Shrewsbury, then past him to Charters, his eye flicking with unconscious professional interest over the empty sleeve of his coat. His voice was solemn when he addressed the Lord High Treasurer. 'Your Grace, it is with regret that I inform you that Her Majesty the Queen has left us.'

Shrewsbury said nothing, merely nodded and lowered his gaze.

The physician cocked his head for a moment, as if straining to hear further breathing from within the bedchamber, but the only sounds were the prayers of the clergy and the soft sobs of the ladies. 'I believe sleep was never more welcome to a weary traveller than death was to her.'

Shrewsbury nodded his understanding. The queen's life had not been an easy one. 'I will have word sent immediately to Whitehall and to the Hanoverian ambassador.'

Such matters were not Arbuthnot's concern and he merely gave them a curt nod, replaced his wig then stepped back into the room behind him, this time fastening the door. To Charters, it was as if he was shutting them off from the past, forcing them to look to the future.

Shrewsbury stared at the closed door, as if gathering his thoughts. Charters allowed him a moment. Finally, His Grace spoke. 'How certain are you that we shall not find it?'

'As certain as any man could be.'

Shrewsbury pursed his lips. 'Then we must bide our time and hope that its existence is little more than gossip.'

'And if it is not?'

'Then it will surface, or it will not.'

'If it does surface?'

Shrewsbury's eye was firm and steady. 'If it does, my dear colonel, we shall have need of you... and your Company of Rogues.'

Part One

London, October 1715

1

They called it Satan's Gullet, and with good reason, for those unwary enough to step into it alone often did not step out again with their purse, virtue or person intact. St Giles entire was no leafy glade, but the Gullet was a hellhole. It did not deter Bess from walking it every night, for it was the quickest way between Covent Garden and her lodgings. She was known here so she felt little fear.

She looked forward to reaching her room, even though it was a poxy little box in a god-rotting tenement at the far end of the alley. Once there she would recline on her bed, always reasonably clean, she saw to that, and lose herself in the bottle she had just purchased from one of the many gin shops in the vicinity. After a night of satisfying the lusts of a variety of culls in the Garden she needed the spirit to wash out her mouth and throat, to erode the memory of hands, both filthy and sweet-scented, touching every part of her body. Men, women, old, young. They were all the same to her. She might be used to such treatment – it was how she made her living – but she still liked to salve her body and her soul with liquor.

The alleyway was ill lit and narrow, a ridge down its centre carrying sewage and garbage thrown there by denizens of the tall buildings on either side. It would rot there until the next heavy rainfall swept it away. Its stench, like those of the culls she rutted, rubbed and, when she was desperate, robbed, was so much a part of her life that she barely noticed it.

The man, though, she did notice, and the sight of him instilled fear. The tall figure stood in the shadow of a doorway with a skinny boy at his side. The lad, too, was familiar for she had often seen him around the Garden. A sly little buz cove, he was, and a cull never felt his touch as his purse was lifted. He was a cocky one and she had caught him more than once eyeing her apple dumplings, but he had not the bunce to pay for a taste.

The man, though, the man.

She most certainly knew the cove for she had seen him in the taverns and gambling dens around the Garden and beyond. He dressed like a Puritan, his long greatcoat, his breeches, his knee-length boots all black. The cane in his right hand was a flash of silver, and his wide-brimmed hat was brown and adorned by a peacock feather which she always thought unusual. Underneath that hat she knew his dark hair was close-cropped, for she had never seen him favour a wig at the gaming tables as he took bunce from dandies who were out of their depth. He wasn't a sharper but he could turn the boards and throw a dice with uncanny skill. She had heard talk of the other side of him, the side that she suspected was employed this night, for there was no gaming profit to be made in Satan's Gullet. Whatever business he had in this alley of the damned was not something she need be a part of, so she told herself it was best to get home, girl, and don't dawdle. Bess hurried her gait, clutching her bottle of liquid salvation close to her bosom.

—

The boy watched her scuttle away, at only thirteen already capable of appreciating the female form, because a lad grew up fast in the streets. Bess, they called her, Edgeworth Bess, though he knew it was not her real name. She was only two years older than him but her face had aged before its time. Still, he would not mind the chance to dance the goat's jig with her when he had the coin. Her profession mattered nothing to him, for most of the women he knew were harlots, apart from those who visited the draper's shop of Mr William Kneebone in the Strand, where he lived and worked. If his employer found him missing this night there would be hell to pay, but young Jack loved the streets, even pisshole back alleys like this one between hell and gone.

The voice of the man beside him forced his mind from any lascivious thoughts and back to the matter at hand. The man spoke softly, his Scotch accent not strong but still there. 'How many in there, Jack?'

'I seen three go in, Mr Flynt,' Jack replied, his slight stammer never evident when he was with him. 'Couple what looks like mumpers, both had campaign coats, but could be rufflers. Dunno how many was already in the crib.'

He watched as Jonas Flynt studied the doorway opposite. It was the street entrance to a decrepit-looking tenement of brick and wood which seemed in danger of momentary collapse. Jack had heard of the fire of 1666 and knew that many structures were thrown up and were prone to collapsing with little warning. St Giles, being beyond the city wall, had been untouched by the flames so this building was crumbling due to age and lack of care, rather than overly hasty construction work.

'Do you know where they went once inside?'

'Course I does, Mr Flynt, you take me for an addle-pated ninnyhammer? I followed them in, cased the crib for you, saw them go into the basement.'

'And did you see their upright man?'

'No sign of him, Mr Flynt, but the rogues I saw looked like hard coves. For their upright man to keep them in line he needs to be even harder and you needs to be careful in your dealings with 'em.'

'I am always careful, Jack.' Flynt reached into the pocket of his coat and withdrew a coin. 'You head back to your bed before old Kneebone notices you are gone.'

The boy peered at the coin, saw it was a croker and his heart leaped. A groat was more than enough to get his wick dipped. There were doxies out there who would do anything for four pennies, maybe even Edgeworth Bess, and still have some left over for a swig or six of gin.

'Mr Flynt, you're a decent cove.' He thrust the money in his own pocket and glanced once more at the door. 'They got a lock on that door to the basement, Mr Flynt, I saw it myself. You got a dub?'

'I have no need for a lockpick.'

'So what will you do? Just knock on the door and ask to be let in? I doesn't see that working, I really doesn't.'

Flynt was still studying the door. 'Don't worry, Jack, I will employ Tact and Diplomacy...'

The outer door was unlocked, Jack had seen to that. Flynt glanced back to ensure the boy had done as he was told. He was a bit wild, and his penchant for thievery added to his youthful eye for women would get him in trouble before he was much older, but at heart he was a good lad and Flynt did what he could to look out for him.

The corridor beyond was in darkness, which suited Flynt. He closed the door then paused and listened. Somewhere a man coughed, a great rasping hack, and a baby began crying, followed by a woman's scold, whether to the infant or the cougher he knew not. Ahead he heard scratching at the floor as tiny claws scuttled away. Rats. How many he could only guess, for he would not risk a lantern even if he had one with him. He had no love for the creatures but he pushed them from his mind with a shudder, for he knew there were larger foes in this place.

He thought about the three men Jack had seen. 'Mumpers' or 'rufflers', the lad had said, using the thieves cant in which he was fluent. So they had looked like beggars judging by their clothes, but could just as easily have been legitimately wounded soldiers or merely claiming to be. Jack had not thought any of them a leader, though. The upright man would have been an easy spot for a sharp-eyed child of the streets such as he. So that meant there could be at least four men in the basement, the door to which Flynt had now found in the gloom at the foot of a short flight of steps. It was a decent portal for a hovel like this but still far from quality. At any rate, it was only as strong as the lock and on inspection that was a shoddy piece of work. He leaned in, his ears straining to catch any sound from within. He detected indistinct voices but could not discern how many. He could be walking into an army of rogues for all he knew, but the dice had been thrown. All of life was a wager and he had never shirked from one yet.

He peeled back the front of his greatcoat, thrust the silver cane into his broad belt and drew the two pistols free. They had been made specially for him and were perfectly weighted for his hands. He had used many weapons since leaving Edinburgh years before but none had ever felt as much part of his whole as these. Tact fitted easily in his left hand and Diplomacy in his right. Together they had served him well.

The weapons held high in both hands, barrels upwards, he took a step backwards, his body tingling with anticipation, every nerve ready to respond should someone of a sudden emerge from the basement. He felt something brushing past the toe of his boot but he swallowed back his revulsion and ignored it.

A deep breath.

Out again.

His stomach broiled like a raging sea and a tremble vibrated along his arms to quiver the pistols but he forced his flesh and muscles to still. He took another breath and held it for a moment longer than usual, waited for the turmoil that beset his gut to settle. He focused on the doorway, tried to visualise what lay beyond. He had to be vigilant, ready for anything, prepared to improvise. He took a third breath, a deep one, retained it even longer than the last. The trembling in his hands stopped. He closed his eyes briefly and allowed the air to seep from his lungs.

He was ready.

Raising his right leg, he rammed the sole of his boot against the door just below the metal handle. The shoddy lock broke with the first kick, the wood splintering with a crack. He sprang into a room lit by two candles on a table, their light glinting from the running sewer down the centre of the floor. The stench was like a hand grasping his throat, making him wish he'd had the foresight to wrap his kerchief around his mouth and nose. No matter, he had work to do. In the split second after his entrance he surveyed his surroundings and counted five men and the boy, tied to a chair. One, wearing the campaign coat Jack had mentioned, sprang at him from the right, a cudgel raised. Flynt crouched, triggered Diplomacy while also aiming and firing Tact at a second man lurching towards him from the left. He had loaded large calibre manstopper balls and at this range they tore bloody holes in flesh and sent his attackers spinning into the gloom.

A burly rogue who Flynt knew instinctively was the upright man darted behind the boy in the chair. The remainder of the band, one with a cheek puckered by a ragged scar, the other a lad barely older than Jack, his face white with fear, had been frozen in place by the suddenness of Flynt's entrance.

The upright man tilted the boy's head back and laid a knife blade to his neck. The boy was gagged and bound but Flynt saw the terror scream in his eyes. His firepower had been exhausted and he would not have time to reload, so he slowly straightened and thrust the pistols back into his belt. The men watched him as he held up his right hand in a placating manner while he eased his silver cane free with his left to let it dangle at his side. They knew not how much their inactivity at this juncture would cost them.

'Let us take our ease here, boys,' he said.

The upright man sneered. 'Take our ease? You say that after you have murdered two of my fellows?'

His voice bore traces of culture and Flynt surmised he had been born to some comfort but had somehow fallen on harsh times.

'I did not come here to kill,' asserted Flynt, even though in his heart he had known there would be no other outcome to this night's adventure.

'And yet, there they lie.' The man jerked the boy's hair and dimpled the flesh of his throat with the blade but did not draw blood. 'And here we are.'

Flynt allowed his hand to lower slightly. 'Let us not be hasty here, my friend. Just give me the lad and there will be no need for further loss of life.'

The man laughed. 'If there is to be loss of life it will not be that of any of my remaining crew, you can take my oath on that, damn your blood. For we are three to your one and you no longer have the advantage of surprise.'

Flynt smiled, taking a single step closer. 'Surprise can come in many forms.'

'Yes, it can,' agreed the man as he shot a look at Scarface, who took it as a signal to move. He leaped at Flynt, a knife held high ready to strike. He was fast on his feet, very fast, but Flynt was faster. He gripped the handle of his stick, twisted and pulled free the long, thin blade secreted within. He spun away from the thrust of the man's dagger, twirled and slashed the rapier across his throat.

'Surprise,' he hissed.

Scarface's free hand dabbed at the wound and he stumbled back a pace or two, gazing at the blood on his fingers as if puzzled over how it got there. What had been a thin trickle from the wound soon became a dark torrent, and the man looked down as it soaked his coat then regarded Flynt again, his face reflecting both the knowledge and terror of death. He tried to speak but could manage only a bloody gargle before he pitched forward, his face splashing into a pool on the dirt floor, his blood becoming one with the filth.

Flynt whirled to face the young man, who was staring at his former comrade in horror.

'Do for him, Nate,' urged the leader, and the youth's face first jerked in his direction, then back to Flynt. He too had a knife and he began to raise it but the movement was slowed by indecision.

'Don't listen to him, lad,' said Flynt. 'You don't want to die, not for this doomed venture.'

The boy could not have been many years older than Jack, Flynt judged. He was still fresh-faced but where Jack's eyes sparkled with good humour and a lust for life, Nate's carried the shadow of knowledge that his existence was mired in the filth that surrounded him in this dingy basement.

'Look what he did to our friends, Nate,' said the upright man. 'Do for him.'

The youth cast a glance at the bodies of his erstwhile friends, then at Flynt once more. Fear rose from him over the stench of the ordure on the floor. He shook his head, as if trying to clear the terror from his mind, but it did not move.

'Go, Nate,' Flynt pleaded, deliberately using the boy's name. He wanted him to at least have a chance at life, ugly and squalid though it may turn out to be. 'Leave this place. Leave it now.'

Nate swallowed, his eyes falling to the knife in his hand as if someone had placed it there without his knowledge. He lowered the weapon and edged towards the door. 'I am sorry, Gus.'

Flynt suppressed a smile, not only because it meant Nate had made the correct decision, but because he now knew the upright man's name, which put him at a further advantage.

'You goddamned cur, Nate Hopkins,' Gus growled but made no move to stop him from leaving. Flynt did not expect him to, for the boy under his knife was the villain's only bargaining chip and he was not about to relinquish it.

Nate had apparently seen the wisdom of retreat so Flynt did not hinder him, but his senses were alert. He retained his focus on the leader while listening to the young man's movements behind him. But a flicker of triumph in Gus's eyes and a footfall at his back saddened him, for it told him that the boy's acquiescence had been a feint. That, or misplaced loyalty had spurred a change of heart. Flynt's sorrow was not sufficient, though, to prevent him from taking action. He swung his thin blade up and under his arm, thrusting it back until he heard Nate suck in a sharp breath as the steel slid through cloth and flesh that offered no resistance at all.

Flynt jerked the sword free, heard the boy stagger backwards, his steps splashing in the sludge underfoot, then there was a single groan and the crumple of his body hitting the dirt. Flynt had no need to turn to confirm the boy was out of action. He stared hard at Gus. It was between them now.

'Looks like the odds have evened.'

Gus jerked his captive's head back with considerable force, prompting a moan of pain. 'I think not. I still have him and will bleed him dry before you reach me with that fancy sword of yours.'

Flynt was well aware of how the cards had been dealt and needed time to consider how he played his next hand, whatever it would be. This was the part of the game he loved. The mystery. The gamble of it. All in or not at all.

'Do you like it?' he said, studying the blade himself. 'It's German steel, hollow ground blade. Quite illegal but I find it useful.'

'I prefer good English steel.'

'Of course you do. I am sure you are a good Englishman and yet you are involved in the abduction of an innocent lad. I am a Scot, but I do wonder if that is the English way?'

A small laugh from Gus but Flynt heard the nervousness behind it. 'It is a living.'

Flynt's gaze did not waver. 'It will be a death sentence.'

For the first time unease flashed in the man's eyes and he looked to his dead comrades then beyond Flynt to the door. There was a sharp intelligence working there and Flynt knew what he was calculating.

'Let me help you, Gus,' he said, as if they were conversing in a salon over a glass of wine. 'You can't get past me to the door, I think you know that. Even if you let the boy go, you know I'll not let you live. I could tell you I will, I could promise you safe passage, but we are both men of violence and you would know I am lying. Your life is forfeit because of poor Nate back there. You should have allowed him to go from this place without urging him to do what he did. However, I also am certain that if I were to rush you, the boy would die. Am I correct in my assessment?'

'You are correct, with the exception of the certainty of my death.'

Flynt allowed a smile to twitch his lips. 'We shall see.'

Gus's confidence wavered further as he shifted his stance slightly and licked his lips. 'We are at an impasse then?'

Yes, Gus was definitely not born of these streets. No one from St Giles would use such a word.

'Perhaps,' said Flynt. 'Do you know chess?'

Gus nodded once, but the question had not been directed at him. Flynt hoped the boy in the chair was paying attention and not totally paralysed by terror.

'The way this game stands, we are at a stalemate. I fired two shots but here in the Gullet the men of the watch are unlikely to investigate, not while it's dark. So here we stand, neither able to move, neither able to seize the advantage.' He paused for a quick smile. 'The boy is but a pawn. If I move, I sacrifice him. If you move, you sacrifice yourself. But there is something that players forget about pawns.'

Flynt allowed himself to lapse into silence as his eyes found the captive's. Gus filled that silence, as Flynt hoped he would. 'And what is that?'

Flynt fixed his gaze upon the boy in the chair. 'That pawns can move. They can also take pieces on the board. And, in this game only, they can move backwards.'

He prayed the boy understood before Gus could comprehend. He prayed the boy had some courage. He prayed the boy had the heart of a gamester.

His prayers were answered.

The boy rocked back on the chair, which was already teetering on its two back legs under Gus's harsh treatment. The move caught Gus unawares and he lost his grasp of the lad's hair, being left with only a few strands between his fingers.

As soon as he saw Gus's focus shift, albeit slightly, Flynt was in motion. He surged forward, leaping over the upturning chair legs and pushing the man back against the rear wall. Gus recovered sufficiently to raise his knife but Flynt clamped his left hand round his wrist and held it fast against the brickwork while his right slid the sword blade in and up below the man's ribs. Gus's eyes widened and his fingers slackened on the hilt of his weapon, letting it fall. He struggled but Flynt thrust his steel deeper. A high-pitched scream grew in the man's throat and his eyes bulged as he bucked and trembled, his free hand beating weakly at Flynt's coat as blood bubbled from his mouth. One final thrust and the last traces of life left him in a gore-frothed sigh. The body slumped against Flynt's, the head drooping to one side, blood trailing from his chin and jaw like red ribbons. He let him slide to the floor, sheathed his weapon then picked up the man's knife and moved to the boy. He loosened the gag and cut at the bonds.

'Are you hurt?'

'Only my head, where he tugged at my hair.' The lad's voice shook with fear and his skin was pale. Once the ropes were cut, Flynt helped him to his feet, checking for signs of injury nonetheless. He nodded in satisfaction when he perceived no wounds or bruises. At least the rogues had not had sport with the lad.

The boy stared at him. 'Who are you, sir?'

'Who I am is of no consequence.'

'It is to me, sir.' He waited for an answer, and seeing none was forthcoming, displayed a flash of irritation. 'Damn you, sir, you will not at least give me your name?'

How quickly the gentry show their true faces, Flynt thought. 'All you need know is that *you* breathe while *they* do not.'

The boy's eyes flicked to the bodies strewn around them, then he asked, 'Did my father send you?'

'Indirectly,' said Flynt, studying Gus's knife. It was a sturdy blade, a fine piece of work. He dropped it in the pocket of his coat just as a groan reached him from across the room. He tensed, his hand on the handle of his sword again, but relaxed when he saw the weak movement of Nate's leg. He stepped across the noisome flow of sewage and stood over the young man, whose eyes bore a look that Flynt had seen many times, that of a soul staring into a darkness that would never end.

'Kill him,' said the boy at his side.

'He is killed already,' said Flynt, kneeling beside the stricken Nate and pushing a strand of hair back from his forehead. His flesh was cold.

'He is a villain and must die,' insisted the boy.

'And he will. There is no need for me to hurry it along.'

Nate's hand rose, the fingers shaking as if palsied. 'I don't want to die,' he said, blood bursting forth along with the words. 'Not alone.'

Flynt did not reflect on whether he could have done more to prevent this, for such thoughts were worthless. He had done what he had done because he had been forced to, just as Nate perhaps believed he'd had a duty to Gus. He gripped the boy's trembling hand. 'You will not die alone.'

Nate's eyes moved beyond Flynt to where Gus's body lay against the wall. 'You killed us all so easily. So easily…'

'It is never easy,' said Flynt. 'But sometimes necessary.'

The boy standing at his side sighed his impatience. 'We must be away. Let this wretch die here in the filth, it is little more than he deserves.'

Flynt gave him a sharp look. After all that he had been through, he truly had reverted to type very quickly. 'You are of noble birth, are you not?'

The boy drew himself erect. 'I am Bartholomew, the eldest son of the Earl of—'

Flynt did not want his family history. 'You are a nobleman's son, I know. Why don't you surprise me and show some real nobility.'

'You are impertinent, sir. I am grateful for your deliverance but I will have you know your station. Now, I command you to leave this wretch where he lies and take me to my father.'

Flynt jutted his chin towards the door. 'There's the way out and you are free to go if you wish. But I'll not leave this young man to step into eternity alone.'

The boy tutted his displeasure and picked his way delicately across the room to avoid coming into contact with the muck and filth and blood. Flynt let him reach the open door before he said, 'But think on this. You were with a servant when these men snatched you. That servant was no match for them and died to save you. Should you leave now, you will be out there alone. An easy mark. You won't travel two streets before some footpad or bully ruffian takes you down. Without me, your lordship, you will not survive.'

The boy could not have missed the heavy sarcasm Flynt laid on the words *your lordship* but he was not dim-witted and recognised the truth when spoken. He gave the darkness beyond the doorway a longing glance then moved back to Flynt's side. Nate coughed up blood as he looked up at the boy over whom he had so recently had dominion.

'I never wanted you hurt,' he said, his voice liquid crimson. 'I'm sorry.'

His lordship ignored him and addressed Flynt. 'Why do you do this? Just a few moments ago this man was your enemy and he would have killed you had events turned out differently. He deserves no such gentle feeling.'

Flynt sighed as he felt Nate's fingers spasm slightly and then loosen. A final slight cough, a small blister of blood rose and burst at his lips, then his head slowly drooped to one side, the dim light in his eyes guttering until they, like the rest of his body, were lifeless. Whatever abyss he had faced, he was now lost in it.

'No, you do not understand, but that is not the tragedy of it.' He gently laid Nate's hand across his chest. He was so young, so very young. 'The real tragedy is that you probably never will.'

2

A fiddler scratched a lively jig but struggled to be heard over the hubbub in the Black Lion. It was a popular Drury Lane tavern, where all manner of flash coves and doxies rubbed shoulders and other portions of their anatomy against swells from Mayfair and St James's in search of illicit pleasures in exchange for coin. Flynt knew the innkeeper, a burly dark-haired man by the name of Joseph Hines, who boasted arms like the beams of the Tyburn tree and the quick watchful eyes of one who saw much and stored it away for future use. He and Flynt had transacted business in the past, for Hines was a purveyor not only of ales, gin, wines and food, but also whatever he saw and heard. Flynt had long suspected the innkeeper was an informer, what Jack would call a 'queer rooster', and the fact that he had been instructed to attend his establishment at this time went a long way to confirming it. The man he was here to meet made great use of men such as Hines.

The landlord saw Flynt enter and with a jerk of the head directed him to the door at the far end of the tavern. Visibility was limited, for the dark-panelled room was lit only by candles and the glow emanating from the large fireplace. Smoke belched from the hearth and mixed with that drifting from myriad pipes to cloud the air, and Flynt held his breath as he picked his way between the tables, for he had never developed a taste for tobacco. Although he spent many of his leisure and working hours in such drinking dens, or the gaming halls and coffee houses of the West End, he also did not indulge in alcohol overmuch as it dulled the senses and made a man incautious. Such a lack of attention, even momentary, could be lethal. He was alert for faces he knew and spotted young Jack, his hair as ever tousled, his slim face sporting its customary cocky grin.

'Jack, lad – you are absent from your employer's premises once again, I see.'

Young Jack's grin widened. 'There's a world I wants to see, Mr Flynt, and I can't do that from a crib in the Strand.'

Flynt understood, for he had once shared that desire to venture beyond his youthful surroundings. A memory of Nate lying in the shit and blood in the basement in Satan's Gullet came to his mind, and he vowed to do what he could to keep Jack from a similar fate. 'I wouldn't be doing any dipping here. The landlord is known for taking a dim view of his patrons being fleeced.'

'No worry, Mr Flynt, I am fly to old Joe and wouldn't lift as much as a damp rag from a gent's pocket within these walls, let alone a silken wipe. I has other work this night.'

Flynt knew better than to ask the boy to expand but was reassured. Jack Sheppard was fly, as he said, and perhaps that sharp intelligence meant the odds of not dying in some rat-infested hole were in his favour.

Jack's smile faltered and his eyes became guarded. He looked around and lowered his voice. 'I hears the thieftaker is after you, Mr Flynt.'

There were two such gentlemen operating in London but Flynt knew which it would be. 'Mr Wild, I take it?'

Jack's head bobbed in assent. 'You must be careful, Mr Flynt. Jonathan Wild is not a man to fall foul of. I'm thinking he might have got wind of last night's work and wants to wet his beak.'

Wild's intelligence network was impressive and Flynt had little doubt he would have heard something of the events in the Gullet. Hearing something and proving it were two different matters, but not mutually exclusive, as Flynt already knew to his cost.

'I will deal with Mr Wild presently, Jack.'

Jack was canny enough to know that 'presently' meant perhaps never. 'He'll send someone for you, Mr Flynt, you knows that, and his boys, they ain't gentle.'

'Neither am I.'

Jack nodded as if Flynt had delivered wisdom to match that of Solomon.

'You be wary, lad, and stay away from Wild, if you can. Your youth will not protect you from the Tyburn jig.'

Jack gave him his wide grin once more. 'Don't you trouble yourself, Mr Flynt, I ain't afeard of the three-legged mare. I knows that's my destiny. A short life for me, and a merry one.'

Jack moved on then, heading to the street door. Flynt watched the boy, small even for his age, eye up a red-haired, buxom doxy whose breasts were near free from her neckline, but he did not tarry to talk to her. Whatever the boy's other work was, it had greater call than slaking any youthful lust. A sharp melancholy settled over Flynt as he watched the boy swagger between the tables. There may be no bloody end in a basement for Jack, but neither would he see old age.

He could not consider that future now, however, for he had business here. As he laid a hand on the door to which Hines had directed him, Flynt was aware of the young woman studying him briefly, before looking away.

The wooden stairs leading aloft were narrow and dark but at least the air here was relatively clear, and Flynt's eyes were sharp so he ascended without stumbling. Another door at the apex took him into a small private room to find a man seated at a table. His face was thin but handsome, and his head was topped with a curling black wig. He wore a thick blue velvet coat of finest quality, and cupped a glass of red in his right hand. The sleeve of his missing arm was pinned against his shoulder. Heavy curtains covered the window that looked upon Drury Lane and candles guttered in holders on the walls, while lanterns dangled from the black beams above. In the corner a screen obscured an area set aside for gentlemen guests to fulfil their private offices into a bowl. A door that Flynt knew led to an adjoining chamber where those same gentlemen could attend to other personal functions was closed.

'Close the door, Serjeant,' the man ordered, and Flynt did so, blocking the laughter, the music and raised voices from below. He peeled off his greatcoat and draped it and his hat over a chair in the corner of the room.

'Our host sears a fine beefsteak,' the man said as he motioned Flynt to sit opposite him. 'I took the liberty of ordering it for you. I know you are not one for the grape so I will not offer.'

He watched as Flynt slid his pistols from the belt beneath his long undercoat and set them on the table. His silver walking stick he propped against the arm of the chair before sitting down. An eyebrow was raised in the direction of the weaponry and amusement flickered in the man's eyes. 'The beast has already been butchered, Serjeant, there is no need for you to hunt it. Or perhaps you expect to go to war once more?'

'Never again,' said Flynt. 'At least not for king or country. Of such folly I have had my fill.'

He sat back, rested his left arm on the tabletop, by habit keeping his right free to reach for either sword or flintlock, even though there was little likelihood of anyone attacking. He knew the man before him did not venture abroad alone night or day. There would have been eyes upon him below, watchful men ready to protect their master should there be any sign of attack. Had he wished, Flynt would have picked them out, but he knew they were there and that was enough.

'I take it, Colonel, this is not a social occasion.'

Colonel Charters sipped from his glass. 'Cannot two old comrades get together to reminisce about past glories?'

'There was little glory in Flanders. A lot of blood, as I recall. Especially at Malplaquet.'

'Come, sir, it was a glorious victory for His Grace the Duke of Marlborough.'

'The thousands who died for his cause might take issue as to how glorious that victory was,' Flynt remarked. 'It was such a glorious victory that Corporal John lost his command shortly thereafter.'

Charters shrugged that aside, and did not comment on the lack of respect towards their old commander. 'Political manoeuvring, is all. He was a fine commander and he cared for the rank and file.'

Flynt believed John Churchill was more solicitous of his own advancement than that of his forces but he kept his counsel. He knew Colonel Charters to be loyal to Marlborough. 'Victory it may have been but at what cost? Thousands dead in a war fought over the succession to a throne thousands of miles from here, a squabble between royalty sanctioned by politicians who with a scratch of pen or finely turned phrase shed blood from a safe distance and called it patriotism. And then, after all the death, a treaty made by politicians in secret. And you the lesser of an arm.'

'But I live, thanks to you. And we both shared in the glory.'

Flynt made no reply but his mind travelled to that day in September six years before. He had been returning from the front line against orders, having had his fill of death, of seeing comrades fall, of causing other men's comrades to fall. He had shed a lot of blood that day, by ball and bayonet, and he could do it no longer.

'Glory is for officers and politicians, not the common soldier,' Flynt said.

Charters shrugged. 'As for the Treaty of Utrecht, I agree there was an element of secrecy, but such matters are best attended in shadow, and it did end the bloodshed and pinioned the arms of the French. Old King Louis' death has left them with no appetite for open war.'

'For now.'

Charters inclined his head in agreement, then smiled. 'As you see, Serjeant, we are two old soldiers discussing our joint past after all.'

Flynt banished the memories of that day from his mind for he knew demons lay in wait among them. 'But that is not why you instructed me to meet you in this place.'

'It was an invitation, not an instruction.'

'The word "invitation" suggests I had a choice. I detected no hint of such in your missive. You have a task for me, have you not?'

Charters laughed. 'Flynt, this is why I prize you above all others among my Company of Rogues. You know I wield the power of life and death over you, yet you seem to care not and still talk to me as if I were not your superior.'

'I do your bidding, for I do not care to be paraded through the courts. I do not care to be used as entertainment by the wealthy while I languish in Newgate. I do not care to take centre stage at Tyburn, to be gawped at by high and low while I struggle for breath on the rope and soil my breeches. I care not to be subjected to any of those due processes of law which you hold so dear and yet I see as more corrupt and vicious than the bloodiest rogue in the kingdom. You have power over me, I cannot deny it, and I do not care for that, either. As for you being my superior, you issue orders and that is all. I do not see you as superior even to the lowest beggar in the streets.'

Charters showed no sign of insult. He sipped his wine again. 'What is important is that I alone prevent you from such ignominy, and in return I use your undoubted skills to the purpose of securing this nation.'

'And last night's adventure? How did that fit this noble purpose?'

Charters had the decency to look slightly shamed. 'That was a favour for an old friend whose son had been taken by ruffians. I knew you would find them. Was it really necessary to kill them all, by the way?'

'It seemed like the thing to do at the time.'

A thin smile from Charters. 'Indeed. It so often seems the thing to do at the time when you are involved, Serjeant.'

'Is that not why you employ me?'

'That is so, that is so. You are a resourceful man and your skills, even your propensity to save a hangman the trouble of unfurling his rope, are invaluable to the nation.'

29

He dropped a pouch on the table between them. The sound of jangling coin as it landed was a welcome one, and when Flynt hefted it he was reassured by the weight.

'And how much of the reward did you pocket, Colonel?'

The door opened and a girl of no more than ten years entered carrying two plates. Flynt quickly transferred the pouch to his lap as she laid the food before them then left without a word.

'His young lordship was correct,' said Charters, his smile languid. 'You are damnable impudent, Flynt.'

'I am fluent in it,' replied Flynt. 'So what say you, Colonel Charters – sir? Shall we set aside any pretence of brotherhood or comradeship? You did not summon me hence simply to pass on my share of the booty. You have further work for me, so tell me what you need me to do, what you need me to find or to steal, who you need me to seek, to intimidate, to kill. As you said, such are my skills, so speak and let me go about my business.'

He knew he was goading the colonel but he did not care. Charters was correct in one thing – he had an aptitude for taking lives. He did not particularly enjoy it and did not take such action lightly. Had he been a spiritual man he would fret for the wellbeing of his soul but he did not believe in any deity.

The colonel's meat had been pre-cut for him. With only one arm he found it difficult, though not impossible, and in Flynt's mind this was a fresh sign that he was no stranger to this establishment. Charters speared a morsel with force then conveyed it to his mouth and proceeded to chew slowly, while regarding Flynt with that damnable hint of mockery in his eyes. Flynt had never seen the man fly into a rage, despite his many attempts to entice him. His coolness had been legendary in the field and he had been trusted, even loved, by his men. That did not mean he would not sacrifice them when he had to, for to Charters the ends always justified the means, both on the battlefield and in the work in which he was currently engaged.

The colonel took a sip of wine to wash the meat down. 'The nation faces many foes,' he said.

'It always does,' said Flynt.

'The French may be licking their wounds – they have not the appetite nor the means to finance a war for now – but we still have the Stuarts nipping at the throne like annoying lap dogs.'

The Stuarts had ruled Scotland for centuries and on the death of Queen Elizabeth had also ascended the throne of England. The late Queen Anne's line to the throne had been assured when her father, James, was ousted for his adherence to the Roman Catholic faith, which was ever a sticking point in politics. Anne had been Protestant and that was more palatable to the politicians. Catholic or Protestant, Tory or Whig, it all meant little more than the bite of a flea to Flynt.

'The Jacobites have no teeth,' Flynt said, taking up his cutlery to attack his steak, finding himself hungry of a sudden.

'They may have found some. There are those on these isles who would see the Stuarts return to power. There were riots in cities across England on the day His Majesty King George was crowned, you know this. There are powerful members of parliament who have connived with the exiled Stuart court. Even now, the Earl of Oxford lies in the Tower and others have fled across the Channel. Intelligences have reached me that there is new-found enthusiasm in your own country for the return of their King Over the Water.'

Flynt's own country. Scotland. He had not seen Edinburgh for many a long year. 'Aye, talk there may be, for there is always a sufficiency of words, but a paucity of action.'

'Talk is how it begins, Flynt. There is talk that even the old queen, God rest her, was minded to have her half-brother take the throne. She was guilt-ridden over her part in the Glorious Revolution that forced her father to relinquish England, even to the point of believing that her inability to birth healthy children was the result. A Herod curse, if you will.'

Flynt chewed a forkful of steak. Charters was correct, it was decidedly succulent. 'I recall a rumour that she did not believe her half-brother to be legitimate.'

31

'The warming-pan baby, he was called. She said that the child had died at birth and a substitute was smuggled into Kensington Palace in such an implement. That was merely a means of discrediting his claim to the throne and bolstering her own power, and if she ever believed it, it seems she may have come to regret it.'

'And how do you know this?'

Charters waited a moment before answering. He laid his fork down and leaned across the table. After a quick glance at the closed door, he said quietly, 'Her Majesty died intestate, that much is common knowledge. But though she left no will, the Act of Settlement ensured that George of Hanover took the throne. She did not much care for our new king, Flynt, for he rejected a suit of marriage many years ago. She agreed to the Act only on the provision that he never set foot on English soil in her lifetime.'

'So a German took the throne of England and he is not universally popular. He also cares little for this country and prefers to spend as much time in Hanover as he can. But he is a Protestant and that is all that matters. The Act of Settlement was legal, was it not?'

'It was.'

'And the old queen left no further instructions as to her wishes following her death, so what is the issue? Ferment will always be in the air, no matter what royal arse warms the throne and no matter what way that arse worships its God.'

Charters ignored Flynt's disparaging tone. 'There may have been a will of sorts.'

'May have been?'

'A number of people close to Her Majesty insist they saw a document, which she carried on her person at all times. None read it fully but they believed that in it she stated her wish that James Francis Edward Stuart become king following her death.'

'And if this document exists, where is it?'

'As the queen lay dying I was among those who searched Kensington Palace under the instruction of His Grace the Duke of Shrewsbury. It was not found.'

'So its existence was merely rumour.'

'That was what we surmised.'

Charters said nothing further but Flynt knew there was more and he was suitably intrigued to ask, 'You surmise that no longer, I take it.'

'As I said, there is unrest in Scotland.'

'There is always unrest in Scotland.'

'The Act of Union to bring the two countries under our single parliament is yet an open wound, even though eight years have passed since it was agreed. There is a belief, promoted by the Jacobites, that it was corruptly obtained.'

Flynt laughed. 'It was a negotiation between politicians and nobles. *Of course* there was corruption involved.'

Charters ignored yet another barb. 'Nonetheless, feeling burns hot,' he said, his tone remaining even. 'John Erskine, the Earl of Mar, fled London out of pique at failing to obtain office at court. He headed north on a ship carrying coal, I believe, and on the way he felt compelled to embrace the Jacobite cause. He did so with such zeal that a few weeks ago he gathered some like-minded Scots for what is called a *tinchal*, which I understand is Scotch for a hunting party.'

Flynt saw the colonel expected him to confirm that but he had no knowledge of the word. 'I will accept your word on that.'

Charters continued, 'Mar damned the Act of Union, even though he had a hand in its creation, and last month he raised the Stuart standard at Braemar and declared for the Pretender. You have not heard of this?'

Flynt shrugged and continued to eat. He had heard talk in coffee houses but he paid little heed.

'No matter,' said Charters, 'although you should take more interest in your nation's affairs, Flynt.'

'Not my nation,' said Flynt. 'I thought I had made that clear.'

'Quite so.' Charters poured himself more wine. 'The raising of the standard was not without incident. The gilded sphere atop the pole fell off. Hardly an auspicious start to rebellion, don't you agree?'

Flynt did not reply.

Charters said, 'A fire has been kindled, Flynt, and such a testament in the old queen's own hand would only fan those flames.'

'Again, if it exists.'

'There has been talk here in the streets of a document that is rumoured to have the power to change the course of history. If that is the case, and not mere hyperbole, then we must have it before it reaches Mar or the Pretender, or knowledge of it girds the loins of France to back the Jacobite cause.'

Flynt forked a morsel of meat, his lack of interest apparent in his expression and unhurried movement. 'I take it you want me to find this mysterious document. If it exists.'

'I do.'

'And steal it back.'

'Yes, that is your mission, Serjeant Flynt. As you can see it is of vital importance to our nation's security. I do not believe it to have left the city yet. I want it intercepted before it goes beyond our border or shores and into the wrong hands.'

'And if it does? What harm can it do if Herr Hanover's succession is lawful?'

'Propaganda, Flynt, do you know this word?' Charters did not provide time for an answer, thus sparing Flynt from revealing his lack of knowledge. 'It is from the Latin and was used by the Vatican some hundred years since for the propagation of their faith. Should such a document fall into Jacobite hands it would be used to call the succession into question. Half-truths and lies. The Jacobites have used it as currency for forty years.'

Flynt knew the Crown and its ministers had done the same, and for longer, and would do so forever more, but he kept his counsel. He had already been outspoken enough and no benefit would be gained by pointing out something as inconsequential as the truth.

'The simple fact of the matter is that this document can muddy constitutional waters and strengthen the Stuart claim in the eyes of our enemies at home and abroad,' Charters said. 'There was a time in recent memory when, if he had agreed to renounce Catholicism or had at least managed to keep his own counsel concerning his refusal to do so, then James Edward could have come within a hair's breadth of gaining the throne. Her late Majesty was beloved, not by all but by a majority, and her final wish to have her half-brother take the orb and sceptre would be a powerful tool in any attempt to delegitimise the Hanoverian claim. As you have already stated, our current Majesty is not overwhelmingly popular, and a foreigner to boot. James Edward may be a Catholic but he is at least English-born, even though he has spent his life among foreigners. Should that document leave these shores or reach the hands of those behind the rising, it could become more than a powerful tool, it could become a weapon. I am not willing to leave such matters to fortune.'

Flynt continued to eat, his mind turning the issue over. 'And what do these intelligences of yours tell you of the document's whereabouts? Where has it been for the past year?'

'It is my belief it was smuggled from the palace by a servant, who perhaps knew not what he or she carried, and delivered into the hands of someone on the outside, perhaps stolen for financial gain, perhaps hidden at the instigation of one of Her Majesty's advisors, or even Her Majesty herself. I stress this is speculation, Flynt, for I have no evidence. What I do know is that my sources tell me that a certain middleman seems to have some knowledge of the document.'

'A middleman?'

'One who makes a living from the return or dispersal of stolen goods.'

It had to be a thieftaker, and this was the second time in the past hour that the unofficial office had been mentioned to him. It was wont to make him feel that forces were working against him. 'Which is it? Wild or Hitchin?'

'It is my understanding that Hitchin's star is in the descent while his erstwhile pupil's travels in the opposite direction. I would suggest you begin with Jonathan Wild. I shall be at the Bear Garden tomorrow night and I would be obliged if you would attend me at this same hour with a report on your progress.'

Flynt had eaten his fill and knew the conviviality, such as it was, had reached its conclusion. He stood, thrusting his pistols into his belt before shouldering into his greatcoat and reaching for his hat. 'Thank you for the meal.'

Charters acknowledged him with an incline of the head. 'I cannot overemphasise the importance of this mission, Serjeant Flynt. Nor the danger. These are perilous times and we could very easily be tipped into civil war.'

Flynt remained unimpressed as he flicked some ash from his hat brim.

'Tell me, Flynt, you do not believe in kings or princes,' said Charters. 'You do not believe in nobles or politicians. Not the law nor the judiciary. Not God nor clergy. Is there anything in this world that you do believe in?'

Flynt thought for a moment before he answered. 'I believe in Tact and Diplomacy, Colonel.' He picked up his slender silver stick from where it rested against the arm of his chair. 'And when that fails, Surprise.'

–

There was a delay of but a few moments, during which a thoughtful Charters sat back and studied the door through which Flynt had just left, before Charles Talbot entered from the ante-chamber, a glass of red wine in one hand, a hat in the other, and a thick coat draped over his arm. He was no longer in government but Charters knew the political warhorse had a special interest in this issue and so had invited him to listen in on his conversation with Flynt. If there was one man he knew he could trust, it was the Duke of Shrewsbury.

'He is a surly fellow, is he not?' the former Lord High Treasurer said as he dropped the hat and coat over the arm of the chair vacated by Flynt, before sinking into it with a subdued groan.

His skin was pallid, his voice throaty. Charters knew the statesman had been unwell of late but he fought back any desire to inquire as to his wellbeing. The duke would not thank him for being so indelicate. They were not close friends.

'He is a useful surly fellow,' Charters said.

Shrewsbury pushed Flynt's half-finished meal away from him and set his glass down. 'So that is who rescued you from the battlefield.'

'It was, and for that service I will be forever grateful.'

Shrewsbury's good eye focused squarely on the colonel. 'But not so grateful that you would not blackmail him into your service.'

'No, Your Grace. My duty transcends my gratitude.'

'Of course, of course.' Shrewsbury picked up Flynt's knife and idly pushed the remains of the meal around on the plate. 'Do you trust him?'

Charters sipped his wine as he considered. 'He is a man with his own peculiar sense of honour. He will see the task through.'

'But he is a criminal, is he not?'

'Of course, else he would not be part of my Company of Rogues.'

Shrewsbury acknowledged that logic with a wave of his hand. 'And this charge he spoke of, the one you hold over his head. Of what nature is it?'

'It's what they call a "toby lay", Your Grace.'

Shrewsbury wrinkled his brow in irritation. 'The King's English, if you please, my dear colonel. I am not a denizen of the streets and their cant means nothing to me.'

'A robbery under arms on Blackheath. A certain lady of high station and a young gentleman who is more than just a friend. A necklace valued at one hundred guineas was taken and the lady's companion beaten. I have witnesses who would swear it was Flynt who was the highwayman that night.'

'And was he?'

'Truth matters little in the face of evidence.'

The duke smiled. 'There is something of the rogue in you too, is there not?'

Charters returned the smile. 'It is my duty to do what I can to protect England, by fair means or foul. We have all committed dishonourable acts for the greater good, have we not?'

Shrewsbury lowered his gaze to the table and Charters wondered if his dishonourable acts now haunted his memory. He was respected by many but not by all, and some of those even said he had once been a Jacobite himself.

'How aware is this fellow Flynt, do you think, of the situation in his homeland?'

Again Charters thought this over. 'The question, I believe, is not how much he is aware but how much he cares. As you no doubt heard, he cares for very little, or at the very least, purports thus.'

'You think it a feint?'

'I think it is self-delusion. You heard his assertion that the Act of Union was obtained through corrupt practices. Is that true, I wonder?'

Shrewsbury's mouth twitched as he continued to rearrange the scraps on the plate. 'Commerce, by its very nature, lends itself to a measure of corruption. The commerce of government is not immune. Money, favours, promises can smooth the path towards an equitable outcome for all parties.'

Charters let the duke's words hang between them. He had been otherwise engaged during the negotiations for the Act of Union between the two nations but he had little doubt that the path spoken of was smoothed to a considerable degree.

His Grace sighed. 'Which brings us to Bobbing John.'

Bobbing John was the disparaging term used for John Erskine, the Earl of Mar, due to his habit of switching his allegiances seemingly with the change of the wind. Charters had met him only once and found him to be personable enough but his lack of deliberation was clear. Like many such men, he would do what was best for him and not his country.

'His forces hold Inverness and the Highland fastness, but he yet bides his time in Perth,' Charters said. 'Had he moved more forcefully to take Stirling and Edinburgh we might be facing a greater problem. But it would appear that his lordship appears to have no stomach to carry through with his rebellion.'

'Ah yes. The Right Honourable Earl ever lacked determination, I am glad to say. Except when it came to his fit of pique when His Majesty declined his services in government. He had campaigned ardently for Union, yet when he fled the city aboard that collier he must have experienced a conversion of Damascene proportions, for when he disembarked he was reborn an ardent Jacobite. He has been sufficiently persuasive to gather many other Scottish lords to his cause, correct?'

'He has. Some motivated by patriotism, some by self-interest, some sharing the earl's pique over lack of a cabinet position. Mackintoshes, Macdonalds, Macleans, Camerons, MacGregors – all have declared for Mar and his cause. I hear tell that the elder Lord Moncrieff has also left London for his Edinburgh house.'

Shrewsbury's face puckered with distaste. 'Moncrieff! Now there is a man for whom the word slippery was coined. If he has joined with the other Scottish lords then he must see profit in it for himself and his family.'

Charters was aware of the Scottish nobleman's reputation for self-interest. He had never encountered him either professionally or socially but he had met his son in various gaming houses and it was his opinion that if the elder was the tree, then the younger was the proverbial apple that failed to fall far from it.

'Perhaps so,' he said, 'but these rebels have together amassed a considerable force, though it lies stymied by their commander's indecision.'

'They face Red John, do they not?'

Charters had served with John, the Duke of Argyll, known as Red John of the Battles, under Marlborough. He had acquitted himself with distinction and Charters was of the opinion that there was no better soldier to quash this rebellion, if it ever progressed.

'Yes. The delay in advancing has given him time to bolster his own forces.'

Shrewsbury was heartened by this news and nodded as if satisfied that Charters had the matter well in his sole hand. 'I need not emphasise the importance of this mission. There is little threat at the moment – the stock exchange can act as a barometer to such conditions and it remains unconcerned – but that could change. If Mar and his supporters somehow rally the English Jacobite lords to their standard, or obtain support from France, then the tide could turn. We have many home-grown traitors on this side of the border and their support would be vital.'

'France has couched many fine words with empty promises in the past. As for the English Jacobites, they are timid beasts who confine their sedition to wild talk after too much wine.'

'Nevertheless, as you pointed out to your man, they may feel emboldened should this document surface, as could France. I pray your faith in this fellow Flynt is well founded.'

The sound of female voices drifted from the stairway and the door opened to reveal two statuesque beauties wearing gowns that revealed somewhat more than polite society might wish, but this room was not polite society. Shrewsbury took this as his cue to leave.

'Why not stay, Your Grace?' Charters said as the other man rose. 'Take your ease.' He lowered his voice, glanced at the two women grinning by the door and leaned over the table. 'They are clean, I assure you. My men take the utmost care to ensure there is no disease.'

The duke shook his head. 'Thank you, my friend, but I will decline. My wife is quite enough for me, and should she discover that I dallied with a doxy she would have me emasculated with a blunt knife.'

Charters knew Charles Talbot's Italian wife was the subject of much gossip herself and was reputed to have had an affair with a notorious womaniser, but he kept his silence. The duke gave the women a final appraising glance and sighed. 'Enjoy your recreation, Colonel. And keep me informed on developments regarding our enterprise.'

The former Lord High Treasurer pushed himself to his feet, retrieved his hat and coat and, with a courteous bow to the ladies, took his leave. The women smiled at Charters and he waved them to take their ease at the table. 'Come, my darlings, some wine before the games, eh?'

–

The fiddler had managed to galvanise some of the drinkers and they were singing 'Lilluburlero' in voices roughened by drink and smoke. Flynt had lingered after he had descended the flight of stairs to listen for a few moments, the anti-Catholic sentiment expressed in the lyric the patrons bellowed somehow fitting considering the work on which he was embarking. Charters was correct, he cared little for how a man worshipped his God or whether they favoured monarch or Pope. He held neither in high regard. He donned his hat and set it over his eyes as was his custom, allowing himself a moment to scan the crowd, making sport of picking out the colonel's men. He spotted them with ease, tall silent men standing alone, their gaze never far from the doorway in which he stood. He recognised the stance of the elite soldier, for these were not the rogues Charters employed in his shadow work. These were men for whom honour and duty were like bread and water, and he recognised a certain kinship with them, though his own sense of such matters was uniquely personal.

As he listened he became aware of the young woman Jack had been admiring weaving her way towards him, a gin bottle in her hands, her pale face smeared with dirt, the slopes of her breasts on display, her long red hair loose and matted. She would be pretty if she washed herself now and then, he thought. She stepped in front of him and peered at his face, her eyes struggling to focus through the gloom and the smoky air.

'I knows you,' she said.

He did not reply. He knew her to be a young whore by the name of Bess but that was all.

She leaned in closer. 'I sees you earlier, with that kinching cove, Jack Sheppard.' Flynt seldom spoke in the cant himself but he understood it well enough. She was suggesting that Jack was on the run from his master and had turned to thievery, which, in a sense, was true. He had not absconded from the employer to whom he had been bound but he did moonlight on the streets. The young woman edged ever nearer. 'And I sees you before, didn't I? Last night. Down the Gullet.'

Flynt looked around quickly but no one paid them the slightest heed. A pot boy hurried by, his hands full of empty tankards, no attention to spare a drunken doxy. Bess's words were slurred but the girl at least had wit sufficient to lower her voice when she spoke again so that only he could hear. 'Aye, I sees you, down there, last night. Just before all them coves was slaughtered in that cellar.'

'You are mistaken, girl,' he said and stepped to one side in order to pass, but she swayed into his path once more.

'No, mister, I knows you. I knows who you are. I sees you there, I did. I knows you.'

He fixed his gaze upon her but she was too lost in the gin to notice the menace. 'You would do well not to repeat such libel, lass.'

She laughed, and it might have been a pleasant sound were it not made ugly by drink and sin. It was loud enough to cause a head or two to turn in their direction. Flynt was not ruffled by this fleeting attention, for to all intents it would look as if she was merely seeking his business. The girls who frequented the Black Lion were brazen in their approaches and the patrons cared little.

''Tain't no libel, mister,' she said. 'It's the truth and be damned.'

It was time to take this conversation away from any prying ears. He gripped her by the upper arm and propelled her between the tables towards the door. Again he was unconcerned, for anyone watching would simply assume the bargain had been reached. He took care not to hurt her, as he was not a man who took pleasure from such behaviour, but he had to get the woman out of that tavern. Bess did not struggle against his grip, for she was used to being mishandled by men.

The air outside was cool but far more foetid, for the stench of waste and manure replaced that of woodsmoke and tobacco. In the tavern, a solo voice had begun singing 'England's Triumph', obviously intent on keeping the anti-popery feeling in the room high. The fiddler joined in, halting at first, the tune perhaps unknown to him, but he soon caught up.

Flynt hauled the young woman across Drury Lane to a narrow alleyway and pressed her against the wall. From further along he heard the sounds of breathing and groaning as another of Bess's profession made her living against the bricks. Carnal pleasures knew little shame in these decaying streets.

'So, if you want to tup, that will cost you,' Bess said, her free hand reaching under his coat to rub the front of his breeches. He reached down and jerked her hand free.

'Bess is your name, am I correct?'

'That's right, but what's wrong with you, eh? The way you dragged me out of there I thought you wanted some business.' She jerked her head in the direction of the rutting in the darkness. 'Does that give you some ideas, my big fellow?' Her hand snaked back towards his groin but he struck it away again. She looked first disappointed, then angry. 'You not like women, is that it? You a molly, or something?'

She was goading him by suggesting he preferred men but he ignored it. 'Bess, you would be well advised to forget what you think you saw last night.'

Her anger gave way to gin-addled confusion. 'Last night...? What you...?' Her gaze cleared as she remembered. 'That's right. I sees you, didn't I?'

He reached into the pocket of his coat and withdrew some coins, which he pressed into her hot, damp palm. 'No, you did not.'

43

She stared at the money. Drink may have made her incautious but she could still count. Flynt knew there was enough there to see her insensate for a week. She looked back at him and he saw a sly half smile creep across her mouth. 'Maybe I didn't see you after all, mister.'

He nodded and stepped away from her as she returned her attention to the money in her hand. 'You sure you don't want nothing?' she asked, licking her lips in what she obviously thought was an alluring fashion. She was young and perhaps could be pretty but the abuses of men, and her own reliance on gin, had removed any appeal.

'I regret you are not my type.'

'What is your type, then?' A finger trailed in her tresses like a little girl. He felt sadness as he realised that she was little more than a child who had been forced to become a woman too early. 'You don't like red hair? Maybe I could find you a friend...'

'No,' said Flynt with finality, moving closer once again. 'But one thing more, Bess, and I need you to listen with care. That is all the coin you will get from me. If I hear you have been spreading such infamous libels about me again, I will seek you out, and that is a day you will rue. Do you understand, girl?'

She looked into his eyes and this time she saw the menace and heard the promise in his voice. She had faced the threats of men before, he was certain of that, but in her face he saw reflected the certainty that he meant what he said. She thrust the money into a pocket of her dress before he could take it back. 'I understand, mister.'

He felt sudden pity for her. He knew nothing of how and why she had ended up selling her body on the street and he did not like having to threaten her, but he could not have her peaching on him, even indirectly. A careless word to one of her culls could then be relayed to a magistrate and Flynt would have to answer some difficult questions. He could rely on Charters to intercede but that could in turn leave Flynt open to questions from the underworld, not to mention finding himself even further enmeshed in the colonel's web. That he could not have.

He gave her one final look and pulled his neckerchief up over his mouth and nose to intercept the rank stench of the city streets, then walked from the alley. In Drury Lane a swell stepped delicately through the muck on the cobbles, a linen square pressed to his face. He could have been returning from a performance at the Covent Garden theatre, but it was more likely he was heading to a night of debauchery. The well-dressed gentleman's way was lit by a young link boy, the flaming torch in his hand bathing his features in red light. Flynt saw Jack giving him a sly smile as he passed. So this was the work. In a matter of minutes the fop would be led into the clutches of a crew who would end his dreams of a night's bacchanal with the loss of both consciousness and purse. Flynt watched them go, the two figures silhouetted against the glow of the torch, before he turned towards Covent Garden. What happened to that man meant nothing to him.

3

Insipid grey morning light drifted through the lace curtains to catch the smoke snaking from the hollow stump of the candle on the sideboard. Flynt watched it twist and twirl upwards until it finally dissipated. He reached under the bed covers and stroked the hip of the body beside him, enjoying the silky smoothness under his palm as he recalled the pleasures of the previous night. The woman stirred at his touch and rolled over to face him, her own hand moving between his legs.

'Oh my,' she said, smiling as she gripped his hardness. 'It would seem we are ready for another session.'

'Always,' he lied and kissed her. She responded, her hand expertly working at him below before she pushed him onto his back and tossed the blankets aside in order to straddle him. He stared up at her face and wondered at her beauty before he closed his eyes and thought of another.

Afterwards, she lay her head against his shoulder as they listened to the daytime sounds of the Covent Garden Piazza beyond the window: the street sellers calling their wares, porters cursing and laughing and whistling jaunty airs as they manhandled the fruit and vegetables, the beggars appealing for charity, and over all the clip of hooves and rumble of cartwheels on dirt and cobble. The Covent Garden of daylight and its moonlit counterpart were each places of industry, except one retailed that which was fresh and healthy while the other specialised in that which was often rotten and spoiled. Flynt was never certain in which world he belonged.

The sound of men singing a bawdy ditty drifted upwards, no doubt a group of swells still abroad after a night of sup and sin, their refined voices coarsened by drink and debauchery but already running out of words and enthusiasm as they made their way back to their fine homes and polite society. There were those who walked in both light and shade; not just men like the drunken singers, but also milliners and seamstresses and servant girls who supplemented their meagre income by taking to the streets when darkness fell. Flynt had more in common with them, perhaps, than the poor lost souls like Bess. He thought of his young friend Jack's words – a short life but a merry one. Aye, perchance the lad would lead the world a sprightly dance before he performed one himself at the end of a rope. But that lass? A short life, no doubt, but far from merry. She would drink herself to death, catch some dreadful scourge or perhaps even be murdered by a cull blinded by gin and rage.

The woman by his side was no milliner, seamstress or servant girl, but she was no streetwalker either. She was Annabelle St Clair, known to many as Tawny Belle, and one of the most popular girls working out of Mother Grady's fine house on the west corner of the Garden. She was West Indian by birth, African by race, and a harlot by circumstance if not choice. She had arrived from the Indies, an innocent of twelve years, as part of a consignment of young slaves selected for their beauty, bought at the Kingston block so the likes of Mother Mary Grady could bring 'exotica' to her house of erotica. Her new owner was as caring as a bawd could be, given the life was hard. That is to say, she was not quite as brutal as the other madams, but Flynt knew she had her moments. Belle had spoken English, which was why she and others had been selected from the West Indies rather than straight off the boat from Africa, but Mother Grady saw to it that the young woman was educated to a degree. While Belle was tutored in the delicate arts of a lady, she was also inculcated in the less than delicate arts of the courtesan. Her maidenhood was sold to the highest bidder during an auction conducted in the plush salon on the ground floor. Belle had been fourteen. Mother Grady had sold many girls much younger to be broken in by culls who savoured young flesh.

47

'Can I ask you a question, Flynt?' she asked, her voice deep and mellifluous, still bearing traces of her childhood.

'You need no permission.'

'Who is Cassie?'

He did not reply at first. He was aware he had breathed the name in the heights of his passion and Annabelle was not one to let it pass. He did not mind the question, for she asked not out of jealousy but mere curiosity. All the same, he felt guilt stab at him along with the question as to why, after all these years, he should think of her.

'Someone I knew many years ago, when I was but a lad,' he said.

Belle propped herself up on one arm. 'And where is she now?'

'I know not. Home, perhaps. Wed, probably.'

'In Edinburgh?'

'Aye.'

'You have not returned since you left?'

'No.'

'Why not?'

'There is nothing for me there.'

'You have no family? No friends?'

He paused, not sure he wished to continue this conversation. 'Yes, I have family and friends there still but I am not the person I once was, Belle.'

Her dark eyes flicked quickly to the pistols within easy reach on the table beside the bed and then she laid her head back on the pillow. 'We are none of us the people we once were.' There was a note of sadness in her voice which he had never before detected. 'This Cassie of yours, you broke her heart, did you not?'

He affected a smile. 'What makes you think she did not break mine?'

'People like you and I do not have hearts to break, Flynt, for they are luxuries we cannot afford.'

He lay in silence, staring at the ceiling and considering her words. He understood Belle believing she had an empty space in her chest, for the life she had been dealt had been tough. She was well fed and comparatively well taken care of, but she remained someone's property and could be sold if she grew too old to be of interest to the house's clients, if Mother Grady experienced a financial downturn or even on a whim. For her, Mother Grady's comfortable house with its fine furniture, tastefully erotic art and elegant decor was little more than a prison. Flynt had his freedom: he was nobody's man, despite the sword in Charters' hand that forever dangled over his head. Many years ago he had left his home to walk his own path, but had those years and that journey left a callus where his heart should be?

Voices from outside the doorway snatched him from his reflections and he instinctively reached for one of his flintlocks. He tucked it under the bedclothes just as the door was thrown open and two men bundled in thick coats pushed their way past Jerome, Mother Grady's nephew and the house bully. He was a heavy-set country boy from Yorkshire with the muscles of a shire horse and the ability to heft two unruly gentlemen at once, something he had to perform on a regular basis as the house's protector, but he was brushed aside as if he was nothing by the two men. The fact that one wielded a cudgel and the other a flintlock may have had something to do with it.

'You can't burst in here and disturb customers,' Jerome protested. 'I'm sorry, Mr Flynt, but they come through the front door before I could do anything...'

The man holding the pistol levelled it in the direction of the young man but he seemed uneasy in the movement, as if he was an inexperienced player in a game with rules that were a mystery to him. His companion, a swarthy, burly fellow, was entirely comfortable in brandishing his hefty club and ordering, 'Keep your mouth shut, country boy, or I will shut it for you.'

Belle sat up in the bed, the sheets clutched to her neck with her left hand, her right trailing behind her. There was no fear in her eyes, despite the weaponry. 'What is the meaning of this villainy?'

The man ignored her to address Flynt directly. 'You are to come with us.'

Under the bedclothes, Flynt eased the hammer of the pistol back until it locked. 'And what makes you think I will do so?'

'Because you knows who I am and you knows who sent me. And you ignore his summons at your peril.'

Flynt did know who he was although they had never actually met. His name was Joseph Blake, known on the streets as Blueskin, and he was Thieftaker Jonathan Wild's man. He was known to be a brutal individual and Flynt was grateful he had his weapon trained on him. One twitch of that club and he would send him straight to hell. Blake's friend with the pistol was a problem for the moments that followed.

Flynt kept his voice smooth. He wished to see the thieftaker himself but he was not about to make it easy for his lackeys. 'And why does Mr Jonathan Wild seek my society?'

'That is not for me to know, or care. Alls I know is, he says, "Blueskin, fetch me Jonas Flynt." So here I am, fetching you.'

'And how did you know to find me here?'

Blueskin smirked. 'We knows you has a taste for the dusky ones.' His eyes strayed towards Belle and studied her as if he could see through the sheet. 'There ain't that many high-class tail twitchers like her. It was a – what would you calls it? Process of elimination?'

Flynt doubted if that was true and began to wonder if someone had peached. His first thought was Bess but he had left her in that alley off Drury Lane. He thought about Jack but dismissed that notion immediately. A thief he may be but he was loyal. Any number of other rogues, beggars, doxies and drunks would have witnessed him walk from the Lane to the Garden and thence to Mother Grady's establishment, and any one of them could have recognised him then passed the intelligence to Wild.

Blueskin was still admiring Belle. 'Got to say, Flynt, you has an eye for 'em, and no mistake. She's a pretty one. I wouldn't mind me a glimpse of the rest of her.' He reached out to tug at the bedsheet, trying to jerk it from Belle's hand, but she steadfastly held on while displaying no fear.

'Do not examine the goods unless you have the coin to pay for them,' she said, snatching the material from his fingers.

'Bashful, ain't you, for a whore what would open her legs for the mere sight of tuppence.'

'It would cost you a damned sight more than tuppence to even breathe in my direction, you foul-smelling wretch. Perhaps you would be best advised to find yourself a Covent Garden Nun sleeping it off in a ditch in order to gain your pleasures. I am sure even the meanest of whores would need to be insensate before she let you lay a finger on her, let alone go near her with your cock.'

Blueskin's smirk became a snarl and he raised his club but froze when Belle's right hand snapped up to train a small Queen Anne pistol upon him. Her aim did not waver and there was steel in her eyes. Flynt was surprised at the appearance of the firearm but not as much as Blueskin's companion, who still trained his weapon on Jerome but watched the scene before him with his mouth agape. Flynt knew it was only a matter of moments before the man realised he should amend his aim, so he flung the blanket back and steadied his own flintlock upon him.

'Easy, cully,' he said. 'Let us keep our congress polite.'

The man's confused, frightened eyes moved from Blake immobile under Belle's gun to Flynt as he palmed his other weapon and eased himself naked from the bed. He kept one barrel on the fellow with pistol, the other on Blueskin, still frozen as if in aspic, though his initial look of shock had transformed into a glare.

'I'll wager that thing ain't even primed,' Blueskin said to Belle.

'Test me, friend,' she said, her voice low but steady.

For all his unpleasantness, Blueskin Blake was no coward. His mouth twisted into a disdainful sneer. 'You ain't got the balls to use that little thing.'

Belle's eyes flared and she lowered her aim until level with his groin. 'Shall we see who does not have the balls? Not to mention a little thing?'

Flynt could not conceal his grin. At this range, even that tiny firearm could wreak havoc with Blueskin's vitals. 'I would take a step back, friend, and drop the toothpick if I were you.'

His face noticeably blanching at the thought of his manhood being blown away, Blueskin did as he was bid and let the club fall to the floor at his feet.

Flynt looked to his companion. 'Jerome, relieve our visitor of that barking iron, if you please.'

Blueskin's partner, as surprised by Flynt's nakedness as he had been by the turn of events, meekly allowed Jerome to ease the flintlock from his grasp and turn it upon him. Blueskin had regained his composure and now scowled at Flynt with considerable heat.

'Mr Wild will not take such abuse of his officers kindly,' he said.

His officers. Flynt smiled at the man's pretence towards any official capacity but refrained from making comment. He had become acutely aware of his nakedness and it was damnably chill in this room.

'My compliments to Mr Wild,' he said, 'and convey to him that I will attend him at my convenience.'

'He will not like it,' said Blueskin.

'That is not my concern. Now, I would be obliged if you and your companion would take your leave, for the lady and I have business that does not require an audience.'

For a moment it was evident that Blueskin contemplated rushing him but thought better of it. Flynt was disappointed as he would have happily blown a hole in the bastard's forehead. The man gave him a stare that should have raised the temperature, then transferred said gaze to Belle before stooping to retrieve his cudgel.

'Leave that as it lies,' ordered Flynt. 'I will return it and your friend's barker when I call on your master. Jerome, show the gentlemen out, if you please.'

Blueskin began to back away, his eyes darting malevolence, but Flynt knew he was an experienced enough rogue to know that any action now would be foolhardy. There were four firearms in the room and not one was on his side.

'Before you take your leave, Mr Blake,' Flynt said, his tone conversational, 'I would ask you to apologise to the lady.'

A smile that was close relative to a sneer crossed Blueskin's broad face. 'Apologise to this bunter?'

Belle's voice was tight with rage. 'I am no bunter, you puff-gutted bull calf. I make more in one week than you do in a year entire.'

'Apologise for your behaviour, my friend,' insisted Flynt, raising the pistol slightly to advertise that he would brook no further argument, 'or you will never split the beard of a bunter again.'

Blueskin knew Flynt would not hesitate to pull the trigger so he swallowed back his outrage and gave Belle a slight bow. 'I apologises, my lady, for any offence what I has caused by word or deed.' Flynt heard the heavy sarcasm in the words but he let it pass.

'That's better,' he said. 'Now, be off with you – and Jerome? Have a care that the door does not strike their ample buttocks on their way out.'

Jerome smiled and waved the pistol in his hands. He was a sturdy man, as caring as he might be under the circumstances for the wellbeing of the ladies who toiled under this roof, and this incident would not sit well with him. 'Right, my lads, let's be having you. You know t' way.'

Blueskin, his wide shoulders tight with rage, left the room without a further word, followed by his friend who, by his perplexed expression, seemed to be having difficulty compre-hending what had transpired. Jerome gave Flynt another grin and departed in their wake. Flynt crossed the room and peered down the hallway to watch them go, pistols still at the ready, then closed the door.

'That was not necessary,' said Belle.

'What was not necessary?' He returned to the bed, uncocking the pistols and setting them back on the table.

'The apology. I've had worse said to me than being called a low-class harlot. I just did not like him saying it.'

Flynt hauled up his breeches and sat on the edge of the bed to pull his boots on. 'It was impolite. Manners maketh the man.'

'You are not my bully, Flynt. I have Jerome for that, and when all else fails, Mother Grady.'

Flynt laughed. Jerome was a capable fellow in a fight but Mother Grady was a fearsome creature in her rage. She was obviously not at home that morning for had she been present Blueskin and his friend might not have walked from the house without the support of a few stocky men.

'Anyway,' Annabelle went on, waving her firing piece, 'I was prepared should he continue with his disrespect.'

Flynt reached for his shirt as he nodded to the weapon. 'And where did you hide that?'

'I secrete it under the mattress.'

He stood up. 'It is there always?'

'Always. A lady can never be too careful.'

'Do you not fear that there is danger of it going off should a cull prove overly vigorous?'

Belle smiled and replaced the small weapon from whence she had drawn it. 'Many a cull has gone off half-cocked, not to mention misfired, but my weapon has never suffered such a malady.'

Flynt hauled his waistcoat on and thrust his pistols in his belt. He draped his greatcoat over his arm and held his hat and silver stick in his hand. Moving around the bed, he stroked her cheek with a finger. What they had was a business arrangement but he still harboured tender feelings for her. She was good company and had a fine mind. 'I am sorry I brought this to your door.'

She caressed the back of his hand with her own long, slim fingers. 'Be careful of Wild, Jonas. He is a dangerous man.'

He kissed her, gently, fleetingly. Her words echoed Jack's warning the evening before. 'As am I.'

He retrieved Blueskin's weapon from where it lay then opened the door, but paused when she asked, 'Did you love her… Cassie?'

He thought about it as he placed his hat on his head. 'Annabelle, I am unsure what love is.' He fixed the brim over his eyes and smiled but could not hide the sadness he felt. 'For such an emotion, you need a heart.'

Mother Grady was at the front door, still in her hat and coat, as Flynt crossed her house's wide reception hall. Jerome was informing her of their unwelcome visitors and she was far from pleased. Small and round and fiery, she gave Flynt a glare as he approached.

'I always knew you would bring trouble to my house, Jonas Flynt.' Her accent was pure Dublin but Flynt sometimes suspected that she pulled it on like a mask. Mary Grady was the best-known of Covent Garden's bawds but her past was kept hidden. Apart from the knowledge she had a sister, and that only discovered by the arrival of her nephew, nothing was known of her. They said she had been a titled lady in Ireland who had fallen into disgrace, that she'd had multiple affairs with cabinet ministers. They said a great deal of things, but when someone inquired of her on the subject she answered with a thin smile, a tiny flick of an eyebrow and a chuckle. She was quick to laugh and equally as quick to rage and it was the latter she visited now upon Flynt. 'I don't like the thieftaker's men at my door. It's bad for business. I don't wish my girls bothered by those lickspittles.'

'I think it was they who were bothered, Mrs Grady.'

'No matter. You will keep your business beyond that door in future.' She fixed her ire on her nephew. 'And you, you useless gobshite, what were you doing? Playing with yourself, were you?'

'They forced their way in, Aunt,' explained Jerome. 'They were up them stairs before I could do owt.'

She made a sucking, dismissive noise. 'I've told you before to keep your eyes on that front door. We're a fine house and have a reputation to uphold. Don't make me regret my affection for my poor sister, God rest her.'

Jerome's big face seemed to crumple under the withering gaze and harsh words from this diminutive woman. Flynt spoke up in his defence. 'Jerome acquitted himself well, Mrs Grady. He faced them bravely, even though one had a barker, and had those men out of here in an instant. You should be proud to have such a fine bully watching over your house.'

Mother Grady gave Jerome another look but its harshness had softened slightly. 'That's his job. And he'd best be getting about it now. Make sure the girls are breakfasted and cleaned with their rooms tidy, for men's lusts recognise no clock.'

It was a phrase Flynt had heard her utter many times, as had Jerome. The big Yorkshireman gave Flynt a grateful nod and hurried off to the kitchen. Flynt saw the pistol he had taken from Blueskin's companion resting on a table and he thrust it into the pocket of his greatcoat alongside the stout cudgel.

'A word, if I may, Mrs Grady,' said Flynt when they were alone. 'About Belle.'

Mother Grady took off her hat and threw it onto a small table against the wall behind her. 'I know what you're going to say and the answer is no.'

Even though he had expected the response, Flynt was still disappointed. This was the third time he had offered to buy Belle's freedom and the third time he had been refused.

'I've told you before,' said the madam, 'that girl has some fine coin between her legs for many years yet, with proper care. I can give her that.'

'Do you think it right that you own another human being?'

Mother Grady dismissed that with a grimace. 'She has a good home here. She leads a comfortable life.'

'She is a slave.' Flynt was not a religious man but he knew Mother Grady was a believer, although whether Roman Catholic or Protestant was a mystery, so his next words were designed to stir that part of her conscience. 'Slave owners will be judged harshly in the afterlife, I believe.'

She laughed. 'I think when that column of the balance sheet is studied I will be well down the line, behind plantation owners, lords, ladies and ministers of the king. Anyway, I don't hear you complaining about her ownership when you are bedding her. If I grant your wish, if I allow you to pay for her liberty, what would you do? Would you wed her? Put her in high keeping? I don't think so. You are not the marrying kind and though you often have funds to spare you are not so flush that you can keep a mistress. Save your pious words, my friend, for you use her as I do, for your own ends.'

Her words stung and he struggled for a response but found himself wanting.

'But don't you be worrying about that lass,' Mother Grady went on. 'She's got a solid head on those shoulders. She knows what she wants.'

'And what's that?'

The madam smiled. 'She wants to be me. And one day she will be. Yes, I hold her papers, I hold her very existence in my hands, and perhaps that is wrong. It may not be the way of the next world but it is the way of this one, and has been since the beginning of time. But let me tell you a little secret...' She leaned in closer. 'Belle will have her freedom but not because some man wills it. She will have it because she wills it. She will work for it and she will have it, you should have no fears on that score. And when that occurs, she will either have all this or a house of her own. You are like all men, you either wish to ruin us or save us and you cannot fathom that women are capable of doing both themselves. No, Mr Jonas Flynt, you are not Belle St Clair's salvation. You are no white knight. You are merely a cull.'

He had no words to offer in rebuttal. He had seen Belle as a victim, and that was what she was: a victim of a society who saw fellow human beings as somehow less than them. What he had not understood was that Belle had a clear plan for her future, and Mother Grady was part of it.

He decided it would avail him nought to continue with the subject. 'I would have a care, Mrs Grady, for Blueskin Blake was today shamed and he might not take that kindly.'

She snorted. 'That festering bag of pus? Should he return here he'll wish whatever hell creature squeezed him out had kept her legs crossed, you have my promise on that.'

4

The sedan chair listed sharply to the side and Flynt reconsidered his decision not to walk down Holborn to where the thieftaker held court. He had wanted to be fresh and rested when he faced Wild, but this bumpy journey was leaving him storm-tossed as he clung to a strap above the window to keep from bouncing around in the seat.

The long thoroughfare was not unusually busy but the two burly chairmen conveying him did seem to cry out 'Chair' and 'Have a care, there' more frequently than was customary, as unwary pedestrians ventured across the narrow roadway with nary a thought. The bearers' feet intermittently slapped against cobbles or splashed through puddles and the chair often lurched as they avoided soft mud or stinking manure. Beyond the open window, people moved from store to store, to coffee houses, to taverns and, some discreetly but others brazenly, to brothels. Carriages and sedans and carts rocked by, horses whinnied and whips cracked. There were oaths and laughs and everywhere there was humanity. The roadway was overlooked by buildings of varying styles, some dating back to the time of Henry and Elizabeth, for Holborn had been untouched by the great fire fifty years earlier. The chair tilted sharply to one side again as the men negotiated the narrows created by the Middle Row, a three-storey building that jutted into the road.

Flynt only absently took in the scene as he considered what he knew of Jonathan Wild. They had never met, which in itself was a surprise given their respective careers. Wild had adopted the title of Thieftaker General, although not an official designation, but the irony was that he was the biggest villain in London. He organised crime, he manipulated criminals, he returned stolen property to those who offered a reward – and pocketed cash from city officials for the service. He also saw to it that rogues who did not allow themselves to be tucked away in his pocket were tucked away in gaol. Some were guilty of the crime of which he accused them, others most certainly not. In that regard, Wild and Colonel Charters shared common ground. Belle had been correct – he was a dangerous man and Flynt had to tread warily.

Wild had headquartered himself in a room at the Blue Boar Tavern in Little Old Bailey near Fleet Lane, and Flynt was grateful when the chair came to a halt there. Nevertheless he bade the bearers to await his return, promising a healthy tip, and as he stretched his muscles, he gave an idle glance to a hackney carriage resting at the corner of the Bailey and the tavern. A gentleman was demanding that he be conveyed to Westminster but the driver, a diminutive elderly man with a face that was no stranger to blows and who looked as if he had been squashed into a heavy greatcoat, replied that he was already engaged. The broad face of a man with dark hair appeared at the carriage window and glowered at the gentleman with such ferocity that he shrank away and walked swiftly towards the Bailey. The passenger's gaze found Flynt watching him and held his eyes for a moment before he sank back into the gloom of the interior. Flynt thought nothing further of it as he entered the tavern.

The Blue Boar was like any other such establishment in the locality, a step or two above watering holes such as the Black Lion but still prone to rowdiness, drunkenness and licentiousness. At this hour of the day, just before noon, it was relatively quiet, with a handful of dedicated soakers hanging heads over tankard and glass while a group of lawyers from the Bailey drank coffee or more likely something stronger at a corner table. Flynt saw no face he recognised and climbed the stairs to the first floor where the entire London underworld knew Wild held court.

Blueskin stood sentinel by the door to the upstairs room, his hands clasped before him as if he were a butler awaiting the signal to serve cake. He gave Flynt a sour look as he approached.

'As promised, I am here,' said Flynt.

'Mr Wild is engaged,' said Blueskin, with the forced formality of a minor functionary. He jutted one beefy finger in the direction of a wooden chair against the wall. 'You can set your arse there until you is summoned.'

For a moment Flynt considered telling Blueskin he would return when Wild was ready for him, but that would be petty. He had reason to be here and little desire to return. The thieftaker's chosen centre of operations was too close to both the Old Bailey and the gaol of Newgate for Flynt's comfort.

He took his ease in the chair, which was no easy task as it had no padding, but, unlike the sedan, it was at least stationary. The sound of voices floated up the stairs towards them as the tavern grew busier.

Flynt fixed his eyes on the other man and said, 'I would stay away from Mother Grady's, my friend.'

Blueskin's head turned slowly as if he had forgotten Flynt was present. 'I will go where I please. And I ain't your friend.'

'Nonetheless, I will take it ill should I hear you have irritated Miss Belle again. Very ill indeed.'

Blueskin was amused. 'Am I expected to be fearful of you?'

Flynt give him the mere suggestion of a smile in reply, then tipped his hat low over his eyes, stretched his legs out in front of him, folded his arms and allowed his chin to drop towards his chest. To the observer he would look as if he was in repose, but in reality he was tensed to spring should Blueskin attack him. They shared the hallway, the silence between them broken only by the voices and the rattle of pot and tankard below.

After a few minutes the door opened and a lady of obvious quality stepped from the room, with Wild himself following. He gave Flynt a cursory glance then returned his attentions to his guest, whom Flynt found far more interesting even though she hardly registered the presence of any other person in the hallway. She held out her hand in the manner of someone who was used to deference, and Flynt studied her. She was wearing a blue silken mantua partially covered by a dark cape, the hood already over her head. Her skin was fashionably pale, her hair auburn, but her eyes were deep dark pools, all the better for keeping secrets hid. She was uncommonly beautiful and he would wager that she knew it.

'It is a pleasure to be of service, my lady,' Wild said, his Staffordshire accent yet strong despite his attempt at refining it. Flynt had been told that the thieftaker often treated those in his immediate circle roughly but he had pretensions to gentility and was so obsequious towards the gentry that witnessing it was likened to the ingestion of a strong emetic. It was said that there was many an alderman in the Guildhall and MP in the Commons who, before sitting down, first hitched up their coat to remove Wild's lips from where they had been firmly fastened.

Wild affected a slight bow and gently brushed those lips against the back of the lady's hand like a gallant. As he did so, her dark eyes flicked briefly in Flynt's direction and he knew in that swift glance she had studied him as intently as he had her.

Wild straightened. 'I trust I have assisted you to bring this matter to a conclusion you will find satisfactory.'

The lady said nothing, merely dropped her eyes in gratitude, extricated her hand from Wild's and walked away, lifting the hem of her dress to avoid it brushing against the dirt on the floor. Flynt caught sight of delicate blue damask shoes embroidered in great silk which he thought were of French design. Unusual, though he was no expert. He had once known a lady with similar footwear but she had been the mistress of the French ambassador to Spain. Flynt did not know for certain if Wild's visitor was aristocracy, landed gentry or simply a merchant's wife with airs, but she carried with her the arrogance of one who was used to comfort and the compliments of men. Wild was obviously useful to her for some reason and so she granted him the grace of her attention but that was all. Flynt had no doubt the thieftaker would ensure that she also granted him the grace of her gold.

Wild watched her leave, then turned when Blueskin said, 'This here is Jonas Flynt, Mr Wild.'

Wild, all trace of sycophancy now replaced by self-importance, jerked his head towards his office and stepped back inside. As Flynt moved to follow, Blueskin stepped in front of him in the doorway and said to his master, 'He's heeled, Mr Wild. Carries a pair of barkers.'

Wild turned to face Flynt. His eyes sharpened as he studied Flynt but he did not take a step back in any sign of alarm. 'This true? Are you carrying?'

Flynt peeled back the front of his greatcoat to reveal Tact and Diplomacy. 'Always. You never know what kind of ruffian you might meet who needs a ball in him to teach him manners.' This last was said directly to Blueskin, who bristled. Flynt fished the flintlock and club he had taken from Wild's men earlier from the pocket of his greatcoat and held them out in Wild's direction. 'You might wish to have these returned. Your lads left them behind in their haste to leave my company this morning.'

A smile ghosted Wild's lips as he flicked a finger at Blueskin to take possession of the weaponry. 'I heard of this morning's escapade with you and your doxy. Tell me, Flynt, do you intend to shoot me?'

Flynt turned his attention slowly back to the thieftaker as if considering the proposition. 'Not today.'

Wild laughed, then said to Blueskin, 'Well then, there you have it. The word of a gentleman. Let him come forward.'

Blueskin stepped aside with some reluctance and Flynt entered the room. It was not spacious but it was made smaller by the large desk of dark wood before the window that faced the Old Bailey session house.

Blueskin was minded to follow but Wild waved him away, saying, 'Ensure we are not disturbed. Mr Flynt and I have business.'

Blueskin could not halt a slight click of the tongue before he said, solely for Flynt's benefit, 'I'll be right outside.'

Wild gave this centre of his operations the grand title of Office for the Recovery of Lost and Stolen Property, and from here he spun his web while he sat feeling for which strand twitched. He was not a big man but neither was he slight of stature. At first glance his body looked strong, hardened by his years of prison and street life. Flynt knew well not to underestimate him. Others had done so to their cost. His men, Blueskin being a prime example, were little more than muscle and larceny on the hoof, but Wild was cunning.

The thieftaker wrenched off his wig and threw it on the desktop, running a hand over his close-cropped black hair before peeling off his coat to reveal a waistcoat of blue silk, hanging it over the back of the high chair behind his desk. Gesturing in the direction of a comfortable chair opposite, he moved to a shelf and took down a glass decanter half red with wine. 'Would you care for a taste?'

Flynt declined with a wave of the hand, then made a show of removing Tact and Diplomacy from his belt and laying them on the desktop, before he settled himself down, took off his hat and set it on his lap. His silver stick he held loosely in his left hand, resting its point on the floorboards.

'Ah, yes,' said Wild, remembering while he poured himself a large measure. 'I had heard you did not imbibe.'

'I do, but not when I am working.'

'And you are working now?'

'You think I am here for my pleasure?'

Wild seemed amused as he sat down in the heavy chair behind the desk. 'You are a curious individual, Mr Flynt.' Wild's attention lingered over the pistols on the desktop but he made no comment. The wood creaked as he tipped the chair back, threw one leg over the arm and studied Flynt over the rim of his glass, his steady gaze both assessing and judging. His hands bore slight nicks and gouges, old wounds perhaps gained when he had worked as a buckle maker in Wolverhampton, where Flynt had been told he still had a wife and child.

'I take it the lady is another satisfied customer,' Flynt said.

'Not yet, but she will be.'

'She has lost property for you to retrieve?'

Wild sipped his claret, his tongue darting out to catch the drops like a dog licking blood. 'It is a delicate matter.'

'It always is.'

Wild seemed keen to share but also wished to cling to the appearance of integrity. Flynt had heard he was fond of boasting of his accomplishments. Finally, he said, 'Her ladyship lost a letter. A most indiscreet letter.'

'Lost or stolen?'

Wild shrugged. 'It matters not. She does not have it and wishes its return before some rogue embarrasses both her husband, who is a very influential man, and the author, who is equally as prominent in society. Should the contents of that missive be revealed there would be a considerable scandal.'

'You are confident you can locate the letter and ensure its safe return?'

'Of course,' said Wild, and in that instant Flynt knew that Wild either already possessed the item or knew its location.

A silver sword rested by Wild's right hand. Street culls preferred shorter blades, sticks and firearms, but not the thieftaker, who had taken to sporting the weapon in the manner of a gentleman. He saw himself as a cut above and had the blade to prove it. He had been in partnership with a woman named Mary Milliner, who shared his enthusiasm for profiting from other people's property. That partnership had extended to the bedchamber but Wild had recently divorced himself from the liaison by cutting off her ear, perhaps with that very sword. Nothing demonstrates that a relationship has run its course more than the loss of a body part, Flynt thought to himself.

'So, Mr Flynt,' said Wild, his eyes still smiling at a jest only he could hear. 'We have business, do we not?'

'You tell me, Mr Wild,' said Flynt, even though he did in truth have his own purpose for being in this little room. He would broach that presently, but first he wished to know why Wild had taken such a keen interest in his affairs. 'You sent your message boys to fetch me.'

Wild tipped forward, returning all four legs of his chair to the floor, to lean over his desk with his glass cupped in both hands. 'Come, sir, such obtuseness ill becomes a gentleman such as yourself.'

'You called me that before, Mr Wild, but I am no gentleman.'

Wild smiled. 'There are no gentlemen in Scotland?'

'There are too many if you ask me, but I am not one of them.'

Wild thought about this. 'Perhaps not by birth but I would propose you are one by repute. A gentleman of the road.'

Wild was inferring that Flynt had plied a larcenous trade as a highwayman, and while it was true – Colonel Charters knew that well and used it to his advantage – he was certainly not going to admit it. The man before him was the biggest thief in the city; confessing anything to him could prove imprudent.

When Flynt did not reply, Wild sat back again. 'I know a great deal about you, Mr Flynt.'

'And I you, Mr Wild.'

A slight nod. 'And yet our paths have never crossed. They have followed parallel to one another most certainly but never met. Why is that, I wonder?'

'It is a large city.'

'Not that large and our world, the world of shadows we inhabit, is even less so. My man Blake out there, he knows many people. I know many people. I have other associates who also know many people. And yet, upon inquiry, I find that few of them have ever shared your society. I find that curious, Mr Flynt.'

'I am prejudiced regarding those with whom I share my time,' said Flynt, before adding for courtesy's sake, 'Mr Wild.'

Wild's eyes grew cold, just for a brief moment, but the chill thawed quickly and the smile returned. He was not an easy man to insult, a characteristic he shared with Charters. 'We need not be enemies, Mr Flynt.'

'I did not know we were, even though you sent your men, both armed, to interrupt me in my personal moments.'

'With a doxy.'

'With a lady,' corrected Flynt, 'and one they would be well advised to avoid in future, for she is not one to take such ill-usage lightly.'

Wild dismissed that with a shrug. 'Blueskin is his own man. He will do as he pleases.'

Flynt very much doubted that Blake so much as belched without Wild's permission but he let that pass. 'How came he by the name?'

'Some say it is because he is a swarthy fellow, and his heavy beard gives his chin a blue tinge, even after scraping it clean. Others because he was once befriended by a cove named Blewitt, so in jest they called him Blueskin. Blewitt and Blueskin.'

There was natural wit on the streets but such a 'jest' was not the best example, Flynt felt. 'Mr Wild, delightful though this conversation is, I have business elsewhere. Is it not about time that you told me why you sent your men to fetch me?'

'Very well. As I say, I know a great deal about you. You are Scotch, you served the old queen, God rest her, with some distinction, you turn a card with an ease that borders on the mystical, I hear. You live reasonably comfortably yet have no notable relationships, save the whore and the lad Jack Sheppard.' Flynt must have betrayed something for Wild smiled and said, 'Oh yes, Mr Flynt, I know of young Sheppard. I keep an eye on all the fresh rogues on the streets, for that is my business. Rogues, vagabonds, divers, doxies, cutpurses, footpads.' He paused. 'Highwaymen.'

'Is there a point to this, or is it your intention to bore me into admitting something to you?'

Wild chuckled. 'Yes, I had heard you were insolent too.'

'We all have a talent.'

'You have more than one, I am told. Those pistols, for instance.' He looked upon the weapons. 'I understand you are more than competent with them.'

'I hit that at which I aim.'

Wild's eye fell to the silver stick on which Flynt's left hand rested. 'And your swordsmanship is exquisite also.'

It irritated Flynt that the man knew of the blade concealed within but accepted the compliment with grace. 'We live in a dangerous world, Mr Wild, and a man must be prepared to defend himself against those very desperate individuals of whom you yourself have just made mention.'

'And you do it with such expertise. Two nights ago being a case in point.'

So it was about Satan's Gullet after all. Flynt feigned innocence. 'What occurred two nights ago?'

Wild rose to refill his now empty glass. 'Come, sir, let us not be coy. We are cut from similar cloth, you and I, and there is no need for men such as we to play games.' Flynt did not reply as Wild sat down again and sighed. 'Five men were murdered in a basement in St Giles. You did not hear of this?'

Flynt saw no reason to deny knowledge. 'I heard some talk of it but I suspected it was merely idle talk, a tale that grew in the telling.'

'No sir, it is my contention that you know much about the incident, for, sir, it was you who perpetrated the crime.'

'Crime, Mr Wild? It is my understanding that the men, if men there were, were themselves committing a crime.'

'They were and I was aware of it. My agents, in fact, were in the process of hunting them down to bring them to the king's justice when you intervened so bloodily.'

Flynt wondered how much Wild knew of the abduction of the young lord. It was possible that he was indeed searching for the men in order to claim the reward, but it was equally as possible he was involved in the planning of it and thus had been deprived of the revenue from the unpaid ransom.

'Then, were it the case that I did this thing of which you accuse me, I did you a service,' Flynt said.

'You did not, sir, far from it, sir. You intervened in official business and in so doing committed murder.'

'Official business? I was not aware that you or your men had been granted any official standing.'

Wild drew himself erect in his chair. 'I have the confidence of the council and the magistrates of this great city to help stem the rising tide of larceny and murder on our streets.'

'But no official title,' Flynt insisted. 'Only Mr Hitchin has any official capacity, I believe. He is yet Under-Marshall.'

Flynt mentioned Charles Hitchin purposely, for he knew it would stab at Wild. The man had been his mentor and had for some years been thieftaker. He had recruited Wild upon his release from debtors' prison a scant three years before. Wild was already a sly fox but he learned much while languishing in the Wood Street Compter and even more from the older man. However, Hitchin had appetites. In short, he liked young men, and while Flynt himself believed in live and let live he knew that such preferences in a commoner could lead to the disapproval of society. A different standard was set for those of higher birth.

Flynt was gratified to see Wild's eyes flare at the mention of his rival's name. 'That molly bought the title for seven hundred pounds – and he is suspended for dishonesty.'

'And yet, his title remains.'

'I am Thieftaker General,' Wild replied.

'Self-appointed. You have no warrant.'

'I provide a service.'

'So does a rat catcher.'

Wild laughed at the exchange. 'Aye, but the rats I catch walk on two legs and some of them adopt airs to which they are not entitled by birth.'

Flynt gave him a smile in return. They were conversing like two old friends. 'Do you have proof that I was present at this slaughter?'

'I know it to be true. And I also know it to be true that you made a handsome profit from the blood you shed. A reward was paid by the family of the boy who was taken.'

Here was the nub of it at last. Wild wanted a taste. Flynt would be damned if he would part with a penny. 'If it were the case that

I performed this service for the family and by extension the city, then I would have deserved such a reward. However, as it is, I am not the person you seek.'

A further silence fell between them as Wild searched his face for sign that he was lying. As the man had said, Flynt could turn a card to win a pot as if it were sorcery and part of that was the ability to keep his expression from betraying his thoughts. Wild, though, had survived by understanding men's natures and sometimes that had to be done at a glance. It was obvious he did not believe Flynt but a throaty laugh erupted.

'I like you, sir,' he said. 'You are a man of my own stripe.'

Flynt was unsure that was something to be desired but he swallowed the compliment as he would a bitter draught. 'I thank you.'

'I speak the truth. There are many adventurers such as you who would have acquiesced with such ease that there was hardly any sport in the joust. But you, sir, you...' He wagged a finger in Flynt's direction. 'You have spine and you have wit. There are not many who can retain their composure in this room and under my gaze. I see well why you are a demon at the tables. You and I will be great friends, I believe.'

Flynt knew when he was being handled and at that moment Wild's words were like fingers upon him. He went along with it, for he knew gold was important, but the time had come to raise the real reason for his presence and perhaps appeal to the man's vanity.

'In that spirit of friendship,' said Flynt, 'there is a matter in which you may assist me. It is within your bailliwick and it could prove profitable.' Flynt paused to let that register. 'And your assistance might bring you favour in influential circles.'

If there was anything that enticed Wild more than fattening his purse, it was increasing his standing among those he believed to be his betters. He was unable to disguise the glitter of greed in his eyes. 'What kind of profit? And what are these influential circles?'

'Discretion and honour do not afford me the liberty to identify the principal in this matter,' said Flynt. 'But rest assured, he and the gentlemen at his back are of sufficient rank to, shall we say, open doors that might normally remain closed to men such as you and I. I am a Scot of humble birth, you are a northerner with a chequered past, but these men often have need of us, of our individual skills, and can be most generous indeed.'

He was aware that he should not have been talking in such a manner but he had the feeling time was not his friend. If the will had been floating on the open market then Wild would be the one to know. The thought of profit and power was irresistible to the man.

'And what is this delicate matter?'

Flynt knew that he had him. 'It is a document.'

'What kind of document?'

'I regret I cannot go into detail but it is of vital importance that I recover it.'

Something crept into Wild's eyes, as if he were listening to the echo of earlier words. 'And was it stolen, lost?' he said carefully. 'If so by whom? From whence? And when?'

Flynt breathed in and contemplated how much he could share. He knew he walked a fine line in this conversation. On the one hand he did not care how much he told Wild, for the importance of the will mattered little to him and he was beginning to suspect the thieftaker had already divined the meaning of his words, but on the other if he said too much it could make the man ponder overlong upon for whom Flynt was working. Wild was correct – Flynt had a reputation in the world of shadows they shared and should it be revealed that he performed duties for Charters, albeit unwillingly, his life would not be worth a Frenchman's piss.

He leaned across the desk and lowered his voice in conspiratorial fashion. 'Mr Wild, you are a patriot, are you not?'

'I am.'

As long as there is coin in it, Flynt thought as he made a show of glancing back at the door, as if ensuring it was tightly shut. 'This document is vital to the security of this nation and the wellbeing of the monarchy. If it were to fall into the wrong hands, then both would be threatened, do you understand?'

He again saw the glimmer in Wild's eye. It was the look of a man who has come to believe he holds the winning card, but Flynt was expert in taking that look, the card and the pot away. Flynt sensed Wild knew exactly what the document was. 'I will tell you this. It was lost from Kensington Palace in August of last year.'

The glimmer took flame and Wild pursed his lips, then stood to replenish his glass. He hefted the decanter in Flynt's direction. 'I cannot tempt you?'

Flynt decided he should be more sociable. 'I will, thank you.'

Wild poured the two measures and carried a glass to Flynt, then set his buttocks against the desk so that he stood over him. It was a calculated, if obvious, display of dominance but it held no sway over Flynt. The thieftaker made a show of contemplating what he had been told and Flynt noticed his belly was slightly potted under his fine silk waistcoat. Hard he may be but his prosperity was beginning to show. They both sipped the wine, which Flynt found most agreeable. Wild's tongue lingered over his lips as he chose his next words.

'How came you to hear of this document, Mr Flynt?'

Flynt kept his voice casual, knowing he was snaring the man's interest. 'As you say, I enjoy the gaming tables. Men drink at these tables. The drink makes them talk. I listen to such talk for anything that might turn a profit. If I can find this document, I can negotiate with those powerful men I mentioned to turn us both a handsome sum.'

Wild considered this as he took another sip of wine. Flynt did similar and waited for the man to speak.

'Let us say, Mr Flynt,' he said, his words slow, 'for argument's sake, that I have heard tell of a document that was lost at the time of which you speak. Let us also say that not only have I heard of it but I know for certain of its whereabouts.'

'Then I would say tell me and I will ensure that both our pockets are lined.'

Wild's face was creased in thought. 'Mr Flynt, I am on the horns of the veritable dilemma. I wish to assist my country but my, erm, professional ethics urge caution.'

'Mr Wild,' Flynt began, then took another sip of the claret to hide his amusement at the thought of Wild having any professional ethics. 'This is damnable fine, I compliment you.'

Wild affected a slight bob of the head, pleased his vintage met with approval. 'Nothing but the best, sir.'

Flynt took another sip and made a show of his enjoyment, then said, 'Mr Wild, I understand you are bound by your code, I would expect nothing less of you, but there are greater stakes at play here, as I have stated. If you know where this document is, then I pray you tell me. I promise I will do us both justice and we will be saving the kingdom to boot.'

Wild was also making a show, but his was that of a man of principle struggling with his conscience. He straightened from the edge of the desk and walked around it once again to his chair, his shoulders hunched, his face still a portrait of mental turmoil. He sat down and laid his glass on the desktop, then reached out with his left hand to run a finger along the scabbard of his sword. Flynt instinctively felt his own grip tighten on the handle of his stick. Whenever a man reaches for a weapon, even in idleness, it was best to be prepared for action.

'Mr Flynt,' said Wild eventually, 'I believe the interests of the nation outweigh all else and that is why I will break my word – which is sacred to me – in this instance. Yes, I know of this document you seek and although I am not entirely cognisant of its contents, I am not a stupid man. I was approached last week by a rough fellow by the name of Bates, a ballast heaver at the docks who was once employed in some menial capacity in Kensington Palace. A dalliance with one of the maids led to scandal, for such things are not countenanced in great houses, but she retained her position while he did not. It was she who slipped him the document in question, on the night the late queen died, God rest her, along with a few others she had purloined, thinking she might turn a coin with them. Poor girl had no idea what she had, for she could neither read nor write, but this fellow Bates had wit enough to recognise a few words. He suspected there would be a hue and cry for such an item so he prudently waited until now to venture forth in order to profit from it.'

'Where does this Bates live?'

'Across the river, in the Mint.' Wild took up quill and scribbled an address on a slip of paper and handed it to Flynt. The Mint was part of Southwark and was a seething hotbed of criminals and debtors that made St Giles look like St James's. Flynt studied the scrawl while Wild continued his tale. 'I had heard tell of it a few days since but it was only yesterday forenoon that this fellow came to me with a view to selling it.'

'To whom?'

'To whomsoever has funds sufficient to pay.'

'And you agreed to act as broker?'

Wild spread his hands in an apology. 'I did not realise the full import until this very moment. Had I done so, I would of course have taken this intelligence to the Crown agents.'

Flynt doubted that very much but now was not the time to call the man a liar. He folded the paper and slid it into the pocket of his greatcoat, then stood up. He drained his claret and said, 'Thank you, Mr Wild, for the fine wine and the even finer information. I will ensure that your name is heard in the correct quarters and that you are suitably rewarded for your patriotism.'

'To serve is enough for me,' lied Wild with a humble bow of the head, 'but naturally I would not offend by refusing a just reward.'

Naturally, Flynt thought.

'But there is more, Mr Flynt,' said Wild, causing Flynt to pause. 'Another party was in this very room this very day.'

'Another party?'

'Aye, the lady you saw when you arrived.'

'So she was not seeking return of an indiscreet letter?'

Wild gave him an apologetic smile. 'Your pardon for the slight twist of truth, for that is all it was. Is this document not a letter of sorts? And is it not indiscreet in the cavalier way it might cause havoc in the kingdom?'

Once more, Flynt knew Wild was fully aware of the contents of the document but had been seeking to turn it to his advantage. 'And who was that lady?'

'She called herself Madame de Fontaine.'

'French?'

'By marriage, she said, but she is now widowed. She was originally of your country but she speaks the foul French tongue with fluency.'

'And did you tell this Madame de Fontaine that which you have told me?'

Wild looked shameful again but his lips vibrated with some merriment. Flynt rebuked himself, for while he had wasted time swapping words with this creature, the lady had been making good time towards the river and Southwark. He wasted no further breath on Wild, but merely pulled open the door and left the man at his desk with that curious little smile on his face, the spider having gorged on the fly.

5

The Mint was a liberty zone, where criminals felt safer from the jurisdictional reach of magistrates and men of the watch, and debtors sought a place of refuge from their creditors. The chairmen were unwilling to convey Flynt across the river, believing they would be lucky to escape with their lives, if not their sedan, but agreed to carry him to the northern entrance of London Bridge. He urged increased haste, resulting in an even rockier ride than before. As he clung to the strap and endeavoured to remain in the chair, Flynt thought of Wild. The man was indeed a sly one and well versed in playing on every side of a game. He had without doubt taken payment from the mysterious woman but now relished the prospect of profiting from Flynt. One day he fancied facing him in a game of chance, if only for the satisfaction of separating him from the contents of his purse. The thieftaker did not strike him as a gambling man, though, unless he had weighted the dice or shaved the cards in his favour.

The chairmen deposited him at the bridge and Flynt rewarded them handsomely before he set off on foot, forcing his way through a press of humanity that seemed hellbent on impeding his progress as it congressed in the archway. The bridge was the only way to the city from the south, unless you took a ferry or paid a waterman, so there was a constant stream of people on foot as well as driving carts, wagons, coaches and even livestock being taken to market. The roadway had been widened when the old buildings lining either side of the bridge had been rebuilt to jut over the water, struts and beams holding them steady, but they still loomed as if threatening to collapse upon him.

As he hurried, he thought of his quarry, a buzz of questions revolving in his mind. Wild had said the woman was Scottish but had married a Frenchman and spoke the language. Had she spoken French to him, or did he mean she had an accent? Madame de Fontaine, he had called her, but that could be an alias. She could be a French agent, or an adventurer like himself. It crossed his mind that she could even be in the pay of Colonel Charters, for he was certainly capable of setting more than one hound to follow a scent.

The streets leading to the Mint were populated by a variety of debt collectors awaiting any unwary individuals who might cross the frontier from the safe zone and so be liable to arrest and imprisonment until the debt was cleared. These duns turned their sharp eyes on him as he passed, taking in his features and searching for any identifying marks that might reveal him to be one of the indebted they sought. None molested him, though, and he passed the invisible boundary with ease. He was now in the liberty zone and he needed to be on his mettle.

The address Wild had given him was an ancient three-storey ramshackle hovel that may even have dated back to the days of old Henry when there actually was a Royal Mint in this part of Southwark. It was situated in a narrow street which itself could have been picked up and transported to St Giles and felt well at home. The gutter down the centre of the roadway was clogged with similar waste and garbage and the buildings that crowded on either side possessed the same desperate look. The smell, the olfactory sense that humanity had reached its lowest ebb without actually being beneath the sod, was also shared with the streets beyond the city walls to the north-west.

The hackney he had seen outside the Blue Boar waited here, its squat driver obviously having no qualms about accepting the fare from the comparative safety of the city; Madame de Fontaine had no doubt sweetened the pot with a hefty tip. Nevertheless, he seemed tense as he perched above his pair of horses, his hands fingering a cudgel that had obviously been well used. The city streets could be dangerous places for those eking a living upon them and a man had to be prepared for anything. In the Mint, those dangers were writ large. The driver gave Flynt a long appraisal and, judging he was no immediate threat, resumed casting his gaze about him for any sign of ambush.

The man Bates lived on the second floor, according to Wild's note. The street door lay open and Flynt peered into the gloom beyond, a crawling sensation at the nape of his neck alerting him there was something amiss. He had learned to pay heed to his instincts over the years for they were seldom wrong. He pushed the door open further with the toe of his boot as he thrust his swordstick into his belt and withdrew Tact and Diplomacy, sensing he would have need of them. The street itself was dingy, for even though it was early afternoon the buildings blocked the daylight, but stepping into this narrow foul-smelling corridor was as if night had fallen with unnerving suddenness. He paused and listened in a blackness so intense that it took even his sharp eyes considerable time to grow accustomed. Beams creaked. There was movement somewhere beyond but not human, the scrabble of unseen claws and the image of countless dark-furred bodies flashed through his mind. He shuddered, wishing he could shake off this revulsion while also knowing that the memory of its source would never leave him. From somewhere above he heard a woman's voice, but could not discern her words, and the sound of foot on wood. Slowly a flight of stairs emerged from the gloom and he began to ascend, pistols at the ready. He took each step carefully, cursing every groan of the ancient boards beneath him, nerves tingling in anticipation of some form of attack. The prickling of his skin increased as he neared the first landing, where the darkness was a shade lighter thanks to illumination tip-toeing down the next flight of stairs. As he edged along the short landing, a door opened hesitantly and a woman's face appeared, elderly, fear evident in her lined features. He would be little more than a grey shape in the shadows but she would see the brace of pistols held aloft in each hand.

'Go back inside, mother,' he whispered.

'Have a care,' she said, her accent carrying the breeze of Welsh mountains. 'There is murder above.'

She closed the door and he paused at the first step to peer upwards. Daylight slanted in from somewhere, a window perhaps, even a hole in the roof. The beam pierced the darkness like a spear, bleeding soft light across the wooden walls. Motes of dust infested the shaft as if they were a plague of insects feeding upon it.

The woman's voice was clearer now as it filtered down from the floor above. Her words were French.

Madame de Fontaine was here.

He began to ascend the final set of stairs, eyes fixed for any figures breaking through the luminescent column. At the top he peered through the beam to the dimness beyond and saw a doorway lying slightly ajar. The sound of booted feet stomped across bare boards. Bates, perhaps? But the old woman had said there was murder here. Was Bates the murderer or the victim? The footfalls were definitely those of a man for he doubted the stylish footwear he had glimpsed on the lady's feet would have created such a distinctive tread. He recalled the broad face looking from the darkness of the carriage interior outside Wild's headquarters – was it his step he heard? He edged forward, ensuring he made as little sound as possible even though the floor creaked with each step, tarrying at the partially open door to listen. Another door, another room beyond holding unknown peril. Such was his life, it seemed. How many such doors, how many such dangers had he encountered? And how long would it be before he opened the wrong one? He breathed deeply, flexed his shoulders to ease the tension that had crept upon them and eased the door open with his toe.

The window shutters were pushed fully open and sunbeams climbed over the roof of the building opposite to steal away the dark of the little room. Enough, at least, to make out the man lying on the floor, his head at an unnatural angle, and the woman standing over him as if he were nothing but an old rug. In her hand was a sheaf of papers, which she was reading with great interest. She became aware of the movement at the door and looked up sharply, taking in Flynt and his pistols as if he were a servant bringing afternoon tea.

'Gregor,' she said.

The door slammed into Flynt's side and jammed him against the frame, both arms slightly pinioned by the sheer weight behind it. He pushed back but the pressure was powerful. A large hand reached round the edge of the door and wrenched Tact from the grip of his left hand to toss it across the floor. Flynt strained against his confinement and engineered to twist Diplomacy in his attacker's direction. The sharp edge of the frame bit into the flesh of his upper right arm even through his greatcoat, but he ignored the scraping pain and managed to bring the weapon level sufficiently to blast towards the door in the hope it would hit the man behind. Acrid gunsmoke puffed in his face and a hole splintered the wood. The pressure eased and he was able to leap into the room, believing he had hit his mark, but the hand he had seen earlier reached out again, gripped him by the front of his greatcoat and threw him across the room as if he were discarded laundry. Pain shot through his shoulder where it connected with the bare floorboards but he rolled and in a fluid movement dropped his spent weapon even as he plucked his silver stick from his belt. He rose to one knee and palmed the sword handle, ready to draw it.

He could see his attacker now. Gregor, she had called him, the same broad face from the carriage in the Bailey, a big man, his body brawny, his hair long and held back behind his head like the tail of a horse. His left hand appeared to be gloved but not his right, which Flynt found curious, but this was not the time to ponder it. Gregor looked to the lady for further instructions. She said something in French, which Flynt did not understand, and the man nodded but did not make any move to mount a further attack. He had grey eyes, cold, unfeeling, and he fixed them upon Flynt, a little smile taunting him to mount some kind of offence.

'If you rise further, Gregor will kill you,' the woman said in English, her accent a curious mix of French and Scots.

Flynt had no doubt the man would most certainly try and perhaps even succeed. 'I will stay here then,' he decided. As he had noted in the hallway outside Wild's office, the lady was quite beautiful and her dark red hair, free from the confines of her hooded cape, tumbled down about her shoulders. 'You are Madame de Fontaine, I presume?'

She seemed surprised he knew her. 'You have the advantage of me.'

'My apologies, madame, but circumstances prevented me from making a formal introduction. My name is Jonas Flynt.'

She made a show of studying him as she locked his name in her mind. 'I saw you earlier, did I not?'

He nodded, even though he knew she had recognised him as soon as she saw him in the doorway. This was a woman who saw all and forgot nothing.

She stabbed the papers in her hand towards the corpse at her feet. 'You are friend to this man?'

'I regret I did not have his acquaintance.'

'Then why are you here?'

'I am here for the same reason as you.' Flynt gestured with his chin towards the document. 'For that.'

Madame de Fontaine looked at the paper and smiled. 'You are a Scot.'

'I am.'

'You have been sent by the Fellowship? I assured them I would obtain the document. They need not have sent you.'

Flynt's lack of comprehension would have been fleeting but she narrowed her eyes. 'Ah, I think you are not from our friends in the north, after all. You are one of Colonel Charters' rogues then?' Again, she perceived a telltale flicker for she smiled. 'Do not be surprised, monsieur. It is my business to know of such things.'

Her smile was like sunshine which in any other situation he might find charming, but not when he was taking a knee on the floor while a brute awaited a simple nod giving leave to tear him apart. Flynt's hand tightened on the handle of the sword which remained sheathed within its slender scabbard. He still had surprise on his side.

'I would appreciate it, madame, if you would leave the document here, then you and your companion may leave without any further unpleasantness.'

She laughed. It was a lovely laugh and he wondered how many men had been entranced by it, her smile and her fair countenance, no doubt to their detriment. 'Monsieur Flynt, I admire your courage – or is it stupidity?'

'Madame, I suspect it is a bit of both.'

'Perhaps. But you are in no position to make any demands. Gregor here can rend your flesh as though you were a roast fowl.'

Gregor had not moved an inch but his smile suggested to Flynt that he enjoyed rending any kind of flesh. 'I take your point.'

Madame de Fontaine folded the document and thrust it into the pocket of her cape. 'I would not move, Monsieur Flynt.' She pulled the hood over her head and stepped towards the door.

'Madame, you must know that I cannot do that. I will have that document.'

She looked back at him, the smile now gone, and she regarded him with sadness. 'I am so very sorry to hear that.'

She crooked a finger at Gregor and he leaped across the floor. Flynt, though, was already moving. He rose to his feet, slid his rapier free and sprang in the air to bring the blade swinging down towards the brute's head. Gregor's forward motion did not falter but his left hand shot up to parry the blow. Flynt instantly thought this folly, for the keen blade would slice flesh with ease, even through the glove.

The sword did not strike flesh, however. The raised hand was solid and Flynt realised what he thought was a glove was a sheath. What lay underneath he did not know, only that it was as unyielding as steel and his blade bounced from it without leaving so much as a dent. Gregor clamped Flynt's wrist with his stiff fingers while clasping him by the throat with his good hand, lifting him effortlessly from the floor and pinning him against the wall. Flynt pulled at the man's arm to dislodge the grip that not only threatened to block the air from reaching his lungs but was forceful enough to crush his windpipe. He struggled to free his sword arm from the leathery fist but was unable to wrench it clear. Those fingers may have been immovable but their grasp was tight and they twisted until he was forced to allow the weapon to clatter to the floor.

His boots rattled a tattoo against the wall as his vision began to cloud. Through the gathering mist he saw Gregor's face peer into his, the minutest of smiles showing that he was vastly entertained by Flynt's attempts to retain his hold on life, knowing it was to no avail. This, to all intents and purposes, was a hanging, his hanging, with Gregor's vice-like constriction acting as the noose and his arm the gallows tree. He did not wish to leave this world in such a manner, to have the life squeezed from him in this desolate room and be left as a feast for vermin. He did not wish this brute to take pleasure from seeing his bladder gush and his bowels open.

Forcing the panic from his mind, he endeavoured to focus. His left hand snaked down to the pocket of his greatcoat and his fingers felt the reassuring heft of the dagger he had taken from the basement in St Giles. He snatched it free and would have plunged it deep into Gregor's belly had the man not read his movements. Gregor was too swift even for that. He relinquished his hold on Flynt's throat and caught the thrust before it could reach its target. Both arms were now almost totally immobile but his feet were resting on the floor once more and he could breathe, which was a blessing albeit one that proved short-lived. Gregor wrenched his wrist almost to breaking point and yet another blade tumbled to the floor unblooded before he resumed his vice-like grip on Flynt's throat.

Flynt twisted against the pressure, not to free himself, for he knew he could not, but to position himself in such a way that he could make his next move. He did not know if he had succeeded in doing so but he knew it was a now or never situation. This would work or it would not.

With all the strength he could muster, he lashed out with his right knee, praying he would not strike Gregor's unyielding leg but something more vulnerable. The man was powerful and he was large but a solid knee to the manhood would fell any man. Unfortunately, his prayers remained unanswered for the big man barely flinched when Flynt's knee failed to hit the mark. Flynt tried again but still could not find the tender spot between Gregor's legs.

His muscles weakened and his vision misted again. The pressure on his throat was agonising and it would only take a few more moments to crush the delicate bone. Flynt's mind raced. Do something, do anything, don't die like this...

Flynt unclamped the fingers of his left hand from the giant paw that squeezed his neck and reached out almost blindly to Gregor's face, seeking another soft target, one that was easier to find. Finally he reached the man's right eye and thrust his thumb deep into the socket, probing as far as he could. The sensation of compressing something pulpy yet curiously unyielding was distinctly unpleasant and he wondered how long he could continue before the man either released his own grip, the integrity of the eyeball was breached or Flynt himself expired.

Thankfully it was the first option. A strange muted cry grew in Gregor's throat as blood trickled round the pressure of Flynt's thumb. His grip around Flynt's throat fell away and tried to deflect the fingers from inflicting such pain but Flynt pressed harder, not caring if he blinded the man. He sucked in air as his boots thudded onto the floorboards again. He wanted to twist away to fill his lungs and ease the agonising grip at his throat but he had to somehow bring the man down first. He shifted his body slightly until he knew he was in the correct position then slammed his knee deep between the man's legs. The first attempt generated no response but the second seemed to hit the mark. Gregor squealed, his leather claw released its grip of Flynt's other arm as he doubled over slightly and stumbled away, his good hand wiping the blood from his eye. Flynt followed him, lashing out again, this time with his booted foot, and connected with considerable force on Gregor's knee. The resounding blow gave him considerable satisfaction so he did it again, hoping he could shatter bone. Gregor's face contorted with agony as he pitched to one side, the knee giving way, and landed hard on his uninjured one.

Flynt darted to retrieve his blade and pressed the point into the flesh below Gregor's unbloodied eye.

'That is enough,' said Madame de Fontaine as she aimed a small pistol at him. That was the second one that day, making him wonder how many women carried such firearms.

He affected a nonchalant smile as he rubbed his bruised throat. 'If your man so much as twitches I will run this into his brain,' he said, his voice a painful rasp. He gave Gregor a look that assured him he meant what he said. 'It will only take a slight amount of pressure, my friend. And don't think of clutching the blade. The edge is sharp and will slice through fingers with ease, while your false hand will fail to make purchase.'

Gregor's red-eyed glare was a mixture of blood and hatred.

'And if you do harm to my friend, I will cut you down,' the woman said, her voice as steady as her hand. 'I am competent with this weapon, I can assure you.'

'I do not doubt you, madame,' said Flynt, the words irritating his windpipe and making him cough. 'It would appear we are deadlocked.'

'Not if we agree to cease further hostilities. I will order Gregor to back away slowly. Your blade will remain unblooded. I will not shoot. We leave. You live.'

Flynt studied her over Gregor's head. The pistol did not waver. Her voice was equally as steady. He returned his attention to Gregor's face which still burned with a desire to commit mayhem, although he did not move. He may have been a brute but he knew the sword could penetrate eye and brain before he could move a fraction of an inch.

Flynt considered the lady's alternative to further bloodshed. Them leaving and his living did have its appeal. 'And the document?'

'It stays with me.'

'I cannot accept that.'

'Then we stand here until one of us drops from exhaustion. And I have not recently been choked close to the point of unconsciousness.'

Flynt recognised that she made a good point. His throat still ached from Gregor's stranglehold and his body felt as if it had been trampled upon not just by a team of four but also the cannon they pulled. He considered his options. He could dispose of Gregor, which would give him no small amount of pleasure, but he would then be gunned down, for he suspected Madame de Fontaine was not merely a competent shot but extremely proficient.

'Are you a woman of your word?'

'Of course,' she replied, her eyes twinkling. 'I always do that which I say I will.'

He looked at Gregor again. 'And your man?'

'He will do as I command,' she said with a confidence Flynt did not share. However, he knew when a game was lost. He slowly lowered the blade, his eyes watchful for the first sign of Gregor not being a man of his mistress's word but the big man merely rose slowly and backed away, his gait slightly lopsided but his eyes bearing a promise of pain in the future.

True to her pledge, Madame de Fontaine lowered the pistol and stowed it away in the pocket of her cape. 'A wise move, Mr Flynt.' She and her man backed out of the door. 'Please do not pursue us. I will shoot you. And even if by some chance I miss, I assure you that you will not get the better of Gregor a second time.'

'We will meet again, my lady,' said Flynt. 'I also keep my word.'

She smiled. 'I count on it.'

They vanished into the darkness of the hallway and the sound of their footsteps clattered down the stairs, hers light, his with a slight hitch. Flynt let them go, for even though he knew he should make an attempt to retrieve the will, he did not believe he had the strength for another bout with Gregor or the desire to test the woman's marksmanship. He leaned against the wall and slid to a sitting position, his sword across his legs. He rubbed his throat and took several ragged breaths while studying the body of the man a few feet away. It had to be Bates. He had been a husky fellow, with the thick, strong arms of one who loaded ballast onto ships for a living, and yet Gregor had snapped his neck with apparent ease.

The sound of a whip crack and a galvanising bellow was followed by the clip of hooves and scrape of wheels on dirt. The carriage, pulling away with the woman and her hulk. And, more to the point, the document. He had come so close to retrieving it but now it was gone, carried in the folds of a cape draped around a mysterious woman. As the hooves faded, Flynt consoled himself with the thought that the hand was lost but not the game. He lived to deal again.

6

The two men were not evenly matched. One was tall and heavy-set with head shaved; the other smaller, equally muscular, but his long hair was pulled back and clasped behind his head with a red ribbon. They were naked from the waist up with only loose-fitting breeches to cover their modesty. They circled each other barefoot, their backs stiff and erect, their elbows tight against their bodies and fists held up before them ready to defend or strike. Around them the faces of men and women clustered, each craning to see beyond the head in front in order not to miss a blow or, preferably, the flow of blood. Bookmakers walked among them taking bets and offering odds. Bottles of gin and wine were tipped and passed. Voices cried out encouragement or jeered at each crack of knuckle on jaw. The Bear Garden on Marylebone Fields was not a place Flynt visited regularly and he was glad that on this occasion it was men and not animals doing battle to satisfy the bloodlust of noble and commoner alike.

Flynt found Charters among the crowd, his guards as ever keeping a respectful, if watchful, distance. The colonel did not add his voice to the general din surrounding the spectacle but his eyes glittered as he observed the two men jab stiff-armed at each other. So far the bout was reasonably civilised, a punch here, a duck there, but Flynt knew from experience pugilism was raw and visceral and there was every likelihood the men would resort to grappling and kicking. The noble art of self-defence was often far from noble, as Flynt himself could testify.

'You are late,' Charters said without diverting his attention from the men.

'I have been busy on your behalf,' said Flynt, which was true. He had spent all afternoon and a goodly part of the evening on his investigations.

'I hope you have some news for me.'

Flynt avoided the subject for now. 'It does not seem a fair fight,' he observed, even though he had minimal interest, if any, in the outcome. For him, fighting was what you did to survive, it was not entertainment. He was far more enthralled by the nerve and skill needed at the gaming tables. Luck was required as the cards were dealt, to be sure, but there was luck required in the ring also. A guard dropped for a second, a weakness of flesh and bone discovered and preyed upon, a misstep – all were bad luck for one, but the opposite for an opponent with wit sufficient to capitalise upon it.

'Make no mistake, Serjeant, each of these men is as capable as the other.' Charters grinned. 'The smaller man is Edward Noble. Thirty contests this year and none lost.'

The taller man shot his arm out like a rapier and cracked Noble on the nose.

'And the other?'

'James Figg, up from Oxford courtesy of his patron the Earl of Peterborough. A fighting machine with fist, sword or quarterstaff. We could have done with him in Flanders.'

Noble had staggered back slightly after the blow, wiping blood from his nostrils with the back of his hand and leaving a trail of blood on his cheek like a duelling scar. Figg followed, his other fist already darting forward to deliver another blow to the same spot. Flynt studied him, wondering how he would fare going toe to toe with Gregor, the memory of whose delicate touch lingered in the bruised flesh of his throat.

Charters retained his focus on the fight as he asked, 'I take it from your failure to answer my question that the hunt does not go well?'

'I almost had it.'

Charters gave him a swift glance. 'Almost is not what I wish to hear, Flynt. Almost does not ensure the safety of this nation. Did Wild have it?'

'No, but he knew of its whereabouts.'

'And how did he know that?'

Flynt quickly told him about Bates having the will and Wild being asked to act as intermediary, ending with the encounter in the Mint. He omitted to mention where Bates obtained the document in the first place for he had no desire to have some poor maidservant lose her position and quite possibly her life. If the State was willing to sacrifice a lad for the theft of a kerchief, they would not hesitate to do the same to a young woman who purloined something of national importance, whether she knew it or not.

Charters grunted. 'And yet you do not have it.'

Flynt shrugged. 'Does the name Madame de Fontaine resonate?'

Charters looked back to the combatants, where Figg was once again beating Noble as if his fists were clubs. 'It does. I take it she is the reason for the "almost"?'

'She is. But who is she?'

Charters did not reply as he watched Noble summon strength from somewhere deep within to battle back, lowering his head and slamming into Figg's midriff like a bull. A great cry rose from the audience as Figg crashed his elbows hard into the man's back but he was carried by the charge and he stumbled, tipping backwards. Noble threw himself on top of him, delivering blow upon blow to his opponent's face and upper arms. Figg had to cover himself in whatever way he could but it looked as if his luck had run out.

Charters' lips flattened, whether at the turn the fight had taken or mention of the woman's name Flynt did not know. The colonel cast his eyes around but the throng was too intent on the match to pay attention to what he was saying. 'I thought her still to be in Paris but if she is here in London clearly she has evaded the agents of my Lord Stair.'

Lord Stair was the ambassador to France and had a well-developed spy network in order to monitor French movements and those of the Pretender. The thought that he had somehow allowed the woman to slip through his fingers seemed to amuse Charters as much as it annoyed him that she had somehow bested Flynt.

'She is Scottish?'

Charters nodded. 'Her father fled the country after the Glorious Revolution when William of Orange took the throne from James. Lord Christian Montgomery was a Jacobite to the marrow and he tried to raise his daughter similarly, but like so many of the fairer sex – more than many men would wish to acknowledge – she had a mind of her own.'

His words brought Belle back to Flynt's mind and he felt some shame at believing she needed protection.

'She married a Parisian merchant of no mean wealth, but he died within the year.' A flicker of amusement tickled Charters' lips. 'There are those who say it may even have been by natural causes.'

'And now she works for the French?'

'Yes, but she will also perform services for anyone who will pay her.'

'Including you?'

Charters ignored the question and Flynt took that evasion as confirmation that he had used Madame de Fontaine's skills in the past, which might explain how she knew of the Company of Rogues. On the other hand, the French also had an efficient spy network and were bound to know of its existence if perhaps not who filled its ranks. Flynt doubted no one person apart from Charters himself knew that.

Instead Charters asked, 'I take it Wild informed her of the document's location?'

'Almost certainly.'

'And yet he also told you.'

'I appealed to his patriotism,' Flynt said, prompting another smile from Charters.

'That individual's patriotism lies in his purse, I believe,' Charters observed. 'He will without doubt see a way to profit from both sides in this matter. I will hazard he has already been paid by Madame de Fontaine, and in your entreaties I presume was the promise of further benefits?'

'You assume correctly. I convinced him that it would be to our mutual benefit to enter a loose partnership.'

'The man is a damnable rogue.'

'That he is. Almost crooked enough to be part of His Majesty's inner circle.'

Charters gave Flynt a scathing look. 'Are you certain this woman de Fontaine has it?'

'I saw it, or at least what I take to be it, in her hand with the man Bates dead at her feet.'

'Did she kill him?'

'No, that was a fellow she called Gregor.'

Charters seemed unsurprised. 'Gregor Vasilovich. A decidedly vicious killer. You and he could be brothers, Flynt. You were lucky to escape with your life.'

Flynt was well aware how close he had come to death. As for the suggestion they were alike, Flynt let that pass, although Gregor seemed to take pleasure in such work while Flynt did only what was necessary within the moment. At least, that was how he justified it to himself.

'He was formerly a member of the Streltsy, the Russian praetorian guard,' Charters continued. 'They were very powerful but about, oh, seventeen years ago Tsar Peter had them disbanded – he slaughtered hundreds of them – because they posed a threat to his dominion, not to mention his personal wellbeing. He had good reason to fear for his own head. Some years before he had watched as they threw their own commander and his mother's lover from the balcony of the palace onto pikes because they believed they had been complicit in strangling Peter's half-brother, even though that same half-brother stood before them in plain view.'

'People will see what they want to see, believe what they want to believe, no matter how ridiculous.'

'Quite so. Gregor escaped the purge with his life and became a soldier of fortune. He somehow met up with Madame de Fontaine and now never leaves her side. There are those who say they are more than mere comrades.'

Flynt thought of the man he had battled. He was not a handsome fellow, whereas his mistress was pleasing to the eye, but he was experienced enough to know that there was more to attraction than physical beauty. He believed himself to be no Adonis. His nose was crooked, his face just a little too long, and although his chin and jaw were firm he thought himself a plain-faced man who would not in the ordinary course of romance have caught the eye of a woman as fair as Belle. However, as had been made clear only that day, his arrangement with Belle was a commercial one, even though he did think of her most fondly. No, it was Cassie who came to his mind. How he had ever drawn her to him was a mystery.

'Somewhere along the line the Russian has lost a hand,' Flynt told Charters. 'He has an artificial one now, encased in leather.'

Charters unconsciously twitched the shoulder of his empty sleeve. 'Fortunes of war. I am sure he remains a formidable opponent.'

Flynt once again felt the sensation of the man's fingers at his throat.

Figg had thrown Noble from him and, even though his body had suffered punishment from the man's ferocious blows, leaped to his feet as if he was getting out of bed at the end of a fine night's rest. The two resumed their stance, backs straight, heads up, arms and fists forward, and circled one another once more. Flynt wondered if this was a way of catching their breath as much as seeking an opening for a fresh attack.

'Bravo, sir!' Charters called out, his encouragement suggesting to Flynt he had a wager riding on Mr Figg's abilities. Then his voice lowered again. 'So all is lost?'

'Not quite.'

When he had recovered sufficiently from the encounter with Gregor, he had made haste back to the bridge and across the river. Once there he inquired of hackney drivers and chairmen, describing the driver he had seen. There were not many who would risk the Mint, no matter the sum offered, and though it took him a few hours he finally tracked him down to a tavern on the Strand. The driver was cagey when Flynt questioned him about his passengers but a few coins soon smoothed down the rough edges of his ethics and he told Flynt he had dropped them at the White Hart on Bishopsgate. By the time Flynt reached the inn his birds had flown, but he struck up a conversation with a young groom who told him that they had departed, bag and baggage.

Charters' eyes did not stray from the fight as he listened to Flynt's recitation of his investigation. 'As I said, all is lost,' he said.

'As *I* said, not quite. The woman mentioned that she was in the employ of something called the Fellowship.'

That drew Charters' attention from the brawlers. 'The devil she is.'

'You know of this Fellowship?'

'I know of it. An underground society so secret not even I know who fills its ranks.'

'They are Jacobite?'

'That is the damnable thing about them, we do not know.'

Flynt thought about this. 'If this Fellowship seeks the old queen's will then they must be drawn to the power it represents.'

'Quite so, but what benefit it would be to them I cannot say.'

'Financial? They could ransom it to the highest bidder.'

Charters agreed. 'There have been criminal enterprises in which their name has surfaced but also political acts. There has been mention of them in intelligence reports for some years now, but they are like the mist. Whenever I or those like me reach out to grasp them, they simply slip through our fingers and vanish. Until now, I might even have dismissed them as mere rumour. But de Fontaine was working for them, you say?'

'That was my distinct impression.'

'God damn it, man, if this Fellowship can hide themselves from me then it may mean all is really lost! I do not even know where they are based.'

'I believe she is taking the will to Scotland.'

'That is a wild assumption, Flynt. She could be taking it in any direction – Paris or Rome even. She managed to enter the country without being identified so I am certain she could engineer passage in the opposite direction with little difficulty.'

'Perhaps, but during our exchange she mentioned our friends in the north.'

Charters allowed this to play on his mind. 'You cannot be certain she is headed for Scotland. She could have meant one of the Jacobite sympathisers in the northern shires for all you know. Not all supporters of the Pretender are Scots.'

'It was because I was a Scot that she thought I was with them. I do not think that was an idle thought. No, she is not headed for the Continent or a Yorkshire manor house. The stable lad I spoke to was certain he heard her mention Edinburgh.'

'How certain?'

Flynt could only shrug. 'He said she and her man were unaware of his proximity and were speaking softly but he swore he heard Edinburgh. And they were provisioned for a lengthy journey.'

'She could have uttered it in his hearing to lay a false trail. She is a cunning vixen and would know that you would follow her.'

'Aye, but what other choice do we have? She made mention of the north, she let Edinburgh slip, there is a rising in progress, so where better to take this will?'

Charters fell silent once more and returned his attention to the two men who had stopped raining blows and were now grappling, fingers slipping on sweat and blood-soaked flesh. Finally, Figg threw Noble away from him and lashed out with his right fist. It connected with the man's already weakened nose, sending more blood spraying into the air. He followed with his left, again to the nose. Noble's legs wobbled with the force of the blows but Figg's work was not complete. He clasped his two hands together and swung them with all his strength against Noble's jaw, the force of the blow snapping the man's head to one side. Noble staggered, his upper body swaying, his arms hanging at his side as if devoid of any strength. Figg stepped closer, raised his right fist to shoulder level and then shot it forward, driving it into his opponent's face with considerable force. Even from where he stood, Flynt heard the crunch as bone and cartilage succumbed to the inevitable and Noble rocked back on his heels before he pitched backwards like a felled tree and did not move.

Cheers exploded from those smiling men who had money on the victor while groans and unhappy looks darkened the countenances of those who had not. Colonel Charters nodded in a satisfied manner, confirming Flynt's earlier belief that he had a wager riding on Figg's abilities.

The victor held both arms aloft and walked around the fighting area. 'I am Jemmy Figg from Thane,' he cried. 'And I will fight any man in England!'

His handlers and supporters crowded around him, slapping him on the back. Someone passed him a bottle and he took a long drink.

'A fine victory,' said Charters as he led Flynt away from the crowd, his men trailing behind and around them.

'You will not collect your winnings, Colonel?'

Charters waved his hand. 'I will have them collected anon. It was but a trifle and a gentleman does not lower himself to such a base exchange.'

By his sour expression whenever it had appeared that Figg was labouring, Flynt doubted very much indeed that he had risked a trifle on the man's fists. 'So what do you wish me to do now? You must have agents in Edinburgh who can take up the trail.'

'Of course I do, but there are two types of agents in my employ – those who watch and those who act. You, my dear Serjeant Flynt, are the latter. It is time for you to go home.'

Part Two

Edinburgh, November 1715

7

The laughter of boys reached Flynt's ears from the alleys and wynds but its source was not corporeal, he knew, merely echoes of the past playing on his mind. Home, Charters had called it, but he wondered. Yes, here was family, here was the place of his childhood, but he had left all of that behind as a youth. In London, he had rooms in Charing Cross but he did not think of those as home. The truth was, and he realised this with some surprise, Jonas Flynt thought of nowhere as home.

Even so, as he approached Edinburgh from the south and saw the line of buildings creeping up hill towards the castle, perched atop the rock like an eagle surveying the land below, he felt something stirring within him. He knew not what it was. A thrill of expectation, perhaps. Or dread.

The journey from London took almost two weeks. He could have travelled by coach but he did not relish the thought of being imprisoned for hours on end in an uncomfortable and cramped vehicle sharing air and body odours while making small talk. Such intimacy with strangers was not something he relished. In many ways he preferred the company of his horse and he visited the fine black mare every few days in the stable space he rented to ensure she was being properly treated and exercised. He need not have worried, for the owner, a former cavalry officer, handled all the mounts in his care as if they were his own children, of which he had many, for he was a man of great passion which had led him to three wives and a string of mistresses.

It felt good to be back in the saddle after months of being city-bound and he resolved to get away from the streets more often in future, perhaps further afield than Blackheath and Hounslow where he had followed the life of a highwayman. He had a yen to see the West Country and perhaps when he had such liberty he would visit. Travelling to Scotland on horseback meant he could move at his own pace, halt when he felt the need, overnight at inns of his own choosing, even under the stars if the weather was fair. He need not fret about having to suffer the discomfort of being tossed about as the coach lurched over the ruts on the Great North Road, be delayed by thrown wheels or having to labour to free those wheels when they became mired in mud. Luckily, the elements as he headed north were on the whole peaceful so he was able to enjoy much of the trip. He did notice the change in temperature as he left the comparatively mild climes of the south. It had not been overly warm in London but it was now early November and though dry there was a chill in the Scottish air that hinted at the tough winter ahead.

He passed the Palace of Holyrood and the abbey ruins standing like gravestones to an old religion that had been almost murdered by hatred. On the other side loomed the crags where he and the friends of his youth once roamed. He thought now of them – of Rab Gow and Charlie Temple. And Cassie. Always Cassie, there in his thoughts like a guilty secret. She too had run with them through these streets. She had lain with them in the grasses atop those cliffs, listening as Flynt and Charlie talked of heroes and brave deeds from ancient Rome and Greece, fancying they saw shapes in the clouds. They had been companions, the three boys and the girl, and had vowed to remain so forever. But that, like life, had changed and those days were long gone. He had seen more of life and more of death.

Rab's father was a cobbler while Charlie's parents were reasonably successful merchants but never did he make them feel they were in any way beneath him. Life seemed so different when viewed through the eyes of a boy. The iniquities of class, of station, of wealth and the lack thereof meant nothing. Flynt's father was often away at sea, and his mother Jenny had died when he was an infant, so his upbringing was left to the care of her sister who, though kindly, had little inclination to properly care for a lad growing into manhood, although she did instil in him a love of reading. Flynt was at liberty to run wild and free through the town itself, around the waters of the Nor' Loch beneath the castle and those cliffs above the Palace where he found something close to freedom.

Later, it was here that he discovered his feelings for Cassie were deeper than that of mere friendship. He saw her face now. Her smile. Felt the touch of her hand on his skin. The feel of her lips. He had treated her badly and he hoped he would not have to face her again, though it was inevitable, unless she had left Edinburgh, but that seemed unlikely.

He entered by the Canongate and the voices of those ghosts of his past grew stronger as they called to him from the hidden closes and tiny courtyards behind the buildings. He recalled the last time he had passed this way, many years before, at break of dawn as he left the city with Charlie, two bright-eyed young men in search of adventure. Charlie had also been at Malplaquet but the last Flynt had seen of him was as they both fled the carnage. They were separated in the confusion and though he tried to seek him out, he never learned if Charlie had survived.

He turned his horse under the covered portal leading to the courtyard of the White Horse Inn. The buildings, to Flynt's eyes influenced by continental designs, had been constructed during the previous century but already bore a sense of exhaustion. A stone stairway led to the upper floor and the inn proper but he had little interest in that. It was the accommodations on the ground that drew him here, for this was where he would lodge his mount. He had no idea how long he would have to remain in Edinburgh but he paid the innkeeper for a full week's stabling. The stable lad seemed polite and caring and he patted the animal's nose as he took the reins from Flynt's hands to walk her to her stall.

'What's she called, mister?'

Flynt had been asked this many times and he smiled to himself, knowing the response he would receive. 'She has no name. I merely call her Horse.'

The boy was surprised. 'Och, a fine beast like this should have a name.'

Flynt stroked Horse's long neck. 'She cares not for names. Only that she is well tended.' He handed the boy some coins. 'Ensure that she gets the best of treatment.'

The boy looked at the money in his palm then back at Flynt, his face beaming. 'Aye, mister, I'll do that, right enough.'

'I'll be back every day to check on her, mind.'

'Don't you fret, mister, she's in good hands here, I'll see to her myself.'

Flynt followed the boy and gave Horse's new accommodation a careful inspection. The straw was fresh, as was the feed, the bucket containing water looked clean while the bolt and the door on which it sat were secure. Light streaked through a small window to the rear. Satisfied, Flynt threw his saddlebags over his shoulder, strode across the courtyard and left through the archway to emerge once again on the Canongate. He turned right and began walking up the incline to the city proper.

His time on the road had been filled with rural tranquillity but here the clamour of commerce and the reek of the city assaulted his senses. The smell was the most overpowering but he resisted the impulse to pull his neckerchief over his nose for he resolved to become used to it as swiftly as possible. It was a confusion of odours. Woodsmoke from the chimneys of the tall buildings that lined the street, tobacco from the pipes of the gentlemen as they walked, fish in the baskets of the fisherwomen up from Leith, bread baking in bakers' shops, horse droppings mixing with human filth – all combined to make Edinburgh as fragrant as the larger metropolis to the south. He would shortly come to terms with it but it was almost unbearable at first.

He walked through the castellated gate of the Netherbow Port, where Canongate became High Street, and gazed at the people milling about him as if he were walking into the past. The city had changed little in the years he had been away. It was as thronged and noisy – and stinking – as it ever was. It was as London but writ small, with accents that were' rougher but to his ear more pleasing, though he knew that was but nascent national affection. Though he no longer recognised any nation or flag as his own, he knew within his heart he was a Scot, and now that he was here there was a part of him that was glad to be back among his own folk. The hoarse cries of vendors enticed custom to wares they carried in baskets or displayed on carts used as stalls. Men gathered in groups to discuss business, ladies of quality walked with their servants, idlers sat against walls or reclined against the obelisk at the Cross, some sharing a bottle of cheap wine. The ragged messengers, the caddies, darted hither and yon or conveyed visitors to their destinations. The houses were of stone or of wood or a mixture and accessed by narrow doorways and within them the common would mix with the worthy just as they did in the street. Unlike London, where the poor clustered in the likes of St Giles or Whitechapel while the rich congregated in Mayfair or St James's, in Edinburgh rich and poor often shared the same building. 'Lands' they called them here, tenements in which the wealthy took the upper floors while the less well-off existed closer to the stink and filth that was daily thrown from windows. A gentleman walking below had to have a care that he was not splashed with household and human waste as it showered from above.

Beyond the Cross loomed the Tolbooth, the town gaol, its dark stonework a stark reminder that the harsh hand of the law was always lurking. At its side stood the triple kirk of St Giles, so different from its London namesake. The English church was bright in countenance compared to this Scots edifice, which glowered at the citizens in true Presbyterian spirit.

All this was both alien and familiar to Flynt as he made his way up the hill. He entered one of the closes, one he knew very well, and followed the dingy passageway, trailing his hand along the wall to feel the words carved in times past by someone moved by a fit of religious zeal. Even now he knew them, although he could not see them clearly in the half light from the High Street. *THE LORD IS MY ONLY SVPORT* was one, *O LORD IN*

THE IS ALL MY TRAIST the other. He knew not who had taken hammer and chisel to the old stone to record his thoughts, but as a boy he had often wondered if it was someone who had enjoyed too freely and suffered for that pleasure within the establishment that was his destination.

The alleyway, wide enough only for one man's shoulders, opened into a courtyard much smaller than the one that housed the White Horse Inn. The building before him was of three storeys and leaned heavily in one direction, much like a man at the end of a convivial night. A short flight of well-worn stone steps led to the door on the corner, above which hung a rough-hewn sign announcing this place simply as Gideon's. Flynt knew it well, for this was the tavern his father had bought on his return from sailing around the world. Flynt suspected that Gideon Flynt had been no ordinary sailor, had instead either voyaged with a privateer or outright pirate, for how else could a mere seaman have gathered the wherewithal to purchase one of Edinburgh's favourite taverns? But his father had never admitted to such a past and merely insisted that he had saved prudently all his life.

Flynt hesitated at the foot of the steps, feeling a nervousness akin to that which he had experienced outside the cellar door in Satan's Gullet. This, however, was not a precursor to action or danger that would dissipate once he moved forward, but something he found more difficult to control. He was unsure of the reaction his reappearance would receive but he knew he could not avoid showing his face. Edinburgh was not a large city and there was every likelihood that his father would hear of his presence, for such news would spread through the wynds along with the smell. He could not dishonour the old man in that way, nor hurt Mother Mercy, the woman Gideon had brought back from the West Indies. She had been a slave in a Kingston tavern and his father had somehow managed to either buy, win or steal her. The details of how she came to leave with him were as hazy as sea mist and neither of them spoke much about life in the islands.

The simple fact behind Flynt's trepidation was that the manner of his leaving had been underhand. Both he and Charlie Temple had wished to see more of the world, to find adventure, to seek their fortune away from the confines of this small city and this small, poor country where famine and pestilence often raged. Rab Gow had been party to the plan but declined to follow them for he had not shared their longing to discover what lay far beyond the city walls. He had followed his father into the cobbler's trade and though he had many a summer's day lain with them in the long grass on the rocky hill above the Palace and dreamed of exploration, he knew in his heart that not only his past and present belonged in these streets, but also his future.

So the three – no, four, for Cassie had joined them, become part of them, become part of Flynt – became two and they had stolen away from Edinburgh, their minds filled with the promise and excitement the morrow would bring, and all the morrows after that. He left behind Gideon and Mercy. He left behind Cassie, for though he had often told her he wished to see more of the world, he did not share his plan to leave. He did not even say goodbye. If Flynt had not answered the call to adventure that had coursed through his young veins, he could only conjecture as to how different his life would have been. He might have worked here in his father's tavern, serving liquor and scalloped oysters to men and women, rich and poor. He might have been an honest man and not one who walked the world with a brace of pistols in his saddlebags and a silver sword in his hand. In this alternative world of his imagination, he might not have lifted purses, stolen jewels, taken lives. He might not have felt the spectre of the noose forever cast a shadow over him.

He was certain he would have led a far different life from the one he now followed. One, perhaps, with Cassie.

Two men almost collided with him as they pushed through the doorway of the tavern, snatching him from his thoughts and making him realise he was stationed like a minister debating with himself whether to sin. One was a man in fine garb and carrying a walking stick with a silver head in the shape of an animal Flynt could not make out, his hair grey and unencumbered by periwig, his face ageing well. For a brief moment Flynt felt something like recognition flash through his mind but then it was gone. The other was of sallow complexion, both taller and thinner than the first and his clothes seemed to perch on his bones as if they belonged on a much sturdier frame, and even in the brief moment they shared, Flynt sensed a nervousness from him.

'My apologies, gentlemen,' he said, for he recognised his fault in the near collision.

'You are an impediment, sir, by standing thus immobile,' said the first man, his accent cultured but bearing a trace of the Scots. His eyes were cold and they flitted from face to foot as if taking Flynt's measure.

Flynt had no desire to begin an altercation so soon after his arrival so he affected a slight bow, though in truth the man's tone had irritated him. 'As I say, my apologies. I was in a dream.'

'Then do so elsewhere. You are an obstruction in this entranceway.'

Flynt felt anger kindle. 'I have apologised, sir, and if you cannot accept that then be on your way before my manners desert me.'

The man's grip on his stick twitched and a nerve pulsated in his jaw, though when he spoke his voice was even. 'You must be a stranger to this place, otherwise you would not dare to speak in such a way to me.'

'I was born here, sir, but I am sufficiently travelled to know that I will match any man's tone. I have apologised and that should be sufficient for such a small discourtesy. If that is something you cannot countenance then I am willing to discuss this further at your pleasure.'

A glare stretched time between them, during which Flynt felt that pang of recognition again. He had seen this man before somewhere but he did not know where. It was the man's lanky companion who finally broke the tension, his voice nervous and soft.

'Come, my lord, this stranger is of no import. We have business elsewhere, have we not?'

My lord. This man was of noble birth. Flynt realised he should have known that immediately, for only the entitled would be so self-entitled. There was a further pause as the man regarded him with haughty disdain, then with a slight grunt he brushed past him to stride across the courtyard, the click of his walking stick echoing from the walls of the passageway leading to the street. Flynt noted that the taller man followed the other a half pace to the rear. Whether such subservience was affected or came naturally, he did not know.

Unpleasant though the brief conversation had been, a good point had been made. He could not tarry at the threshold much longer. It was time for him to screw his courage to the sticking place, as Mr Shakespeare had once put it. *Macbeth*, he thought, a fitting drama for the mission on which he was engaged, for it was also about men seeking power.

He hitched his saddlebags higher on his shoulder, took a deep breath, then climbed the three steps to push the doorway open.

The interior was dingy, the single window looking onto the courtyard blackened by generations of soot and smoke. The tallow candles filled the small space with the acrid smell of burning animal fat, overcoming attempts, no doubt by Mother Mercy, to counter it with a sweeter fragrance by burning applewood in the fireplace. Flynt's eyes quickly accustomed themselves to the dim light and he saw the room was only sparsely populated. A group of men sat by the fire, hunched over tankards and talking in low voices. They studied him as he lingered by the doorway, for he was a stranger to them. Flynt understood their mistrust, for though this smoky tavern should have been his home, he felt like an outsider. A wizened jade sat alone at a table in the corner, some bread and cheese sitting before her alongside a tankard. She paid little heed to the newcomer as she broke off a chunk of cheese, laid it on a portion of bread and ate it, washing it down with ale, her eyes lost in whatever netherworld kept her company.

The woman behind the counter did take notice. She was tall, her body full and strong, her face broad but still youthful despite having seen over fifty summers, and the bulk of those in her youth labouring in the sweat of the tropics. She stared at Flynt as if trying to place his face. It took only a moment but he knew she recognised him, for shock flashed like lightning across her face before she brought it under control. Her expression was impassive as she moved through the opening and crossed the short space between them. She said nothing as she gazed at him, her dark eyes searching his features for something he could only guess at. Perhaps the lad he had once been, bright-eyed, filled with the vigour of life. But that lad was long gone. He had been lost in foreign lands amid cannonade and gun smoke.

'Hello, Mother Mercy,' he said. He had always called her that, never simply mother or Mercy. Always the two together but not in the way that Mary Grady used the title. When Gideon returned for good, this woman took over from Flynt's aunt and became his mother, the union of title and name delineating her from the woman he had never known.

He expected her to lay into him, for Mother Mercy knew words that could strip the bark from a tree, but she remained silent as she regarded him. His parting would have caused pain, his lack of contact since then even more so. He fully deserved whatever rebuke was coming and he was steeled to receive it, like a soldier awaiting the sting of the lash.

'We thought you dead and gone,' she said, her voice deep, clear and still familiar despite the passage of years. Where Belle's had retained the lilt of the islands, hers was mixed with the harshness of the Scots. 'I saw you there and thought I was seeing a ghost.'

'I'm no ghost,' he said.

She continued to study him, as if seeking visual confirmation that he was flesh and blood. He still expected a verbal flogging but then her eyes softened and she folded him in her strong arms, pulling him tight against her.

'Welcome home, Jonas.'

Flynt closed his eyes and enjoyed the embrace, the warmth and love seeping from this big woman's body into his own. Home, she had said. Charters had said he was going home. He did not know if this foggy tavern down a dark alley in Edinburgh really was it but, even if only for that moment, he needed to believe it was.

He surrendered himself into the embrace and blinked at whatever burned behind his eyes.

Through the mist of those tears he saw his father staring at them.

–

Gideon Flynt said nothing as he filled the bowl of his clay pipe, lit the tobacco slowly then proceeded to by turns puff and suck life into it, allowing the smoke to billow into the air. It was done with precision, as if it were a ritual, but Flynt knew this attention to detail was no more than a means of dealing with the discomfort they both felt. They sat in what Gideon called his Crown Room, a private apartment on the second floor of the tavern which was available for rent by gentlemen for their private entertainment, Scottish men of quality being as licentious and dissolute as their southern counterparts. The ground floor housed the tavern proper as well as a kitchen, where Mother Mercy and two servants prepared food for patrons, so this space was more generously proportioned and brighter, thanks to the large, clean double window looking out on the courtyard. The dark panelling on the walls still gave the room a murky ambience, however, and even though it was the middle of the afternoon lamps had to be lit. No tallow thankfully, for gentlemen should not be expected to suffer such a stench, so the candles here were of beeswax.

They sat in two high-backed chairs before the fire which a serving girl had lit for them. Flynt remained silent, knowing that it was not his place to speak. Gideon puffed on his pipe as he watched the flames take hold, the orange glow catching his face. His father was nearing sixty and bore the leathered skin of the young man who had faced into the trade winds around the world. His hair was grey, the long strands tied at the back in a black ribbon. He was lean but his body was strong. Looking at him, however, Flynt could not see his own face some thirty or so years hence. Gideon had often told him he favoured his mother, but when he had studied her likeness, held within a medallion of his father's, he saw only a faint resemblance.

'So how have you been, lad?' Gideon said without looking at him. *Lad*, he called him. Flynt was over thirty now, and yet sitting here with his father, he felt like the boy he had once been, waiting for a story from life at sea or a reprimand for some transgression.

'I've been well, Faither.' *Faither*. His tongue had taken easily to calling Gideon that, even after nigh on fifteen years. His accent had roughened too. In London they knew him to be Scottish but his manner of speech was tempered for their ear. Now, unconsciously, he had slipped into the old rhythms and patterns.

Gideon nodded as he stared at the glow in the bowl of his pipe. 'We had no word from you.'

It was a simple statement of fact, nothing accusatory in its tone, but Flynt could not deny it. 'I ken that.'

'Mercy was most concerned regarding your welfare. You should have written, even if only to her.'

He had loved her as if she was his own blood so his conscience stung as if slit by a blade. The writing of a letter now and then would not have been much to ask. He could not explain why he had not and he did not attempt to do so now.

'For a long year she refused to believe you were gone,' Gideon said. 'But after some time even she began to accept it.' The words made the blade turn. He felt another stab of remorse when Gideon added, 'Your aunt died. A fever struck her. Pneumonia.'

'I'm right sorry to hear that,' Flynt said and he meant his words.

Gideon accepted his condolence with a nod. 'She cared for you, in her way.'

Though his mother's sister had not been a bad surrogate parent for the first ten years of his life, ensuring he was fed, cared for and educated, she had always seemed distant, as if she blamed him for some crime he was unaware of having committed.

'She was a good woman.' He could think of no other words. He saw her face now as she told him to tend to his letters while she worked on a garment for some lady or other. She had insisted that he be more than proficient in reading and writing, often leaving copies of books on his bed, predominantly the works of Mr Shakespeare, Malory's *Le Morte d'Arthur* and tales of Roman and Greek heroes, but also the writings of Cicero, Ovid and the lives of Roman emperors.

Gideon cleared his throat. 'So what brings you back after all this time, lad?'

'This place and the people within it have never been far from my mind, Faither,' Flynt said and it was mostly true. He had never forgotten what he had left behind. Especially Cassie.

Gideon's eyes darted in his direction in emphasis as he returned to his previous point. 'And yet no a word from you in all this time. That was cruel, lad. There were – there are – folks here who cared about you.'

It was as close to a rebuke as he would get but it was enough. Flynt felt the barb plunge into his heart again.

'And are you home now to settle?'

'No,' replied Flynt and felt his pain deepen as disappointment flared in Gideon's eyes. 'I have business here.'

Gideon looked away, perhaps not wishing his son to see his regret. 'What sort of business?'

Flynt had a lie ready prepared, one supplied by Jonathan Wild. 'A favour, for a respectable lady in the south. She is blackmailed regarding an indiscreet letter she wrote to a gentleman of note. It has fallen into the wrong hands and I have traced it to Scotland.'

Gideon regarded him steadily. 'And you do this sort of thing regularly, lad?'

'I've developed certain... skills, Faither. They come in useful for some people.'

Flynt sensed his father did not fully believe him. Gideon had the ability to size up a man in an instant, something he had learned while at sea where you had to swiftly judge if the sailor at your side could be depended upon in a tempest or a fight. It had stood him in good stead as a tavern keeper, for he knew with a look which patron was a troublemaker and which was not.

Gideon studied the flames in the fireplace again. 'You have too much of me in you, lad.'

'I am your son.'

'Aye, perhaps that's what it is.' There was sadness in his voice as he now examined the tobacco smouldering in his pipe. 'Adventure. That was what you wanted. Those books my sister gave you did not help, those tales of quests and wars. I saw it in you when I returned home after voyages. You used to revel in my stories of foreign ports and the wonders of the world.' He sighed and sucked on his pipe, held the smoke for a moment then released it with his words. 'I was the same, when I was a boy, and that was why I ran away to sea. Even then I could feel the salt in my blood. But you did not go to sea. You went to war.'

'Aye.'

Gideon's eyes returned to him. 'And what did you find in *your* blood?'

Flynt could not reply. It was not the time to tell his father that he had found a monster within.

A noise beyond the doorway saved him from whatever lie he could formulate. Flynt rose by instinct, his hand falling on the handle of his swordstick. Gideon observed the move but said nothing, instead giving him a look that told him he had taken his stock and knew him for what he was. Shame once again prickled at Flynt's cheeks.

His hand fell away from the sword when he recognised the man who burst in, even though it had been many years since he had seen Rab Gow. Mother Mercy followed, her grin matching that of his old friend.

'It's true, by God!'

Mercy delivered a soft slap to the back of his head. 'Did you think me a liar, Robert Gow?'

Rab winced theatrically and rubbed his pate. 'No, Mother, heaven forbid that I should ever think ill of you.' With an exaggerated wink, Rab strode across the room and pumped Flynt's hand. 'Jonny Flynt. Large as life and twice as bloody ugly. Ach, damn your eyes, boy.' He pulled Flynt to him in an embrace. Flynt was uncomfortable with such displays of affection but he allowed it. They had been close friends once. When Rab released him, he stepped back a pace to scrutinise his face. 'You've changed, Jonny.'

'I'm older, Rab.'

Rab grinned again. 'I'm no.'

Flynt had to admit there was some truth to that. Rab was older certainly but the sandy hair was just as Flynt recalled and the bright humour yet sparkled in his eyes. Life had not drained any of his youthful exuberance.

'It's good to see you, Rab.'

'It's good to be seen, boy. Come, we should be having a wee something to celebrate.' Rab looked from Flynt to his father and finally noted the sombre expression. 'This is a good day, is it no?'

'We had a visitor,' Gideon stated, his voice flat but his eye flicking restlessly in Flynt's direction. 'With Baillie Wilson.'

Rab tilted his head. 'Aye? And who would that be, Faither?'

Gideon's look was firm. 'You'll know who, Rab.'

Rab's grin faltered. 'Moncrieff?'

Gideon's teeth gritted and Flynt became aware of Mother Mercy watching him closely. 'I'll no have his name uttered in this house, you know that.'

Flynt felt something change in the air. The name Moncrieff seemed to hang between his father and old friend. It stirred a memory within him too. It was a name he had heard in his youth, from his aunt, from Gideon, whispered in corners, murmured beyond doors, but why it would generate such friction he did not know.

Rab raised a placating hand. 'I'm sorry, Faither, I ken that. It slipped out.'

'It's only a matter of time before his lordship thinks on visiting your shop and home.'

Flynt sensed hesitation on Rab's part as he first shot a glance in his direction, then over his shoulder to Mother Mercy, still studying him. There was something deeper in the exchange, a secret shared by all in the room but Flynt.

'He'll find nothing there,' Rab said carefully.

'You have a wife there, and a boy. That bastard is no respecter of such things.'

Rab's grin died. 'Aye,' he said. 'The boy is at his studies but, erm,' another glance to Flynt, 'my wife bides at home. Jonny, lad, we must delay our celebrations for a short while, for I've responsibilities that must be attended to.'

Flynt picked up his hat from where he had hung it over the wooden frame of the chair. He paused for a moment looking at his saddlebags but decided to leave them and the pistols tucked away within. 'I'll accompany you.'

Another hesitation and another look towards Gideon. An understanding seemed to pass between them and Gideon shrugged. Rab smiled again, although there was something forced about it this time, and clapped him on the shoulder. 'And right glad I will be for that.'

On their way to the door, Mother Mercy said, 'I'll have your old room made up for you, Jonas.'

He stared into her eyes, saw only love and, despite himself, embraced her, the comfort of her arms welcome once more. 'Thank you, Mother. I am grateful.'

'You are family, Jonas, you must never forget that.'

Gideon watched them from his chair, pipe in hand, his eyes pensive. A brief nod showed his agreement with Mercy, and Flynt replied to them both with a grateful smile then followed Rab, but as the door closed behind him, he heard Mother Mercy say quietly, 'Does he know?'

'No,' his father replied.

He thought of returning and asking them of what it was they spoke, but Rab was already down the narrow stairway and waiting for him below. He caught up with him and his old friend gave him a reproving look as they moved through the tavern.

'Who is this Moncrieff?'

'A man who thinks he owns the world.'

'What does that mean, Rab?'

Rab laughed. 'I feel certain you'll find out before very long.'

'Why does Gideon despise him so?'

Rab took a deep breath and kept walking. 'Moncrieff is an easy man to despise, Jonny… But *you* are a right bastard, you ken that? You should've sent some kind of word, for God's sake.'

'I ken, Rab,' replied Flynt. 'But time has a way with a man that makes him forget his manners.'

Rab's hand fell on Flynt's shoulder. 'We thought you were dead.'

'There were times I thought I was. But I was merely in Flanders.'

'Aye, Charlie told us you were over there.'

Flynt's step faltered. 'Charlie Temple is home?'

'Aye, and still in the military… well, the Town Guard at least. He's their captain.'

As they emerged from the close, Flynt's eyes were drawn down the High Street to the squat building that acted as guardhouse. So Charlie had survived the war after all.

'He said you lost touch,' Rab said. 'That you were separated during battle.'

'Malplaquet,' said Flynt, thinking he and Charlie were parted as they ran away from the battle but now was not the time to let facts get in the way. Flynt had later made discreet inquiries about his friend's welfare and found he was hearty and back with their old regiment. He had not made any attempt to contact him again, having already decided to change the course of his life.

'Aye, he said it was hell.'

'That it was,' said Flynt.

'But he made his way home upon discharge from duty, unlike some bastards I could mention.' Rab gave him a sharp nudge with his elbow. 'His old faither used his money and influence to get him the commission with the guard.'

Flynt smiled. It would be good to see his friend again. They walked quickly in the shadow of the Tolbooth towards the West

Bow, where the Gows had their cobbler's shop, nestling among other artisans. 'Your own faither, Rab, how does he fare?'

'Ach, he's gone, Jonny, these eight years since. A seizure of the brain, the doctor said.'

More death. First his aunt, now Robert Gow. Flynt was used to the fragility of life but these two hit him hard. 'I am right sorry to hear that. He was a good man.'

Rab clapped his shoulder again. 'It was his time, Jonny boy. We will all go when it is ours.'

They walked together on the Lawnmarket, edging past the men loading and unloading carts outside the ornate doorway to the two-storey stone-built Weigh House, where butter, cheese and other goods were weighed prior to sale, to reach the head of the West Bow, which zigzagged down the steep hill to the Grassmarket. Rab kept up a continual chatter of how good it was to see him, how he had missed him, how it was great to have all three friends back breathing the same air. As he talked, the tinkle of hammers echoed up the cobbled road, for this was where the tinsmiths carried out their trade. It wasn't long before Flynt saw the small shopfront with the legend 'Gow's the Cobbler' above the door. Above it were the windows to the personal accommodations. Rab had been born within those three small rooms and many a time Flynt had enjoyed a meal and laughter with his family. Now a new generation of Gows lived there. The symmetry and certainty of such a tradition pleased Flynt, even though he wouldn't know it for himself. He had never thought of having a family of his own, not consciously, but he knew that Gideon's line would die with him. He did not mourn it, did not regret it; it was a certainty.

Rab slowed his pace before they reached his door, then came to a halt. The good humour on his face had been replaced by a frown. He looked towards the shop and his prattle stilled. His teeth worried at the inside of his cheek, an old habit that meant he had something on his mind. Flynt sensed he was preparing to say something important.

'Did you ken I was wed now?'

'I heard Gideon say so.' This had always been the way with them. Father to his face, Gideon when the friends were alone. It was the same with Gow's father. 'And a child too, my congratulations.'

'Thank you,' replied Rab though something yet troubled him. 'Do you ken who it was I married, Jonny?'

'I only learned of your nuptials a few minutes ago, Rab, you know that.'

'It's Cassie, Jonny,' Rab said, the words coming out in a rush. 'I married Cassie.'

8

He tried to find words, but as his mind struggled to comprehend this revelation he could not. Of course she would be married, why should he be so surprised?

He found his voice at last. 'Again congratulations. I am glad she has found a good man.'

Rab seemed relieved by Flynt's acceptance, for his smile returned and he resumed his swift pace towards the shop, fishing a key from his pocket to unlock the door. Beyond it was a small space, little more than a passageway for customers to stand before a rude counter and the workshop itself to the rear. A line of shoes and boots awaited Rab's attention, and the tools of his trade – hammers, awls, knives and leather – hung on the wall or lay on his workbench. The smell of the leather took Flynt's mind back to his childhood and he heard the laughter that had seemed a permanent presence in this household. It had been a bustling little space back then, but this day it harboured a desolate feel, and even from where he stood Flynt could see there was a film of dust over some of the tools and the sheets of leather. He did not remark upon it as he followed Rab to the narrow wooden stairway leading to the apartment above. A sturdy door stood at the head of the stairs and when Rab opened it, Flynt saw her waiting for them at a small table.

'See what the winds have blown our way, my love,' said Rab and stepped aside. Flynt forced a smile to his lips and took off his hat.

'Hello, Cassie,' he said.

Cassie regarded him across the wooden table, her expression reaching out like a sharp slap, but even through her cold fury he saw that she was still as beautiful as ever. There were lines on her skin that had not been there before, of course, and her face had filled out slightly but not to the detriment of her fine features. Her hair was not as long as it had been in their youth, when she had allowed it to tumble about her neck and shoulders, but it remained dark and curled. But it was her eyes that had changed the most, or perhaps only because they now regarded Flynt with such disdain.

Flynt felt nerves tug at the corners of his mouth. Facing Gideon and Mercy was gruelling enough but this moment with Cassie was his fiercest dread. He had sought her out while at the tavern, braced every moment for her to suddenly present herself in his path. Now here she was in his friend's home, in a room in which he had spent many hours as a boy, rage in her dark eyes.

'Jonas Flynt,' Cassie said, her Edinburgh accent strong. 'So it's true. You're a bold fellow to come dancing back here after all this time.'

'I know,' he said, putting as much apology into the two words as he could muster.

She did not move to greet him but continued to talk in a tone that was as chill as the wind from the Forth. 'We thought you dead.'

'So I have heard. As you can see, such reports were something of an exaggeration.'

Rab laughed but Cassie's face remained frozen. 'Is that the way of it? You walk from our lives without so much as a farewell, we never hear a single word from you, you let us believe that you had perished on some pox-ridden foreign field, and now you joke?'

She'd always had a way of making him feel a fool, as well as the ability to be both hot and cold at once. Her beautiful face would freeze and her eyes would frost, but her words would burn. Once again he was that gangling youth, dreaming of adventure but being drawn to her like a moth to flame. Their love was not forbidden – they were not blood, for she had returned as a child with Gideon and Mother Mercy – but they called her his sister and that seemed to generate shame within them both. No one knew they had been lovers, not even Rab.

'Cassie,' said Rab, his voice firm, 'be grateful that Jonny is back hale and hearty and welcome him to our home.'

Cassie gave him another withering look. 'I will not, Rab Gow, for I know in my heart he will bring us yet more pain.'

'Cassie, in the name of God…'

'No!' Her rage was unrestrained now. 'I won't have this. I won't—'

'Cassie, yon bastard Moncrieff and Baillie Wilson are searching for Nero,' said Rab. 'They've been to Gideon's, they'll come here. I'm certain.'

Rab's interruption halted her flow and she took a deep breath. 'Let him, for he will find nothing.'

'I ken that, but Jonny and I wanted to be here when he does.'

The chill of Cassie's ire turned on Rab. 'You think I cannot handle James Moncrieff?'

'Aye, I ken fine you can, my love, and that's what worries me. He's a bastard, so he is, but he's a powerful bastard and Wilson licks at his tail like a cur. My fear is that you'd handle him all too well and he wouldn't like that. You ken he's a contemptible man.'

Cassie nodded slightly. 'Then you may handle him, if he comes, for I'll no remain.'

She rose, plucked a shawl from the back of her chair and draped it across her shoulders as she walked around the table. More than her face had filled out. He felt guilt immediately pierce his chest over such a thought. He had no right to think of her in that way. He had abandoned any rights when he abandoned her. And now she was married to his friend.

'Cassie…' Rab began.

She held up a hand to silence him. 'No. Not another word, Rab, for I'll no hear it. And I'll no bide here either.' She stopped in front of Flynt, looked up at his face and scowled. 'My God, Jonas Flynt, I always knew there to be some coldness in your heart but I never thought you to be this cruel.'

'I'm sorry, Cassie, I...'

She made one last furious sound and brushed past him. The sound of her shoes on the wooden steps was like a drum roll at an execution. The door to the shop slammed and he and Rab stood in awkward silence for a moment.

'You hurt her, you ken that, Jonny,' Rab said at last.

Flynt took a deep breath. 'Aye.'

'She loved you.' Rab paused. 'And no just like a sister.'

So she had told Rab that at least. How much she had shared of what had happened between them, he still did not know. 'And now she loves you.'

Rab's grin returned. 'Aye. And don't you be forgetting that, boy.' He glanced at the door and Flynt felt he was wishing his wife would reappear. 'She'll come around, you wait and see. It was just the shock. I should've kent when the caddie brought word from Mother Mercy. You know Cassie...'

Flynt indeed knew Cassie well and he knew the fire in her blood — which was part of why he loved her — would not douse easily. She would never come around, not fully. She would accept his return to an extent but that was all. In those brief few minutes he had seen that in her eyes and heard it in her words. He did not feel rancour towards her because he knew he deserved such enmity, although saying she had always believed he harboured a cruel heart did wound him. He knew his heart carried much — larceny, violence, guilt — but he did not think himself cruel. And yet, had he not been callous in the way he had left? He had felt remorse for his action over the years but he had never considered it cruel until now.

'Sit yourself down, boy,' said Rab as he reached up to a shelf and brought down a bottle. 'We'll toast your return.'

Flynt hesitated, unsettled by the encounter with Cassie. 'Rab, perhaps it is best if I go.'

'Away! The damage is done now and there is no changing that. Cassie's head will cool, believe me. I ken her better than you, although you may not realise it. We have been together longer now than when you lived as family. She *will* cool, mark my words. Now, sit and have a drink with me.'

Flynt did as he was told, taking off his greatcoat and draping it over the back of the chair. Rab poured the amber fluid into two cups and passed one to Flynt, who sipped it. 'Brandy,' he said.

'Aye, may be the last of it too. They hang my supplier in the morning and such things tend to put a damper on trade.'

'Your supplier is a smuggler?'

'Aye, Somey Barclay, a good man but obviously not popular with the magistrates. After the bastard treaty of 1707, the English increased taxes here on spirits, salt, lace, baccy, printed linen and calico. Anything the Crown can make a profit on they taxed and had their excise men, the bastard gaugers, enforce it. Auld Somey has been in operation along the east coast for maybe six years now, always managed to avoid capture.'

'Until now.'

'Aye, until now. Betrayed he was, by one of his own. The gaugers caught him in a tavern, his cart outside filled with contraband. Poor soul never had a chance to make his escape.'

'And they hang him tomorrow?'

'On the Grassmarket. It's a bad business. Leaves a sour taste, a hanging.'

Flynt sipped his brandy, hoping the warm spirit would burn away the foul flavour of the impending execution. His welcome from Mother Mercy and even his father had not prepared him for the virulence of Cassie's reaction, and now this. He did not know the condemned, and why he had thought he would leave such things behind was a mystery, for Edinburgh was as fond of the noose as London. Here there was even the Maiden, a decapitating machine which was wheeled out for when the gentry fell afoul of the law.

'Poor Charlie is leading the guard,' Rab said. 'There will be trouble, for auld Somey is highly regarded. I fear Charlie will not cope with it well, for he's no suited to such work. He soils his breeks if someone in Leith farts, so how he fared in war is beyond me.'

Flynt was well aware that Charlie was not the man for such a duty yet still felt the need to defend his old friend's honour in some way.

'He was as terrified as the rest of us,' said Flynt. 'The battlefield can make cowards of us all.'

'I cannot see you as coward, Jonny.'

Flynt paused, remembering his headlong flight away from the thick of the action at Malplaquet. He had killed men in peacetime when circumstances demanded, but in war it was different. Death could strike from any direction, at any time.

'I have had my moments, Rab. There is no shame in showing fear. Charlie did his duty, as did I, until it was time not to do so.'

'You didn't find the glory you sought?'

Flynt heard the shrieks of men and horses as they died, the deafening roar of cannons as they blasted death and destruction, the gunfire, the ring of sword striking sword. He smelled the burnt powder and the stink of bodily wastes expelled by fear. And he saw the body of a man between him and Charlie at Malplaquet, and the look they had exchanged when they each decided that they had experienced enough glory for one lifetime.

'No,' he said, 'there is only waste in war, Rab.'

The sound of the door opening below saved him from explaining, or thinking, any further about battle and what he had seen. They waited a moment for the sound of footsteps on the stairs, hoping perhaps it was Cassie returned, but heard nothing.

Then, a voice. 'Robert Gow.'

Rab grimaced. 'Baillie Wilson,' he whispered.

Flynt followed Rab down the stairs to the shop, his silver stick in his hand. As they ducked below the low beams, he saw the two men he had encountered outside Gideon's waiting for them. So, the man who had treated him with such disdain was Lord Moncrieff.

'You again,' said Moncrieff when he saw Flynt.

'Aye, me again.'

Moncrieff studied him and Flynt returned the favour, wondering once more why the fellow was so familiar. Although he was certain he had heard the name mentioned when he was a boy, he could not recall ever seeing the man. His voice was Scottish but there was enough of the English accent to make him wonder if they had met in London. It could mean nothing, for many Scots nobles were educated in the south, but it was possible they had faced each other over a card game.

'We seek Lord James's property, Gow,' said Wilson.

'Oh, aye?' Rab replied, his face radiating innocence. 'And what would that be? I have not repaired any of his shoes.'

'Don't be obtuse, man,' snapped Moncrieff, flicking his cane towards Flynt. 'And who is this fellow who likes to stand outside doorways like a statue?'

'My name is Jonas Flynt.'

Moncrieff's eyes widened slightly at the hearing of his name. More than ever Jonas was certain they had encountered one another.

'Flynt,' his lordship repeated, as if tasting the name and finding it bitter. 'The tavern keeper's boy.'

'That's correct.'

'So the wanderer has returned. I trust the fatted calf was duly slaughtered.'

'I am but arrived only recently. This very afternoon.'

The cane tapped again. 'Then I apologise for interrupting your reunion with old friends.'

His tone oozed insincerity but Flynt treated him to a slight bow. 'Your apology is accepted.'

Moncrieff regarded him for a moment, his eyes hard and calculating, then they returned to Rab. 'We seek the slave, Nero, who has absconded from my home.'

'Perhaps he's gone for a wee walk only,' said Rab. 'It's a fine afternoon.'

'The property has been missing for a night,' said Wilson.

'A gey long walk, then.'

Moncrieff tapped his cane on the wooden floor again. 'Do not play the jester, Gow. We know when it comes to blackamores that you have no notion of property. I want it returned.'

'I don't ken where this man is.'

'And I do not believe you,' said Moncrieff.

Rab clicked his tongue. 'I care not what you believe.'

Moncrieff tired of the exchange and turned to Wilson. 'Do your duty, man, search the place.'

Wilson began to move beyond the counter but Flynt blocked his passage. Rab seemed well capable of handling himself, his demeanour and words were bold and unafraid, but Flynt could not stand by and allow this man to wander freely. 'Mr Gow has not given his leave for a search. Do you have paper that gives you such permissions?'

'I need no paper to give me leave,' said Moncrieff. 'It is my belief that my property is here and I will have it returned.'

Rab said, 'I told you I don't ken where the man Nero is and I can assure you he is not under this roof.'

Moncrieff's laugh was a bark. '*Man*, you call him. It is not a man, it is property, nothing more, and it has absconded. As such it has committed theft, Robert Gow, and I will have it returned. And when I do, I will see to it that the punishment is suitable for the crime.' He looked from Rab to Flynt with equal disfavour. 'I will see Nero dangle from the gallows on the Grassmarket. And anyone who has aided the wretch will be equally subject to the rigours of justice. On that you have my word.'

'I feel sure you will be so vindictive.'

Baillie Wilson coughed in an attempt to divert the conversation from becoming even more adversarial. 'Come, Mr Gow, if you are innocent, then why not grant us leave to search?'

Rab's expression told Flynt he thought little of the town functionary. 'I've told you twice that the man is no here and before I would grant you liberty to roam freely around my business and my home I would ask for evidence that I'm lying.'

Moncrieff snorted his disbelief. 'You are as much to be believed as this one's father.' Once again the cane jerked towards Flynt, then resumed its drumming of the floor. 'After all, both you and the tavern keeper have taken such beasts to your beds.'

Flynt saw Rab's colour rise and he replied before his friend could say something intemperate. 'I can vouch for the fact that the man you seek is not here.'

'And you expect me to take the word of the son of a tavern keeper?'

'I expect you to turn around, go to a magistrate and obtain legal authority to search.'

Moncrieff's eyes narrowed. 'You have been absent for some time, Flynt, you do not understand the way of things here.'

'I understand that a man's home is a man's home and you cannot enter without permission, no matter your station in life.'

Moncrieff's cane tapped an irregular beat. 'And you would stop us?'

'If I must.'

The tapping ceased as Moncrieff and Flynt stared across the small shop at each other. Flynt did not know if the nobleman was armed – that stick could easily be of a similar nature to his own – but he suspected not. All the same, he was ready to react if the man was sufficiently unwise, or arrogant, to let his anger and sense of entitlement lead to action.

As before, outside Gideon's, it was Wilson who tried to be peacemaker. He cleared his throat and raised a trembling hand. 'Gentlemen, we must observe propriety here. Mr Gow, are you steadfast in your position to deny us leave to search for the missing property?'

Rab's face was fierce and when he spoke his words were tortured with rage. 'Indeed I will no. In fact, I'll thank you both to leave my establishment immediately.'

Moncrieff's eyes slithered from Flynt towards Rab as if he could not believe his ears. 'You are ordering us to leave?'

Flynt smiled. 'I believe my friend spoke clearly. You do not understand the King's English, sir?'

Colour rose in the nobleman's face. 'Wilson, will you stand there and allow me to be so abused by these two... these two...' he searched for the correct word but came up wanting.

'Guttersnipes?' suggested Flynt.

'Scum?' Rab offered.

'Free men with rights,' added Flynt, his voice even.

Moncrieff seemed to regain his composure. He was obviously unused to being spoken to in the manner that first Gideon and now his son and his friend had done. He breathed deeply, his mouth set in a firm line as he looked from one to the other.

'You will regret this day, Robert Gow,' he said, then addressed Flynt. 'And you, sir, have impeded my progress twice and you would be well advised against making such an error a third time.'

Flynt inclined his head as if amused. 'Do I detect a threat, sir?'

'You detect a promise, sir, mark me. I am not a man to be trifled with.' He looked back to Rab once more. 'This does not end here. You and your consort...' a sneer coated the word '...and the creature that spawned her are known to have aided runaway property in the past. So far you have managed to avoid paying the penalty but rest assured I have my eye on you.' He glared at Flynt. 'And you too. Whatever runs in your blood will not save you, for you are but nothing to me.'

The tip of his cane tapped the floor once as if to emphasise his words before he whirled and walked from the shop. Baillie Wilson seemed flustered, as if he had never seen such a thing in his life. 'Have a care, gentlemen. You have made a bad enemy in Lord Moncrieff.'

'That's a relief,' said Flynt, 'for there is nothing I detest more than a good enemy, eh, Rab?'

Wilson shook his head as if in sorrow. 'This was folly, Robert Gow. If the property is not here then why not put the matter to rest and let me confirm it?'

'There is such a thing as principle, Baillie Wilson,' said Rab. 'It's something you perhaps should study upon.'

The Baillie gave Rab a long, stern look, under which Rab seemed to flinch as if he regretted being so forthright with the man, then his frown returned as he glanced at Flynt and turned to the door. 'Folly, folly,' he said as he left.

Flynt and Rab remained in their positions for a few moments, their eyes on the door in case Moncrieff thought better of his retreat, but no shadow fell upon it and it remained closed. Rab locked it and he and Flynt ascended the stairs again in silence.

'What did he mean by that?' Rab asked as they entered the private apartments. 'About whatever runs in your blood?'

'Gideon, I would imagine. Over the years he has gained the ear of many a powerful man. Owning a successful tavern can be a conduit to many a secret.'

Rab smiled, knowing that secrets gleaned in Gideon's private rooms were like currency. 'Aye, Gideon is an influential man in this town.'

'So where is this man Nero?' asked Flynt.

'Well on the road to Greenock by now,' said Rab. 'He is posing as the servant of a friend.'

'Why Greenock?'

'It's arranged for him to take ship there. Leith was too close to Edinburgh. He'll join the ship's company and see the world.'

'Gideon arranged such, I assume?'

Rab grinned. 'Aye. He still has many friends in merchant vessels.'

'The poor soul faces a hard life at sea.'

'Aye, but life with Moncrieff will no be easy and at least he'll be free. Moncrieff threatened to have him returned to the Colonies where life is even harder.'

'Why was he being sent back?'

Rab gestured to Flynt to sit back at the table where their unfinished drinks waited. 'He had the audacity to learn how to read and had this outrageous notion that he deserved to be more than a lackey in smart livery being verbally and physically abused by Jimmy Moncrieff and his like.'

'So you gave him aid?'

'We facilitated merely. The plan was all Nero's. He waited for weeks for the opportunity to simply walk away from the bastards in that household.'

'How did he know you would be sympathetic?'

'Mother Mercy and Cassie. In that Moncrieff was correct, for they – and I and your faither – have provided succour to runaways before. Word travels.'

'Aye, but not always in the right direction. You can be certain that if the servants know, then the masters also. There are many such runaways?'

'There are only a few slaves in Edinburgh but a few is still too many. We are right careful, Jonny, and ensure there can be no suspicion that rests upon us for we know we cannot help them from the Tolbooth or at the end of a noose. But we must do what we can to assist them, all the same, for it isn't right for one person to own another. Everyone deserves to be free, Jonny.'

–

Cassie was waiting for him near Gideon's.

The afternoon was waning as he left Rab's shop but the brandy they had shared as they reminisced had warmed his blood. Rab had said he would send a caddie to the guardhouse to alert Charlie and they would reunite in his father's tavern that night.

He was in the shadow of the passageway when he saw a dark shape ahead. For the third time that afternoon his hand fell to the handle of his sword, but when the figure threw back the shawl he knew there was no threat here. Not physical at least. Even in the muted light that crept in from the street he could see she had been crying, but she held his gaze with something like defiance. Or more likely hatred, but he did not wish to think on that. Not with regard to Cassie.

'Why did you come back?' she said, her voice strong.

'Believe me, I had little choice in the matter.'

'Why not?'

'I have business here.'

'What sort of business?'

'It doesn't matter, Cassie. I will leave once it has been completed.'

She nodded, looked over her shoulder at the tavern door to see if anyone was approaching. The courtyard was empty, although through the grime of the lower windows Flynt could see the tallow glow. Cassie turned back to him. 'Why did you leave without a word? Why were you so unfeeling?'

He felt something sting at his eyes, just as he had when Mother Mercy embraced him. This time it was guilt, not relief. 'I was young and uncaring.'

'You were cruel.'

There was that word again, and it bit once more, even though it was coated in that sadness that had haunted her eyes so briefly earlier. He felt a wave of tenderness wash over him and sweep away his voice as he said, 'I did not mean to be.'

'You should have told me you were leaving.'

'You would have tried to stop me.'

'And would I have been able?'

He paused to consider this. 'Yes. If anyone could have diverted me from my course, it was you.'

'Because you loved me?'

He hesitated as the now familiar sharp pain heated his chest. He could not recall ever telling anyone he loved them. Not Gideon. Not his aunt. He had never known his mother. Certainly not Belle, who he cared for, but she and Mary Grady had made it clear love to them was a transaction and not an emotion. He had never said it to Cassie when they were young, even though he suspected he had loved her. He could not say it now, even though he suspected he still did.

Her face betrayed no disappointment at his failure to reply. 'And now you're returned and perhaps you think things can be as they once were.'

'No, Cassie, things can never be as they once were.'

Her eyes flashed in the dim light. 'You're damned right they can't. I am wed now, to a man I love…'

'I know that. And I wish you both well. Had I known that you were Rab's wife I would never have come to the shop this day. You have to believe that.'

'Why should I believe that? Because you've been so honest with me in the past? The night before you left, when we were alone together, that was the time for you to be honest, to tell me you were leaving, but you didn't, did you? You weren't honest. You had me and then you left. And not a word since. And *then*, later, you allowed us to believe that you had perished in battle.'

'I didn't know Charlie had survived and returned to Edinburgh.'

'You didn't make it your business to know. We thought you dead, all of us, and we grieved. My mother, your father, Rab.' Her lips trembled and Flynt could do nothing but watch as she struggled to bring her emotions under control. 'And me.'

He cursed himself for being so thoughtless. He should have written at least once to let them know he was alive and well but life had overtaken his commitment to family. Charlie Temple had not been wrong, however. The young man who had left Edinburgh, bright of eye and head filled with adventure, had died on the battlefields of Flanders. The Jonas Flynt who had unwillingly returned to Edinburgh was not the Jonas Flynt they had known and he had never written because part of him had not wanted to run the risk of them seeing such in the spaces between his words. He had committed sins that did not bear scrutiny. He had robbed and killed. He wanted to explain all that to Cassie as they stood in that shadowy passageway between High Street and tavern, where once they had run together and laughed together, where they would snatch a final, passionate kiss before returning home. And now he wanted to reach out and hold her and tell her that he was sorry. He wanted to feel her body against his once more, to smell the fragrance of her hair and feel the softness of her cheek. But all he did was stand before her as if mute, the pain he had caused rebounding on him one hundredfold.

She held his eyes intently as if sensing his turmoil and willing him to speak. They had been close, all those years ago, and if anyone could somehow divine his thoughts it was she. She had a gift, Mother Mercy used to say – the sight. Ever since she was a child she had seen things to come, not complete, just little shafts of preconception beyond her understanding. Like Gideon she had the ability to sum up a person in one look. She now looked on him as if she had never seen him before and she did not like what she saw.

This time when he failed to respond, her eyes dropped as if in disappointment. 'Do me one courtesy, Jonas.'

'Anything,' he said, his voice a rasp, the single word scraped raw by the emotion he kept trapped in his throat.

'Whatever it is you've come here to do, do it quickly and leave us again.' Her eyes rose to meet his and even in the gloom of the passageway he saw tears glistening. 'There's a darkness that follows you. I see it in you, even if you don't know it exists. Leave us soon and never come back, Jonny, for I fear you carry the stench of death.'

She tugged her shawl over her head and pushed past him in the narrow space. He did not watch her go but he knew he would feel that brief brush of her arm upon his for a long time to come.

London

Charters sat alone at a corner table in the Blue Boar, a tankard of ale before him, ostensibly reading the most recent *Daily Courant* while surreptitiously studying the man holding court at a far table. The colonel had seen Jonathan Wild before, of course, but until now the man had meant little to him. He saw him as merely a common low-life criminal with his eye set on lining his own pockets. Now, though, Charters sensed something different in the man. He had ambition, his fine tuning of the process set up by his mentor Charles Hitchin into an efficient criminal organisation proved that, and that meant he became infinitely more interesting to Charters. He had no intention of inviting the man to join his Company of Rogues, for Wild was not suitable material. Certainly, the colonel could find something in the man's life to keep him in line, and failing that could invent something, but the self-styled Thieftaker General was too unpredictable and devoid of any integrity. Charters chose his recruits with care. Rogues they were, of all genders, religions, political beliefs, but each had that little something extra. It was not enough that they were larcenous or capable of violence. They had to have a quality that even Charters found indefinable and yet he was able to recognise it when he saw it. Call it a sense of honour or duty, call it an innate decency, call it trustworthiness, Charters knew that Jonas Flynt possessed it while Jonathan Wild did not. He had told Shrewsbury that Flynt would get the job done and he truly believed that. Flynt would do as he was bid or die trying. He might consider turning whatever he found to his advantage, but Charters would deal with that eventuality should it arise, though he doubted it would. He understood Jonas Flynt, knew how his mind worked. Charters would always wonder, on the other hand, what devious turn Wild would take. Undoubtedly the man had talents that could be utilised, but such usage would have to be at the length of Flynt's arms. Yes, that was the way to handle him, with Flynt always as intermediary.

Charters' Company of Rogues had a very broad brief. Their remit was to protect the security of the nation, but crime also threatened that security and often went hand in glove with England's enemies. Wild could prove useful but must never know he was working for His Majesty's government.

And yet, he found himself fascinated by the man. He had observed him a number of times since Flynt had departed for Scotland, partly out of this piqued interest, but also because he thought Wild bore watching. He had also had one of his men keep a watchful eye on Tawny Belle after Flynt had told him of her exposure to Blueskin Blake. He may have coerced the good serjeant into his service, but that did not mean he cared nothing for the man, and Flynt's concern for the woman's wellbeing was evident. The least he could do was watch over her. His man had reported seeing Blake outside the Covent Garden house only once, the day after Flynt left, but not since. Charters had also not observed any individual answering Blake's description during his periods of observing Wild.

He could not help but conjecture as to what villainy the man was undertaking on behalf of his master.

9

'My God, Jonny – I had you dead all these years!'

Flynt had been in Edinburgh only a matter of hours but had become well used to the fact that his demise had somehow passed him by, so he merely laughed at Charlie Temple's first words when they met in Gideon's that evening. Rab sported a broad grin but it flitted through Flynt's mind that perhaps Cassie had told her husband of their encounter. She had always been forthright, but Rab hadn't mentioned it so he could not be certain.

Charlie Temple looked trim and fit in his red-and-white uniform, certainly far more dapper than when Flynt had last seen him, with his tunic covered in mud, blood, bone and brain. As boys they had made fun of the red-coated Town Guard as they marched up and down the High Street bearing their long Lochaber axes over their shoulders. The weapon, with its spike, hook and blade, was to them a daunting sight, but the men who carried it were often too young, too old, too fat, for it to be of any great use. Although soldiers were garrisoned in the castle at the top of the hill, the guard were responsible for policing and keeping order on the streets and so were unpopular, which was why the boys felt it their youthful duty to mock them before being chased away, generally accompanied by curses and threats of bodily harm. When the Edinburgh mob gathered, which was often, the brave defenders of the city tended to make themselves scarce by hiding in their guardhouse near the Tron Kirk or within the walls of the Tolbooth gaol and what little security that afforded. The mob could be a fearsome creature when roused, and the guard well knew that the better part of valour is discretion, as Mr Shakespeare put it.

Flynt reminded Charlie of this as they sat by the fire, pots of ale before them, although Flynt barely touched his. Wine and brandy he could sup if he had the notion but he had never developed a taste for ale, finding it bitter. Flynt had ensured his back was to the blackened wood panelling, from where he could see not only the door to the courtyard but also the way to the kitchen and the stairway to the upper floors. He had done this unconsciously, just as he had placed his silver stick within easy reach. Lord Moncrieff aside, he had little reason to expect an attack here, but old habits, like old loves, do not die easily.

'We were young and foolish,' said Charlie, a slight smile playing across his lips, 'but I now know they are a fine body of men. It is my honour to command them.'

'Of course it is,' said Rab, giving Flynt a surreptitious wink. 'Sweeping up the drunken flotsam from the streets is a fine pursuit.'

Charlie gave Rab a weary look that told Flynt the two had sparred like this in the past. 'We do far more than that, as you know, Rab. We maintain order in our streets so that decent people can go about their business without fear. We guard the citizens, no matter their station in life.'

'And hang folk who should not be hung,' Rab retorted.

Charlie fidgeted in his seat, clearly not comfortable with the task that lay ahead but resolute in defending the honour of his office. 'We're escort only tomorrow. It's not our function to comment on the right or wrong of the sentence, it's merely our duty to ensure the execution is carried out peacefully. The lockman yonder will officiate.'

He jerked his head in the direction of a slender man sitting alone in the corner. He was hunched over his table, a tankard near to hand, a pipe smouldering between his lips, as he stared into the flame of the candle perched in the holder in front of him as if seeking the meaning of life. The lockman, Charlie had called him, using the local term for hangman. As such, he was entitled to some meals and other supplies – his lock – on market days. Flynt knew not his name but had heard someone mutter that he had 'cheated the widdie' – avoided the noose himself – by accepting the position of executioner.

'Aye, peacefully,' repeated Rab. 'It'll be far from peaceful for auld Somey Barclay.'

'He knew the risks in smuggling. He enjoyed the dance, now he must pay the piper.'

Rab smiled. 'Aye, and many a time you enjoyed the fruits of that dance in my parlour, Captain Charlie Temple, so I'll thank you not to be so sanctimonious.'

Charlie looked as if he expected the retort. 'I don't condone the sentence, Rab, but it will be carried out, mark me.'

'And if the mob turns ugly?' Flynt said. 'Will your men be able to ward it off with only Lochaber axes at your hand? They are fearsome weapons to be sure but designed to counter cavalry. I doubt the populace will attack on horseback.'

'We'll be armed with musket and ball,' said Charlie. 'But I truly hope we'll have no need to discharge them.'

Talk of the impending hanging made Flynt uncomfortable so he had the need to divert the subject. 'When we fought together I would never have thought you to attain the rank of captain, Charlie. You have done well.'

Charlie gave him a bashful look and Flynt saw the boy that was yet in the man. 'I am lieutenant only. The rank of captain is but an honorary one given me by the guard. And the truth of the matter is that I did not earn it – it was bought for me.'

Rab had already told as much so Flynt merely nodded. 'I thought you would've had your fill of the military after what we saw, Charlie. In truth, I didn't think you suited to the life.'

Charlie accepted his opinion with grace. 'In equal truth I don't think I am either, but what else will I do? I'm unsuited to trade, like my father. I could enter politics but lack the necessary self-interest. So it's either the guards or thievery and I don't think I have the nerve for that.'

Flynt remembered Charlie's face, ash white, as they looked at each other amid musket fire and clash of steel at Malplaquet. He remembered the body of a Cornishman who had found himself between them during the fighting. They did not even know his name but Flynt recalled the man whistling under his breath, perhaps to calm his nerves, then felt again the sudden splash of blood and sting of shattered bone on his face as the man's head was torn off by a cannon ball. Realisation struck them both immediately that had the munition veered a foot either way it would have been one of them lying on the ground.

They had each lost their nerve that day and little wonder, with the blood and death that had surrounded them for months. Flynt had decided that it was not his war and he was damned if he would die for a monarch who gave not a single damn for him. He did not know if Charlie felt the same but he suspected it was more blind fear than a distaste for royalty, for his friend had always shown a respect for authority no matter how misplaced. They did not discuss it as they ran and were eventually separated in the general confusion. They did not discuss it now in this dark room with the smell of tallow and the snap of firewood, but even in the dim light he saw by the slight loss of focus in Charlie's eyes that he too had been transported back to that hell.

Charlie lowered his head and took a mouthful of ale. When he looked back the mist had gone and he smiled. 'I'm glad to see you, Jonny.'

'And I you, Charlie.'

'It's good to be home, is it not?'

Flynt did not reply but he saw Rab's eyebrow flick. Although the three of them had been inseparable as boys, he and Rab had shared a special bond and he knew now that his friend was well aware of Flynt's discomfort at being back in Edinburgh. It was more than shame at not having kept in touch, it was that solid lump in his gut that told him he no longer belonged. Moncrieff had stated it, Cassie had made it clear and Flynt agreed. Rab understood that.

Charlie took another sip and his face grew more serious. 'I received a complaint from Baillie Wilson today concerning you both.' He looked to Flynt. 'You didn't waste any time getting into a scrape, did you, Jonny?'

'Yon Andy Wilson is a lickspittle bastard, so he is,' said Rab. 'Was his laird and master with him?'

Charlie's eyes crinkled in amusement. He did not need to ask who Rab meant. 'No, Lord Moncrieff was not present.'

'Just as well, for you'd never hear what auld Andy had to say with his lips stuck to yon bastard's erse. I take it he told you they wished to ransack my shop and apartments?'

'He said they were in search of stolen property they thought might be in your premises.'

'They were looking for a man, Charlie, no property. A *man*.'

Charlie sighed. 'Be that as it may, this – eh – man remains property, rightly or wrongly.'

'Wrongly.'

Charlie held up both hands. 'I won't debate the issue with you, Rab.' Listening to them, Flynt felt once again that these two had argued this point, and others, many times before. 'The fact is that under the law this man…'

'Nero.'

Charlie looked puzzled.

'The man has a name,' said Rab, 'and it's Nero. It's no the name he was born with, of course, for they took that from him along with his liberty when he was a child.'

'The fact is, Nero is property under the law and Lord Moncrieff had every right to see that property returned.'

'But no to search my premises.'

'Not without your permission, no. Or an official warrant obliging you to accede to his request.'

'And that is exactly what they were told.'

Charlie sighed. 'Rab, I ask you this as a friend, do you know anything of this man Nero's whereabouts?'

Rab took a moment to reply during which Flynt believed he was considering whether to be truthful. Friends they might be, but Charlie was still in command of the Town Guard and, no matter the right of it, under the law Nero was legally, though not morally, bound to Moncrieff. No good would come of Rab admitting to any knowledge, so he said simply, 'No.'

Flynt reasoned that Rab had not lied to their friend. The fact was, although he knew the man's destination, he did not in all honesty know exactly where he was at that moment. It was a fine distinction but one that Flynt felt Rab could live with.

Charlie seemed satisfied. Rab, though, did not, and was not going to allow the matter to rest. 'And if I had such knowledge, Charlie, would you arrest me? Would you report back to Wilson?'

Charlie's expression was a mixture of shock and pain. 'You know better than to ask that.'

'Do I? I'm no so sure.'

Charlie looked to Flynt. 'This is a matter Rab and I have argued about for many a year, Jonny. We stand on opposite sides of what is legal property and what is not, he and I. He will not accept the order of things.'

Flynt pursed his lips. 'It's an ill-balanced world, it's true.'

Rab sat back. 'Aye, but we must do what we can to even that balance, must we not? Else why are we on this earth, if no to assist other souls? Gideon kent that, when he snatched Mother Mercy and Cassie from the West Indies.'

Flynt was surprised. 'He told you about that?'

Rab shook his head. 'Cassie. She was but an infant but she remembered well the desperate flight in the night, fearful of being caught. Your father had paid for passage to England for them both and he followed later in his ship.'

Flynt looked to Charlie, suddenly concerned at Rab's openness before a law officer, even though he was a friend, but there was no sign of any official interest. In fact, Flynt realised, this was not news to him. 'You know of this?'

'Aye,' Charlie replied, 'but the West Indies are far from my jurisdiction so what happens there is not my concern.'

Cassie had shared Gideon's reticence regarding the details of their leaving the Indies and Flynt felt a pang of what he thought might be envy that she had entrusted this intelligence with Rab and not with him when they were younger. He asked, 'The master of the vessel on which they sailed was anti-slavery also?'

'Perhaps…' Rab reassessed his reply. 'Probably no, as there are but few people who would risk their all for these unfortunate souls, but there are men who will swallow fears when it's leavened with silver. Principles too.' A glint of mischief shone in Rab's eye. 'Take your Lord high and mighty Moncrieff, Charlie…'

'He is not *my* lord,' Charlie argued, then permitted a slight smile. 'Although he is both high and mighty, something you would do well to keep in mind.'

Rab ignored him and spoke directly to Flynt. 'He was involved in negotiating the bastard Treaty of Union. He took English gold in return for our freedom…'

'Come, Rab, you exaggerate,' said Charlie. 'You throw the word *freedom* out like bread to the starving. Scots are not slaves. Yes, I agree that slavery is a thorny subject…'

Rab's eyebrow raised. 'A thorny subject?'

Charlie pressed on this time. '…But that gold was to pay the debts incurred during the Darien enterprise. The country was on its knees, man, and something had to be done.'

'Aye, and who ensured that enterprise failed? The English. Whose unfair legislation prevented our merchants from trading abroad? The English. Who effectively forced this country to embark on the scheme to expand trade in the first place? The English. And who then conspired to prevent it from being a success?' He put a hand to his chin and adopted a quizzical expression. 'Now, let me think…'

Charlie was not to be bested. 'You oversimplify it as usual, Rab. It was commerce, pure and simple, and the English merchants were merely protecting their interests as *we* would have done had the situation been reversed.'

'Aye, backed by their parliament.'

'As our merchants were backed by ours. And remember, His Majesty King William gave his leave for the Company of Scotland to be established.'

Rab dismissed this with a grimace. 'Only because his Commissioner gave the royal assent without consulting him. If William had known, he would have refused and he later did everything he could to block it. It was meant to be a joint venture between England and Scotland, mind, but the English traders refused to take part and moved to destroy it.'

Charlie's voice grew slightly weary, conveying to Flynt that these two had argued this point before. 'Again, commerce. It is a cut-throat business. And the men behind the Darien company chose their location poorly, a marshy strip of land in far-off Panama, in the name of God. It was an ill-advised, ill-chosen and ill-fated scheme from the start and as such was plagued by disaster, disease and Spanish opposition. There is no wonder that it collapsed amid a welter of blood and fever in those pox-ridden jungles. And the result? It sucked up much of Scotland's fortune and left an already poor country even poorer. Perhaps we did get a bad bargain but in the end we had no choice but to agree to a union.'

'A union with the very people who had either caused, or at least capitalised on, our misfortune. English colonists could have come to the Darien colony's aid but they sat back and did nothing, under orders from London. No, Charlie, they knew what they were about and they made sure that the venture failed. And then when we were desperate, they came for our freedom and lined the pockets of our nobles to make sure it went through.'

'And paid off the country's debts.'

'Which they were instrumental in creating.' Rab's voice had risen slightly and Flynt saw his father look in their direction from the counter. A group of men, perhaps the same he had seen when he arrived, also began to take note of the conversation.

'Let us remain friendly, Rab,' Flynt said quietly.

Rab took a deep breath and lowered his voice again. 'We lost our parliament, we lost our independence, we lost our souls to English gold – and men like Lord Moncrieff were ready and waiting with their hands out. They sold us, Charlie, blood and bone. And now his lordship calls himself patriot and proclaims Jacobitism.'

Flynt became interested. 'He supports the Pretender?'

Rab smiled again. 'He does but he is canny with it. Do you remember what my faither used to tell us about William Wallace, Robert the Bruce and the wars of independence? Mind what he said about the Scottish nobility then?'

Flynt remembered well, for he had often seen it in men of noble blood since. 'That they looked to themselves while waving banners of either Scot or Englishman, depending on where the power and profit lay.'

'Aye, and they do it still. So the old man makes it appear he has come out for James Stuart while the younger mouths loyalty to Hanover. They look to themselves and their fortunes, Jonny, and the devil take the people and the country.'

'He has a son?'

'Aye, he bides in London, looking after the family's interests in the south. He has embedded himself in the government's hide like a tick while his faither plays the Scottish patriot here, along with Bobbing John, the Earl of Mar.'

Flynt noted Charlie did not object to the use of the Earl of Mar's nickname. In opposing what Charlie believed was the natural order of things, the earl had lost the right to any respect.

'They both were refused lucrative government posts under the wee German lairdie and came back in a rage,' Rab added. 'So when Bobbing John raised the Stuart standard, Moncrieff cleaved to the cause. Or at least, pretends to.'

Flynt asked, 'And was Moncrieff present at the gathering on the Braes of Mar?'

Rab was astonished. 'You ken about that, Jonny?'

'I was in London, Rab, no the other end of the earth.'

Charlie coughed diplomatically. 'Well,' he said, then drained his tankard and forced a smile, even though he was decidedly discomfited by the turn this reunion had taken. 'If you lads will indulge in seditious talk, I regret I must leave you.'

Flynt asked, 'So soon, Charlie?'

Rab rose along with Charlie. 'Charlie boy, I apologise, please don't pay me any heed. We have been through this too many times for you to take any offence.'

'Ach, Rab, away with you, man – I'm well used to you and your pontifications. I would be more than happy to sit here and argue with you, as we have done so many times, but I must ensure my men are prepared for the morrow.' He gave a quick glance towards the men around the corner. 'And it does not look well for an officer of the loyal Town Guard to discuss such events. I'm sorry, Jonny, your return comes at a bad time.'

Flynt rose and offered his hand. 'Charlie, I'm glad to see you.'

'And I you, my friend,' said Charlie, his grip firm. Rab laid his hand on theirs and suddenly Flynt felt a kinship he had not felt for many a year. He did not share blood with these two men but they were linked by friendship and it was a bond that would endure, no matter their differences of opinion.

Charlie felt it too. 'It is good for we three to be together again. How did old Cicero put it? Life is nothing without friendship. I feel as if all is right with the world, at last.'

'Aye,' said Flynt, and in that moment he believed it too.

'We will meet again, spend more time together, once this dread duty has been performed, on that you have my word,' Charlie said, then turned to Rab and delivered a playful backhanded blow to his shoulder. 'And *you*, you rebellious scum, you keep an eye over your shoulder for his lordship and Baillie Wilson.'

Rab laughed. 'I've little fear, for I know the gallant men of the Town Guard are there to protect me.'

Charlie's lips pursed in mock severity. 'Aye, perhaps I will order them to look the other way in your case.'

He donned his three-cornered uniform hat and with a final mock glare at Rab, followed by a sly smile to Flynt, he left. The group of men watched him go, their mutters not reaching Flynt's ear but by their expression it was clear that the presence of the Captain of the Guard in their midst was obviously not to their liking. Flynt kept a surreptitious eye on them as he and Rab resumed their seats. He had seen them shoot glances in their direction while Rab and Charlie had argued but he did not know if they posed a threat. It was always best, he had learned, to fully comprehend the tone of any room and he resolved to study them further, just in case.

'He's still the same old Charlie,' Rab said with a smile. 'He always did favour those in authority.'

'While you did not,' said Flynt.

'And you always occupied the middle ground, as I recall. Do you still not hold views on the nature of life and society, Jonny?'

Charlie's departure had not dispelled Rab's argumentative nature, Flynt noted. 'Holding views can be a dangerous thing. Or, at least, expressing them.'

'You don't seem to be the kind of man who would fear such things.'

'I have learned that a man does well to keep his thoughts to himself,' Flynt said. 'The more that is known on the workings of his mind, the easier he is manipulated.'

Rab sat back and studied Flynt carefully. 'So you don't believe a stand should be taken on such matters as the ownership of human beings simply because of the colour of their skin?'

'I lived for a number of years with Mother Mercy and Cassie…' Flynt felt a shard of pain pierce his chest as he said her name but pressed on. 'I could not think otherwise than that slavery is wrong. But the likes of you and I are too few and those who support it too numerous, not to mention powerful, for our words to make a difference.'

'But if we don't speak, if we don't act, then such a difference will never be made. And it will change, Jonny, it has to.'

Flynt saw the wisdom in Rab's words, but he had also seen more of the world than his friend. He knew the tilt in the order of things envisaged by his friend was massive and those opposed to the tipping of the scales held the most weight. He suspected change would come but not in his lifetime. However, at that moment, he had other matters with which to deal.

He sat back in his chair. 'May I ask you a question?'

'By Christ, Jonny, you don't need permission.'

Flynt carefully rotated his still full tankard on the tabletop before him. 'Charlie called you rebel.'

Rab said with a smile, 'Ach, he has called me worse.'

Flynt paused a moment before his next words. 'Are you a Jacobite?'

Rab's face grew sombre as he understood there was serious intent behind the question. 'Would it matter if I was, Jonny?'

'No, but I have reason to ask.'

Rab glanced over his shoulder at the men behind him, then leaned across the table, his voice lowered. 'I've no love for kings or queens, Jonny. House of Stuart, House of Hanover, they're all the same to me. Why would I support a king who cares more for his electorate in Germany than he does for the land he rules? And why should I support a claimant to that throne who is more English than he is Scot and more French than he is English? Neither of these pampered, entitled buffoons have the slightest care for the common man.'

'And yet you often speak like a Jacobite.'

'I speak like a man who believes the people have a right to be ruled by men they put in power, not by men or women born into power. Or who bought their way to it.'

'You favour a republic?'

'I favour justice and liberty and the right to choose your own destiny and not have to go cap in hand to people like Lord Moncrieff and his ilk to beg leave to draw breath. He and men like him are a canker on the hides of the common people. I know you believe that too.'

Flynt's own view of the ruling classes was formed not just in Edinburgh but by what he witnessed while serving in the army, where the incompetence of many officers was masked by their arrogance. There were some who were able, of course, and yet others who were brilliant, but it was his view that military proficiency was something that was born with a man and honed, and not as a result of having the means to purchase a commission or patronage at court in order to smooth the way.

When he nodded his agreement, Rab took it as leave to continue with his personal manifesto. 'I favour a Scotland with the right to make its own decisions. I favour it free from the stranglehold of London, which thinks it has bought us for a handful of gold.'

'And you think this small country capable of standing alone?'

'We did it for hundreds of years, through fat and famine, war and peace. We can do it again. But this time we would be free of royal blood. The Stuarts ruled this country for centuries. Some were good, others bad, but since Mary Stuart it has overwhelmingly been the latter. She cared only for herself and obtaining the English throne. Her son was a bitter, mewling little creature who saw conspiracy and witches on every corner. And the arrogance of his son and grandson brought nothing but war and contempt for the Kirk. We are better off shot of them and any fat German. Does that answer your question, Jonny?'

Flynt knew the matter was far more complex than Rab had described but he did not intend to become embroiled in a political debate. 'Let me ask you another question.' He paused, debating briefly with himself whether he should, but knowing in his heart that if he could not trust Rab, he could trust no one. 'Have you heard of a group known as the Fellowship?'

Rab frowned and was silent for a moment as he studied Flynt. He cleared his throat and once again looked to the men at his back. It was a swift glance to see if they were listening to their discourse. Flynt had been monitoring them while he and Rab talked and was satisfied that they were not eavesdropping to any great degree. Rab lowered his voice even further. 'Where did you hear of them?'

Flynt remained casual, even though he had to lean closer across the table to catch the words. 'I heard mention, in London, in relation to Mar's rising. Your talk brought them to mind. Some kind of secret society, is it?'

Rab weighed carefully his next words. 'You would be well advised to never mention them to anyone but me, Jonny, and even then think carefully before you do. The Fellowship is secretive, it is true, and they don't like to be spoken of. It is comprised of men who support the return of the Stuarts to the throne, or at least claim they do. Some have grown fat since the Treaty of Union yet they wrap themselves in the Saltire and tradition, but the reality is they see profit in the return of James Stuart and increased power for their families. I told you the wee German lairdie down there in London has turned against many of the Scots who helped husband the treaty and they don't like that. They think themselves betrayed and so they came home, drank the health of the King Over the Water and plotted.'

So they were Jacobite at heart, Flynt mused. It was not often that Charters' intelligence network was so lacking. 'And will they succeed?'

There was a further silence and Flynt felt Rab was growing suspicious. 'Why do you ask about this, Jonny?'

Flynt had a lie readily prepared but he did not give it breath. He was uncomfortable with deluding his friend. He took a deep breath. 'They are connected to the business that brought me home.'

'Connected in what manner?'

Flynt had already decided he would tell Rab the real reason why he had come to Edinburgh. In a hushed tone he told him of fleeing the battle, of finding Charters and fighting his way back to his own lines. He told him of his life in London, of gambling and stealing. He told him of the blackmail that forced him to work for the Company of Rogues. And he told him of the queen's document, of Madame de Fontaine and her mention of the Fellowship. He told his old friend all and he felt the better for it.

Rab remained silent for a long time after he had completed his tale. He drained his ale and stared at the flames flickering in the grate. 'And if you find this document, what will you do with it?'

'I'll take it back to London. That was what I agreed to do.'

'You show such honour to a man and government who have shown none to you?'

'I gave my word, Rab, and a man has nothing if he has not his word. I've committed many crimes but the one constant is that when I give my oath, I honour it. I'll do so now, if I can.'

'Come what may?'

'Come what may.'

'You see this as duty, Jonny? Like Charlie does tomorrow's execution?'

'Aye. Duty and honour, Rab. They are a draught we must swallow and oftentimes they are bitter.'

'Yet you care not who is on the throne, Hanover or Stuart?'

'Not a fig. As you say, they each are as useless as the other. But believe me when I say I will do what I have to regardless. So what more can you tell me about the Fellowship? Do you have names of its members?'

Rab once again considered before speaking. 'Rumours only. One name.'

'At this point I will accept rumour, as that is all I have.'

A little half smile tickled Rab's lips. 'Can you not guess, Jonny? You've already met.'

Flynt knew immediately. 'Moncrieff.'

'The elder, perhaps even the younger, but as I say, they play the double game of old.'

'Where can I find the elder?'

'They live off the Lawnmarket, close by the castle, but I would not march up there and hammer at the door if I were you. You have already irked him and I doubt very much that you would receive a warm welcome.'

'Then where does his lordship frequent? What tavern, brothel?'

'Ah, Lord Moncrieff is not one for bending an elbow with the commoners or unbuttoning his breeches in a bawdy house. He is far too upstanding for that. He has the doxies brought to his

149

home when Lady Moncrieff is not in town and a fine old time is had by all accounts. Age has not withered him, it would seem.'

'So how will I make his further acquaintance?'

'I doubt after today he will welcome your society, lad, but tomorrow, the hanging, down on the Grassmarket. He will be there, as will most of Edinburgh, high and low.'

Flynt felt his heart sink.

10

A multitude of bobbing heads crammed into the open area beneath the castle like sand in an hourglass. The Grassmarket, bound by tall lands and buildings of varying antiquity, was a wide and airy piazza, for it was here that markets and horse sales were held. This day it had a cramped feeling, such was the press of humanity. A judicial death was as much an attraction in Edinburgh as it was in the south, so the townspeople had flooded in from West Bow and Cowgate to pack themselves into the space stretching to the King's Stables, a liberty zone for debtors at the western end. Windows overlooking the execution site were open and further bodies projected from them, eager for a view. Peddlers moved through the throng, hawking food and drink, but Flynt did not sense the festival atmosphere that would have been prevalent in London. There the crowd's mood was a mix of sympathy, of fascination and even mockery towards the accused, but here he could smell rage in the air. Rab had said the execution was unpopular and he saw this in the faces and demeanour of the people clustered around him.

The Edinburgh mob was well known for its short fuse and the flame was being put to it as Somey Barclay was brought to the site of his death. From where he stood Flynt saw the cart emerging from the Bow, having carried the condemned man up the High Street from the Tolbooth gaol. The Town Guard formed a double-lined wedge around it, their red coats gleaming in the brisk sunlight, their muskets shouldered, the clump of their feet in time to the drummer at their head. Charlie strode before them, head high, his sword drawn and held upright against his shoulder in mirror of his men's arms, a pistol his only other weapon. The crowd eased aside to let them pass but there was a great deal of jeering and insults thrown, although no missiles. Even so, Flynt could tell it would take very little for the mood of the assembly to explode.

The procession passed by a wooden platform that had been erected against a building at the Bowfoot known as Templar's Land. Flynt's aunt had once told him that it was named such because the land was owned in perpetuity by a band of Knights Templar who escaped the purge of their brethren centuries before by fleeing to Scotland. He did not know if it was true but the name had clung through the centuries. On this platform judges, magistrates, baillies and Edinburgh's quality would bear witness to the finishing of the law, for it was ridiculous to expect them to crane their necks while watching another's stretch. They would sup fine wine there before retiring to a private room in a tavern for the *deid-chack*, a sumptuous meal served after every hanging, there being nothing like watching a felon breathe his or her last to make a rich man right sharp set.

The dignitaries were already filing up the staircase to the platform so Flynt stepped down from his stool and began to thread his way through the crowd towards the structure, for if his quarry was present, that was where he would be. He had little space in which to manoeuvre in the press of bodies so his progress was slow, leaving him able to observe the activity around the gallows as he moved. The hanging tree itself was, unlike London's Tyburn, not a permanent structure. It was a sturdy wooden inverted L-frame inserted when required into a wide sandstone block at the eastern end of the piazza. The guest of honour, Somey Barclay, was not as Flynt had expected. He had met a few smugglers in his day and almost to a man they were weather-beaten, muscular men well used to dealing with heavy seas and heavier excise officers as they transacted their moonlight trade, but the soul now being led up to the block was a frail, elderly man who looked as if he would be more at home reading catechism. His hair was thin and his face was narrow and he wore a pair of spectacles that perched on the end of his nose as if preparing to leap to safety at any moment. He stood, his hands bound behind him, his head bowed as if in prayer, which perhaps he was. Flynt had no notion of the man's piety but it was not unusual for even the most dedicated sinner to find his faith miraculously resurrected as he stood in the shadow of the gibbet. A minister with the stern visage of one who would brook no suggestion of sin stood by him and mouthed platitudes, perhaps even lecturing the man on his transgressions. Flynt wondered if his deep-set expression masked sympathy for the man, for though the Kirk officially condemned the free traders, the clergy themselves more often than not turned a blind eye.

A ladder had been placed against the cross-beam and the lockman Flynt had seen the night before leaned against it in a nonchalant manner, his pipe between his lips. Normally the ire of the crowd would be directed at him, for executioners were as unpopular here as in London, so perhaps this day was something of a relief as the bulk of the crowd's spite was levelled towards Charlie and his men.

Flynt alternated his attention between the gallows stone and the platform. He did not seek any familiar faces among the crowd for he was aware none of his now extended family would attend. Years before, Mother Mercy had said she and her daughter had seen enough of hanged men and women in the West Indies to last them a lifetime so she never joined the crowds on execution day. Flynt himself would not have been present, had the occasion not offered him the opportunity to engineer a chance meeting with Moncrieff and repair the breach caused by their previous encounters. He had no notion as to how best to attempt it but much of his work for Charters was at best improvisational, at times chaotic. Given the circumstances, this particular episode would be a mixture of both.

The men of the guard were deployed in twin ranks around the base of the stone as a barrier, their weapons at the ready position. Above them, Charlie stood slightly behind the accused, his face quivering with nerves, his restless feet moving constantly beneath him as if dancing to a fiddler only he could hear. His eyes darted to and fro as he looked upon the sea of faces below him, his trembling hand never straying far from the butt of the pistol in his belt while the fingers gripping the sword hilt twitched as if in spasm. Sweat sheened his forehead under his three-cornered hat and his tongue darted out to dampen his lips. Mouth dry, face and palms wet; Flynt knew those sensations well and he knew Charlie was experiencing the same terror they had felt when the cannonball narrowly missed them at Malplaquet. He hoped the execution would pass without incident because Charlie was not a man to act with reason when his mind and body were in such turmoil. At the first hint of trouble he would panic, and that would be catastrophic in this heady atmosphere of hatred, rage and grim anticipation.

Somey stepped forward to address the crowd. A hush fell as his voice rose, thin and reedy, warning them about the temptations of strong liquor and exhorting them to follow the teachings of the Lord Jesus Christ. Flynt detected an element of coaching in the speech, for the Kirk was ever keen to hear of redemption at the moment of meeting eternity. The minister's mouth adopted what might have been a small smile of satisfaction as he listened.

Flynt focused on the viewing platform as he eased his way between the congregated bodies as sinuously as he could without jostling. He did not wish to push or thrust himself through, for should he cause friction enough to allow a row to flare, it could spark the tinderbox of emotions that heated the air around him.

A fresh restlessness moved among the crowd. Somey had completed his speech, ending with an admonishment for all to lead a life of decency and adhere to the laws of both God and Man, and was being led to the foot of the ladder. Flynt heard mutterings as the man was assisted onto the bottom rung, his step faltering. The lockman reached out to steady him, for it would not do if a nasty accident were to befall the man before he was officially turned off.

'Let him free!'

The woman's voice came from behind Flynt and he twisted to see its source but could not. The cry was taken up by other voices.

'He doesnae deserve a hanging!' Another woman just ahead of him yelled, and those around her nodded their approval.

Charlie glanced towards the officials on the platform to his right, as if looking for guidance, perhaps even hoping for a commutation of sentence. Flynt followed his gaze and saw a cadaverous man dressed in black wave a hand as if he was batting away an irritating insect. It did not make Charlie happy. He murmured something to the lockman, who nodded and began to guide Somey further up the ladder.

Disapproval rumbled through the spectators like thunder with the lightning yet to come, but Flynt tried to ignore it as he fixed his eye on the platform. While watching the man he presumed to be a judge give his casual order he had spotted Moncrieff, with Baillie Wilson at his side like a faithful dog. His lordship stood with his hand as ever resting on his cane, his expression reflective, perhaps contemplating his own mortality. Then his head turned to his left, away from Wilson, as if listening to someone speaking to him from behind.

Flynt began to move again, gently edging his way forward, for the ire of the people rose with each faltering step Somey took up the ladder. Demands to have him set free grew in number and became more threatening, while a gang of boys carrying stones and balls of mud weaved between the adults to reach a better vantage point. Flynt caught sight of men further back handing out more missiles to others.

This was about to erupt, Flynt could feel it pulse in the air around him. And when it did, he might lose his prey. He forced himself to keep moving, his eyes fixed on the platform party. Lord Moncrieff had turned fully away to talk to the person behind, as if he did not wish to see what followed on the makeshift stage below. Flynt tried to see to whom he spoke but from his position could not.

155

A moan from those near to the gallows stone drew his eye back to Somey, who had climbed as far as he could without standing on the overhead spar. At his back, the lockman reached up to grasp the noose dangling from the beam.

Lord Moncrieff moved slightly to allow the person behind a clearer view.

The lockman looped the rope over Somey's head, pulling the knot tight, and Somey teetered, causing the crowd's displeasure to erupt in a roar. The lockman steadied the ladder and began to descend again.

The person on the platform behind Moncrieff stepped forward. Even though he had expected to see her again he felt something flutter in his stomach, but still his eyes were dragged back to the execution block.

The lockman was safely back on the stone and without any hesitation he grasped the edges of the ladder in both hands and twisted, sending Somey into space. It was a sudden movement, made with no flourish, and it caught many in the crowd by surprise.

Flynt dragged his eyes away, not wishing to see Somey's final moments. He had seen death in many forms but he found the formality of judicial execution distinctly disturbing, not least because of the noose hung over his own head thanks to Charters. Around him the men cried out and women screamed. Hands darted to mouths while hoarse voices called out against the injustice, and guttural oaths were levelled at the hangman and the guards. He could not help himself from looking back to where the limp body now swung on the rope, the head at a slight angle to the neck. The lockman might have been an unwilling recruit to the post but it appeared he had positioned the knot perfectly. That, coupled with the length of the drop, had snapped the neck. Somey had been lucky, for he did not slowly throttle as did most victims of the hemp. He could not say if it was the result of the hangman's skill or simple good fortune, if such circumstance could be so described.

On the platform, Madame de Fontaine watched, her mouth slightly open at the scene before her. She, like Flynt, must have seen men die in such a fashion before but it was to her credit that she appeared so discomfited by the sight. Perhaps she shared Flynt's presentiment that such a future lay before them. Then, as if sensing his eyes upon her, her gaze moved to the crowd, which had fallen into a sullen silence as the body swayed gently from side to side. When she found Flynt's face staring back at her, her frozen shock melted into a smile, as if pleased to see him. One eyebrow cocked slightly and her head tilted a fraction in greeting. Moncrieff saw the look and turned, his eyes resting on Flynt, a frown already puckering his face.

Flynt became aware of a renewed restlessness growing in the bodies around him. Two young men in dark clothing had stepped up to the gallows stone and were preparing a large sack to receive the remains. Medical students, Flynt surmised, for the surgeons were allowed the use of the corpses of the hanged to study the mysteries of anatomy.

'No,' a woman's voice cried out – Flynt thought it the first woman he had heard earlier, but could not be certain. 'Has he no suffered enough?'

A man shouted, 'Aye, ye have taken his spirit, leave his flesh be, in the name of God!'

The lockman faltered and the students, their sack now ready to receive the corpse, looked to each other as if asking why they had volunteered for this task. Charlie stepped forward.

'The sentence has been carried out lawfully,' he announced, the break in his voice giving lie to the confident manner in which he stood. 'You will now disperse and allow the remains to be removed as dictated by the court.'

'No!' The same woman's voice, hoarse now, roughened by rage and emotion. A friend of the dead man, perhaps? A loved one? 'It's an abomination to cut him open! Leave him be!'

More voices joined in assent, chanting 'leave him be', and Flynt could smell the approaching storm.

It was the boys who set it in motion. The missiles they had been given were now utilised, thrown at the guard, the medical students, the lockman, even the minister. The degrees of accuracy varied but a few hit their marks and the targets fled the block for the comparative safety of the ground, all save Charlie who, to his credit, remained below the still suspended corpse, waving his sword. In anyone else it might have been bravery but Flynt knew his friend was in fact frozen by fear. Again he found his mind jumping back to another day and another land where he had been forced to physically push his friend in order to galvanise those limbs.

Flynt looked for the men who had supplied the ammunition but they had been either swallowed by the crowd or had taken their leave, not wishing to be part of what they'd had a hand in creating. If their intention was for the volley of rocks, mud and other missiles to act as a signal to the crowd, it had worked, for around him anger was exhaled in bellows as Flynt was carried by a torrent of bodies towards the gallows stone. He tried to resist the flow, for he saw the platform being hastily cleared, Moncrieff gallantly ushering Madame de Fontaine ahead of him, his body shielding her from harm. As Flynt was swept away by the tide of fury, he saw her look back to find him. She gave him a little wave, a waggle of the fingers, a flash of a brilliant grin, before she vanished down the steps. Despite the palpable atmosphere of violence and impending tragedy, he could not help a small smile himself. She was plucky, he would give her that.

A rock flew upwards and caught Charlie on the temple. His hat had already been lost and there was a visible wound on his forehead. He dabbed at it with his fingers and stared at the blood as if perplexed. When his head rose again Flynt knew by the vacant expression and slightly slackened jaw that his friend had been momentarily stunned. What action he took when his senses – and his fear – returned might prove catastrophic.

Men and women drove themselves at the red-coated barrier on the ground, striving to reach the stone to liberate the hanged man's body, but the guards held them back with their muskets. A serjeant, swinging a hefty club to keep the nearest at bay, looked to his commander for guidance, and Flynt dreaded what order Charlie might give, for he saw the terror rising in his face. At Malplaquet they could at least flee from the violence, but here Charlie was at the centre of a whirlwind of rage and rocks.

Flynt thrust his way towards the gallows, ignoring protests as he shouldered men and women from his path. He had to get to Charlie, had to talk him down.

The serjeant at the foot of the block called out, 'Captain, what are your orders?'

Charlie's head swivelled towards his men and then back to the jeering crowd, the chants fraying and fracturing into a general roar. Flynt saw something creep into his friend's eye, something that infected his fear. It was fury and it would lead him to make a mistake.

Don't do it, Flynt willed as he jerked a bulky man aside, who objected in a coarse verbal fashion and swung a huge fist, but Flynt ducked under it and moved on. The man continued to curse and reached out with both hands to seize him but was stopped with a warning look from Flynt. When he was satisfied the man had reconsidered, he returned his attention to Charlie, who was backing from the edge of the gallows stone, his head shaking as his fingers fumbled for his pistol.

'Charlie!' Flynt cried out. 'For God's sake, man!'

But Charlie could not hear him over the din. He looked back at the serjeant, nodded and said something Flynt could not hear. In his heart he knew what order had been given. Disperse the crowd. Using any means necessary.

The serjeant stared at his commander for a second or two, as if considering debating the order, but the soldier within overcame any doubts and he acknowledged it with a curt nod, then told his men to ready their weapons. One or two of the rifles raised were matchlock hackbuts, Flynt noted, decades old by the looks, but well maintained. The remainder were flintlocks and Flynt was certain one was a smooth bore fowler, more used to bringing down birds than men but capable of inflicting damage at close range. Some of the rioters at the front saw the firearms swivel in their direction and began to push away from the guardsmen, but those behind continued to press ahead, determined to reach the dead smuggler who still hung above their heads. Flynt rammed another couple of men aside as he tried to reach the stone.

'Charlie! In the name of God, don't do it!'

The serjeant's mouth tightened as he looked to his captain and received another nod. 'Over their heads, boys,' he yelled above the noise.

Flynt glanced behind him to the buildings facing the stone, at the people still at their windows watching the scene below, the barrels raised in their direction. The hackbuts and fowler did not have the range but the more modern weapons might just have power enough.

'Charlie, rescind that order!' he yelled, moving forward with renewed urgency. 'Look to the windows, man! The windows!'

The serjeant heard him but he had received his orders. The arm holding the club dropped. 'Front rank, fire!'

The stutter of gunfire stunned the crowd into silence and all movement seemed to freeze, with faces staring at the line of guards or at each other in bewilderment and terror. In that instant, nobody spoke, nobody shouted, barely anybody moved.

Then Flynt heard another sound, a high keening emanating from the lands behind him. He had expected something but he still felt the sadness engulf him.

'They've shot wee Jeannie Robertson,' someone called from one the windows. 'The guard – they shot the wee lassie...'

A child. They had hit a child who had been witnessing the spectacle from one of the windows, perhaps not fully understanding what was developing below. A child seeing only thousands of people and thinking herself safe. A child, now wounded or dead. He heard the news circulating around him, like a shared breath, passing from one to another.

A child, they had shot a child.

A child, dead.

A child, murdered by the guard.

The whispers became a hum that grew in intensity with alarming rapidity, and where there had recently been panic, now the fury returned and the mob was once more a vengeful creature, its roar that of a maddened beast.

Charlie was transfixed on the block, his head still shaking as if denying the reality of the situation, his mouth opening and closing like a fish out of water. The serjeant, his face sliced with deep lines, looked to him for further guidance, but when none came he addressed the men himself, a tremor in his voice the only sign of his own nervousness.

'Second rank, ready!' he ordered. 'Hold! Wait for the command!'

It was an easy order to issue but not as easy to take. Flynt, still fighting to close the gap, studied the faces of the red-coated men. Some would be sufficiently disciplined to obey, others would follow suit but fear would eat at them. All it would take was one who was so abjectly terrified that his reason failed him. Just one.

Flynt's eye fell on just such a guard, standing in the second rank. Little more than a boy, really, the dark fuzz on his cheeks yet a stranger to a blade. He aimed his weapon but it trembled in his hand like a leaf in a high wind. The more intently Flynt looked, the more he could see the tremors that travelled through the boy's entire body. He flinched at every insult spat at him and also at the attempts on either side to break through the guard's ranks as they were rebuffed. He was confused and terrified and feeling lone and helpless. Beads of sweat rose on his forehead and began to trickle into his eyes and he wiped them away with a sleeve. But when he looked back, his vision cleared, there was something different about him. Flynt changed course to reach him.

'Serjeant!' Flynt cried out. 'Order shoulder arms!'

He had seen the change bleed into the young man's eyes, as if the sweat had washed away the fear and replaced it with a certainty that there was only one course of action he could take, order or no order. He lowered his musket a few inches.

'No!' Flynt cried, stretching out as if to push the barrel upwards.

The young guard fired directly into the crowd. Flynt saw a man spin, try to steady himself by clinging to the person closest to him, but his legs failed him and he slid to the ground. Those around him froze for a moment, unsure of what had happened, but then realisation dawned and Flynt could hear the murmurs build again into full-throated clamour. The remaining guards thought the order had been given and they too fired, the bark of their weapons rising over the harsh cries of the people. Screams rose with the white puffs of smoke. Those at the front, realising they were in the line of fire, pushed back with renewed vigour but were held in place by those in the rear thrusting forward. The crowd around Flynt swayed back and forth like waves. Bodies stumbled and fell, were trampled upon. Flynt was jostled, forced away from the stone, still calling out to Charlie. But Charlie could not hear him above the screams and bellows.

The serjeant gave the cease fire command, but the first rank had reloaded and paid no heed. Fear now dictated the orders of the day. Fear and survival. They discharged their weapons in ragged order. A woman beside Flynt stopped in her tracks and tumbled backwards, what looked like a bloody rose flowering on her chest. He stooped to help her but was forced back as others fled the gunfire. A young boy cradled the head of a friend with a red, bubbling hole where his left eye had once been, crying as he tried to wipe the blood away and calling out the lad's name, impervious to the feet pummelling the ground around him. The boy hunched over his friend as if protecting him and then vanished from view beneath the stampede.

Flynt was growing tired of being treated like flotsam on an ebb tide, so he steadied his feet and braced himself against the tide of humanity before pushing his way through it to reach the guards, as the second rank, their blood up, levelled their weapons again.

'In the name of God, stop this!' he yelled, but still they paid no heed. Another angry blast of gunfire and more bodies fell. Flynt looked at Charlie and was about to appeal to him again but he was staring in an uncomprehending fashion at the killing ground below the stone. He could expect no assistance from that quarter.

The serjeant's continued demands for calm were ignored by his men who had allowed fear and rage and possibly even bloodlust to dictate their actions. He grabbed the man nearest him and threw him away.

'I said stand down, man!' he screamed just as the first rank loosed another volley. Flynt felt musket balls displace the air around him, heard the sickening splash as metal ruptured flesh. He reached the two lines of guards and stood in front of them. He gripped the barrel of the nearest firearm and thrust it upwards with one hand, doing the same with his stick to another. The guards swore at him but did not retaliate. The moment seemed to have passed. The mob had retreated from the field of fire, the din had abated into a comparative silence, with only a few oaths volleyed at the guards, and the groans of the wounded. The acrid smoke of burnt powder swirling in the air around them stung Flynt's eyes and left a bitter taste on his tongue.

'Stand down, men!' Flynt yelled at them. 'Get your men in order, Serjeant.'

The serjeant gave him a defiant look. He was a small man but powerfully built and his face was broad and weathered. Flynt would wager he was the only one of these men who had ever seen any kind of action beyond a street fight. 'You have no authority, sir.'

'I need authority to stop a slaughter?'

The serjeant saw the sense in this and also the quiet command in Flynt's voice and stance. 'Stand down, men. Shoulder those arms.'

All anger spent, the men were now merely confused. Weapons were lowered and their bearers looked to their neighbour for a measure of guidance, but each man's thoughts were as muddied as the next. Fear had made them act without considering the ramifications but now, with Flynt enforcing a lull, the reality was beginning to sink in.

The serjeant looked beyond Flynt at the crowd. 'Will they come at us again?'

Flynt turned and studied the shredded line of protesters. Figures lay on the ground, some writhing and screaming, others moving only slightly, still others not at all. A few of the able-bodied were brave enough to move closer in order to tend to the casualties.

He turned back. 'Return your men to the guardhouse, Serjeant.'

'I cannot, sir,' the serjeant said, and Flynt thought he caught the salt of the Fifeshire coast in his voice. 'No without an order from my captain.'

Flynt looked up at his friend. 'Charlie,' said Flynt, 'give the order to dismiss your men.'

Charlie seemed not to hear. He was looking over the edge of the stone at the dead, the dying, the wounded. His head quivered as if he had been stricken with a palsy.

'Charlie!' Flynt snapped. 'Give the damned order, man!'

His voice pulled Charlie's gaze from the bloody piazza. He finally focused on Flynt, seeing and hearing him for the first time that day. He blinked as he began to comprehend the situation. He licked his lips and said in a hoarse voice, 'Stand down, men. Form ranks and prepare to return to the guardhouse.'

The men did as they were ordered, all now lowering their weapons completely or shouldering them. As the serjeant cajoled, cursed and even pushed the guards into some sort of order, Flynt turned and walked onto the Grassmarket, stooping now and then to inspect a wound and calling on people to give aid. This had been a small war but war nonetheless. It had not been declared, there had been no pomp, no ceremony, no call to patriotism, but as usual the bill was paid in blood. He swallowed back the bitter taste that now had nothing to do with the still redolent gunsmoke.

He finally alighted on two little bodies, the boy shot in the eye and his friend still holding him in an embrace, his lifeless body draped protectively over him. The sight took his breath clean away, and he blinked at the welling tears. He had seen and caused far too much death in his life, but the sight of those two lads motionless on the ground was almost more than he could bear.

'Murdering bastards,' someone shouted, causing a few of the guards to raise their weapons again.

'Easy, men,' said the serjeant. 'It's only words.'

Flynt felt no sense of real threat from the remainder of the crowd but it would take very little to spark the flame again. He looked away from the pitiful little bodies at his feet and returned to the guards, now in two trim ranks thanks to the serjeant's orders and the occasional prod of his club.

'Get them out of here,' he said, his voice hoarse. He squinted up at Charlie again, motionless once more atop the stone. 'I will tend to your captain.'

'Aye, sir,' said the serjeant, then issued the order for the men to march towards the West Bow. The fringes of the crowd parted, allowing them to pass like blood through an open wound, although there were a few angry taunts. Nobody made a move to attack and Flynt watched the double line of red snake up the hill. Satisfied there would be little more than insults thrown now, Flynt turned his attention to Charlie.

'Better come down, Charlie,' he said, his tone gentle.

Charlie nodded and wordlessly slid down the block of sandstone to Flynt's side, his pistol still in one hand, his sword in the other. 'I had better take that,' said Flynt as he eased the pistol free and sniffed the barrel. There was no smell of burnt powder. Charlie had not fired a shot. 'It would be best if you sheathed your blade.'

Charlie's movements were slow, his muscles numb, as he did what he was told. His eyes roamed over the scene again. 'What have I done?'

Flynt did not reply. There was nothing he could say, for Charlie knew well what his lack of resolve, his inability to control the situation, had caused. Flynt took him gently by the forearm and led him away from the gallows stone.

Above them, Somey's head tilted downwards, as if surveying the carnage.

11

Flynt sat alone in his father's tavern, a cup filled with the Highland spirit on the table before him, and ignored the looks from the other men. It was the same group who had been present when he had first arrived and when he had supped ale with Rab and Charlie the night before. They regarded him now with their previous suspicion leavened by more than a little curiosity. He presumed they had been present in the Grassmarket earlier that day, or had heard of the bloody events and his involvement in them. They would most certainly already know by now he was Gideon's son returned from abroad. They did not approach him, and for that he was thankful as the events of the day had made him even less inclined to interact with strangers than normal. He was a man well used to the sight of violent death yet he had been sapped by what he had witnessed, even though the death toll was not as high as he had feared. The Town Guard were not marksmen, it seemed, for only six had died of gunshot wounds, while an equal number were wounded but clung to life. More were injured in the panic, with another five losing their lives. Compared to the thousands lost in battle it was nothing, but still so unnecessary. The child who was first shot, the one who had been at her window, was not among those dead. She had been only slightly injured by a masonry chip to the cheek. There was an irony there that made the events that followed even more tragic.

He sipped the spirit, feeling its fire in his throat and wishing it could burn away the sight of the young boy holding his dead friend in his arms, the two locked together even in death. He downed a deep draught of the whisky in an attempt to wash it away but knew it would return and would, during his bleaker moments, jostle for position with other deathly images from his past.

He was aware of a figure standing before him and looked up to see Gideon observing him. Such inattention to his surroundings could be lethal and he had to regain his focus. He must cast off this black mood and consign the day's sad memories to the darkest recesses of his mind, where the others waited.

Gideon placed a hand on the back of the chair opposite. 'May I sit?'

Flynt waved a hand. 'It's your tavern, Faither.'

'Aye, but sometimes a man wishes to be left to his own thoughts,' said Gideon as he lowered himself into the chair.

'And sometimes a man should never be left with his thoughts,' said Flynt, 'for there be dragons.'

He discerned from his father's face that he understood. Gideon sighed deeply. 'That was a bad business today.'

'Aye.'

'From what I hear the city has you to thank for it not being worse.'

'It was bad enough,' said Flynt, his voice bitter. 'I could have done more.'

'You did more than anyone else, son.' He reached out and patted Flynt's hand. 'I'm proud of you.'

Flynt felt something solid in his throat, as if hot pitch had lodged in his gullet. He could not recall Gideon ever saying he was proud of him before. Of course, he had done little as a boy to make him proud and nothing as an adult. Until today, it seemed.

He gave Gideon a wan smile in thanks for his words, then asked, 'What do they say of Charlie?'

Gideon had inquired of friends on the town council and in the courts. 'He's been detained, pending an inquiry. They've lodged him in the Tolbooth for his own protection.'

'That hellhole? He does not deserve that!'

'It's more secure than the guardhouse,' said Gideon.

Flynt's laugh was short and cynical. 'Aye, but that says little. Men escape the Tolbooth with the foul stench. Anyone wishing to get in would find it an easy matter.'

Gideon had to agree but his face was sombre. The candle guttering in the holder on the tabletop cut deeper lines into his face than had the years. 'It doesn't look promising for the boy, Jonas.'

Flynt suspected as much but he felt the need to speak up for his friend. 'He didn't give the order to fire into the crowd. It was a guard who lost his reason.'

'Aye, but he ordered the first volley and began the tumult.'

'The tumult was preordained, Faither. I saw men hand the young ones ammunition to throw.'

Gideon thought upon this for a moment. 'Aye, there may have been those with other motives involved, but he was in command, so if there is responsibility – if there is blame – then Charlie must shoulder it.'

'And what will that mean for him? Cashiered? Dismissed? What?'

Gideon shrugged. 'That's for the courts to decide, should it get that far.'

'Is there a possibility it will not?'

Gideon turned his head to look at the men in the corner. 'There is fear that the authorities believe no action should be taken, that they would prefer the matter to be forgotten. The honour of the Town Guard is at stake and there are those who argue that it was the mob that caused the riot.'

'And those who fired up the lads to volley their stones and mud? Who were they?'

Gideon looked around him then hunched forward. 'There are some who wish to see anarchy in the streets.'

'Who, Faither? Jacobites?'

'Some perhaps, not all. But the people don't see that. All they see is the merchant classes and those above them looking after their own.' He was silent for a moment. 'There's talk of the Blue Blanket being unfurled.'

Flynt had seen the Blue Banner when he was a boy and knew its importance. It had been given by a grateful king when the common folk rescued him from the castle during an insurrection and its presence at a convocation of the mob gave it some validity and acted as a rallying point for all.

'And there are those who are listening to such talk, am I right?'

Another shrug from his father. 'We are a small city. What is whispered in the West Port can be heard in the Canongate.' He took a deep breath. 'Feelings are high, son. You have returned home at a most delicate time. Rebellion, disruption, suspicion that people are not what they seem.'

Flynt suspected from the long look his father gave him that he waited for him to admit something. When he remained silent, Gideon's eyebrow flicked and he continued speaking.

'Edinburgh is, in the main, loyal to the king. Did you hear that a small force tried to take the castle?'

'I did not.'

'Aye, Lord Drummond and around eighty men planned by stealth to raid the armoury and the treasury, a few weeks ago it was now. They were betrayed and the attempt failed. The town council and magistrates are in a state of alert. They have repaired the old walls and the gates. The guard has been augmented, such as it is, a further militia armed and trained. But tensions remain, son, and there is much talk of spies in the city, from both sides. You'll have noticed that your coming has excited much curiosity in some corners.'

Gideon half turned as if to imply that such a corner was within striking distance. Flynt caught one of the men shooting a furtive glance in his direction then looking swiftly away. 'Aye, it has not been hidden.'

'They know not what to make of you, but you are my son and that goes a long way. Some of them saw what you did today and that goes further. But Charlie's actions have tapped into the tensions and they may have need to be released somehow.'

'And is there a likelihood direct action be taken?'

'At present it is talk only. Ale-soaked oaths and wine-coated words,' Gideon said. 'It may die down when the drink wears off, it may not.'

'And if it doesn't? If those who seek to disrupt manoeuvre further?' Gideon said nothing but Flynt saw it in his eyes. He jerked his head towards the men at the table. 'Are these men I should watch, Faither?'

Gideon did not turn this time. 'Aye, some of them at least. If there is to be any action taken, they will perhaps not be in the vanguard but they will most certainly be encouraging from the safety of the rear.'

'And are any of these men in the ranks of the disruptors?'

'I can't say, Jonas. They are sleekit and underhand, these people.'

The Fellowship. It had to be them of whom his father spoke, though he did not name them. What purpose they would have for causing such carnage he could not say, apart from stirring up hatred against the authorities and perhaps bringing more to the Stuart cause, if that was their aim. He thought of Moncrieff and Madame de Fontaine and wondered if even now they were transacting over the document. He felt a sensation of events moving without him and he did not like it. He gave the group another study, purposely storing away their features in his mind.

'And what of Lord Moncrieff?'

'I won't talk about him.' The vehemence in Gideon's words caught Flynt by surprise.

'Why not?'

'He is a vile creature.'

'Because he owns slaves?'

Gideon seemed on the verge of saying something but then thought better of it. 'That man is not to be discussed, Jonas. The mention of his name is like a plague that contaminates the very air. Speak no more of him, son, I beg you.'

Flynt was puzzled by the heat that burned in his father's face but he decided not to press the matter. They sat in silence for some time until he heard Gideon say quietly, 'You saw Cassie.'

That now familiar ache thrust itself into his mind and chest. 'Aye.'

'You broke her heart, you know that, do you not?'

Flynt was unsure whether he wished to discuss this, so all he did was nod.

'I can understand why you didn't tell me you were leaving, you know I would have done everything I could to dissuade you.'

'I believe you would have locked me in my room.' And perhaps that's what should have happened, Flynt thought. Once more he wondered how different his life would have been had he remained in Edinburgh.

'Aye, I would have done that and more to prevent it. But what's done is done. What you did was hurtful to me, to Mercy, but to Cassie it was more than that, do you see?'

Again, he could do nothing more than nod.

'Of course, we didn't know then why she was so distraught,' Gideon said. 'It took her a time before she told us what had taken place between you two.'

'It was not planned, Faither.'

'These things never are. They simply happen. Two people meet, there is a joining of souls. That's what happened between Mercy and I. She was working in a tavern on the New Providence waterfront, I went in there and... Well, to say I was transfixed does not do it justice. I knew there and then that she was the one for me and I moved heaven and earth to make it so. So did Mercy. *We* made it so.'

Flynt already knew but he didn't want Gideon to think Rab was talking at his back, so he asked, 'Did you buy her, Faither?'

Gideon produced his pipe from the pocket of his long waist-coat and began to fill it with tobacco. 'No, it didn't seem right to me for one human to buy another. I had sailed with too many former slaves to countenance the trade. Good men, decent men, brave men. The man who claimed ownership, of wee Cassie too, was a foul bastard and I had no qualms in stealing them away from him.'

'And this man, did he not come after you?'

Gideon pressed down on the tobacco in the pipe bowl. 'He was in no condition to come after anyone, son.' He looked across the table. 'D'ye understand?'

Flynt did. The man, whoever he was, foul bastard that he was, was dead and by his father's hand. Flynt had often wondered about Gideon's past and now he knew there was violence there. Like father, like son.

'It had to be done,' said Gideon. 'I don't regret it. He was a black-hearted scumsucker, and believe me I knew many like him. I was willing to do anything, even that, to be with Mercy, that was the way of it, right from the first moment I saw her. I knew she was a fine woman and I was right. In an instant I was hers.'

'It wasn't that way with Cassie, Faither.'

'No, I know – you were too young when you first met. It was a gradual thing, and a natural one too, I suppose. Living under the same roof, both blossoming from boy and girl to man and woman.' He paused. 'Also, there was no shame to it, not the attraction at any rate. You did not share blood.'

'I was not ashamed but it was, in its way, awkward.'

The pipe was lit and aromatic smoke drifted from between Gideon's lips. 'Aye, that I understand. Was that one of the reasons you ran off? Cassie?'

Flynt had never admitted that to himself but he did now. 'It was part of it.'

'You feared what you were feeling?'

'Aye, that would be the size of it.'

Gideon nodded as he picked up the candle from the table and put flame to pipe. He puffed once, twice, three times, the pungent aroma managing to vanquish the smell of tallow. 'We're cowards, we men,' he said. 'We feel that by admitting to such emotions we're somehow unmanned, that it makes us weaker. But we're wrong. Such feelings make us all the stronger. We're not built to be solitary, Jonas. We're not whole when alone but are built to be part of a whole. Family, community, nation, call it what you will, but we need to be with others. The solitary man is not a complete man.'

'No man is an island, entire of itself,' Flynt quoted and saw the puzzled look on his father's face. Gideon Flynt had never been much of a reader, although he had always encouraged his son to continue with his studies. 'The words of a poet, Faither. John Donne.'

'Aye, seems like a wise man.' He smiled. 'Must be a Scot.'

Despite his mood, Flynt smiled along with this father. 'What you say may be true, but some men are best left to their solitary course.'

'And you thought that when you left?'

'No, but I think it now.' He felt the need to unburden himself, if only partially. 'I have not led a blameless life, Faither.'

Gideon took the pipe from between his teeth and made a show of checking the burn of the tobacco. 'There's none of us who have, son. We all have our sins. We all must atone, in this world or the next.'

The words surprised Flynt. Gideon had never been a religious man. 'You believe in the next world now?'

Gideon looked sheepish. 'Aye, Mercy finally got through to me. She's a devout woman, your mother.'

Flynt knew that, for she had taken it upon herself to teach her new-found son the ways of the Lord, but they had never taken with him. 'I believe only in this world. If I must atone, it has to be here.'

'And will you?'

Flynt thought about it. 'I think, for the sins I have committed, there is not the time.'

'They are that bad?'

'Aye.'

Gideon studied him closely. 'You know you can talk to me, son. Perhaps by giving the sins breath it will go some way to purge you of the guilt that seems to weigh heavily upon you.'

Flynt looked at the tabletop. 'A man acts according to his nature, Faither. I have done what I have done, and I will do more, of that I have no doubt, but I must live with it.'

Gideon let that sit between them for a time, his pipe between his teeth, as he considered what he had heard. He filled the space by rising to his feet. Finally he found the words he was looking for. 'With every sin, a man loses a little bit of himself. You must be careful that you do not lose all.'

Flynt looked up at him. 'I have already lost much. There is little more than can be taken from me but my life. And I intend to hold onto that for as long as I can.'

Gideon stared down at him for a few moments, his expression a mix of compassion and curiosity. Flynt could tell his father wanted to know more about what he had lost, but he would not probe further. 'You ken where I am if you need to unburden yourself, son.'

Flynt nodded his thanks and Gideon cleared his throat as if something was lodged there, took the pipe from his mouth then inspected it as he left him alone at the table.

Flynt remained in the bar for a time more but the looks he continued to receive soon grew tedious so he retired to his small room on the top floor of the tavern. He stretched out on his bed still fully clothed and stared at the ceiling. How often as a boy had he done similar in this very same space? Simply lain there, listening to the sounds beyond the small window. People making their way through the dim passageway and across the courtyard to and from the tavern or to the lands opposite. The life of the city beating from the High Street, faint here but still ever present. Voices. Footsteps. A vendor's cry. Carts being pushed and dragged to and fro. He would hear this and stare at the ceiling and dream of what life was like beyond the city walls, not merely just outside the West Port or the Netherbow, but what lay beyond the ruined abbey and the palace and the Nor' Loch, further even than he could see from atop the crags.

He closed his eyes and tried to sleep but saw once more the events of the day unfolding in his mind and smelled the powder smoke as it drifted over the dead on the Grassmarket.

He was thankful when a tentative knock at the door forced him back to the present. He opened it to find Cassie before him and felt the same thrill of pleasure he felt whenever he saw her, a sensation undimmed by the years or even the severe expression she had sported the day before. This time, though, there was a softness to it.

They regarded one another for a few moments in silence, the sound of voices drifting from below, where Gideon carried on a roaring trade. It was late but not yet too late for conviviality. Cassie seemed to be waiting for him to speak but he found he did not have the words.

Finally, she said, 'Well, will you invite me in or must I stand here like a caddie awaiting instruction?'

He felt a shy smile break out on his lips. 'Of course,' he said, stepping back. 'Please...'

'Your time away has not improved your manners, Jonas Flynt,' she said as she passed, looking around her. 'Mother kept this room free for you, did you know that? Even after we heard you were dead, she kept it thus. Cleaned it. Fresh linens.' She looked to the small window where a nosegay sat in a vase. 'Even flowers.' She turned to face him. 'She said she'd given up hope of your return but I know she never did. She knew in her heart that you lived and you would come back to her.'

Flynt decided he could feel no further guilt. His heart was already full of it. 'Cassie, if you've come to chastise me further, I beg you not to. I've apologised and there's no doubt I was, and am, in the wrong but further scolding will not change it.'

'I didn't come to berate you,' she said, her voice low. 'I came to apologise for being so ungracious yesterday.'

He held up a hand. 'No need, Cassie. I deserved it.'

'Damned right you did,' she said, but her smile removed the sting from her words. He had loved that smile. He did love that smile. It made his heart both sing and break, for in that smile he saw all the things that might have been but never would.

There followed another silence, even more awkward than the first. He remained unsure as to what to say and felt it prudent for his tongue to remain still, while Cassie seemed at a loss as to why she had even come. She looked to the bed and he thought for a moment she had considered sitting upon it but then thought better of it. He understood why. It had been on that bed, the night before he left, that they had made love. It had been the first time for them both and it was a clumsy, uncoordinated act but the remembrance of it always stirred him. She was beautiful and the thought of her body and the sweet scent of her skin was even now a stimulant to him. That was why he had cried out her name when with Belle. For in his mind he was not with Belle, but with Cassie.

He gestured to a wooden chair in the corner. 'Will you sit?'

She seemed relieved and she did so, her hands clasped in a prim manner on her lap. Flynt sat on the edge of the bed.

'You're quite the hero of the hour,' she said. 'Stopping the slaughter from being worse than it was has you discussed on every street corner. Most don't know your name but they talk of the stranger who faced down the Town Guard.'

'I don't feel like a hero. I feel like a failure.'

'You did what others couldn't or wouldn't do.'

He shrugged that away, hoping she would understand he did not wish to speak on it. The old Cassie would have sensed it but he was unsure if this new one would.

She did. A playful look pranced in her eyes. 'So you're a thief and a gambler now?'

He was neither surprised nor angered by this but relieved that he did not need to lie to Cassie at least. 'Rab told you?'

'We have no secrets, as it should be between husband and wife.' The short silence added emphasis to her words. She was with Rab now. Whatever might have been was mere fantasy, a wisp of memory mixed with longing. 'I don't recall you ever expressing ambitions for such occupations. They were always somewhat loftier.'

'Life has a way of making a mockery of our dreams.'

'It does do that, Jonny.' A wistful tone crept into her voice. 'It does do that.'

Silence again. This time he broke it. 'You have a son.'

'A fine son.'

'He was at studies when I called.'

She nodded. 'Aye, Rab is determined he will not be a cobbler like him or his faither and his before that. It is the law or medicine for his boy, he says.'

'Worthy ambitions,' said Flynt, hoping life would not mock them. 'How old is he?'

The hesitation was slight but it was there. 'He is twelve.'

'And his name?'

This time the pause was more pronounced. 'You do not know?'

'No, else why would I ask?'

'Perhaps because you wish to hear me say it?'

'Why?'

'I don't know.' She hesitated again but said finally, 'Jonas. We called him Jonas. Rab insisted upon it.'

Flynt blinked. They had named their son after him and it moved him. He tried to make light of it. 'A fine name.'

'Aye.' A glint of a smile. 'Let's hope he carries it more proudly than the one after whom he's named.'

Flynt hoped that too. 'I'm honoured, Cassie.'

She looked away. 'Aye, well. Rab felt it was time to break with another Gow tradition – his faither, his grandfaither, him, all named Robert.' She fixed him steadily. 'And we missed you, Jonas. We thought we'd never see you again.'

It all came back to that. He felt that, had he had the courtesy to make contact over the years, the gulf between them might have been narrower. As it was, despite her being only two feet from him, Cassie seemed on the other side of the world. Out of reach. Untouchable. Lost.

'You are happy?'

'Aye. More than I thought possible,' she replied. 'Rab's a good man. He works hard to provide for us. He stands by me when I help runaways and has made enemies because of it, even though they cannot prove we give these souls assistance.'

'Lord Moncrieff, for instance.'

Once again mention of Moncrieff's name provoked unease and Cassie's look towards the door seemed to be a reassurance that Gideon was not listening. 'Aye, he's chief among them.'

'He's cruel to his servants?'

She considered this. 'Not cruel, not overtly. But he treats them as he would a beast of burden. He is one of those men who looks down on anyone who is not like him, be it in colour, religion or politics. I saw him not long ago as I came here, walking with his lapdog, Andy Wilson. He looked through me as if I was nothing. I remember little from the islands but I do remember his like, men who would lie with women like my mother and yet still see them as no more than animals. He and Rab have argued publicly about slavery but my man is in the minority here.'

'He believes in the justice of the cause.'

'He believes a great many things.'

'Yes, I heard some of that last night. He has strong opinions.'

'He does that. The failure of Darien and the Union caused so much bitterness here. The mob took to the streets and you will remember what that was like.'

He nodded. He had watched when, in jubilation over the commencement of the Darien scheme, they had set the Tolbooth door aflame in their exultation. The nation had high hopes the trading mission in the southern hemisphere would bring riches, but in the end, as Charlie and Rab had said, it had failed miserably with loss of life and capital, leaving many investors, and the country as a whole, near penniless.

'They hung three English sailors down by Leith, claiming piracy against a Scottish ship off the Africa coast,' Cassie said. 'Did you hear of this?'

He shook his head. 'The mob did this?'

'No, but that would have been the case if the magistrates had not. There was rumour that the men would be pardoned and the people took to the streets in their thousands to ensure the sentence was carried out.'

'Did these sailors deserve their fate?'

'Who can say? They were condemned on the word of seamates who may have been speaking to what they needed to in order to save their own necks from the noose.'

Flynt's mind turned to Charlie in the Tolbooth and his father's warning of dark talk on the streets.

'Rab tried to speak out against it but no one paid him heed, him being such a young man then. He resented the Union but he thought such behaviour was unseemly in his Scotland. Between that and his support for my people he has lost many friends and customers.'

Flynt recalled the workshop and its apparent lack of industry. Had Rab alienated so many people by his beliefs?

'Being so outspoken will one day find him in trouble,' Cassie continued. 'But when it does I will stand by him.'

Flynt swallowed. 'You love him.'

Her eyes burned with light. 'More than I thought possible.'

Her words wounded but he was glad she and his friend had found happiness together. He also suspected that was the reason she had come to visit him. She had to make sure he understood how much life had changed.

She rose and smoothed her dress. 'I must be away. I said I would not tarry.'

Flynt also got to his feet. 'Rab knows you are here?'

'Of course. No secrets, I told you.'

'And he knows of…' He waved a hand at the bed behind him.

'Us? What happened here in this room? Yes. Not even that is secret.'

So Rab did know all and yet he still welcomed him. Flynt doubted if he would be so magnanimous to the man who had first lain with his wife and then treated her so shabbily. Rab Gow was a better man than he. He told her he would escort her home and pulled on his coat and hat. Naturally, she objected, saying she had walked the streets after dark many times and never been molested, but he was adamant. He was well aware that Cassie could take care of herself but he had another reason for going abroad. They left the tavern in silence, followed by a soft look from Mother Mercy that to Flynt's eyes was both fond and filled with sadness.

In the passageway he asked, 'Do you still wish me to leave as soon as possible?'

Her answer came swiftly. 'I am glad you live and I regret my harsh words but aye, I do with all my heart.'

'You still sense death around me?'

She stopped before they reached the street and stepped closer, so close that, if he so wished, he could reach out and touch her. He did not do so. He had abandoned that privilege fifteen years before.

'More than ever, Jonny,' she said, her voice soft. 'And I fear whose...'

12

The hour was late and the night held the threat of the winter yet to come. His years in London had seen Flynt grow used to a slightly more temperate clime, so he pulled his greatcoat tighter to his body and hunched into the collar turned against his neck as he walked. His recent conversations had troubled him. To his father he had made a confession of sorts but he still had not been totally honest. He deeply regretted lying about his business the day before, for he knew Gideon would have accepted the true reason for his return, even if not with ease. However, had he been more forthright, he would have had to explain why he was undertaking such a mission and that would entail revealing more about his life than he wished. Being truthful with Rab had been a different matter, for he was more a brother than friend, but Flynt was unsure how Gideon would have reacted to the news that his son was guilty of crimes sufficient that he could be blackmailed on a trumped-up charge into performing murky duties for the government of first Queen Anne and now King George.

Cassie most certainly had accepted that he was a rogue. It was as if something within her had always known, which given her prescient gift was possible, though she had never expressed it when they were younger. Being in close proximity to her and talking like old friends had also troubled him but in a different way. That he still loved her he could no longer deny; it took only one look and he knew. He was truly glad she and Rab were together but the twin demons of envy and regret told him that perhaps he could have been as happy as they, had he been a different person. A better person.

They said little as they walked the canyon created by the Tolbooth on one side and the tall land on the other. Flynt scanned the blank face of the old building, wondering if Charlie was lying in a rude cot within, unable to sleep. Mindful of Gideon's warning that there were factions planning to take the law into their own hands, whether or not encouraged by those with reasons of their own to create mayhem, he scrutinised the streets but saw no men clustering in dark corners and heard no sound of boots hitting ground. The Edinburgh Mob was not renowned for being circumspect in its actions and Flynt was moderately confident that should they wish to storm the town gaol, emboldened by the Blue Blanket, they would do it in a heavy-handed and obvious manner.

A soldier of the Town Guard rounded the corner of the building facing the Lawnmarket, his long Lochaber axe over his shoulder. He regarded Flynt and Cassie with wary aspect as they passed within a few feet of each other but did not challenge them. Flynt gave him the courtesy of a nod but the guard failed to respond. There was every possibility that the rumour of which Gideon had spoken had also reached the ears of whoever was in charge of the men now that Charlie was in custody, and, if so, the young soldier's caution was well founded. Flynt was aware too that he presented a slightly sinister figure, bundled as he was in his greatcoat, its collar covering neck and lower jaw, his wide hat pulled low, as he surveyed the steep walls of the Tolbooth. As he recommenced his journey, he sensed the guard's eyes upon him all the way.

The High Street was not deserted despite the lateness of the hour. A few men weaved homeward from tavern or brothel, some led by caddies now acting as link boys, while others faced the shadow of the dark streets with the security of long acquaintance. There were a few lamps here and there to brighten the way or illuminate a passageway but it was after nine of the clock and most had been extinguished.

They reached the Bowhead and turned down the hill. Outside Rab's shop Cassie stopped and thanked him for his escort. 'It was not needed,' she added.

'I know,' he said. They stared at one another in silence, she looking into his face as if seeking the boy who had left long ago, he wishing a look could traverse those same years and change events. Finally, she turned away, a key drawn from the pocket of her dress and she was gone. He lingered a moment, staring at the closed door, imagining. Her climbing the wooden steps within and greeting her husband in their parlour. A kiss. An embrace. And then to bed. But in his mind it was not Rab's face he saw. It was his own. The image of them locked together in his room appeared behind his eyes. There had been touching before that night, of course, for they were young and when attraction had taken hold they found they could not hold from physicality of some sort, surreptitious though it might have been. There had been kissing. There had been stroking. He had tasted her and she him, but until that night, in his room above the tavern while Gideon and Mercy were working downstairs, their two bodies had not become one.

He put further thoughts from his head. He had work to do this night. Cassie had seen Moncrieff here with Wilson. Circumstance had stymied his plans to confront him earlier; now he sought to engineer another meeting. The odds were long, he knew, but as Gideon had said, Edinburgh was not large and the areas where the likes of Moncrieff would allow himself to be seen were limited. If their paths did not cross then all he would have lost was time, but if they did then there was at least an opportunity. He didn't know what he would do or say, he merely planned to throw the dice and see what turned up.

The Bow was a much different street in the night. The shops and businesses were closed and few lights guttered behind windows. There was no rattle of hammer against metal at this hour, no buzz of commerce. His footsteps echoed from the walls around and above him as he passed the entranceway to the house of Major Weir, the wizard strangled at the stake then burned to ash a few years before Flynt was born. His aunt had told him the story of the seemingly devout Presbyterian whose secret life was one of depravity, incest with his sister and, they said, witchcraft.

As boys they had dared each other to explore the dark corridor that led to the courtyard beyond and face the Major's spectre that was said to walk when night fell, the tap of his long black cane echoing against the walls. Only Cassie had been brave enough to do it, though she later confessed to him that she thought she might soil herself with fear as she ventured through the dark to the doorway. He smiled at the memory of her admission. They were simpler times, when their greatest fear was a story to scare the superstitious, the weak-minded and the young. The house remained empty, potential tenants too fearful of the black arts said to have been practised within its walls to take up residence, and Flynt was tempted to hammer on the door to dare the malevolent spirit to face him and put to the test whether the fine steel of his swordstick could match the satanic strength of Weir's black rod.

Still combating memories of Cassie and himself in passionate embrace, Flynt drifted onwards, his feet carrying him in aimless fashion to the Bowfoot and then once again onto the Grassmarket. The wide, open space was now devoid of people and even the skeletal finger of the gallows had been removed from its socket in the stone. He wandered across the ground that only that day had been the site of massacre to stand before the sandstone block again. A breeze drifted from the Cowgate and floated towards the West Port as he stared at the slab before him. It had witnessed many a death over the centuries, some merited, others like Somey perhaps not. Major Weir's sister, also found guilty of witchcraft and unnatural acts, had met her end here, attempting to throw off her clothes to die, she said, with all the shame she could. Her restless spirit was not reputed to lurk around this stone, and nor were those of the countless others who had preceded and followed her into eternity. He thought of the innocent people who had perished facing the gallows earlier. Would they forever be tied to the spot? The two young boys, the adults who fell under a hail of musket balls? He stopped, closed his eyes and listened for the echo of gunfire or groans of the dying on the wind, but heard none. If such spirits existed, then they were otherwise engaged.

The faint scuff of footfall and soft murmur of voices drew his attention to the shadows at the foot of the lands on the far side of the stone. Three men had emerged from the darkness of a wynd and were parting company, one making his way towards the Cowgate with the rolling gait of a former seafarer, a way of walking Gideon shared, as if they still expected the land beneath them to pitch and yaw. Flynt could not make out any features but he was sturdy rather than stout and wore the clothes of a worker, with a flat bonnet perched on his bullet head. The other two were obviously more refined in their apparel and walked together in the direction of the West Bow, their heads bent close in quiet conversation. They had not seen Flynt standing at the dark centre of the Grassmarket, but as they passed beneath a solitary lamp burning late in a close mouth, Flynt recognised the sharp features of Baillie Andrew Wilson and Lord Moncrieff. Now, what were such as they doing here at this hour in congress with a working man, Flynt wondered. There could be an innocent explanation but Flynt's instincts told him there was not.

He lingered for a few minutes to give them time to make their way up the street before he followed. He kept himself as distant as he dared without losing sight of them, hugging the shadows where he could and mindful not to make any loud footfall, but they were deep in conversation and unaware of his presence. He retraced his steps up the Bow, stopping when he saw the men halt beside the Weigh House, exchange a few more words, then part ways: Wilson heading down the Lawnmarket, Moncrieff turning on Castlehill. By the time Flynt reached the Weigh House, the Baillie was striding towards the Tolbooth while Moncrieff was entering a close mouth on the far side of the road, looking over his shoulder directly at Flynt. So he knows I am here, Flynt thought, but could not decide if that was fortuitous or not. He hurried across the road, his boots echoing on the cobbles for he had no reason to be stealthy now, and entered the narrow passage. It opened onto a courtyard with Moncrieff's home on the left, a tall, narrow building of grey stone with a single circular turret. A lamp burned above the door set in the corner and he was careful not to step into its glow as he evaluated the structure with an expert eye. It was a fine house, the doors and windows sturdy, and there was little chance of him forcing or entering by stealth. It was unlikely that Nero had been the family's only servant so it would seldom, if ever, be empty.

'You are haunting me, sir.'

The voice came from an inset leading to a doorway to the right of where Flynt stood and he recognised it immediately. Moncrieff stepped from the darkness into the dim light of the lamp above his own door.

Flynt had expected the man to be waiting for him. 'I would speak with you.'

'What could a rogue like you possibly have to discuss with me?'

'I believe you know, sir,' Flynt replied, any subterfuge meaningless. 'After all, you have the acquaintance of Madame de Fontaine.'

'What concern is that of yours?'

Flynt took a step closer, concealing a smile when Moncrieff flinched and raised his silver-topped cane a little as if primed to defend himself. He was nervous and he should be. However, in that moment Flynt was once more struck by how familiar the man looked. 'Games, my lord? Is there need for subterfuge? You know why I am here, I am certain that Madame de Fontaine will have informed you of my mission.'

'I was a dear friend of her father.'

Flynt doubted very much if Moncrieff was a dear friend to anyone. He took yet another step and Moncrieff edged back.

'Keep your distance, sir,' he warned. 'One cry from me and my staff will be upon you in an instant.'

Flynt smiled again but came to a halt. He had briefly considered attacking the man and rifling his pockets for the will but that struck him as too crude. Such an act was not to be carried out within sight of his front door, for there was too much danger in that. If force was ever a necessity then it must be employed subtly, away from the eyes of others.

'You are in no danger from me, sir,' Flynt promised. Then added, 'Tonight, at least.'

Moncrieff caught the threat but he obviously believed he was safe for he grew more confident, his expression a sneer. 'Then be on your way else I shall send someone to fetch the Town Guard.'

Flynt ignored the retaliatory threat and struck directly at the point of their conversation. 'Do you have the will?'

Moncrieff's innocence was feigned. 'Will? I have no knowledge of any will.'

Flynt affected a deep sigh. 'Come, Lord Moncrieff, we are both men of business so let us play no more games. The lady possessed the will, I believe she has sold it to you and I would have it.'

Moncrieff relaxed a little, leaning on his cane with both hands clasped on the silver handle. Even in the light of the lamp, Flynt saw calculation in his eyes, for this had become a transaction and such matters were his lifeblood. 'And if I had such a document, what would you give me for it?'

Flynt had no intention of negotiating with this man, was resolved to have the testament by stealth or by force, but he could play games too. 'What would you ask?'

Moncrieff made a show of pursing his lips as he considered. 'To begin with, to prove I could trust you, I would require information.'

'Of what nature?'

'My property. My stolen property. I would know of its whereabouts.'

'What property?'

Moncrieff sneered in slight irritation. 'Who plays games now, sir? The slave, Nero, I will know where your friends have it hid.'

In that moment Flynt knew Moncrieff was not yet in possession of the document, for he doubted if he would barter it in such a manner, notwithstanding his bruised pride, outraged ego and need to lash out at Cassie and Rab. It was possible that his demand was little more than a probe to see if Flynt would betray his friendships. Men without honour needed to know how far the honour of others reached. 'I know nothing of Nero's whereabouts. He might as well be on the moon.'

Moncrieff stared at him, his expression one of disdain and dismissal. 'Then if you will not assist me in this, you have no further need to waste my time. I bid you goodnight, sir, with a repeat of my warning earlier – do not cross my path again for you will regret it. I know not what Gideon Flynt has told you of me, but it will most assuredly not help you.'

He turned for his door but stopped when Flynt said, 'My father has told me nothing of you that I like, sir.'

'And all lies, of that I am sure.'

A stirring within the house and the light of a candle passing by a window near the door told Flynt he had no time to defend Gideon's name. 'If you wager on our paths not crossing again then you will lose. If you do not have the will, then I will take it before it reaches you. If you do, then I will take it anyway. And that, sir, would be a winning bet. I care not how many strong your Fellowship may be.' What may have been surprise crossed the man's face. 'Yes, I know of your society and I give you notice that they will not impede me in my mission. Of that *I* am certain.'

Moncrieff was about to make some sort of denial but Flynt didn't give him time. He spun and walked swiftly through the passageway to Castlehill, turning over in his mind the brief conversation. Moncrieff's final words were mere braggadocio, arrogance masked as confidence. Flynt was certain that some opportunity of obtaining the document would arise. The trick in his trade was having the wit to recognise such kind circumstance when it appeared and the intrepidity to act upon it.

Providence, however, did not smile upon him that night.

He was tired, at least that's what he told himself later, but in his heart he knew he had allowed his attention to wander. Being back in Edinburgh had blunted the defence mechanisms he had perfected over the years. It had been exemplified in the tavern when his father was at his side before he knew it and now, with the whisky still firing his blood as he turned into Castlehill to head towards the High Street, that inattention manifested itself once again. Normally upon exiting he would have exercised caution, checking his surroundings, but he did not. It was a momentary lapse of caution as his mind turned over his odds of success, but for it he paid the price.

The initial blow was heavy but misplaced, missing his head and striking him firmly on the shoulder, but it was weighty enough to pitch him forward and send his silver stick clattering to the ground. He spun as he fell and caught sight of his attacker, a large man, his body encased in a heavy coat, his face obscured by a kerchief, a vicious-looking cudgel in his hand. Landing heavily on his back, Flynt rolled immediately as a booted foot swung towards his head. The kick missed him but he could not avoid the crashing blow from the heavy club into his ribs. The thickness of his coat absorbed much of its power but it still shot through his body. Another kick was delivered, this time connecting with his shoulder. Again there was pain but he was once more thankful for the protection of his apparel. He searched the ground for his swordstick, spotted it a few feet away and tried to twist towards it, his arm reaching out to grasp the weapon, but a boot heel stabbed at his hand and he snatched it away, agony throbbing through his fingers despite his gloves. He heard the man panting above him as he levelled kicks and rained the heavy end of the club down on Flynt's upper torso. He tried to regain his feet but was beaten down. He wrapped his arms around his head, for if that cudgel connected with his skull it would be all over for him, and his sleeves went some way as a defence, but the sheer volume and force of the pounding took its toll. His skin was now aflame and each new strike was excruciating, but to lie there and take it was not an option.

He lashed out with one foot. It was a blind strike but he connected with something, for he heard a sharp intake of breath followed by a wheezed curse. There followed a lull of but a moment in the assault, but it was enough. Flynt wriggled on the ground, ignored the pain from his protesting bones and muscles, and managed to get some distance from his assailant. He hauled himself to his feet and adopted a crouch, ready to either fend off the next attack or mount one of his own. The man was doubled over, so Flynt's boot had caught him in the midriff or, he fervently hoped, between the legs. The club dangled in a loose manner from his hands and his spluttering epithets questioned Flynt's parentage. Flynt stooped to retrieve the cane at his feet. He would not run the man through but he would make him think twice about highway robbery in the future.

His inattention plagued him once more. There was a golden rule: where there is one bully, there is usually another, and he had failed to survey the perimeter.

The blow to the back of his head was sudden and it was sure. His vision exploded with light and his ears erupted with a high-pitched whine as he lurched forward, his feet suddenly unsteady. He managed to turn to face the new attacker but his eyes had misted and he could feel the world around him pitching and yawing. He was aware of something swinging towards him from the left but was unable to avoid or intercept it. The hard object cracked against his cheekbone and his head snapped to his right, his body following it, and down he went with considerable force. He landed badly, his head a confusion of noise and colours. He felt another blow to his body, a kick perhaps, but its force was lost among the storm of agony that engulfed him. He tried to move but his body would not respond to the commands of his brain. The scream in his head grew and through it he discerned footsteps echoing like the tap of Major Weir's cane. A dark chasm opened up before him, black mist swirling around and within, and he teetered on the edge, staring into it. It would be so easy to step into it, to let it consume him. He fought the temptation.

Hands upon him. Turning him over. The world behind his eyelids was a swirling blaze of lights and sound. A voice took shape amid the cacophony. Familiar. He forced his eyes to open, to focus. A face. Blurred. Without proper shape. A man. Saying his name. Over. And over. And over. Flynt tried to force his eyes to fix upon that face, the voice known to him, and yet unable to put a name to it.

And then the black mists blew in to obscure the material world and he felt himself plunging into the abyss, falling without end.

13

The mists swirled like sinuous creatures writhing around his feet. The unseen ground on which he walked was rough yet soft, the earth pulling at each step as if it had fingers that wished him to stay and become part of it. The air around him rumbled and the sky flashed, briefly illuminating a land that was stark and unreal yet familiar. The thunderstorm circled him and there was something about it that he recognised. He had experienced this before. No matter, he had to keep moving, had to get away. Another crack of thunder and a burst of light irradiated the dark clouds above, illuminating the tendrils of mist now wrapping around his legs. He tried to run but he couldn't for his feet sank into the clinging, uneven ground, and when he looked down, the mist parted to reveal that the earth was not black but red, deep red, blood red, as it crept over his boots. He struggled to free himself but the red mud pulled at him, drawing him down, his struggles proving useless for it had him held firm in its oozing grasp. The land seemed to inhale him as if he were a sweetmeat, something to be enjoyed, savoured, then allowed to disintegrate before being swallowed whole. The scarlet mire crept over his chin, slid into his mouth, open in a silent scream, then filled his ears and his eyes until finally he was submerged, the filth dripping down his throat to block his lungs and invade his stomach, bloating his flesh until he thought he would burst.

Then all was still, and he opened his eyes to find himself lying in a crater. The mist floated overhead but did not venture into the cranny. It hung back as if there was something here that kept it at bay. The thunder still raged in the distance and the sky still flickered. He knew what he would see if he looked to his left. He struggled to keep his eyes averted for he did not wish to see it again.

And yet…

It had once been a man, but part of the face had been blown away. The head lay at a slight angle, its single eye fixed in a blank stare directed at Flynt and what was left of the mouth set in a rictus grin. He could not tell which army the man had belonged to, for his uniform was caked with dirt and blood and grey matter. The body beneath the cloth was distended just as Flynt had felt his own change when being drawn through the red clay.

Something stirred beneath the tunic. The material undulated, as though the flesh was desperate to break free. Flynt knew what was coming and wished to avert his gaze but found he could not. He was transfixed by the sight of the cloth rising and falling and swelling until it began to tear from within, finally breaching into a bloody maw of pale, veined flesh that had been ripped open not by steel but by teeth. Tiny, sharp teeth. Flynt could see them now, nibbling at tissue, gorging on muscle, gnawing at bone, sucking on marrow, their brown and black bodies writhing over each other as they sought out the most succulent portions.

And then they surged from the cavity, their mouths stained with the blood. Dozens of them, hundreds it seemed, disgorging themselves from the body which they had picked clean to go in search of another feast. They had much to choose from, Flynt saw. There were other men here, some dead, others dying, but the rats cared little, for they chewed on whatever they could, those men too weak to beat them off having to endure the ordeal of being feasted upon while they breathed, feeling the teeth at their flesh as the rats excavated to reach the warm, juicy organs within. There were thousands of them now, swarming over the dead and the near dead, scurrying and scratching across the mud, their claws making a curious clicking sound as they moved, squeaking and squealing and hissing at each other as they fought over the tastiest morsels.

And then, as he lay there unable to move, unable to flee, unable to do anything but watch, they turned to face him, as if an officer had given them a signal. The squeaking, squealing and hissing ceased as they edged across the crater floor towards him, dark little eyes glittering with each flicker of light from above. They crept closer, not hurrying for they sensed he was not prey they were likely to lose. At his feet now, on his legs, their sharp claws piercing his clothing, moving upwards, surrounding him, covering him, enveloping him like the mud had done, their teeth nipping and tearing and shredding.

He screamed then.

He screamed.

He screamed.

When he awoke with a start he did not know if the scream he heard was an echo of the dream or if he had in fact cried out. It was with considerable relief that he found himself in his room at Gideon's, encased in clean sheets and with the reassuring sight of twigs with yellow sycamore leaves and others sporting red berries in a vase on the windowsill.

And yet he still felt the cold, moist earth beneath him, still smelled the decay of that crater on the foreign field, still heard the sound and fury of the battle all around, still saw the rats feast on the dead and dying, and felt the sensation of them crawling over his body. He sank back onto the soft pillows and fought the tremors that raced through his muscles as he willed the echoes of the dream to fade. He opened his eyes to banish the memory and found Cassie watching him from the open doorway.

'You live then.' Her tone was casual, but she could not hide the relief in her eyes.

He tried to sit up but was defeated by the pain lancing through his body and drumming in his head. 'I'll let you know, for it's too early to say.'

She moved across the small room and laid her hands on his chest to gently ease him back to his pillow. 'You need to rest.'

He tried to fight against her but had not the strength. 'I cannot lie in bed. I have business. I need to rise.'

She withdrew her hands and folded her arms, her expression a challenge. 'Very well, rise.'

He attempted to force himself upright, to swing his legs over the edge of the bed, but his body refused to heed his brain. He fell back, the air leaving his body with a grunt.

Cassie smiled a little, relaxed her arms and sat in a wooden chair beside his bed. 'Lesson learned, I trust. You have taken a considerable beating. You were lucky you were not brained.'

'The advantages of a thick hat.'

She made a little sniffing sound. 'Thick head is more likely.'

She was enjoying this, he felt. 'How long have I been insensible?'

'Most of the night and this day,' she said.

He looked to the window and saw that the sunlight was dying. Damn, he had lost precious time.

'You cried out just now,' she said. So it had not been a dream memory. 'You said something about rats.'

'A remembrance,' he said.

'And it plagues you?'

He felt a curious discomfort with the exchange. The battlefield from which he had fled had not been as it manifested in his sleeping mind. The terror was real, though, and the rats, though they too had been exaggerated by his imagination. He had stumbled upon them as they feasted on the bodies in the filth and even now when awake he could see them scurrying around his feet, though in reality he had not fallen victim to them. Others had, however, and the sight of their gnawed flesh was what haunted his dreams. It was there that he had found Charters, lying among them, what was left of his arm shattered and bloody, a particularly large creature ripping away a portion of the dead flesh. He had kicked the vermin away but the big one had fought back, snapping at the toe of his boot as though it were a large dog. He had never told anyone about what he had seen in that hollow, not even Charters, though the surgeon who removed his arm had told him later of the bite marks. Perhaps there was a time when he would have unburdened himself to Cassie but that time was long since gone.

'You were lucky your friends found you,' Cassie went on when she saw he was not going to reply. 'Else you may have lain in the street for hours.'

Memories of a face he knew and a voice he recognised filtered through the fog of his mind. 'Friends? What friends?'

'From London. They found you and brought you here.'

He was puzzled. 'Who?'

Cassie rose and left the room without answering. Flynt's mind struggled to make sense of what she had said. First he had lost valuable hours and now she spoke of friends from London. There were precious few he termed friend here at home and none in the south. Young Jack perhaps, but he would never vacate the city. There was Belle, but similarly she would not be inclined to leave her lucrative profession. Had Charters sent someone north to assist him? Again, unlikely, as the colonel preferred to keep his rogues a mystery to all, even each other.

The answer came when the door opened again and Cassie ushered in the two men. He recognised them immediately and knew them to be no friends of his.

'Jonas, me old mate, it is good to see you in the land of the living,' said Blueskin Blake, a smile on his lips, raising a heavy stick in greeting. His companion, the same one who had accompanied him in Mother Grady's house, remained in the rear.

'Blueskin, what the hell are you doing here?'

'Now, that is no way to greet an old friend, is it? Especially one who has come all the way here to Scotchland to aid you in your, erm, endeavours? And it is as well we did, for you seem to have got yourself into a bit of a scrape. I'm impressed, for you cannot have been here more than a day or two. But then, you have a way of making enemies, do you not?'

Though he smiled, Flynt detected the menace in Blueskin's words. 'Cassie, perhaps we should offer my... friends... some refreshment. Some wine, perhaps, if Faither would spare it.'

Cassie seemed to have guessed that these men were indeed not the friends either they had claimed or she had assumed. She gave Blueskin a wary look. 'Will all be well here?'

'Aye,' Flynt said, giving her a reassuring smile. 'Blueskin and I have matters to discuss.'

Cassie nodded and, with a final glance at Blueskin as if delivering an admonition to behave, she left. He gave her a little bow as she passed, his smile transforming into a leer as he studied her from behind. As soon as she closed the door, he said, 'I see now why you likes them dusky, Jonas. She is a fine piece, even if she is Scotch and a tavern wench. I takes it you is slipping her a length too?'

Flynt retained control of his anger, the very thought of Blueskin even looking at Cassie an outrage. There was nothing he could do about it now, for his earlier attempt at rising had indeed taught him a lesson, so he ignored the lewd talk and forced the conversation in a fresh direction. 'So what are you doing here?'

Blueskin sat down in the chair Cassie had recently vacated. 'Oooh,' he said, wriggling a little, 'still warm from that pert behind.'

'Blake,' said Flynt, injecting as much warning as he could into his tone but knowing it was not nearly sufficient and barely indicative of his growing anger.

Blueskin merely smiled. 'We was sent by Mr Wild.'

Flynt had already surmised as much. 'For what purpose?'

'He said we was to look after his investment. That being you, friend.'

'Wild has made no investment in me.'

'He has invested his trust and friendship, and neither is freely given by him in the main.' He reached to the pocket of his coat to produce a letter which he handed to Flynt. 'He said I was to give this to you personal.'

Flynt studied the missive. Its seal was unbroken so Blueskin had not read it. Flynt strongly doubted whether the bruiser could, even if he wanted to. He ripped it open and scanned the fine handwriting.

My dear Jonas,

I make the assumption that you were not responsible for the foul nature of the deeds that occurred in the Mint, for I do not see the snapping of the neck belonging to the unfortunate Mr Bates an act of which you would be guilty. I am disturbed that the lady to whom I had shown both courtesy and assistance proved to be such a she-devil, although again I am sure she did not commit the foul deed herself.

Being deeply concerned for your welfare, dear friend, I made my inquiries and was decidedly relieved to learn that you breathed still and in fact had earlier that day decamped for Edinburgh, said journey I presumed to be in connection with our joint venture.

I have despatched Mr Blake and his colleague with this communication to offer you what assistance they can. Mr Blake has been instructed to obey your every command to the letter. There is dirty work afoot, my dear friend, and I could not countenance any harm to befall you.

I also feel that by engaging Mr Blake thus your lady friend in Covent Garden will be safe from his attentions until you return and can proper watch over her.

I remain yours,

Jonathan Wild, Thieftaker General

The signature was flamboyant and displayed all the presumption of the title with which Wild had dubbed himself. Flynt suppressed a sigh as he crumpled the paper in his hand, watched by Blueskin with a knowing smirk.

'Do you know what is in this letter?'

'Mr Wild gave us our orders before we left.'

'What were those orders?'

'That we was to come up here to Scotchland, to find you and thenceforth not to let you out of our sight.'

'He does not trust me?'

Blueskin's smile broadened. 'Trust ain't a thing in which Mr Wild readily trades. Speaking personal, I would not trust you to even take breath. There is something rum about you, something I cannot quite fathom, but I will, you has my oath on that.'

Trust did not come easily to Flynt either, so that was something he and Wild shared. As for Blueskin's sense of Flynt's rumness, he could not argue. 'How came you to find me last night?'

'We arrived here yesterday afternoon but it took us till last night before we tracked you down to this place. We spoke to the old tavern keeper, your father as it turns out, and here was me thinking you was some kind of gentleman given the airs you adopt, and he told us you had stepped out.'

'You followed me?'

'Not followed. We was walking up that street in search of you when we saw you being put upon by two coves.' He smiled as if he had enjoyed the sight and in that instant Flynt suspected they had allowed the attack to continue. 'They gave you a proper going over.'

'It was your face I saw before I lost my senses.'

'It was. The two fellows slipped away into the darkness before we reached you.'

'Would you recognise them again?'

Blueskin shook his head. 'They had their faces covered. We would have given chase but we is unfamiliar with this place and we thought it best to have you returned here to be cared for.'

'That was very solicitous of you.'

'Speaking personal again, I would have left you where you lay, but Mr Wild needs you healthy. He says you have a debt and you must honour it.'

'We have an agreement, not a debt,' said Flynt.

Blueskin's head waggled from side to side. 'Agreement. Debt. It's all the same to Mr Wild. Call it what you must, he will see it honoured. I will make sure of it.'

'What did he tell you of this "agreement"?'

'Nothing. All he said was we should follow your instructions but remain close to you and to keep you safe.' He paused and a curious glint crept into his eye, as if he was thinking of a secret only he knew. 'Unfortunately we was too late to prevent them footpads from doing the low toby on you.'

The attack may well have been committed with intent to rob, but it crossed his mind that it could easily have been Blueskin and his colleague who had ambushed him, in revenge for being shamed at Mother Grady's. Judging by Wild's comments about sending Blueskin from the city in order to keep Belle safe proved that a grudge was harboured and perhaps even remarked upon. If such was the case, Blake might be satisfied that his honour was salved, but Flynt resolved to never turn his back on him. However, it occurred to him that he could use them while he was confined to quarters.

'I have work for you then,' he said, trying to study the stick in Blueskin's hand without being too obvious. 'You must call at the home of Lord Moncrieff. It can be found along the passageway at which I was assaulted.'

'To what purpose?'

Flynt could not say for certain if the stick was the same he had glimpsed the previous night. 'Information only. Keep watch for a servant entering or leaving and intercept them – peacefully, do not draw attention. Ask them if his lordship is at home.'

'And if they ask me why I am so interested?'

'Tell them you are my servant…' He took pleasure in seeing Blueskin bristle at this. 'Tell them your master – that is I – pays his respects and wishes to call upon his lordship with information to his advantage.'

Blueskin's displeasure over having to demean himself in such a way was obvious. 'And if they ask what this information regards?'

'Tell them it concerns the location of their man, Nero.'

Flynt had no qualms about using Nero, or Blake, in such a manner. Blueskin had no intelligence regarding the man and would not be guilty of betraying a confidence.

Blake asked, 'And who is this Nero?'

'A servant who has absconded.'

'And do you know where he is?'

'No,' Flynt replied, 'but that is unimportant. It is a ruse only. I must know where his lordship is.'

'Why is this lord so important?'

'He may have that which I – and Mr Wild – seek,' said Flynt.

He mentioned Wild purposely, for if Blueskin was minded to disregard the mission on which he was sent, a reminder of the thieftaker's interests should serve as a warning. It worked, for he rose from the chair and motioned his companion to open the door. 'We will do this immediately.'

'Report back to me as soon as you have information.'

Cassie returned bearing a tray carrying two glasses of wine. 'The gentlemen are just leaving, Cassie,' Flynt said. 'I regret they do not have time for refreshment.'

Blueskin made a point of taking a glass and swallowing the contents down in a single gulp. He made a satisfied noise and placed the empty vessel back on the tray with a surly glance towards Flynt. His companion made no move to down the other, so Blueskin disposed of that too. He was sending Flynt a message. He would do as he was bid to a point, but Wild's instructions notwithstanding, he remained his own man. Flynt doubled his resolve not to be as distracted in the future as he had been the night before. It was a mistake he could not make again.

Blueskin propped his stick on his right shoulder in what could have been a jaunty fashion and departed, followed by his silent companion. Cassie closed the door behind them. 'I am not sure I like your friends.'

He didn't wish to enter into a discussion about their implied friendship. 'They are an acquired taste.' Like hemlock, he thought.

She sat down in the chair again, setting the tray on the floor at her feet. Flynt made a point of noting the two glasses only. 'I was not to enjoy a glass?'

He had expected a reproving look of the sort only Cassie – and Mother Mercy – could make but she seemed distracted. She flicked a finger at a jug and cup on a low table beside his bed.

'Water only for you,' she said, but there was no strength in the words.

He sensed there was something wrong but her demeanour had nothing to do with his injuries, as much as he would have liked that to be the case. 'There is something amiss,' he said.

'It is nothing.'

'Cassie, there is a gulf between us, I understand that, but we were once close...' Her flashing eyes told him he was on dangerous ground but he pressed on. 'I may have been away for many years...'

Her body stiffened. 'Yes, you have.'

'...but I know you still. So, tell me, what is wrong?'

He feared that he was inviting yet another verbal lashing for his behaviour and it was with some relief that he saw her muscles relax again and she seemed to slump a little. 'Cassie...' he began but she raised a hand to stop him.

'There have been developments this day,' she said carefully. 'With regard to Charlie.'

Ignoring the protests of his bruised flesh and battered bones, Flynt forced himself to sit up. 'Developments of what sort?'

'There has been talk of no action being taken by the courts.'

'I know, Gideon told me.'

She acknowledged that with a slight nod. 'It doesn't sit well with the people.'

'Gideon told me that too.'

'They hold him responsible and mean to take matters into their own hands.'

Flynt was realistic enough to know that his old friend did bear some responsibility for the tragedy but the determination of such guilt or innocence should not rest with an angry crowd liquored up on wine and gin. 'Gideon said it was mere talk.'

'It's moved on from words. Gideon has heard that action is planned.'

He had no doubt of the accuracy of his father's intelligence. 'Does Charlie still bide in the Tolbooth?'

'He does.' She fell silent and he waited, for he knew she had not yet reached the nub of her concerns. He could see she was wrestling with it, but finally she said, 'Rab means to break him free.'

Flynt was shocked by this. 'Has he taken leave of all sense?'

'He says he can't allow his friend to be cruelly used by the mob.'

'And if he is caught he will lose all – his business, his family, his life.'

'He's bound and determined to do it.'

'You have to stop him, Cassie.'

'Do you no think I've tried? You three are grown men but remain foolish boys. Stubborn and careless. Charlie should never have commanded that day, you knew it, Rab knew it, I knew it. I think in his heart he knew it but he was too pig-headed to stand down.'

'He's an officer of the guard, Cassie. He saw it as his duty.'

'*Duty!* Men do foolhardy things and they call it duty while women have to tend the wounds and clean up the blood. And mourn the loss. The rich do the talking, the poor do the dying and the women do the crying. All in the name of duty. And honour. Country. Flag. All false gods.'

A large part of Flynt agreed but he felt obliged to defend his friend. 'Cassie, when we were boys all Charlie ever wanted to be was a soldier. And now he's an officer, even if only of the Town Guard. He did what he thought he had to, whether he liked it or no.'

'And Rab? He didn't share this notion of glory that you and Charlie did. And yet he's below right now, planning to attack the gaol single-handed in the name of loyalty. The Tolbooth is no fortress, Jonas, but what he intends is folly, can you no see that?'

Flynt could see that. 'He won't listen to you?'

'Of course not. I'm merely his wife and the mother of our child. Why should he listen to me when he's already decided on a course of action? My words have no more effect than they would've had with you had you told me you were leaving, no matter what you say.'

He did not wish to follow that thought with a comment for fear that the rage simmering within her would boil over onto him. He threw back the bedsheet and began to swing his legs free. 'I'd be obliged if you'd fetch me my clothes.'

She stood up and tried to force him back but he ignored the agony pulsing through his body and struggled to his feet. He felt the world tilt slightly but he remained upright. He realised for the first time that he was naked and felt abashed. 'Who was it who stripped me?'

Despite the concern still evident, a glint of laughter crept into her eye. 'Mother Mercy and myself. Your clothes were blood-stained and the menfolk were too *manly* to undertake such a task. They have been laundered.' There was a slight pause before she added, 'And no before time.'

He covered himself with both hands. 'Cassie, my clothes, if you please.'

'I have seen you naked before, Jonas Flynt, or do you not recall?'

The image of their young bodies entwined, her breath in his ear as he thrust deep within her, her voice husky with passion as she told him she loved him flashed in his head and, despite the pain and the light-headedness, he felt that familiar tingle in his groin. He shoved the memory aside. This was not the time. It would never be the time. 'Please, Cassie, my clothes.'

She saw the determined look on his face and moved towards the wooden cabinet in the corner of the room. When she opened the door he saw his clothes folded neatly atop his saddlebags and his sword stick propped up at the back. He would hazard a guess that his purse still nestled in the pocket of his greatcoat, which meant that the attack was not a robbery, unless Blake and his friend's arrival interrupted them before they could relieve him of his valuables. Flynt suspected that he had been targeted for some other reason.

Cassie took out his clean shirt, breeches and stockings and carried them to him. 'What do you intend?'

He took a breath as he tried to steady his spinning mind. 'I'll speak with your husband.'

'What makes you think he'll listen to you?'

He took the breeches first and pulled them on, sitting back on the bed to do so. He knew he was moving slowly, as if in a dream, and every contusion and wound screamed at him to get back into bed but he could not. 'I'll reason with him.'

'He'll no listen.'

He eased one arm into the shirt, then the other. His muscles protested. 'Then I'll make him,' he said, as he flexed the hand his attacker had stamped upon, loosening the stiffness from his fingers, his mind trying to overcome the sharp ache. 'Will you fetch my saddlebag?'

–

Rab sat alone at a table, a bottle of brandy half-empty before him, his brow furrowed, his eyes lost in private thoughts, completely unaware of his surroundings. Flynt emerged from the stairwell, noting the concerned look of Mother Mercy. 'You shouldn't be out of bed,' she cautioned, then looked at Cassie behind him. 'What are you thinking, girl? Allowing this…'

'He must speak with Rab, Mother. Someone must talk sense into that bull head of his.'

Mercy understood but she still gave Flynt a stern look. 'You're not one of those Greek gods you used to read about, Jonas. You're mortal.'

He was very much aware of his mortality as he tried to counter the swaying of the tavern around him. 'I shouldn't be long, Mother,' he said.

'Aye.' Her gaze remained severe. 'Be sure you're not, lad, else I'll carry you back up those stairs myself. And don't think I wouldn't shame you in front of all the people here.'

Despite his discomfort, despite the fact that he thought he might collapse at any minute, Flynt smiled. There were many uncertainties in life but Mother Mercy's ability to do as she said was not one of them.

She jerked her head towards her son-in-law. 'There he sits, girding his loins with brandy. Good luck, Jonas, for he'll no listen to reason. Gideon has tried, I've tried, not even Cassie can make him reconsider this foolhardy notion of his.'

He laid his saddlebag on the counter. 'A glass, Mother, if you please,' he said and she handed one over. His gait was stiff and laboured as he crossed the room to where Rab sat. 'Is this a private wake or can anyone join it?'

Rab was startled when Flynt spoke. His head snapped up and the lack of focus in his eyes told Flynt that he had consumed the bulk of the brandy missing from the bottle. Flynt lowered himself gingerly into the chair opposite, laying his cane on the tabletop. He had his back to the door, which he did not like, but he had learned his lesson and had already surveyed the room and it was empty of threats. The knot of whispering men was not present but there were a few who bore the look of the law courts and the council chambers about them, while the old woman he had seen when he first arrived was seated at the same table, bread and cheese and tankard of ale in front of her as before.

'Should you be up and about?' Rab asked, his words clear but his voice carrying the abrasive qualities of the liquor.

Flynt did not reply as he poured himself a measure and threw it down his throat. It was not a fine vintage but it burned away some of the ache, if only temporarily. He set the glass down and scrutinised his friend.

A smile quivered at Rab's lips. 'Did they beat the voice out of you last night?'

Flynt poured himself another drink but left it in the glass. 'You can't do this thing, Rab.'

Rab glanced towards Cassie, watching them from her mother's side at the counter. 'Cassie told you?'

'She did.'

His friend shook his head and drained what was left of his own drink, then reached for the bottle. Flynt laid his hand on top of his and held the bottle in place. 'This is not the way, Rab.'

Rab accepted the denial of another drink with grace, his hand falling away again. 'It must be done.'

'Anything that requires a man to liquor himself up is unwise.'

'He's our friend, Jonny. Aye, I have my differences with him but he remains close to me. Does he not remain close to you? Or has your time away eroded such brotherhood?'

The words added further pain to Flynt's list of injuries. 'No, it hasn't and well you know it, Rab. All I'm saying is that you can't follow the course of action you are planning, if you even have a plan.'

'Oh, I've a plan, don't you worry,' Rab said, freeing the bottle and pouring a measure. 'Access the Tolbooth, find Charlie, walk out again.'

'Sounds foolproof.'

'You have a better one?'

'Not doing it comes to mind.'

'So you'd let them drag Charlie from that place and murder him? 'Cos that's what they intend, Jonny. Murder. I wouldn't let them do it to my dog, much less my friend. Your friend.'

'You could alert the authorities.'

'You think I've not already done so? He's in the Tolbooth, they say. The mob can't reach him there, they say.' He sneered. 'Safe in the Tolbooth. If that place was a ship it would sink. I urged them to place him in the castle but they refused.'

Flynt felt the spirit helping to dull his pains so he quaffed the contents of his glass and reached a decision. 'Then I'll do it in your stead.' He spoke again when he saw Rab was minded to argue. 'Listen to me, Rab. You've a life here. If you do this and you're caught, then that life is over. You have more to think of than yourself. You have Cassie. You have a son. I have nothing.' He gave Rab time to see the wisdom of his words before he added,

'And this is more my line of work than yours. You're a cobbler. This is what I do.'

'Perhaps, but do you no have a mission to accomplish? Involvement in this could place that in jeopardy.'

There was truth in those words but at that moment Flynt cared little for wills, Charters or even his own wellbeing. 'It can bide. I'll attend to it when Charlie is safe behind the castle walls.'

He hoped he sounded more confident than he felt but he could not allow his friend to attempt this. Flynt knew he had more chance of success than a cobbler who had never fired a weapon in anger. Rab considered this, staring at the glass before him, then raised his eyes once more and Flynt noted the determination set within. 'No,' he said, 'this is my responsibility. You've been away too long, Jonny, for this to be your duty.'

'True friendship does not wane by time or distance,' Flynt said. 'Like wine, it improves with age.'

Rab's eyes softened. 'Very well. But we do this together or I do it alone and there will be no further bargaining.'

Flynt had expected that and he nodded then poured them each another drink. 'A final tincture and then we'll begin.'

Rab smiled and downed the drink, not noticing that Flynt's hand failed to pick up his own glass.

'Let's be away then,' said Flynt as he rose, grasping his stick. 'If this is to be done, it's best done swiftly.'

He moved to Cassie and Mother Mercy and retrieved his saddlebag, which he draped over his shoulder. 'Follow us to the door,' he whispered.

Rab failed to notice his wife and her mother trailing in their wake as he moved unsteadily across the tavern. Flynt held the door open for him to pass and motioned the women to linger until they were in the courtyard. He gripped Rab's elbow with his left hand as they moved down the steps, searching the gathering darkness, but the courtyard was empty and he saw no figures in the passageway leading to the High Street. A quick glance over his shoulder to ensure Cassie and Mother Mercy were still watching, then he leaned into his friend's ear.

'I'm sorry, Rab, you leave me no choice.'

He hefted his cane and struck Rab on the temple, catching him as he slumped to the side with a groan. He had weighed the blow carefully to ensure his friend was merely stunned. Rab hung like a child's doll in his arm as Cassie and Mother Mercy rushed to assist.

'He'll have a welt and a thundering ache but that, at least, was already in his future given his brandy intake,' he said. 'Take him to my room, let him rest for as long as you can. He'll come after me, so you will have to be firm, Mother.'

Mercy had her charge held tightly. 'Leave that to me.'

Flynt gave her a thin smile, knowing she would do as she promised, even if it meant Rab getting another welt. He turned towards the passageway.

'Where are you going?' Cassie asked as she looped her husband's arm over her neck.

His step did not falter. 'To finish what he would have begun.'

'Alone?'

Flynt felt the weight of Tact and Diplomacy in his saddlebag. 'No,' he said. 'I have old friends with me.'

14

Mindful of his recent failings, Flynt paused at the mouth of the passageway to reconnoitre the street. A few townspeople milled around but the vendors were making their way home, baskets over their arms or trundling carts down the hill. A glance at the Cross revealed even the caddies had given up for the day and the usual loungers had found somewhere else to recline. Lights already burned in the windows of the guardhouse beyond it. Lanterns had been lit in closes and wynds and would burn until nine, before the majority were extinguished. In the opposite direction the Tolbooth loomed dark in the gathering gloom, the faint glimmer of candlelight behind some of the grime-crusted windows the only sign of life.

He hesitated, unsure of his next step. He had helped break men free before but they had been carefully planned operations. Certainly the Tolbooth was among the least secure gaols he had ever seen, but what he was about to do required by necessity a considerable degree of improvisation. He did not know how many guards the prison held or how they were armed. He was unacquainted with the layout within and would have to study it as he went along. He considered fetching Blueskin and his companion to assist but was unsure if they would agree or, if they did, whether he could trust them to play any part. He decided against it. He did not much like Blake but still felt it wrong to place him in harm's way.

A figure approached him from the direction of the Cross. A woman, her face obscured by the hood of her thick cape, but he did not need to see her features to recognise her.

'Madame de Fontaine,' he said with a courteous bow, while he searched the street for Gregor, finally finding him in the shadow of a wynd opposite, watching the way a hawk hovers over prey in the grass.

The woman swept the hood back and again he was taken with her beauty. She smiled when she saw him dart another look across the street. 'Gregor will maintain his distance unless you molest me, Mr Flynt. But I don't think you'll do that, will you?'

Like his, her native accent was far more pronounced now she was in Scotland. 'I assure you, madame, I won't give your brute the chance to lay his hands upon me a second time. One step in this direction and it'll be his last.'

'Brute, you say? Gregor is really rather sweet when you get to know him.'

Flynt felt the man's hands constricting his throat once more. 'Aye, I well remember his gentle nature.'

'Nevertheless, you're safe as long as our discourse remains civilised. But then, I don't think you're the type to strike a lady.'

'It depends on the circumstances – and on the lady.' He gave her a brief smile before adding, 'My lady.'

Her laugh was like music as she laid a hand on his arm. 'Ah, Mr Flynt, I liked you from the first moment we met.'

'And that would be when you tried to have me killed?'

'Business, not pleasure, and dictated by the circumstance of the moment. And I am very much a woman who lives by the moment. However, all is well, for here we are conferring like two old friends.'

He allowed the idea that they were friends to hang between them like a threat before he said, 'And why did you seek me out, madame?'

'I felt the need to remake our acquaintance,' she said, 'before I leave.'

'You move on after so short a stay?'

She gave him a mock shiver. 'I find Edinburgh such a dank and dismal place, don't you? There's no gaiety here, no wit. I prefer

Paris, Vienna, Madrid, even London. It's as if the spirt of John Knox has covered all with drab piety that smothers any light.'

'And yet you are a Scot.'

'I'm a Scot by birth but an internationalist by inclination. As I suspect you are, Mr Flynt.'

He had little desire, nor time, to discuss his views on nation with her. 'May I assume you've completed your business with the Fellowship?'

'You may assume what you wish, sir. May I in turn assume that you're not in Edinburgh in these dangerous times for your leisure but that you still act on behalf of our friend Colonel Charters?'

'You also may assume what you wish, madame.'

'Then I would advise a return to London, Mr Flynt, to inform our mutual friend that the cause is lost.'

'The document has changed hands?'

She contemplated declining to answer but then said, 'Not yet. It will very soon but not in this drab place.'

'Why the delay? Has Moncrieff and the Fellowship not met your price? And to where do you go next?'

A tiny frown lined her forehead. 'I regret I don't discuss business with parties who have previously attempted to deprive me of my means to conduct that business.'

'Even if I made a bid for the item?'

She weighed this eventuality then smiled. 'I don't think you have the proxy to make such a bid.'

'How can you know that?'

'Because I know our Colonel Charters. He doesn't bid, he takes. No, my dear Mr Flynt, you must return to London and inform him you have failed.'

He longed to know what delayed the transfer of ownership but the woman was too canny a player to show her hand. 'I regret I cannot do that,' he said. 'I gave my word that I wouldn't return empty-handed.'

'The word of a rogue?'

'A rogue can have honour, madame.'

She conceded with a slight curtsey. 'That we can, Mr Flynt, that we can.'

Her inclusion of herself pleased him for some reason. 'But if I can't return the document, then I could always take you back with me. I feel sure Colonel Charters would be most pleased to have you in his custody.'

She laughed as a seductive gleam shone in her eye. 'Oh, the good colonel has had me in his *custody* more than once, I can assure you of that. I have persuaded him to give me my liberty every time.'

He had thought in London that Charters was acquainted with her but he had not imagined in a sexual way, though the man was a notorious rake. 'I imagine you can be very persuasive, madame.'

'When the need arises. However, you forget I have my guardian angel just yonder and I very much doubt you would live to take me anywhere.'

The Russian still watched them intently and Flynt had no doubt that if he made any kind of attempt to seize the woman, Gregor would close the distance between them with some speed, regardless of his size. Tact and Diplomacy nestled within his saddlebag, already loaded, but despite his earlier threat to drop him in his tracks, Flynt knew he would not have the time to remove either and loose a shot before he again became acquainted with that cold dead hand. He had the feeling even his blade through the man's heart would fail to stop Gregor.

'I was impressed by your actions yesterday at the execution,' Madame de Fontaine said, one hand unconsciously fingering her own neck. 'A dreadful business.'

'I did what I felt was needed,' he said. 'The commander of the Town Guard was unable to retain control of his men.'

'And he's an old friend, I understand.'

He looked back at her. 'You have been investigating me?'

'I like to know who I am up against.'

'And you are up against me?'

Her lips puckered slightly. 'Not yet, but the night is young.'

This had to be the strangest conversation he had ever had with an adversary. But then, he had never had an adversary like Madame de Fontaine. They were generally dirty men who stank of sweat, liquor and tobacco, not a beautiful woman whose scent reached towards him like a caress. He reminded himself that this woman had not only set her attack dog upon him a scant two weeks before, but had also had him under her gun and would not have hesitated to shoot him if the circumstances of that particular moment had drifted in a different direction.

He treated her to another slight bow. 'I regret, madame, that I am at present otherwise engaged.'

''Tis a pity,' she said with a mock sigh. 'However, a man must be about his business.'

'May I ask, given your work here is almost done, why you have sought me out this evening? Do you have further business with me?'

'Not the kind I would perhaps like, but maybe another time. I come with a warning, regarding your old friend. The one who now sits within the Tolbooth.'

'And why would you take such time to warn me?'

'Call it professional courtesy.' She held his eye. 'One rogue to another.'

He was intrigued. 'And what is this warning?'

'There are forces at work which intend to ensure their version of justice is done.'

'I am aware of that.' He paused, wondering why he was about to say his next words. 'In fact, it is that very circumstance that prevents me from tarrying further with you.'

Her eyes lingered on the saddlebag. 'I suspected as much.'

He gave her another curt bow and began to turn away. 'So your solicitude was unnecessary but I thank you all the same.'

'That was not my only warning.'

He stopped, turned to her again as she moved closer. Her scent had become even more insidious, French he surmised, and though more subtle than overpowering, coupled with what he now saw as an innate ability to captivate men, it was slightly intoxicating even to him. This woman had perfected her sexual allure in order to wield it in the way a man would a sword.

He asked, 'So what other warning would you have?'

'Have you ever seen inside a timepiece, Mr Flynt?'

'I have not had the need. My attention is in the main on the dial.'

'The dial is merely the public face of the clock. The maker needs you to know only what he believes you must know, that is the time of day, and so will have you look at the face alone where all is straightforward. One hand marks the minutes and in turn moves the hour hand. But to understand how it all works you must look below the surface. There are cogs and ratchets and little wheels.' She held her thumb and forefinger barely apart. 'Tiny little wheels, Mr Flynt, so tiny it is a wonder the watchmaker can operate them at all, and they all work in harmony while at the same time working against each other. One may turn this way, another that, but together they make the timepiece tick.'

Flynt grew slightly impatient. 'Madame, you talk of time and it is beginning to press upon me. Is there a point?'

'The point is, Mr Flynt, that there are wheels within wheels working here. All is not as it seems.'

From his experience, most of life was such. 'I would be obliged if you could be more transparent.'

She stepped away again, her smile once more playful. 'There is no pleasure in making the game simple. Then all would be able to play.'

He was beginning to understand this woman, and had not expected her to tell him so readily, so he returned her smile. 'Yet I am to trust you? Are we not enemies?'

She drew back as if stung but remained impish. 'You wound, sir! Rivals, perhaps, but surely not enemies.'

'You would have rivalled me to the grave only two weeks ago.'

She dismissed that once again. 'All part of the game, Jonas – may I call you Jonas now? I feel we two grow closer by the minute.'

'By all means, yet you have the advantage of me in that I do not know your Christian name.'

She laughed. 'But it *is* Christian, as was my father's before me! I do so like a name that is utilitarian. You may call me Christy.' She began to back away. 'I will leave you to your business, Jonas, but mark me. You must have a care. You are a capable man, an honourable man for a thief, but there are dangers in this place for which you may not be prepared. An honourable man can be at a disadvantage when dishonour is the name of the game. Please accept this as I mean it, as a friend's concern for your wellbeing.'

'So now we are friends?'

She was halfway across the street now and Gregor was moving to meet her. 'Friends, enemies, rivals. One can become another in the simple tick of a minute hand.'

She gave him a small wave, just as she had done the day before, and even blew him a kiss, then hitched up her hood and turned to meet Gregor. Flynt's hand had by instinct strayed to the opening of his saddlebag when he saw the Russian move, but relaxed when he made no attempt to approach him. The man treated him to a long stare before he followed his mistress down the High Street. Flynt wondered where they were headed. They must have lodgings somewhere and it was doubtful they would leave Edinburgh after nightfall. If she spoke true and her business here really was at an end, she would move on at first light. He felt he understood her for he was cut from similar cloth, both rogues but with their own peculiar sense of honour. That did not mean that, should their paths cross again, she would not hesitate to have her man end his life, or do it herself, if it suited her purpose. Beautiful she was, even charming, but those charms masked a deadly heart.

As he watched them go, it occurred to him that Gregor might have been responsible for the attack on his person the previous night, but he almost immediately dismissed the notion. Had the big Russian been involved Flynt very much doubted he would still draw breath. They vanished beyond the Tron Kirk, he believed turning into the opening that led to Marlin's Wynd. He knew duty to his mission dictated he should follow but he had a deeper duty to fulfil and that matter was, at this moment, more pressing.

Now alone, Flynt became aware of a chill stealing over him that had nothing to do with the breeze drifting up the canyon of the High Street from the Forth or even less the breath of winter carried on the night air. Thoughts of the fair Christy de Fontaine would have to wait as he carefully studied the street around him. He saw no one. Heard nothing.

And that was what was so disturbing.

Flynt walked beyond the gaol to the Lawnmarket but not a soul was to be seen. He could not recall this part of the city being this peaceful at this time of night, for there was usually some element of bustle. Behind him, the shops at the western end of the Tolbooth were dark and shuttered. No one walked, no carriages clattered, no sedan chairs were hefted, no link boys shone the way with their lanterns. He thought it was as if someone had abducted the entire population and transported it to a foreign shore. No, he amended, it was as if the city was holding its breath as it awaited some titanic disruption.

He returned to the Tolbooth, his footsteps unnaturally loud in the unearthly stillness, and approached the main door, which faced the stern stone of St Giles Kirk and Parliament Square beyond. The look of the gaol on this side was greatly different from that on the High Street, where the high wall was flush and featureless, the stone broken only by small windows. On the kirk side it was more commanding, more Scottish in aspect with two turrets rising at what he thought might have been either end of the original building, erected centuries before but since enhanced. There was a series of doors on this side – one to the private residence of the gudeman, as the gaoler was known, another two to separate sections of the gaol, but the principal entrance was at the foot of the turret nearest to St Giles.

Finally he saw another human being. A burly, red-coated figure armed with a musket moved from his post outside the gaol entrance to intercept him. Flynt was heartened to recognise the serjeant from the Grassmarket but could not discern if the man reciprocated as his countenance might well have been carved from granite.

He had known there would be a guard and had not decided how best to approach this moment, but as the man approached Flynt decided to be candid. He ensured his voice was low so that anyone beyond the door could not hear. 'Serjeant, we must talk.'

'Must we, sir? And about what, may I ask?'

His voice was guarded but again Flynt detected traces of Fifeshire, across the river to the north. It had been many a year since Flynt had heard it but he recognised it well enough. He had found the natives of the ancient kingdom to be level-headed and dependable in the past and he prayed this man was a prime example of his people.

'There's trouble heading this way,' said Flynt.

'Oh, aye?' The man seemed unimpressed, thus informing Flynt that intelligence of the impending attack had not reached the ears of the Town Guard. 'And what sort of trouble?'

'Look around you, man. Listen. Have you seen the High Street thus deserted at this hour? Have you ever known it not to have some sort of din?'

The serjeant cocked his head and his expression tightened as he registered the silence. Without a word he turned on his heel and marched through the narrow opening between the walls of Tolbooth and kirk to emerge on the High Street, where he stood for a moment and gazed upon the empty thoroughfare around the Cross. He walked to the far end of the gaol's gable wall and inspected the street towards Lawnmarket and the castle. Flynt followed him, impatient to gain access but knowing it prudent to allow the man to draw his own conclusions.

Finally, he looked at Flynt and nodded. 'What's afoot then?'

'They're coming for Captain Temple. We must get him to safety.'

'I have men in the guardhouse yonder...'

Flynt interrupted. 'The guardhouse is not near secure enough and, no disrespect, your men are no match for the mob in full

219

throe. No, we must transport him to the castle, while we have the chance. They won't breach those walls, not without cannon and siege engines. So, Serjeant, speed is of the essence. Are you with me?'

To his credit the man saw the wisdom in Flynt's words and he nodded. 'The gudeman won't be for giving up his charge easily.'

Flynt had predicted the gaoler might prove an obstacle. 'We'll have to convince him.'

'How?'

'Assist me in getting through the door and leave me to employ tact and diplomacy.'

Flynt ensured his saddlebag was open as they retraced their steps to the main door where the guardsman hesitated for a moment. Flynt gave him an encouraging nod. The man took a deep breath then banged his closed fist against the heavy door, the echo of the sound dying within like the hopes of many of the inhabitants. Flynt resolved to ensure his friend's hopes remained alive.

The serjeant thumped at the wood again and after a delay of a few minutes a panel on the upper section of the door opened and the gap was filled by the face of a man with the engorged nose and blue veins of one who enjoyed too close an acquaintance with the bottle. He recognised the serjeant but when he saw Flynt behind him he grew suspicious.

'What's all the noise, Balfour?' the gudeman demanded, his voice carried on a waft of breath that Flynt swore could intoxicate an entire room if the windows were shuttered.

'Let us in, Andra,' said the serjeant. 'We have urgent business.'

'What's so urgent that you interrupt a man when he is at his dinner? And there's no entry to this place after dark, you know that, Balfour. This is decided irregular.'

'Andra, your dinner will not grow cold in the glass. Open the door.' The serjeant paused. 'It's official.'

The man's eyes narrowed, Flynt knew not whether through offence at the jibe about his liquid meal or if the suspicion with which he had regarded Flynt now extended to Serjeant Balfour, as Flynt now knew him to be named. 'Official, is it? Is that a fact now? What's so official?'

Serjeant Balfour sighed with exasperation. 'If you let us in we can explain.'

Andra's gaze returned to Flynt. 'And who is this gentleman, if I may be so bold as to ask, Balfour? For there's no visiting at this hour and it's decided irregular to allow the public within these walls when there is no visiting.'

'One of your charges is in peril,' explained the serjeant. 'We've come to carry him to safety.'

The information seemed to confuse the old man. 'In peril, you say? One of my prisoners? To safety, you say?' His confusion gave way once again to suspicion. 'And you'll have warrant for this transfer of custody, have you not?'

'There's no time for such procedure. We must take the captain away before harm befalls him.'

Enlightenment dawned. 'Ah, the captain, is it? Your captain, for whom you've no written authorisation to remove from this place and yet you expect me to just open this here door and let you spirit him away quick as you please? Is that the way of it, then? Such a thing is decided irregular, so it is, and you ken that fine, Thomas Balfour.'

Flynt tired of the exchange. He had hoped the presence of the serjeant would have carried the necessary authority to gain access but he now recognised they must be more emphatic.

'There is no time for this,' he muttered, and in a single fluid motion withdrew a pistol from his saddlebag with his right hand, stepped around the serjeant's bulk, jabbed the point of his silver cane against the panel to prevent it from being slammed shut then thrust the muzzle of the weapon into the gudeman's face. 'Open the door, friend, or the council will require a new gaoler.'

In his shock, the gudeman had failed to notice that the pistol at that moment only inches from his bulbous nose was uncocked. For a moment, Balfour's expression reflected that surprise, then disapproval, but swiftly accepted the situation as being necessary. A twitch of a smile revealed that he had observed that the pistol's hammer had not been pulled. Meanwhile, the gudeman nodded, tried to speak and failed, then proceeded to follow the order. A heavy bolt was drawn, the sound echoing against the stone walls within, followed by the rattle of keys and the sturdy click of the big lock. The solid door swung open and Flynt stepped through, his pistol still trained on the man's head, finding himself in an entranceway lit by a single candle hung on the wall. It was a gloomy, cramped space that opened to a flight of stone steps leading upwards, where Flynt saw the flicker of further candles. The gudeman stepped back as far as he could, his back pressed against the damp wall, his trembling hands raised before him as if he could catch the round should the flintlock bark. Serjeant Balfour closed the door behind them, threw the bolt into place and then turned the lock, removing the thick ring bristling with keys. After a final look at the street, he secured the panel door.

'Now, friend,' said Flynt. 'Take us to Captain Temple.'

'You are off your heads,' observed the gaoler, 'the pair of you.'

'Aye,' said Flynt, pressing the barrel of the pistol against the man's cheek, 'but I would much rather be mad than dead.'

It pained him to see the terror wash across the man's face but there was nothing else for it. He had no intention of harming him but he had to make him believe it was not just possible but imminent. Flynt transferred the pistol to his left hand and followed the gaoler and the waft of alcohol up the stairs. Even though older and somewhat the worse for drink, the man's ascent was considerably more sprightly than Flynt's, whose body protested at the strain he was placing upon it. His right hand steadied his aching bones by holding onto the thick rope secured to the stone walls by metal rings. The hemp was greasy to the touch and had no doubt been handled by many hundreds of prisoners and visitors over the years. There were about twenty steps and each one put a strain on his muscles, sending waves of pain through him, but he forced himself to keep moving. He still had no clear idea what he was doing but he was committed now.

Behind him he heard the serjeant's heavy, laboured breathing as he followed them upwards, physical fitness obviously not being a prerequisite for recruitment to the guard. He took no comfort from the harsh exhalations for the man had a good twenty years on him.

They reached another thick door at the top of the stairs, this time with two candles burning yellow flame on either side.

'Open it,' ordered Flynt.

'I cannae,' said Andra, 'for it can only be opened from inside by my neebor. He locks it at my back when I attend at the main door.'

'Then call him and get it done.' Flynt prodded him with the pistol. 'And if you attempt any kind of warning, be assured that I will recognise it as such and it'll be all the worse for you.'

Andra's eyes were filled with fright but Flynt did not know how long it would be before he noticed the pistol remained uncocked. Even so, the man made an attempt at authority, though made feeble by the tremble in his words that marked time with the quivering in his hands and face muscles.

'I must warn you of the folly of your actions, sir. This is the town gaol and I am the duly appointed gudeman. What you are doing is decided irregular, so it is, and you will feel the full weight of the law for it.'

'Well said, sir,' said Flynt. 'And now get the damned door open before I lose patience.'

Andra, his courage sapped by his speech, leaned towards the door and rapped on it with gnarled knuckles, then called out, 'Turn your hand, Davie.'

There was a pause during which Andra began to hop around on both feet as if in urgent need to void his bladder, while his eyes continually darted from the door to the pistol. Eventually, muffled footsteps could be heard and then a key in a lock. The door opened to reveal a small man with lank hair hanging loose around his shoulders and a face bearing what looked like a perpetual scowl. He looked about ready to say something to the gudeman, and Flynt guessed it would have been something ill-natured, but he was struck dumb when he saw the musket at the ready in the serjeant's hands and Flynt with his weapon at the gudeman's head.

'Step back, if you please,' ordered Flynt and pushed the gaoler before him, forcing the smaller man to reverse whether he agreed or not. The serjeant again followed, locking the door behind him and taking the keys. They were now in a larger hall and Flynt could see shabbily dressed prisoners lounging beyond a wooden rail, some at tables with glass in hand. The air was redolent with wine, boiled cabbage, tobacco, pipe smoke, candle fumes, piss and sweat. Many of the men and women here were laughing and making merry but there was a sense of despair that hung above the various odours like a headsman's sword. Three soldiers of the guard patrolled the rail that obviously delineated captivity from freedom within this long room, for one was in the process of ordering two inebriates to move away lest they feel the heft of his Lochaber axe. His two comrades, seeing the armed stranger but also their serjeant seeming relaxed at his side, looked to each other in confusion. They fingered their muskets nervously.

'Attend to me, lads,' Balfour ordered. 'We have ourselves something of a situation.'

Some of the prisoners began to cheer at the sight of the armed man holding the gudeman captive but the serjeant moved to the guard's side and yelled, 'Bide your wheesht, you lot. These matters are no concern of yours.'

Flynt was wary as he watched the men and women clustering beyond the rail and he finally eased the hammer back on his pistol. On seeing this, the gudeman realised how little danger his person had been in and, although still in a state of alarm, he appeared crestfallen at his gullibility. Flynt gave him an apologetic shrug.

The serjeant turned away from the prisoners. 'You proceed while I stay here and watch this rabble.'

Flynt eyed the prisoners warily. 'Do we have a problem?'

Balfour wrinkled his nose as he gestured behind him. 'Not from this lot. Debtors, mostly. They'll make noise but that's all.

But these here privates of the guard and me will keep them in line, don't you worry. Eh, boys?'

His men remained perplexed by the turn of events but they each murmured or nodded their assent. Flynt considered the wooden rail separating them from the prisoners a flimsy defence, but the serjeant seemed confident he and his men could quell any disturbance so he left them to it. All the same, he drew and cocked his second pistol. This alarmed the gudeman further, while even his turnkey's glower melted into unease. However, he did manage to address the gaoler. 'What in the devil's name is all this, Andra?'

Flynt furnished the reply. 'We've come to take Captain Temple away from here and lodge him in safety in the castle. The mob intends to liberate him and visit their own justice upon him.'

'They canna fuckin' dae that!' said Davie. 'This is the fuckin' Tolbooth!'

Flynt found it difficult to understand the veneration these men felt for an institution held in such poor regard by the majority of the city. Perhaps it helped them fulfil their duties. 'Nevertheless, that is their intention. Now, where is he?'

'I'll need my keys,' said the gudeman, holding a hand out to the serjeant, who handed over the weighty bundle, then joined his men to quell those prisoners who had been emboldened sufficiently by wine and gin to crowd the partition rail and jeer. The gudeman motioned Flynt to follow him and led him to a tall wooden pulpit of some antiquity, which Flynt regarded with curiosity.

The gaoler saw his quizzical look. 'This room is also the kirkhouse of the Tolbooth,' he explained. 'They say John Knox himself preached from that pulpit.'

Ordinarily Flynt would have been fascinated but he had more pressing matters with which to deal. Behind the pulpit was yet another heavy door, which was duly unlocked and opened to reveal a further flight of stairs upwards. Andra searched through the collection of keys hanging from the ring as he began to climb. Flynt hauled himself in his wake.

Beyond the next door, as substantial as the others, lay another large room. Its inhabitants were not free to roam as were those on the floor below, but were instead chained to a metal bar that ran along the centre. The bare stone walls were damp and the musty air was redolent with body odour and lost hope. The prisoners stared at Flynt, some with curiosity, others with defiance, but yet more with the hollow-eyed look of men who knew their time on this earth was short. Unlike their fellow inmates milling on the first floor they made no sound but simply watched as the gudeman turned towards a room to the right, which he opened with a fresh key selected with ease from the bundle. Flynt wondered how he told each one apart.

Charlie sprang to his feet from a hard wooden cot as the door opened, his mournful expression becoming a beam when he saw Flynt at the gaoler's back, then transforming to consternation as he took note of the weaponry. 'Jonny, what is the meaning of this?'

'You have to come with me, Charlie. No questions.'

Charlie made no move to pick up the red coat that lay across the cot. 'But why? What...?'

'God's teeth, Charlie,' Flynt snapped. 'Do you no understand the concept of no questions?'

'I need to know why you're here, bearing arms and holding this man hostage.'

'He's not a hostage, he's a guide. And I bear arms because there's tumult afoot.'

'Tumult? What—'

Flynt held up a hand, his ears catching something.

Charlie said, 'Jonny, tell me what is—'

'Will you wheesht, Charlie!'

This time Charlie did as ordered and watched in bewilderment as Flynt strained to identify the sound that had reached him. At first he heard nothing and thought he had imagined hearing it, but as he concentrated, he began to make it out. It was faint, emanating from somewhere beyond the walls of the gaol, but growing in intensity. A drum, beating a slow march, and accompanying it were raised voices and, if he listened intently enough, the tramp of myriad feet.

'God damn it to hell!' he said, cursing for allowing himself to be delayed by Christy de Fontaine. He was too late. The mob was coming.

Charlie heard the growing roar from the street and the same abject horror flared in his eyes that Flynt had witnessed first in Flanders and then in the Grassmarket.

'Jonny...' he began, his voice constricting around the name and squeezing the life from anything further he might have intended to say.

Flynt's mind raced as he moved to the small window set deep into the wall and looked down onto the street. To his left he saw the entrance to St Giles Kirk, ahead a wynd squeezing through to Parliament Square, and to his right, from the direction of the Lawnmarket, was the first faint glow of red that signified the approach of torches. The drum rattled slow and steady, setting the pace for the ragged tramp of feet, the clamour of voices now much louder. He had hoped to get Charlie out before the mob arrived but that was not possible now and it was unlikely they would succeed in stealing him through the streets without being spotted.

'How sturdy is the door below?' he asked the gudeman, who was growing visibly edgy as the din intensified.

The man swallowed. 'It has never been breached, not by sword or musket.'

Flynt thought about the flambeaux already coating the stone of the buildings in a scarlet hue and now spreading from the canyon between gaol and kirk and recalled what he had witnessed as a boy. 'Aye, but can it withstand fire?'

The gaoler knew it could not but declined to reply.

'Jonny, what is going on?' Charlie's voice was little more than a croak.

Flynt delayed an answer, for he knew his friend could not be so addled by fear that he did not know what was occurring.

Eventually, knowing he could not leave it unanswered, he opted to be blunt in the hope that it would cajole Charlie into doing whatever was required of him. 'They are here for you, Charlie. They believe you'll no answer for what happened yesterday.'

'But… but it was not my fault. It was them –' he waved a hand to the window '– they caused it. They threw stones and attacked my men. They rioted, Jonny. You were there!'

Flynt had no time to debate the matter. He would do all in his power to thwart the mob in their intent, but he knew that Charlie did have a bill to pay. His crime may have been as little as weakness or lapse of judgement, it may have been cowardice, it may even have been murder, but it was for a court to decide, as arbitrary as that could be, and certainly not an angry pack.

Charlie must have seen something in Flynt's expression for he began to plead. 'You can't let them take me, Jonny. I did nothing wrong!' He ran to the window. 'It's blood they want, Jonny, you know that. Not justice, blood.' He began to weep and sank to his knees, his body scraping against the damp stonework. 'I did nothing wrong… I did nothing wrong…'

Flynt was overtaken by a sudden sadness, tinged with pity. Looking at Charlie as he wailed, he once again saw the child in the man, the boy with whom he had laughed and dreamed. His own hot tears burned behind his eyes, so he turned away from the sight and contemplated his next step. Escape was impossible. All the doors opened to the front of the building where the throng awaited. Even if there was an exit of which he was unaware, he was willing to wager that the High Street was similarly clogged with townspeople. They could settle in, hope the mob did not think to set the door aflame and pray that soldiers would be sent from the castle to quell the disturbance or that the Town Guard would sally forth. He knew the latter was a vain hope, for they were not known for their steadfastness when it came to the mob and the events in the Grassmarket had probably sapped them of all courage. He also suspected they might be trapped within their guardhouse, for the mob was no crazed monster but a sentient being. This assault would have been planned like a military operation by its leaders.

No, the best hope was aid from the castle and all they could do was wait it out. All they needed was time.

'Stay with him,' he told the gudeman, nodding towards Charlie who still kneeled upon the dirty floor, his body leaning against the wall, wracking sobs and moans erupting with his tears.

'What do you intend, sir?' the gudeman asked.

'I don't know,' Flynt said as he turned to the door, paying little heed to the blank faces of the felons chained to the bar watching him. 'But whatever it is, it'll be decided irregular.'

15

He hesitated in the small entrance chamber on the ground floor for a few moments, his eyes closed, his head filled with the hammering of his heart, his stomach roiling with tension. He was unclear what he was going to do once he opened the Tolbooth's heavy wooden door, for he was still making it up as he went along.

Yet another door. Always another door. He'd had no clear idea what lay beyond that basement door in St Giles and the one in the Mint but he could guess what awaited him on the other side of this one. The odds previously, though hazy, had been on the manageable side, but here he knew he would be outnumbered. What this situation did have in common with London was the element of surprise, for those on the other side would not expect a lone, armed man to emerge.

'Are you ready, sir?'

Flynt opened his eyes and saw Serjeant Balfour giving him an intense study, perhaps suspecting he had lost his nerve. The truth of it was, as he listened to the angry voices beyond the door, that his fixity of purpose was wavering as he wondered what in the name of God he was doing here. This was not his mission.

Nonetheless…

Charlie, for all his faults, was a friend, one of the few Flynt had and one he had let down before, in Flanders, when he had allowed them to be separated, had even written him off as a casualty. Had he taken more care then, perhaps he could have helped steer him away from taking the commission with the guard and the episode of the day before would have been someone else's burden to bear. Charlie needed him now, more than ever before, and he would not, could not in all honour desert him. Not again.

He forced a smile. 'When I give the word, unlock, unbolt and open. Close the door immediately and don't open it again unless I tell you it's safe to do so.'

'And you're certain that I and my men shouldn't accompany you?'

The serjeant had already made such an offer as they left the chamber above, but Flint thought it prudent they remain behind lest the debtors felt encouraged towards some form of anarchy. The actions of individuals could be predicted to some degree but those of a pack could not. Debtors they may have been, and not hardened criminals, but they were still crushed together in that confined space and there was no saying what they would do if they thought there was a chance of liberty. More importantly, given the events of the day before, sight of the guards' red-and-white tunics was likely to enflame the passions of the mob outside even further.

'No, you stay here, defend the upper door with deadly force if you have to.'

There was some relief in the serjeant's eyes as he nodded and laid a hand on the bolt.

A loud voice reached them from the street. 'Gudeman, turn your hand to the key!'

Though the words were muffled by the door, the owner of that stentorian bellow must have been standing directly outside and both Flint and Balfour were startled. They shrank back, each automatically levelling weapons before Flint allowed himself a rueful chuckle at their display of nerves. He leaned against the wall to concentrate on his breathing and quell the thunder of blood in his ears, just as he had done outside the cellar door in St Giles and that grim apartment in the Mint. Was that really a mere half month before? So much had happened since that night. As then, he knew that when he stepped beyond this threshold he had to leave all semblance of nerves behind. Like the gang in that dismal basement, the mob would respond only to power, and confidence was power.

A few deep breaths further, each one slower than the last, and he was ready. He nodded to the serjeant, who slid the weighty metal bolt to the side, turned the key and then stepped back to swing the door open. Flynt stepped through, pistols held before him.

'You show sense, old man,' said the voice they had heard, but its owner's satisfied smirk died when he found himself facing not the gudeman as he had expected but the lethal end of Flynt's weapons. He was a tall, barrel-chested man, with unruly hair bursting from under a blue cap. He had the face of a brawler and the body of a man used to manual labour, but he backed away, his arms outstretched to warn those behind him. Flynt swept the barrels of both weapons ahead of him as, behind him, the door closed quickly, and the crypt echo that followed coupled with the sound of the bolt being thrown and the lock turning underlined how lonely he suddenly felt. He wondered once more just what he was doing facing a multitude with only two pistols and a sword, but the cards had been dealt and he had to play his hand.

He examined the faces ranged before and around him, the flicker of flame from the flambeaux cutting shifting lines into their features and sending tall shadows dancing on the walls of the kirk and the buildings opposite. Men and women crammed into the space and their number stretched, as far as he could tell, all the way to the Lawnmarket, perhaps as far as the West Bow. He glanced to his left and saw the corridor between the gaol and kirk was similarly clogged. The sheer weight of what lay before him worked at his guts again but he fought to keep the barrels of his pistols still. Don't show weakness, he told himself. Don't let them smell fear.

The man in the blue cap had recovered sufficiently from the shock of seeing a stranger armed with a brace of pistols to edge closer, his careful eyes examining Flynt as an anatomist would a cadaver. Flynt studied him in turn, sensing something familiar about him. Something in the way he carried himself.

'Who are ye, friend?'

Before Flynt could answer, another man stepped forward from the crowd. He had the look of a merchant and the sharp eye of someone who could estimate to the penny the amount of silver in your pocket. Flynt had definitely seen him before – he had been among those men in Gideon's who muttered and watched and perhaps plotted.

'He is Gideon Flynt's boy, Hugh,' the man said.

'Aye, he was the one who stopped the guard yesterday from killing more of us,' said another voice, again one of the men from the tavern.

Hugh studied Flynt, his mouth compressing in a show of respect. 'I ken your faither,' he said. 'He's a good man.'

'He is,' agreed Flynt.

'And do ye ken me?'

'I regret, sir, I have been away for many a year and I am unfamiliar with whom my father consorts.'

The man laughed. It was a loud laugh and it boomed around them. 'He speaks well, does he no, for the son of a tavern keeper? "With whom my father consorts", by God!'

He laughed again and the shared mirth scattered through the crowd. When he stopped, he pulled himself up to a considerable height and threw out his chest. 'I'm Hugh Gordon, friend, once shipmate with Gideon. The good people of Edinburgh have seen fit to nominate me as their commander when they have the need and tonight they have that need. They like to call me General and right honoured I am by that, though I would prefer Admiral. But only in these streets can a ditch-digger by trade be accorded such respect, eh, friends?'

There was a cry of assent from all around. The mob was notoriously egalitarian and welcomed all, no matter their station. Before him hawkers, whores and beggars rubbed shoulders with students, merchants and clerks. On this night, as on others, they had come together for a single purpose, to right what they perceived as a wrong, and it mattered little how a person made their living in the daylight. Here, on the street, with the dark kept at bay by the guttering torches, they were all one.

Flynt kept one pistol trained on the man they called the General while the other continued to range in the direction of the crowd. '"Accorded such respect",' he repeated. 'You speak none too badly yourself, sir. For a ditch-digger.'

Hugh smiled. 'Aye, I've read a book or two in my time and learned to communicate. All the better to relay the thoughts and, aye, the demands of my fellow citizens to them in power.'

Flynt suspected that 'General' Hugh Gordon may have come from low beginnings but that was no bar to keen intelligence. Like Flynt, he had elevated his mind through reading. That, coupled with natural leadership qualities, stood him in good stead when assuming command of an unruly mob. It was essential he focus on this man, that he keep him talking, something he suspected this unbraided general relished, and thus give time for any rescue party to reach them.

'And what are the thoughts and demands of these good people?'

The General gave him a mock serious look. 'Come, friend, ye ken fine what work we are about this night.'

'Indulge me.'

A sigh, its overemphasis a touch of theatre for the crowd. 'Very well. We have come for the Captain of the Town Guard, who I believe ye ken bides within those walls.' He paused, Flynt suspected for dramatic effect. 'For now, at least.'

'Aye, and he knows him right well,' said the sharp-faced merchant. 'He drank with him two nights since in Gideon's.'

The General raised an eyebrow. 'He is friend to ye?'

'He is,' confirmed Flynt.

A look of sadness crossed the mob leader's face, which may even have been genuine. 'Then it is extreme sorry I am for what must happen.'

'Nothing will happen.'

'Ah, friend, there are few certainties in life but I regret something will happen this night and it will no be to your liking.'

'You forget, *friend*,' said Flynt, coming down heavily on the last word, 'I have the firepower. And it is my promise that should

234

one person make a move to this door, that person will be the first to fall. If that person is not you, then you will be the second.'

The threat fell on fallow ground for the man merely laughed. 'And to what effect? Two will lie dead and your firepower will be spent and the people here will still access the Tolbooth and find our man. What must be done will be done whether I live or die.'

'Aye,' said Flynt, despite seeing the sense in the man's words, and noting that improvisation was in this case a poor substitute for careful planning. There had been no time for such, however. 'You may be happy to sacrifice your life, but which of your fellows here wants to be the first to die?'

There was a silence then and Flynt noted with satisfaction that questioning faces turned to one another and a murmur of doubt rose. It was the General's turn to see the sense in Flynt's words. He considered them for a moment as he cast his eye around his followers. Flynt was one and they were many but none of them wished to put his marksmanship to the test.

The General returned his attention to Flynt. 'You're proficient with those weapons, I'll hazard.'

Flynt gave him his customary response. 'I hit that at which I aim.'

The man allowed this to hang between them as he considered the ramifications. 'You're delaying us intentional, friend.'

'I am urging you to disperse and let the law run its course.'

Another laugh from the big man. 'The law? The law is not on the side of those poor souls who perished yesterday. The law is on the side of those who make the laws, not those who have to follow them. But let's leave that aside, eh. You hope for rescue, friend, do ye no?'

Flynt did not reply but the casual way the man seemed to have broached the subject troubled him.

The General shook his head. 'It won't come. The gallant members of the Town Guard lie besieged in their citadel down yonder. They'll no engage my people even if they had the stomach for it. The good aldermen and burgesses and magistrates cower in their homes and their chambers awaiting this night's work to be done so they may emerge come the morrow to puff and prance their outrage.' He paused, fixing a knowing eye on Flynt. 'And that leaves the detachment of soldiers billeted in the castle.' Another shake of his head, this one mournful. 'They'll no come, friend. Their commander has ordered the gate sealed. They've no wish to face the people's army. They know that if the soldiers engage there will be further blood running in these streets and no one wishes that, not even the council leaders cowering behind pisspots under their beds.' He laughed and those around him, those who heard, joined him. When it subsided, the General's tone sobered. 'There's a word, friend. Expediency, d'ye ken it?'

Flynt inclined his head to confirm.

'Aye, thought ye might. They are politicians, friend, and they live by such. In this case, it is better that one die so the majority may live.'

Flynt recalled Moncrieff and Baillie Wilson in hushed, shadowed conference with a man in the Grassmarket. That man had shared a similar build with Hugh. 'There will be repercussions,' said Flynt.

'Aye, there will. They will froth and fume and issue arrest warrants but I predict they'll come to nought. For this is the Edinburgh way. In their mind that man in there, your friend, is a liability. If they take action against him then they betray their class and their caste by siding with the mob. If we take him and mete out justice, natural justice, street justice, then they can publicly denounce us but privately thank us for saving them the trouble.'

Flynt was troubled by the man's relaxed attitude, and worse, by how much his reasoning held true. In his heart he knew he was on the losing side, that if the castle commander had ordered no relief be given, then this could only end with Charlie in the mob's hands.

The General continued. 'The question is, friend, do ye need to die too? Is your life so worthless that ye'll throw it away on a lost cause?'

Flynt had no desire to throw his life away but he could not back down. 'Then we have reached an impasse, for I will not leave this door while there is breath in me.'

The General sighed again, less exaggerated than before and therefore more sincere. His eyes slid to his right and Flynt realised that while he had been trying to delay them, the General had also been playing for time. Flynt followed the man's gaze and saw two men had thrust their way through the press of bodies and now had muskets trained on him. He swung the weapon in his left hand in their direction.

'As you can see, friend, ye're no the only one with firepower,' said the General. 'Now, I beg you – see sense. Put up your pistols. Let us gain access. Let us do this business and be done with it.'

Flynt felt something sink within his breast as he realised that he had been outmanoeuvred. His one hope was of rescue, but if the man spoke the truth, and there was a certainty in his tone that told Flynt he did, that hope was dashed. He could not stop them, for though he would drop two, and one of them would indeed have been the leader, he would not be able to reload before he was rushed. He might not even let loose more than a single ball before one of the armed men took him down. The ground was lost. The wisest course was to relinquish his weapons and let them force their way into the gaol.

He took a deep breath. Swallowed. Shifted his grip on his pistol butts. Then he said, 'I cannot.'

It may have been the wisest course but it was not one he could bring himself to travel. His friend relied upon him and he would do his damnedest to protect him, even if it meant the loss of his own life. He had let too many down in the past, he could not allow himself to do so again.

The General seemed genuinely pained. 'Friend, I applaud your sense of honour and your loyalty to your friend, but this is foolhardy. Ye cannae win. Your sacrifice will come to nought. Let us pass. Live your life.'

'Live my life knowing that I allowed my friend to be taken by a rabble? What kind of life is that?'

'A wise one, friend.'

While they debated, the people immediately around them had fallen silent but further afield there were still cries and shouts. The majority of the mob did not know what was happening in the vicinity of the entranceway and were becoming impatient. It would be but a matter of moments before those at the rear would begin to press forward, forcing those in the vanguard to proceed, and all talk would cease. Flynt and the General stared at each other across the ground. The pistols in Flynt's hands did not waver, he was pleased to note, even though he could feel the terror of death rising within. His rational mind exhorted him to back down but that other part, the part that often ruled his actions, still insisted he could not. He thought of his life. He thought of what he had that was worthwhile and came up with nothing. He was a thief and a scoundrel, he knew that. He had stolen and he had killed. If he had to die, then let it be for a lost cause. He was ready.

Raised voices to his left drew his brief attention to the alleyway from the High Street. Someone was demanding to be allowed through and at first he felt the faint hope that it was relief from the castle, then realised they would approach from the other direction. The Town Guard, perhaps, having somehow broken their siege? But as bodies shifted or were shouldered aside and finally the line at the front ruptured, it was only two figures who stepped into view.

Gideon came first, one of his old flintlocks in his hand, followed by Cassie, similarly armed. The two men with muskets swung towards them but Gideon raised his weapon. 'Now, lads, let's keep fingers off triggers, eh?'

Hugh gave his men a nod and they swivelled their aim back in Flynt's direction, allowing his father and Cassie to join him.

'What in the name of Jesus are you two doing here?' he hissed through gritted teeth.

Cassie said nothing as she crossed before him to stand on his right, but Gideon spoke while covering his left. 'Did you think I would let my son do this alone?'

Despite his anger, he felt warmth steal over him. He turned to Cassie. 'You declared this to be folly.'

'And so it is,' she said, her pistol sure and steady. 'But Gideon was right, you couldn't face this alone.'

'And Rab?'

'I believe you hit him harder than you meant to. When last I saw he was still too groggy to even walk. Mother Mercy tends to him.'

He risked giving her a sideways look, which she sensed and returned. Her voice was even but her eyes danced with excitement and fear.

'This is a mistake,' he said. 'I told you to stay safe.'

'Aye,' she said, 'but this was my mistake to make. You don't rule me, Jonas Flynt.'

The General had watched the reunion with amusement. 'Reinforcements, I see, friend. It'll make no matter. The end result remains the same, apart from how much blood is spilled.'

Flynt whispered to Cassie, 'Can you shoot that thing?'

'Aye, perhaps not as well as you but I'm proficient.'

This surprised him. There was not much call for marksmanship in Edinburgh. 'Who taught you?'

She jerked her head towards Gideon. 'The same person who taught you.'

Gideon heard the exchange. 'May I suggest we concentrate on the situation before us? We can discuss the wisdom of our presence and who's the better shot when all is done.'

'Gideon,' said the General, taking a step forward, then halting again as Flynt steadied the pistol trained on him. He raised both hands before him in a calming fashion. 'Gideon, you are a reasonable man, can you no make your boy see sense?'

'Hugh,' replied Gideon, 'you were always a sea lawyer, ever ready to argue. But there is a time to be reasonable and there is a time to do what's right, no matter how *un*reasonable. This is one of those times.'

Sea lawyer, his father had said. So Hugh had spoken the truth about that, he had been a seafarer like Gideon. Again Flynt recalled the rolling gait of the man in the Grassmarket and became even more convinced it had been Hugh. Had he been discussing this action with Moncrieff and the Baillie? Was this a means of ridding themselves of a troublesome issue without betraying their class and own interests? Or was this an example of the hand of the Fellowship at work once again, disrupting, causing chaos, undermining order?

The General widened his arms as if to embrace all around. 'You're hopelessly outnumbered.'

'What's right does not lie in force of numbers, Hugh. What's right is merely what's right.' Gideon raised his voice beyond the General to the faces around and behind. 'Most of you know me and you know I would not be here if I didn't think this action was wrongheaded.'

'And what of the slaughter on the Grassmarket, Gideon?' The voice came from an unseen source further back in the crowd. 'What was that?'

'It was wrong, aye, there can be no denying that. But you know the saying about two wrongs and a right and this is just as wrong.'

The General countered. 'And for what you think right you will sacrifice your boy and the lass?'

'I have a name, Hugh Gordon, and well you know it,' said Cassie. 'And Gideon is not sacrificing anything. I'm here because I wished it.'

A patronising smirk crossed the man's lips. 'You've been too much influenced by your man, Cassie. I'm surprised he is not here.'

'He is indisposed.'

'So you're here in his stead.'

Cassie's eyes narrowed. 'You don't listen, do you, Hugh Gordon? I'm here of my own volition and at the behest of no man.'

Despite his strong feeling that their presence was foolhardy, Flynt felt a sense of pride. Much of his adult life had been solitary, shunning close contact. Now they were together, his father, the woman he had come too late to realise he loved. They may be facing death at the hands of this mob but a sense of wellbeing flooded his body, a feeling that perhaps anything was possible. He could see unease drifting between the faces of some of the crowd, Gideon's words having more effect than anything Flynt – a stranger to them – could do or say, while Cassie's bravery was also taking its toll on their resolve. He began to think that there was a chance they could all walk away from this situation.

And then he heard the bolt behind him sliding free and the lock being turned. Voices rumbled in the throng and a few smiles. Flynt did not turn, thinking it was the serjeant come to assist and was ready to order him back inside.

Then he heard Charlie's voice say, 'Stand down, Jonny.'

He turned and saw his friend standing with Serjeant Balfour, and what was worse they had emerged unarmed. 'Damn you, Charlie, what are you doing? Serjeant, I told you to stay inside.'

'He's still my captain,' said Balfour, his hands raised in apology. 'And these were his orders.'

Charlie was at his side now. He had donned his tunic and his three-cornered hat and he faced the people with a determined look. His skin was pale and his eyes leaked fear but his voice carried some measure of command as he spoke over his shoulder. 'Return to the main hall, Serjeant Balfour. You have prisoners to guard.'

The serjeant ducked back behind the door and again it was locked and bolted.

'You're a bloody fool, Charlie Temple,' Cassie muttered. 'We felt the tide turn.'

So she had sensed that too. But now it was lost.

'I will not let you die for me, not one of you,' said Charlie. 'I lost you once, Jonny, thanks to my cowardice, I will not lose you again. I will not lose any of you.'

'Charlie,' Flynt objected.

'No,' Charlie said, his voice firm, despite the terror that was obvious to Flynt. 'What occurred in the Grassmarket was my responsibility. I was in command. I must face justice.'

'Not this way.'

'This way or another, it makes little difference. The people may be correct, perhaps the authorities would not press charges, but I disagree. I think they will and there can only be one sentence. It might as well be tonight. It is as good a time as any.'

'The garrison will come...'

A calm that was quite unnatural to Charlie had settled upon him and his smile was ghostly. 'No, Jonny. This man speaks the truth. They will not risk another massacre, not to save my life.' He laid a hand on Flynt's arm, gently forcing it down. 'Give it up, Jonny. You tried and I love you for it, I love you all, but this is not Thermopylae, you are not Leonidas and that godforsaken hole back there is not Sparta. You need not forfeit your own life, none of you need do so.' He stared deeply into Flynt's face. 'We both know I am unworthy of such a sacrifice.'

Flynt remained ready for action but his rational mind told him Charlie's words were true. His friend was intent on giving himself into the hands of the mob. He had finally found the courage that had escaped him so often in the past. What would more blood on the streets avail anyone but martyrs, and the world had more than enough of them.

'You're a bloody fool, son,' said Gideon but his tone advertised that he had reached a similar conclusion.

Gideon lowered his pistol first, then slowly Flynt followed. Only Cassie kept hers steady, her eyes glinting with fury.

'No,' she said, 'we can stop this.'

'Cassie,' said Flynt. 'It's over.'

'No!'

Flynt laid his hand on the muzzle of her pistol and gently forced it towards the ground. 'It's done, Cassie. Charlie has made his decision. Our cause was lost as soon as he unlocked that door.'

Cassie glared at him but allowed him to slip the weapon from her hand. She transferred the heat of her gaze to their friend behind them. 'We had them, Charlie. We had them.'

Charlie looked towards the multitude. 'No, Cassie, it was a stalemate is all. It would have ended in bloodshed and I can have no more of that on my conscience.'

With their firepower no longer levelled men rushed forward to seize them and hold their arms fast. The General forced his way through and eased Flynt's pistols from his grasp, giving them an admiring glance before he faced Charlie. 'You're a brave man, Captain.'

A nerve quivered in Charlie's cheek even as he affected a weak smile. 'I wish that were true. If it were, we would not be at this work.' He tried to shrug away the hands restraining him. 'I will walk unaided, if you please.'

The General nodded and signalled that the men should set him free. Charlie clasped Flynt's shoulder. 'Thank you, my friend. You're the best of us all.'

Flynt felt something lodge in his throat. 'I doubt that, Charlie. I really doubt that.'

Charlie gave Gideon a grateful nod but could not face Cassie, who retained a defiant expression as she stood ramrod stiff between two captors. As Charlie passed her, he said softly, 'Take care of them, Cassie, Rab and Jonny both. They need you.'

And then he walked away, the crowd parting before him. The General watched him go then turned back to Flynt.

'Ye did what ye could, friend,' he said. 'No one will blame ye for it, on that ye have my oath.'

Flynt struggled with anger and fear, not for himself, but for his friend who was walking so bravely to his death. 'This is wrong,' he said.

'You are damned right this is wrong, Hugh Gordon,' Cassie said, her mouth little more than a slit. 'And you will pay for this night's work, by God.'

'Aye,' said the General, and there was sorrow in that single word, 'but sometimes what is wrong is the only right thing to do.' He held out Flynt's pistols. 'I trust you on your honour, all of you, that you won't attempt to use these again.'

Flynt nodded. He knew he was beaten. The General gently eased the hammers back in position and handed them over, then motioned that Gideon and Cassie should also have theirs returned to them. 'Those are fine weapons, sir,' he said to Flynt.

'You know of such things?' Flynt said, noticing that the man motioned for the two musket bearers to position themselves at their flank. Flynt's word may have been given but the mob leader would know well that promises were easily made and just as easily broken.

The General smiled. 'I was no always a ditch-digger, friend. We all have a past that we would wish to forget, even though life has a way of reminding us of it. Even you, I suspect.'

As Flynt stowed the pistols in his belt he considered if General Hugh Gordon's past had included military service, given his commanding ways and the ease with which he had handled the pistols.

'Ye'll accompany your friend to his destination?' the man asked.

Flynt did not wish to but knew he must. 'I will, but my father and Cassie will not.'

'You don't speak for me,' Cassie argued.

He turned to face her. 'Cassie, you don't want to see this.'

'I've seen men die before. We are over-fond of such in Edinburgh.'

'Not a good friend and not like this. It will be ugly.'

'Listen to him, Cassie,' said the General.

She turned her ire upon him. 'You do not get to be so familiar, Hugh Gordon, not after this night's villainy.' She withered him with the fire in her eyes then returned them to Flynt. 'I will see this through. We cannot let him face this alone.'

Flynt looked to Gideon for support but saw none forthcoming. He sighed and held up his hands in submission. 'Where do you take him?'

'To where it began,' said the General. 'To the Grassmarket.'

16

There had to be thousands of people now crammed into High Street and Lawnmarket, perhaps even as far as the Canongate. Flynt had suspected a greater number than he could see, but now that he was enveloped in the heart of this behemoth of humanity he felt more than a little overwhelmed. They could never have won. The very idea that he could have stemmed the anger that oozed from every pore in those around him was ludicrous. And yet he knew, somehow, he would have seen it through.

With bodies jammed this close together, forward motion was difficult and part of him hoped, thus impedimented, he would be unable to reach the Grassmarket before it was over. He had seen more than enough death, he knew he would see more before his time was over, but he did not wish to see his friend die even though he knew within his heart that he must. The General used his size and his powerful voice, not to mention his very presence, to clear a way for them to catch up with the vanguard around Charlie. Seeing the man push his way through, Flynt once again noted a familiarity in the way he moved. He was convinced now that it had been Hugh he had seen with Moncrieff and Wilson.

Now walking a few feet behind Charlie, Flynt felt something like pride when he saw how well he carried himself. He knew that his friend would be terrified to his very bowels but no observer would have been aware. His back was straight, his head was high, his stride was steady. He had to know what faced him and yet he was determined to meet it with dignity.

Down the West Bow they marched, a piper blowing a lament, the drummer marking the time in funereal fashion. This was a parade but there was no jollity here, no sense of triumph despite the pent-up rage. It was a solemn business and it would be conducted as such. They passed Rab's shop and Flynt wondered if he had by now regained his senses and was somewhere behind this vast host, trying to reach them. There was an interlude at a mercantile while the owner was roused from her private rooms. A length of rope was duly purchased, an unexpected display of honour, Flynt thought, for though this was a mob intent on an unlawful killing, they were not thieves.

Finally, they reached the Grassmarket. The gallows stone was denuded of the gibbet but that mattered nothing. On the far side of the open space stood a dyer's shop with a sturdy pole protruding above the window. Charlie was positioned beneath it and the end of the rope thrown over the wood. They pinioned his arms and looped the noose over his head.

The General stepped before him. 'Is there anything ye would wish to say, Captain?'

Charlie appeared not to hear his words. He appeared even more deathly white than before, but as he searched the faces behind the General and picked out Cassie, Gideon and himself, Flynt saw a warm smile crease his friend's eyes.

'Remember Cicero, Jonny,' he said, his voice broken, struggling to make itself heard through the terror he swallowed down like a poisoned draught. 'Friends, though absent…'

'…are still present,' Flynt said with him. Charlie's wan smile seemed pleased.

'Is that all?' the General asked.

'Aye,' said Charlie, stiffening his stance. 'Let's get it done, damn you.'

A movement on the far side caught Flynt's attention and he saw Blueskin and his companion push their way to the front of the crowd. Blueskin barely glanced at Charlie at the end of the rope before he took note of the armed escort still at Flynt's back. Flynt had no idea how seriously the man took Wild's instruction to safeguard his person but he did not wish to risk an incident

246

now. He shook his head to dissuade him from any action and Blueskin shrugged then refocused on Charlie. Despite the nausea building within him, Flynt did the same.

The smuggler's death had been a merciful one, whether by accident or design, but there was to be no drop for Charlie, no welcome snap of the neck. This hanging was basic and brutal. It took four men to heave him aloft, their faces straining, their breath expelling in grunts. Charlie's legs kicked and he spun in the noose, his face contorting in a hideous grimace and even in the torchlight the colour change was evident. Whereas before he had been almost white, blood now enflamed his cheeks. A hoarse gasp escaped between his clamped teeth, becoming a rattle as the life was choked from his struggling body. The hanging party fought to retain its grip as the rope tightened and twisted. Charlie had earlier resigned his body to his fate but now his spirit battled to cling to life, his visage distorting ever further, the discolouration seemingly swelling his misshapen features. His eyes bulged and his tongue grew engorged and forced itself from between his lips. His shoulders writhed and jerked as his hands attempted to free themselves from the ropes that bound them.

A woman's wails rose from nearby to join sobs from all around them. Marching to drum and pipe to demand their version of justice was one thing but now that it was being done they recognised the horror of it. Flynt shot a glance at Cassie and saw she was fixated upon the ghastly sight, her eyes wide and liquid, the light from the torches reflecting like fire on a dark pool. She had seen men die before, she had said, as had the majority of those around them, but this was not like the judicial murder of the daytime with its procedure and speeches. This was work done in darkness, with the only sounds being the sobs, the scrape of rope against wood, the rasping exhalations of the men holding it and, over all, the croak of Charlie's dying breaths. He wanted to turn her away, to shield her from the savagery of it all, but he knew she would not thank him for it. If she wished to hide from it, she would, but he knew the hold such things can have. His eyes were drawn back to Charlie as he spun and kicked against the hemp biting into

247

his throat and scraped away the flesh, his face even more swollen and flushed. Flynt felt his bile burn from gut to gullet and he himself wanted to avert his eyes from his friend's suffering but he could not. Charlie had shown strength of character that he had not during life by facing this reckoning, and he would not let him down by displaying weakness.

'Dear God,' said a man nearby, the two words sounding like lumps in his throat.

And then, of a sudden, it was over. Charlie's frame convulsed one final time, his legs stiffened as if trying to reach the ground and a dark stain spread across his groin as his bladder voided. His muscles and sinews and nerves stilled as a misty effusion of breath, all that was left of the air trapped in his mouth, floated into the chill night air to vanish beyond the glow of the torches.

The woman's keening faded. The men at the rope tied their end to a hitching post nearby and then took their ease, each one avoiding the sight above them as if they were now ashamed of their labours. Others among the crowd stared at the body as it swayed in the noose, the creak of the pole unusually loud in the silence.

Then, as if a sign had been given, they began to disperse, melting away like water into the earth. They vanished into wynds and closes, they slipped down the Cowgate and along Candlemaker's Row, they scattered to the West Bow and beyond the West Port. Flynt's two guards seemed to evaporate into the exodus and, now at liberty to move, he stepped forward to stand below his friend's body, staring up at the face, still warped by his death throes, his distended eyes looking down at him as if accusing him in their blankness. A shoe had come off during his struggles so Flynt reached down and gently replaced it, his hand lingering on the foot to steady the slight undulation of the whole. He thought of that final breath and idly wondered if it would continue to rise and rise into the night sky, a part of his friend becoming one with the heavens forevermore.

He sensed rather than saw the General at his side. 'I am truly sorry, friend.'

'This was senseless,' replied Flynt.

'This was barbarity,' Cassie interjected.

The General stared at the body and stated in a solemn tone, 'This was justice.'

Flynt whirled on him with such vehemence that the man took a few paces back in alarm. 'Justice? There is no justice in a life for a life. That is only vengeance. What occurred here yesterday was tragic and even criminal but it was done in panic, in fear. What you and your mob did this night was done with cold heart and calculation. Charlie did not set out to kill but you did. So no, *General*, this was not justice but murder, and God damn you for it. God damn you and all your accomplices to hell.'

The General absorbed Flynt's rage in silence. Even Cassie was taken aback by its intensity, and in truth it had also surprised Flynt. The passion had burst forth unbidden and unheralded by thought. He seldom spoke without consideration of his words but he did so now and did not regret it. The General gazed at the body above them and Flynt thought he saw tears there.

'God may well damn us, friend, for who among us has no sinned in one way or another,' said the man, his words tinged with sadness. 'But there was a butcher's bill to be paid for the deaths he caused.'

'And Charlie might well have paid such a bill but through legal means.'

'We could not be certain.'

'You did not give it a chance,' said Cassie. 'You convinced yourself the law would not act to provide excuse for murder. You may dress this up as much as you will, but Jonas is correct, that was what this night's work was. Murder. And I am ashamed that I saw so many good people here tonight. Neighbours. Customers. Even friends. This brings disgrace upon us all, Hugh Gordon.'

The man the people had named General now looked at the ground as if ashamed. 'I regret this is a matter on which we will never agree. But it is done now and there is no undoing it.'

A shout from the West Bow drew his attention and Flynt saw a line of torches approaching. The Town Guard, emboldened by the absence of any peril, come to save their captain. Too late, though. Far too late.

'Goodbye, friend,' said the General to Flynt, backing away. 'I hope we never have to meet again, for I fear one or other of us will come off worst.'

As the man turned to make his escape, Flynt said with heavy irony, 'I hope you sleep well after your labours here, General.'

The man did not turn but his words were coated with sorrow. 'I fear I will not.'

Flynt watched him run beyond the range of the torches that had been tossed to the ground, regretting that his grief and his temper had prevented him from thinking clearly and interrogating him on his meeting with Moncrieff and Wilson. He had hinted heavily that some council members would be happy to have this matter taken from their hands, that they could not be seen to betray their class but at the same time knew that only Charlie's death would calm the blood of the people. Questions now rolled around his mind as he watched the man vanish in the darkness. He wondered if some deal had been struck that the mob would meet no opposition. He recalled de Fontaine's words about all not being what it seemed and considered whether mob and council were two wheels working against each other to reach an agreed outcome. Or was the hand of the Fellowship at work here, meant, perhaps, to stimulate unrest in the city, to promote instability? It occurred to him that Moncrieff may himself have plotted to undermine authority by beginning the rumour that Charlie was to be allowed to go unpunished.

Blueskin grabbed Flynt's arm. 'We must be on our toes too, Flynt. It will not do us well to be caught here.'

The guard rushed across the Grassmarket and Flynt nodded. Gideon instructed them to follow him and they ducked into the lane leading to the grounds of Heriot's Hospital and thence to Greyfriars Kirkyard, where they scaled a wall, his father showing surprising agility. Once there Gideon felt sufficiently safe to stop and allow them all to catch breath.

'That was a rum deal,' said Blueskin. To his credit he appeared shaken. 'Ain't never seen nothing like it outside of bloody Tyburn.'

Flynt did not reply for he had no wish to discuss his friend's death with Blake. He did have need to distract himself from it so he walked ahead, giving the man a curt signal to follow. Flynt ensured Cassie and Gideon were sufficiently to the rear before he asked, 'Did you have any luck in your mission?'

Although Blueskin's expression was not clearly visible in the dark, he heard a self-satisfied grin in the man's voice. 'Aye, we encountered a maid who was sneaking out to join the hullabaloo in the street.'

'Did she tell you anything?'

'She did, after I used my charm on her.'

Flynt suspected that Blueskin's charm merely extended to a stout club and a painful journey up a back alley. 'You did not harm her?'

'No need. A few silver words from me as we offered to escort her to the show and her tongue was well loose.'

Flynt felt the rub of irritation at the casual way Blueskin had described Charlie's death, as if it was an entertainment for the pleasure of the masses. 'And what did this maid tell you?'

'You man has left Edinburgh this very day.'

Damn, Flynt thought. Madame de Fontaine had told him that the transaction was not yet complete and she was leaving Edinburgh. Now came news Moncrieff had already moved on. It did not take a huge feat of deduction to conclude that where one went, the other followed.

'Did you glean from her his destination?'

'She did not know. Her master is not in the habit of discussing his movements with the likes of her, she says.'

'Damn it,' Flynt said, the vestiges of his frustration still evident.

'She did say one other thing, that he was dead keen to be furth of the city before nightfall. That's the word she used, *furth*. I takes that to mean away from here, right?'

'Aye,' Flynt said absently. He had to discover where Moncrieff had gone, for that was where he would find Madame de Fontaine and the will. There was only one man who might now tell him where that was. He stopped and faced Gideon. 'Faither, where will I find Baillie Wilson?'

London

His father had once told him that a man who watched, studied and, above all, listened would rule the world, and though Charters had little desire to be any kind of potentate, he did rule his world of shadows, and he did that by watching, studying and listening. The men who surrounded him in the private room of a tavern off Holborn were all rulers of their own little worlds of politics, commerce and the military. They had dined well and the talk was flowing as freely as the liquor. Female company had not yet arrived but was imminent and Charters knew this was the period when tongues were loosened by alcohol, convivial like-minded company and the anticipation of priapic adventure. There was gossip aplenty, of course, but there can be secrets in such loose talk and Charters knew well that the man who listened and soaked in such secrets was powerful indeed.

The man at his side, Sir Francis Spooner, who Charters knew only vaguely as someone of authority in the East India Company, was discussing the Scottish situation with another man, Raymond Blaine, an adventurer in the financial sense if not the physical. He was Irish by birth, although he kept that well hid, but Charters knew of his antecedents and had tucked the intelligence away for future use.

'They are damnable barbarians, the lot of them,' said Sir Francis, his voice bloated by wine and his face the colour of rare beef. 'Running around in skirts, eating grass like beasts, no doubt. They should be thankful we are come to civilise them.'

Blaine had drunk little, Charters had noted, and he sat back in his chair in a relaxed manner, his hand fingering the stem of his wine glass. He was in his fortieth year but his hair remained as black as coal and his smooth features were thoughtful. 'Perhaps,' he said, 'they feel aggrieved by the additional taxes imposed following the Act of Union. They had relied much upon the linen trade and you must admit the export duties imposed were deeply unfair.'

'Damn them, sir! Did we not buy them and are we not then entitled to tax them? And now they rebel against their betters, such as it is, for I hear they sit on their ragged arses and do nought…'

'The Earl of Mar awaits the Pretender, I understand.'

Sir Francis dismissed this with a splutter, spreading gobs of red wine and what looked like fragments of meat onto the tabletop. 'That cur will not venture forth from where he hides, mark me, sir. No, the Scotch have no stomach for the fight, let me assure you, and they will sit there until they give up or are forced out.'

'I understand they are on the move,' Charters said, seeing no reason to keep secret the contents of a despatch he had received that very evening. The news would be on the streets by morning. The intelligence report had said they were only preparing but Charters felt certain they would be on the march by now.

Sir Francis regarded him with astonishment. 'The devil you say? And do they move forward or backward?'

'To Stirling, I believe,' said Charters, raising his glass.

Sir Francis digested this as he attempted to hook a sliver of mutton from between his teeth with a fingernail. 'No matter. Their inactivity has given Argyll time sufficient to muster his troops. Bobbing John is no match for His Grace, mark me.'

Charters' intelligence suggested that the Jacobite forces still outnumbered the government troops by at least two to one but he kept that to himself. Some facts are best not bruited abroad. But Sir Francis was correct in his assessment, even though the closest he had ever come to action was grappling with a doxy in the room next door. The Duke of Argyll was a superior commander to the Earl of Mar and Charters hoped that would be enough in the conflict that was bound to come.

Sir Francis succeeded in loosening the fragment of meat and licked it off his finger. 'This ridiculous uprising will soon be over, I will take my oath on that. Mar's head will tumble at the Tower, the Pretender will cower abroad and the skirted Scotch will run back to their holes in the ground like the pitiful wretches they are.'

'It will not end there, I fear,' said Blaine. 'There is deep resentment, and not just in the north. The Scots will not lie down for long.'

'Nonsense,' Sir Francis said. 'They are a beaten people. We have catched them, sir, and we will hold them fast. Our nation will be the strongest since the age of the Caesars, thanks to English brains. The Scots will benefit from it when they understand they are a beaten people and come to respect their masters.'

'Perhaps, Sir Francis,' said Blaine, 'that is the very issue and attitude which vexes them most. It was an Act of Union, was it not? A union of equals?'

Charters agreed with Blaine's assessment but he would never give voice to it. He believed that the kingdoms united could be a force to be reckoned with, but it had to be on an equal footing. London had a habit of viewing anywhere to the north and west as mere provinces and that must change if there was ever to be true harmony. Unfortunately, he feared the likes of Sir Francis – ill-informed, patronising and downright insulting – would exist long into London's future, while there would always be those men on the opposite side who would view anything from the south with deep suspicion if not outright hostility.

'More nonsense, sir.' Sir Francis waved his hand. 'Did you not hear me when I said they are barbarians? How can a people who dine on sheep's blood ever be seen as equals to the greatest nation on earth? They all but sank themselves with that preposterous Darien endeavour, an act of mercantile empire-building that failed through shoddy planning, and needed England to bail them out. No, sir, a union it may have been but it was between a greater and a lesser, and the sooner they learn that, the better it will be for all concerned. This rising is but a piece of comedy that will soon be over.'

Again, Charters knew it was not as simple as that but this too he kept to himself. News that a detachment of Jacobites had struck at the north of England was not something that should be shared. As Sir Francis exemplified, there was more irritation than alarm over the rising, but that could change if it was known that even as they argued and dined and drank, a band of Scots and hard-fighting border troops were closing on Preston. They had already overcome a detachment of militia. While the conflict remained in Scotland it seemed so very far away and to many in London even the northern towns were like foreign lands. However, the idea that English noblemen had joined with the Scottish rebels might cause consternation in the city among men such as Sir Francis and Raymond Blaine, and that had to be avoided.

Charters was troubled, however, but not by the news of the assault on the northern shires, for in that Mar had made a fatal error. He should have had the border forces attack from the south and catch Argyll on two fronts but instead he had sent some two thousand of his own men to rally with them. They had then struck out south rather than north. Sir Francis was correct in one thing – the Highland troops had a habit of heading for home when they grew tired or felt they had gone far enough and some had already deserted the Jacobite host. The borderers apart, there had not been the hoped-for flood of English recruits to the Stuart standard, and a strong Hanoverian force was already hot-footing from Newcastle to Preston. The government commanders were competent men and Charters had little doubt they would over-come the Jacobites when they caught up with them.

There remained the vexing question of the will. It still had the potential to turn the heads of those English nobles who hesitated to join the Jacobite forces. If it existed, if its contents were as they feared, and it fell into Jacobite hands, then it could prove just the tool required to bolster the timid hearts and minds of other men in England – not just those Roman Catholic borderers but also disenchanted former military commanders who had lost their commissions, Tories who had lost their power when His Majesty favoured the Whigs, and the power-mad who saw a way to increase their influence. It could also embolden the French to at the very least send munitions and supplies, if not manpower, and French gold was spent just as easily in England as it was in Paris.

Not knowing the lie of the land regarding that blasted document was damnably annoying. He should have arranged some kind of conduit for Flynt to keep him apprised of events, but then Flynt would probably never have used it. He was his own man in many ways and while that was useful it could also be vexing. Confident as he may be that, under present circumstances, the Scottish rising and its offshoot in the north could be contained, the continuing possibility of that damned document's existence remained an unknown factor. And Charters did not like not knowing.

Edinburgh

That Andrew Wilson was surprised to see Flynt standing over his bed was evident by his expression, though the terror in his eyes was more likely due to the pistol that he found wedged in his mouth.

'I would have you rise, Baillie Wilson,' Flynt said softly so as not to wake the woman sleeping on the far side of the bed. 'And gently, for any move to resist will most surely result in this pistol going off, and we wouldn't want that, would we?'

Wilson did as he was bid, easing himself from the bed and reaching for his breeches at its foot. Flynt shook his head. 'We'll have you just as you are, my friend.'

The man was covered in a thin shift, for which Flynt was grateful as he had no desire to gaze upon his skinny, grey body. However, although his modesty was covered, he would feel exposed. The fact that the lady snoring in the bed was not his wife made him doubly vulnerable. Gideon had told him that Baillie

Andrew Wilson was a man who loved his wife, a rotund woman with a ready laugh that hid a steely nature and a whiplash temper. He was a man who was stern but fair in the upbringing of his three children, two daughters and a son. He was a man who nodded solemnly in kirk when the minister preached against sin. He was also a man who visited this widow at least twice a week in order to comfort her in her grief. That the widow was Annie Gilchrist, whose married status had never been sanctified by Kirk or God and whose adherence to whatever bond she had with her dead husband was tenuous even while he was alive, meant that such visits were kept from his family. But people see and people talk, and they often did so while sharing a convivial ale in Gideon's tavern.

Flynt had first visited Wilson's home, being told by his wife that he was off on council business. 'Although what kind of council business he would have on this night, I don't know,' she had said, her face clouding. 'There is dark work afoot.'

Flynt knew well what dark work had been afoot but the news had obviously not yet reached Mrs Wilson. He had thanked her and then moved to Annie Gilchrist's home on the second floor of a close by the house once occupied by John Knox, both addresses supplied by Gideon.

Now he was in the cramped parlour of the small apartment, Wilson shivering with both cold and fear, the pistol still wedged between his teeth.

'I'm going to remove the weapon from your mouth now. If you cry out I will shoot you. Have a care, sir, for I am in no mood to be patient. I've watched murder being done, I suspect at your behest, so believe me when I say that I need only the slimmest excuse to put a ball into your black heart.'

He eased the pistol barrel free and took two steps back but kept the weapon levelled upon Wilson.

'Now, I need to know where Moncrieff has gone.'

Wilson seemed entranced by the flintlock's unwavering aim and was at first confused by the question. 'My Lord Moncrieff?'

'Do you know of another Moncrieff with whom I may have business? He has left Edinburgh. I need to know where he is headed.' A sly look filtered through the continuing terror in Wilson's eyes and Flynt raised the weapon slightly. 'You are about to lie, sir, and I would urge you to reconsider. Now, I ask you one last time, where has he gone?'

Wilson's mouth opened, closed. He swallowed. He was calculating whether Flynt meant what he said and by the way his body slumped a little he had obviously decided that he did. 'Stirling,' he said, his voice little more than a croak. 'He has gone to Stirling.'

'Why Stirling?'

'He did not say and I did not ask. My Lord Moncrieff is careful in his dealings.'

Flynt turned this over in his mind. Moncrieff did not yet have the will, Madame de Fontaine had confirmed that. She was leaving the city too, and he would bet his weapons, his horse and, yes, his life that she was bound for Stirling. Were they planning to meet with Red John to perhaps negotiate a price with the Crown? Christy de Fontaine bore no love for the English throne, that much Charters had told him, but she was a mercenary and silver salved many a wounded ideal.

'Are you of the Fellowship too, Baillie Wilson?'

The question came as a surprise to the man. 'The Fellowship? What Fellowship?'

Flynt sensed he was feigning lack of knowledge and not very well. He withdrew his other pistol from his belt with his left hand, risked diverting his aim while he cocked it with the heel of his right, then trained it on the man's legs. 'I will blow a knee. It will not kill you but it will be agony. I will then proceed to grind the heel of my boot into the wound for some time. You will faint from the pain but I will revive you and I will continue my attentions. This can be avoided by answering my question truthfully with no prevarication.'

Wilson was disturbed by the prospect but he found some courage. 'You will betray yourself for the pistol shot will be heard and the Town Guard will come.'

'Aye, perhaps, but the majority of the company are busy at the Grassmarket seeking those who murdered their captain. By the time they reach here I will be long gone, but not before I put an end to the agony of your existence. Now, once more, are you of the Fellowship?'

He swallowed again, his Adam's apple bobbing as if in a barrel. 'No.'

'But you know of them?'

'I have heard of them. Rumours mostly.'

'And Moncrieff? He is of their number?'

'He is unlikely to tell me if he were.'

'You are not his confidant?'

'I am of use to him only.'

'And yet you and he helped provoke tonight's tumult?' Flynt saw a denial about to flourish so he stamped on it. 'I saw you both with Hugh Gordon. A little later I was set upon by at least two ruffians. You wouldn't know anything about that, would you?'

'The streets can be perilous after dark.'

Flynt waved both pistols slightly. 'Aye, that they can. And the homes of widow women too. You do not deny that you induced the mob to attack the Tolbooth?'

Another lie seemed to form but Flynt gave him a warning look. 'No, it had to be done,' Wilson admitted. 'If Captain Temple was not sacrificed then the damage to the city would have been greater.'

'So you conspired with the mob leader?'

'Expediency can make for strange bedfellows.'

Flynt sensed that was a line the man had used many times before. Also, Hugh Gordon had used the same word. 'And you would sacrifice the security of the Tolbooth for it?'

'It has happened before. It will happen again. They would have demolished the door somehow. A door can be replaced.'

Flynt could take no issue with that. 'And Moncrieff? What was his interest in this?'

Another cunning look reflected in Wilson's expression. 'You.'

That took Flynt somewhat aback. 'Me? Why?'

'He has particular enmity for you. By striking at your friend, he struck at you.'

That they were at odds was obvious but why would Moncrieff have such a hatred for him that he would engineer Charlie's death? 'For what reason?'

Wilson shrugged. The movement was almost nonchalant. 'You should perhaps question Gideon about that.'

'I am questioning you.'

'Whatever it is, it is between the two of them and you are in the middle. I know of nothing further that I can tell you.'

'Or that you *will* tell me.'

Another shrug, confidence obviously growing. 'I've told you all I can, all I know. If you're a man of honour then you'll leave now and let me cover myself and go home. It's late and my dear wife and bairns will be worried.'

Flynt wondered if he thought of his dear wife and bairns when he was tupping the grieving widow. He could tell he had learned all he would from the man, and further threats would avail him nothing. He uncocked one pistol and replaced it in his belt but kept the other at the ready. 'I wouldn't tell the guard or a magistrate of my visit, friend. For then I would have to tell all I know about your clandestine meeting with Hugh Gordon.' He backed towards the door, his remaining pistol still beaded on Wilson. 'And your lady wife would hear of your nocturnal visits to the widow yonder. Think of your position at the kirk should the session clerks hear that you are an adulterer.'

Wilson's blanching face told Flynt that final threat was the one that hit home.

17

Flynt was resolved to do the decent thing. Fifteen years before he had left without a word and he would not make the same mistake twice. On the surface, Gideon and Mother Mercy did not seem to hold his previous failure overly much against him, but he could not vouch for their inner feelings on the matter. He appeared to have rebuilt a bridge with Cassie and he did not want to risk rending that asunder once again.

They gathered in the Crown Room, seated around the long dining table, Gideon and Mercy at its head, Cassie and Rab side-by-side, their hands entwined on the tabletop. Flynt felt a twinge of envy but he ignored it as best he could. This was not the time for emotions.

The tavern was not yet open but daylight hung from the windows with all the grey promise early November could deliver. The sound of High Street commerce awakening dangled from that limp light as if the night's events had never occurred. There had been death, but life was but a creature that had to be fed. The room was chill, there was nothing but ash and the ghost of the previous night's smoke in the fireplace, but the cold mattered little because he did not intend to linger too long. He could not.

Flynt was tired. He had lain awake for some time, the events at the Tolbooth and on the Grassmarket re-enacting time and again in his mind. When he did sleep it was fitful, his dreams now not of rats feasting on the dead in Flanders but of women and children wilting under fire and above them Charlie's body floating in the air, the telltale mark of the noose on his throat. When he awoke he attempted to determine if there was anything he could have done differently, but he was as certain now as he had been then that what he had attempted was doomed from the start. Yet, knowing this, he had both breached the Tolbooth door and faced the mob alone. He had not known the why of it then and he was no wiser now. There was something within him that made him take such gambles and he knew that one day he would be the loser. That might have been the case on this occasion if it had not been for the arrival of Cassie and Gideon and, more tellingly, Charlie's act of valour, for that was what his friend's final act had been. Inevitable it may have been given the collusion between council, mob and Fellowship in the shape of Moncrieff, but Charlie had found in death the heroism he had lacked in life. That knowledge did not make Flynt feel any better.

Now, in the Crown Room in the weak light of the new day, he began by telling his father and stepmother the real reason why he had returned to Edinburgh. He told them about his life in London, his enforced service to Colonel Charters and his search for the will. Gideon did not seem surprised that he had lied. He listened from the same chair in which he had sat on the afternoon Flynt had returned – so recent a memory and yet so long ago – puffing on his pipe, his expression as inscrutable as ever.

'So you are in service to the king, lad?'

'No, Faither, I am in service – unwilling service – to a man who is in service to the king. It is a slim distinction, I recognise, but a distinction nonetheless.'

'Aye, as you say,' Gideon said, a cloud of pungent smoke expelling from his mouth. Flynt could not discern whether he accepted his reasoning. Flynt was unsure he accepted it himself.

'I didn't see you as being a noblewoman's lackey, Jonas,' Gideon added, referring to Flynt's initial story.

Flynt allowed himself a smile. 'It might be preferable to what I actually am, Faither.'

Gideon took the pipe from his mouth and inspected the burn on the tobacco. 'We are none of us perfect, lad. You are still my son and I know you. Whatever you do, there will be some honour in it.'

Flynt was not so convinced there was honour in some of his past deeds but he did not wish to explore that, not now, not here.

'I believe the document I seek is at this moment making its way to Stirling, still in the possession of Madame de Fontaine,' he said. 'I mean to intercept it before any transaction can be fulfilled.'

Rab had been somewhat sullen, either through a continuing ache in his head or because he was in a sulk over having been aggressively prevented from his course of action the night before. Whether he resented his wife being present at the Tolbooth when he was not, Flynt did not know. In truth, that was something else he was struggling to understand. Cassie had placed herself in danger but the reason for it escaped him. Was it loyalty to Charlie? As he had pointed out, she had herself called Rab's intention folly, yet she had pursued that folly herself.

Another reason had come to Flynt's mind as he had lain awake – that she was there not for Charlie's sake but for his own – but he dared not dwell upon it. For to do so would be a failure of loyalty to his old friend, who had suddenly taken an interest in the proceedings at the mention of the will being on its way to Stirling.

'So that woman,' Rab began, 'I forget her name...'

'Madame de Fontaine,' Flynt provided.

'Aye, her. So she has not yet sold it to Lord Moncrieff?'

Gideon looked up from his pipe at the mention of the name. 'He is involved in this?'

'Aye,' Flynt said. 'He may have thrown in his lot with Mar or he may be playing a double game, trying to obtain the will for his own ends, perhaps to use as a bargaining chip with London, or the Pretender, or France, or God knows who.'

Gideon seemed troubled by this but Rab leaned forward, listening intently. 'He is canny with his coin and so he would without doubt drive a hard bargain.'

Flynt allowed himself a small smile. 'I suspect Christy de Fontaine is adept at such haggling and would not give up her prize until her price was met.'

Rab considered this, then said, 'But you know for certain Moncrieff does not have it?'

'Not as of last evening. I spoke with Madame de Fontaine just before...' Flynt stopped suddenly, not sure how to say it was ahead of Charlie's death. It would be raw for some time to come, and though his dreams might dwell upon it, he could not yet bring himself to utter the words. 'I spoke with her and she hinted that it remained in her possession.'

Cassie asked, 'And if you do manage to obtain this will, what then?'

He looked directly into her face, knowing she had already surmised what he was about to say. 'I will take it back to London.'

Her features tightened and he saw the now customary flame kindle in her eyes.

Mother Mercy was genuinely grieved by the news. 'You would leave us so soon, Jonas?'

Wounded though he was by her tone, he was grateful for the excuse to break away from the anger he felt from Cassie. 'I must, Mother. It is what I said I would do.' He paused, again giving Cassie a glance. 'I no longer belong here.'

Mercy said, 'And you belong in London?'

'As much as I belong anywhere.'

'Do you have people there? Friends? Anyone you hold dear and who holds you the same?'

Flynt thought about that and came up with no one, not even Belle. All those who held him dear were in this room but he knew he had to leave them. 'No,' he said, avoiding the yearning to address Cassie directly for he could not with Rab at her side, although he seemed to be lost in thought once more. 'There is no one I hold dear. Not in London. But return I must, with or without the document.'

'When do you leave?' asked Gideon.

'Immediately. My... friends from London are preparing our mounts at the White Horse as we speak. Time is against me and I must try to make it up. If Moncrieff is for Stirling then it's always possible he's switching sides, perhaps making an appeal to Argyll for funds to buy the document for the Crown.'

Gideon considered this. 'No, he may still be on Mar's side. Or he has some plan of his own for this document. I know him. Whatever he does, he does for his own sake. He will play out this string as long as he needs to and may have good reason to make for Stirling.' He looked at Mother Mercy. 'Tell them, my love.'

Attention switched to Mercy. 'A customer came to the tavern late last night, he had travelled from Perth. He said the Jacobites are on the move at last. Mar has left Perth with some ten thousand men. He intends to take the castle at Stirling.'

Flynt knew the fortress on the plain was a key stronghold between Highland, which Mar held, and Lowland, which he did not. To retain a grip on the country entire they must take Stirling and its castle before moving towards Edinburgh and the south.

'Moncrieff may be seeking to meet with the earl and tap into his deeper pockets to meet this woman's price,' said Gideon. 'If they wish to raise further support here and in the south then the document would be a clarion call to sympathisers. But as I say, I know Moncrieff. He will be playing both ends of the game here. He may not wish to risk too much of his silver but he will happily allow Mar to contribute and then still use the will for his own ends. He won't easily relinquish possession, no matter who has invested.'

'And you are certain your Madame de Fontaine knows all this?' Cassie asked.

Flynt thought he detected a tone in her use of the word *your*, but he had not the time to dwell upon it. 'If the deeper pockets are in Stirling, then that is where she will go.'

As he spoke he thought about what lay ahead. Stirling was a distance of some fifty miles from Edinburgh. Horse was fit and healthy – he had ensured during his stay that she was well cared for – and could do that in a day and one half at a steady pace. With luck, he would encounter Madame de Fontaine on the trail and bring this affair to an end. He would have to deal with Gregor, but he had his measure now and would not allow him to come within touching distance. A ball to the head is a great dissuader.

There was little more to be said so they began to break up. Rab was still distracted or annoyed, Flynt could not tell which, and left in a hurry, giving the others only a brief bob of the head. Watching him go, Flynt was saddened, for he expected more from his friend than that. There was the possibility that they might never see one another again and all he could do was nod and go on his way. He became aware of Cassie giving him one of her long, hard looks before she followed her husband but could not fathom the emotion behind it. She knew he could not stay, she had herself urged him to make haste in his leaving, so why was she so angry?

Mother Mercy treated him to one of her rib-threatening embraces. 'You take care now, boy,' she whispered in his ear. 'And come back to us. There are people here who still love you, no matter what.'

She stepped away from him, her hands still on his arms, and examined his face. 'Aye, he's still there, that lad from long ago. Take care you never lose him. For if you do that, if the boy that lies within a man dies, then all that you were is gone forever.'

Her eyes filled with tears and she turned to rush from the room. He felt his own eyes smarting once again and averted his head lest his father see. Damn Edinburgh, damn Charters, damn the blasted will. This mission had opened old wounds and he did not like it. He could not cope with the emotions that the past few days had ignited. He wanted to be away, to get back to his old life, solitary as it was. He may not be an island but he could at least dig a moat around himself and pull up a drawbridge.

He was now alone with Gideon, who had not moved from his chair but stared at the floor, pipe still in his hand, as if thinking hard on a matter of great import. He looked up, studied Flynt for what seemed like an age, his mouth set in a determined line.

'You have something more to say, son,' he said.

'I do, Faither.'

Flynt sat in the chair opposite him and waited as Gideon stared into the bowl of his pipe and considered refilling and relighting, then decided against it. He set it in the pocket of his waistcoat, took a deep breath and regarded his son as if he knew what he was going to ask.

'Moncrieff, Faither,' said Flynt.

'Aye.' The word came out in a sigh.

'Andrew Wilson told me there is something between you two of which I know nothing.'

Gideon avoided Flynt's eyes. He had never done that before. 'Aye.' He studied the dead ash in the fireplace. 'It's something I should have told you a long time since. Something it's only proper that you know, I think.'

Does he know?

Mother Mercy's question overheard on the day he arrived came into Flynt's head. Later he had put it down to Cassie's marriage to Rab, but was there something else?

Gideon had fallen silent again, as if words were unwilling to move from brain to tongue.

'Faither?' Flynt prompted.

Gideon looked up and for the first time Flynt saw real pain present in his eyes. His father had always been a simple man, straight-spoken almost to the point of being blunt. Whatever it was he felt he had to say, it was not easy for him.

'Your mother,' he began. 'Not Mercy, your birth mother – Jenny, God rest her.'

'Aye.'

'She died, I told you, soon after you were born.'

'Aye, of a fever.' Flynt felt suspicion growing within. 'Did she not?'

'Oh, aye, she died.' Gideon paused again. 'She died. But not of a fever, except one of the mind perhaps.'

Flynt began to dread what was coming next. 'She was mad?'

Gideon shifted in the chair. 'It was madness, of a sort. A madness brought on by shame. A shame she should never have felt.'

'Faither, I think you should say what you have to say. What happened? What have you kept from me?'

A ragged breath. A swallow. 'Jenny, may she rest in peace, took her own life, Jonas. She threw herself from the top of the Hangman's Craig above the palace.'

Flynt was stunned. His aunt had told him that Jenny Flynt had died of fever soon after she had given birth to him. Gideon had continued with the tale, though the nature of the fever had never been expanded upon. He struggled to comprehend why the lie had been told.

'And what shame was so great that it made her do it?'

Gideon held his son's gaze steadily now. Flynt knew that look well, it told him his father had begun this and now it was time to finish. 'Something of which she should not have been ashamed because it was not hers to carry. The shame lay with another who believed he was – is – above such feeling.'

Flynt did not need to have it spelled out for him. 'She was outraged?'

Gideon closed his eyes. His voice became little more than a whisper. 'Aye. She died in the autumn, just after you were born, you know that. I was away at sea, had been for over two years.' He stopped talking, his eyes opening again, and Flynt saw they glistened with pain. 'Do you understand what I'm telling you, Jonas?'

Flynt's heart hammered and his mouth dried as the import of Gideon's words, of the timescale he had laid out, impacted upon him. His mother had been raped and he was the result. The shame had landed upon the victim, as it so often did with such things, and she had killed herself because of it. His mother. He felt his thoughts flounder as he tried to fully comprehend what he was being told. He had never had cause to question his parentage. He knew Gideon was often away at sea back then but had never queried the chronology between absences and conception. He had never needed to.

His next question was obvious, even though he had already guessed the answer. 'Who?'

Gideon took a long time to reply.

–

His mind swooped and whirled like a nervous bird as he climbed the stairs to his room. His body still throbbed from the beating he had taken and the stresses it had undergone the night before. Now he had this to contend with. He took each step as if he had lead weights on both feet, gripping the wooden rail for both support and assistance in the climb.

Gideon's words echoed in his mind like fragments of a dream.

She could not bear the shame…

…realised she was with child…

…born from a criminal act but the child was himself not criminal…

…an innocent…

Cassie waited for him in his room, but he felt no pleasure for he saw from her expression that she was prepared to castigate him.

'Cassie, if you have a mind to lash out at me again,' he said, 'I beg you to reconsider.'

Whatever reprimand she had prepared died in her throat as she saw his expression and the weary way he dropped onto the bed. He rubbed a hand across his face. He knew he had to be on his way but he did not have the heart for it. His world had been upended by a few words from Gideon.

'What's happened?'

He looked at her beautiful face and felt something tear within him. Life was never what was expected. He recalled words spoken by his father, by Gideon, many years before. Life was like the ocean, constantly moving, ever changing, one minute calm, the next a squall, then a storm. And humankind rides the waves like a piece of flotsam being thrown back and forward by fate. And secrets. As a youth he had left Edinburgh dreaming of honour and glory but found only venality and needless death. Before that he had never dreamed of a life with Cassie but now he wished he had. His focus had been on fulfilling his mission, not because he believed in the right of it but simply because it was a matter of self-preservation. That now seemed immaterial. As he looked at her face, waiting for an answer, he knew that she was the only one to whom he could talk at that moment.

'What do you know of my mother, Cassie? My natural mother, Jenny, not Mercy.'

Cassie's brow puckered. 'That she died just after you were born. That she worked as a seamstress. That she was beautiful and witty. That your father loved her and was desolate at her loss. My mother says she has never filled the void left by her and she has never sought to. Your mother will always remain a part of him, she says, and that was a part she could never, would never, touch.'

'Gideon is not my father,' he said, his words flat. He was not angered by what he had been told, not now. The anger had drained from him as he dragged himself up to his room. Now he felt hollow and beaten. The men who had attacked him in the street had bruised his body. What Gideon had revealed had bruised his soul.

He told her everything and while he spoke he saw his father's face again as he slumped in his chair, his face immobile as he recounted what had occurred over thirty years before, but his eyes and his voice betraying grief and anger in equal measure. He had let his father speak without interruption because he understood that Gideon had to unburden himself. He also knew why he had chosen this moment to do so.

'She had been working for his wife,' Gideon had said, 'repairing dresses, creating new ones. Her fingers were nimble, her work exquisite and she was much sought after by the quality. She made a good living, her and your aunt both.'

Gideon had paused then. 'I don't know how long Moncrieff had coveted her. Perhaps not long, for he is not one to delay his gratifications. She was a beautiful woman, your mother, and he knew she was married to me – what she ever saw in a man like me I will never know. But Moncrieff did not allow a wedding ring and words spoken in kirk to keep him from what he wanted.

His family were border reivers and they remain so. He wanted something so he took it.'

He had swallowed, closed his eyes again, perhaps picturing the scene in his mind. Perhaps he had done that many times over the years.

'She was told to hold her tongue, for society would never believe, or care, about whatever she claimed.' He shook his head. 'The woman was at fault, always the woman.' A bitter little laugh then. 'She was not even paid for the work she had done. She was sent home with Moncrieff's seed already working within her.'

He had laid his head against the high back of the chair. 'When she realised she was with child, there were steps she could have taken, women she could have consulted, but she did not. The child within her had been created by a criminal act but was himself not criminal. She could not bring herself to harm you, so she carried to term, but the shame ate at her. Your aunt watched her slowly lose herself, as she came to believe she was at fault for what had occurred, that she had somehow acted as some kind of siren, luring the *good* Lord Moncrieff into sin.' His head had shaken as if trying to dislodge the very idea. 'But she would not have. The fault lay with Moncrieff. When I returned, after your mother's death, I confronted him, of course, but he denied all. I should have killed him. I should have taken my pistol and put an end to his pestilence. But I did not.'

There was no vehemence in those final words but there was very real regret.

'He knows the truth of it, though,' Flynt had said.

Gideon's eyes had narrowed in query. 'How do you know?'

'At Rab's shop, he told me my blood would not save me. I thought he was showing some kind of respect for you...'

There had been no humour in the small laugh from Gideon. 'Moncrieff respects only power and silver.' He thought about what Flynt had told him. 'Well, at least in his heart he knows.'

Flynt knew now why Moncrieff had looked so familiar. The face he had seen that first time in the courtyard outside and in

Rab's shop bore echoes of the face he saw in the looking glass every day.

Gideon had risen then, and kneeled before him as if in supplication. 'I am sorry, Jonas, for not telling you before now,' he had said, his voice breaking. 'I had hoped it was a truth you would never need know, for you are my son even though it is not my blood in your veins. You are mine, Jonas, and you were your mother's and now Mercy's. We are family.'

Flynt knew why Gideon had felt compelled to tell him. He was about to pursue the document and Moncrieff might have it. They would come face to face once more but this time Flynt would know all.

In his room, Cassie sat beside him as he repeated Gideon's words, at one point taking his hand and holding it between hers, the touch of her fingers comforting. He became aware of the pressure of her body against his arm, of the proximity of her face to his. She had listened in silence, her only response the slight contraction of her touch on his skin. He tilted his head to look into her eyes and saw that the rebuke she had come to deliver had been drowned by tenderness. For a moment they seemed locked together, time freezing. He had the urge to lean forward, there was only a matter of inches between them, and kiss her as he used to. He longed to do so, to again feel the youthful passion they had once shared, when the world and they were different.

And then the moment was gone. This was not the time, even though they had experienced some kind of connection through his pain. The world *was* different. *They* were different. She was married to his only remaining friend and no matter how much he wanted to close the space between them and once again feel the mix of warmth and coolness of those lips and the sensual smoothness of her skin under his fingertips, he could not. He must not.

He broke away and stood, moving to the small window in order to look down at the courtyard below. He could avoid her gaze but he could not escape his own, scrutinising him from within. The one that laboured to comprehend the enormity of what he had been told. The one that struggled with guilt over the thoughts he harboured for his friend's wife.

There was a tremor in his voice as he spoke. 'I'm sorry, Cassie, I should not have told you all this.'

'Of course you should. We are family.' Her voice bore no sign of her having felt anything similar to that which had stirred within him.

Family. Gideon had said that too. They were all family. And yet he now knew he had another, even though unwelcome and unacknowledged.

He picked up his saddlebag from the floor. He had already shoved everything into it ready for travel.

'You still intend to go?' Cassie asked. 'Even now?'

'Aye,' he said, draping it over his shoulder and facing her again. The moment between them was history now. It would never be repeated.

'You will pursue that creature Moncrieff?'

'I pursue the woman. If Moncrieff is with her, then so be it.'

'And if he is?'

His jaw tightened. 'Then fate will take its course.'

She rose and moved towards him. A hand came up to brush his cheek and he flinched. She let it hang between them in mid-air for a second before allowing it to fall. 'The shadow of death, Jonas, remember?'

'Aye,' he said. 'We're old friends, that shadow and I.'

'It's a fickle friend and it will turn on you.'

Madame de Fontaine's words came back to him. *Friends, enemies, rivals. One can become another in the simple tick of a minute hand*. The same could be said about life and death. When he faced Moncrieff, they would see what happened as the clock ticked.

Cassie followed him to the door. 'If you kill him, it will be murder.'

Flynt halted on the landing. 'If I kill him, it will be justice.'

As he moved down the stairs, aware that she was watching him with horror, he remembered Hugh Gordon saying something similar the night before.

18

Blueskin had Horse saddled and ready for him in the courtyard of the White Horse Inn, but Flynt trusted no one to prepare his mount properly so he checked cinches and buckles himself. He was still reeling from what Gideon had told him, so when he had walked down High Street and Canongate, barely noticing the people around him as he passed the Cross and through the Netherbow Port, no ghosts called to him from the closes and wynds. This new and unwelcome development in his life occupied his mind and now he loosened straps and adjusted the bridle more through habit than conscious thought.

Gideon was not his father. Lord Moncrieff was.

The man had violated his mother and had paid no penalty at all.

All his life Flynt had at best harboured disdain for, and at worst despised, the nobility. Now he learned that he shared the blood of a Scottish lord. There was an irony there that failed to amuse him.

The clip of hooves into the courtyard from the stables made him glance over Horse's back to see Rab leading a grey gelding towards him, a small sack hanging from the saddle. He had a heavy coat on his shoulders, boots on his feet and an old hat, wide like Flynt's, clamped on his unruly hair. Despite his mood, Flynt felt something fly in his chest. He had thought Rab to be in a sulk but he resisted the urge to reach out and embrace him. It was not their way.

He gave him a cool look. 'You're going somewhere?'

'Aye, with you.'

Flynt shook his head and tightened the girth strap. 'This work is not for you, Rab.'

'Aye, as maybe, but I'll go all the same.'

Flynt dropped a stirrup into place and turned to face him. 'Why?'

Rab seemed about to provide a glib answer but then thought better of it. He took a breath to consider his reply more carefully. 'The truth is, Jonny, I don't know. But something compels me to accompany you. I didn't leave with you and Charlie fifteen years ago but perhaps I should have.'

Flynt moved around Horse, stroking her muzzle. 'No, Rab, you were always the most level-headed of us. Look at our lives now, Charlie and I. One is lost to us. I am' – he stopped to find the correct word – 'adrift. I have no home. You do. You have a wife who loves you, you have a son, a business. You have everything you ever wanted and have nothing to prove. Last night you were ready to place it all in peril to save Charlie and that shows you do not lack courage.'

'But in the end I didn't do it. You did.'

'Because I engineered it so, for compared to you, friend, I have nothing and that is easy to lose.'

Rab watched Blueskin and his friend lead their horses around the courtyard to stretch the animals' muscles before they set off. Blueskin gave them a quizzical glance but did not approach. Flynt wondered if the man understood this was between friends. More likely he did not care enough to inquire. Rab's teeth worked at the interior of his mouth.

'Cassie still loves you, Jonny,' said Rab at last.

Flynt did not wish to explore that subject. 'No, Rab...'

His friend held up a hand. 'It was proved to me last night, after you hit me...'

'Rab, I did that to protect you. As I said, you have a life here.'

'Aye, I see that and so does she, and yet she rushed out with Gideon to help you at the Tolbooth. I had time to think as I lay with the world spinning and I suppose I've known it all along.

She loves you, Jonny, she always has. I see it in the way she looks at you when you are together. I see it when I mention your name. I see it when she talks to our son.'

'Cassie's glad to see my back, Rab.'

'Aye, maybe so but that doesn't mean she no longer has feelings for you. When your friends there brought you home from the street, beaten unconscious, did you know she sat with you all night? Nursed you. Cared for you. Slept in that little chair in your room.'

Flynt had not known that and he struggled to find something to say. Mercy's words to him came back – *there are those here who still love you.* The pleasure he felt at the thought was instantly countered by guilt as he looked upon his friend and heard the pain in his voice.

'I always knew I was second best,' Rab said. 'Even when we were children it was always you, but it took you a time to realise it. I don't blame you for it, Jonny, not one bit. I know neither you nor Cassie would ever betray my trust. But I do need to go with you. I need her to see that there's a wee bit of you in me.' He looked down at the ground where he toed at the dirt, dislodging a small stone. 'And I need to get away from this place for a time. What happened last night has sickened me of my people.' He looked up again, his face a little brighter. 'And you need someone to look after you, Jonny. You need a real friend at your back.'

Flynt had to make an attempt somehow to assuage his friend's feelings of inadequacy, not to mention his own conscience. He already knew he would not have betrayed Rab's trust in deed but he had in thought.

'Rab, you imagine all this. Cassie's your wife. She's the mother of your child. She loves you and you alone. Aye, perhaps she has feelings for me but we are not just friends, I hope still, but also family. I allowed my chance at a settled life to slip through my fingers long ago. Cassie knows that too, but she also knows there's no going back. There are no second chances for men like me.'

Rab listened, his head bowed once more, his toe continuing to work at dislodging the stone. A smile began to ease across his face and when he looked up, Flynt was pleased to see the cheeky glint had returned to his eye. 'Aye, damned right, ya bastard. I was always the better man and Cassie kens that fine. I've maybe no got this man of mystery air that you seem to cultivate but I'm better looking and have more wit.'

'Aye, keep telling yourself that. Horse here has more wit in what comes out of her arse.'

They laughed together. It was a short burst of levity and it felt good because, even though he knew Rab remained troubled, it helped Flynt forget his own issues. He grew serious again. 'I must counsel you against this, Rab. It'll be dangerous. You've already enraged Moncrieff, and Madame de Fontaine is not to be taken lightly.'

Rab reached into the sack draped over his saddle and produced an old flintlock pistol. 'I've come prepared.'

'Dear God,' Flynt said, taking the weapon from him and examining it. He had seen this firearm before. 'This was your faither's – and it was old then.'

Rab took the flintlock from him again and held it lovingly. 'Aye, but it's well cared for. It'll hold steady if the time comes.' He gave Flynt an even look. 'As will I. I'm coming with you, Jonny. You may tell me otherwise and you may ride off with your companions but I'll follow.'

'And what of your business? Who will tend to that?'

'Bugger the business. What I said was the truth – at this moment I have no interest in it. Every patron who entered my shop will be suspect to me. I'd ponder if they were present in the Grassmarket last night. Did they put the noose around poor Charlie's throat, did they pull on that rope? Or did they stand by and cheer as it all happened?'

Flynt had heard no cheering but he did not debate it. He thought once more of the dusty look about the workshop and Cassie telling him of custom deserting the business. 'I suspected things were already slow but will you allow the shop to founder?'

Another smile, more confident this time. 'That will change. I'm the best cobbler in Edinburgh, I was taught by the best and he was taught by the best. The customers will be waiting for me on my return.'

Flynt wondered how much was wishful thinking and how much pure fantasy. 'What does Cassie have to say about this?'

Rab looked ashamed for the first time. 'I didn't speak with her.'

'She doesn't know?'

'I left her a note.'

Flynt laughed. After the morning he had had, these moments were a fine release. 'A note, by God! She will not be pleased. The customers may await you but I fear you'll suffer for that on your return.'

A flick of an eyebrow acknowledged the truth of that statement. 'So you agree to my fellowship?'

Flynt clapped him on the shoulder. 'Aye, if only because Cassie will have read that damned note by now and will flay you either way. Might as well be hanged for a sheep as for a lamb.'

Rab smiled. 'I never had the taste for reading like you and Charlie, but what was it you and he used to say about the sun and friendship?'

'It is like taking the sun out of the world to bereave human life of friendship,' Flynt quoted, but his smile faltered. 'Charlie loved Cicero.'

'Aye,' Rab said, his tone sombre. 'And if he were here, he would be joining us on this adventure. So lets us do it for Charlie, eh?'

Flynt was not so sure Charlie would have accompanied them. 'This is not an adventure, Rab, don't think on it in such a way. This may become life or death and the difference between one and the other is a cool head and a steady hand.'

Flynt thought of Lord Moncrieff and wondered how cool his head, and how steady his hand, would be when they faced one another.

Part Three

Sheriffmuir, November 1715

19

November bit deeply into the land. Flynt's journey from England had been reasonably pleasant but in the three days he had been in Edinburgh the climate had begun to show its teeth. That was the way with Scotland, the elements were as undependable as a politician's promise. It could be temperate one day and chill the next; the sun shining on a clear winter's day and then suddenly the snow appearing as if from nowhere. There were no blue skies as they headed north-west, however; the heavens were as grey as a tombstone, the air filled with sharp flecks of ice driven by a north wind and the ground beneath the horses' hooves solid with frost. This was perhaps a foreshadow of a harsh December and January, but there was something about it that Flynt enjoyed. The cold and unforgiving nature of the climate suited his mood.

They kept the River Forth to their right and, following a series of roads that were barely more than a track, rode as hard as they could without tiring their mounts overmuch. Blueskin, naturally, cared nothing for the animals' welfare, but Flynt did. They would need these horses for some time and he did not want to run the heart out of them. Anyway, he was fond of Horse. She had served him well and had never let him down. It felt good to be carried by her again.

They rested overnight in a sheep fold near Falkirk, hunching before a small fire to keep the bitter cold at bay, its flames sending flickering shadows against the drystone walls circling them. What conversation they engaged in was spare and of a general nature. Blueskin was an unwilling ally, only a member of their company through the orders of Jonathan Wild, and his demeanour and responses were surly, often griping about the weather in this cursed country. Flynt had to keep in mind that the man held enmity towards him and would no doubt seize any chance to retaliate for the shaming he had received at Mother Grady's. His companion remained taciturn but Flynt learned that he was called Dan Soames, a Cornishman by birth and a seaman by trade who had been flogged one too many times in the service of king and country so had jumped ship in Portsmouth and made his way to London to hide in the alleyways around Seven Dials. It transpired that he had a fine baritone voice and he kept their spirits up during the cold night singing shanties taught him by his fisherman father.

Later, as Blueskin and Dan slept, Flynt managed to tell Rab what he had learned of Moncrieff and his mother. Rab listened, his features dark with rage in the flicker of the firelight.

'He is a cruel bastard,' he said finally, his voice barely rising above a whisper lest they arouse their companions.

Flynt felt no need to put his agreement into words. Rab kept his eyes on the flames, as if they held him in strange fascination. 'And what will you do when you face him?'

It was a question that had gnawed at Flynt throughout the day along with the cold. 'I have not yet decided. It will be whatever is dictated by the circumstance of the moment, but for now I have a duty.'

Rab looked at their companions as they snored under their greatcoats. 'Your man Daniel has a fine voice but I do not trust him or the other.'

'Neither do I.'

'Do you think you can depend upon them?'

'Not even a little bit, Rab.'

Rab gave himself a satisfied nod. 'Aye, that's my reckoning too. It is as well I am with you then, for *I* will have your back.'

Flynt wondered how Rab would react when weapons were drawn. As boys they had found themselves in scraps with others of their age, punching, kicking, rolling around on the earth, even volleying missiles at one another from a distance. Flynt knew well that flying stones were different from flying lead, however. Rab had never found himself in the heat of battle, so Flynt resolved to do what he could to ensure his friend was kept away from any action.

They pushed on at first light, stopping to buy a breakfast of oatmeal cakes and cups of warm milk from a farmer's wife but they did not tarry long. Flynt had no firm idea how far ahead Madame de Fontaine and Gregor, or even Moncrieff, could be. He did not know if they were on horseback or travelled by coach, and although he hoped for the latter he had strong doubts. A coach on this rutted track would be slow and he suspected they would have caught up with it by now. That is, if they had even taken this route. When all was laid out in his mind, he knew too little – and in other matters, too much.

Flynt was comfortable on horseback but Rab was not a natural. He had little experience of it and was ungainly in the saddle. He was a townsman, born in Edinburgh, lived in Edinburgh and had never been anywhere else. He held the reins in both hands as if he feared the animal would bolt at any moment and stared straight ahead as if searching for any impediment in the road over which the gelding may take it in mind to vault unbidden. Flynt had examined the mount before they set off and he seemed a sturdy, placid beast, capable of speed if the need arose but unlikely to take such initiative of his own volition.

It was close to midday on the second day, although with the sun veiled by the dank clouds and the sleet still stinging it was difficult to be sure. Rab was bundled down into his heavy coat, a scarf pulled around his lower jaw, his hat low so only his eyes were visible, and he squirmed in the saddle. 'This weather is damnable inhospitable and my arse hurts astride this bloody creature.'

Flynt smiled. 'Try to be one with the horse, find its rhythms and go with it.'

Rab considered this. 'Be one with the horse. Interesting. I recall a fellow was flogged at the Cross for such a thing.' He fidgeted again, trying to find some comfort. 'I fear after this any thoughts Cassie would have of another child may be in vain. I believe my man bags have been squashed as flat as those oatcakes this morning.'

Flynt raised himself slightly in the saddle and squinted against the darting sleet. Ahead and to their left the great brooding citadel of Stirling sat above the plain on a rocky crag like a dragon watching for prey, the town itself spreading down the hill like a tail, smoke snaking into the grey air from chimneys as if the creature was letting off steam. To their right was another mound of vegetation upon rock, which Flynt took to be the Abbey Craig, from where, his aunt had once told him, William Wallace watched his forces slaughter the English army upon Stirling Bridge. It was neither castle nor crag that had caught his eye, but a cart heading their way drawn by a single horse, the rattle of goods in the back and hanging from hooks on the side rising above the rumble of wheels on the hard earth as the vehicle pitched and yawed in the uneven furrows. The man at the reins was a wizened creature, a pipe puffing smoke between his teeth, his head bare as if daring the sleet to penetrate his thick dark pate which, despite the lines on his face, bore no trace of the whitening of age. When he saw the horsemen riding his way, his hand edged towards an ancient flintlock fowling piece propped against the seat beside him.

'Steady there, friend,' said Flynt, holding his right hand up in greeting.

The man reined in his horse and regarded them through narrowed eyes. 'If you mean to rob this poor soul then know that he has no silver for you to take.' The man's voice bore the lilt of the Highlands, his tongue proficient in both Gaelic and Scots. 'All is tin here and his purse is light.'

Flynt gave him a reassuring smile. 'We mean you no harm, friend, we are not outlaws but travellers like yourself.' He gave him a small bow. 'Jonas Flynt, sir, at your service.'

The little man pulled himself erect. 'The man before you is Seumus McPhee, traveller, tinsmith, purveyor of cooking and household instruments from Highland to Lowland, clachan to town, rich to poor.'

The words were delivered in a manner that suggested he was well used to their recitation. Flynt guessed he pitched his tent on green and marketplace and called out his profession using those very phrases. Flynt had heard his like called Summer Walkers but that term seemed out of place on such a day. He was a tinker, what an old Highland soldier had told him was from the Gaelic *tinceard* for the profession they followed. He worked the tin and sold it on the road.

'Where are you headed?' Flynt asked. 'Edinburgh?'

'Aye, then on to the borderlands. Seumus McPhee has seen most of this country, apart from the lands of Kintyre and the islands but he'll get there before his time on this earth is done, you have his oath on that. And where are you gentlemen headed, if he may ask?'

'We head north, friend.'

The old man seemed to size them up, as if he was a coffin maker as well as a tinsmith. He craned his neck to look up at the castle high on its rock. 'But not for Stirling, Seumus McPhee will wager his reputation.'

Flynt smiled, wondering how much stock was held in that reputation by anyone other than Seumus McPhee 'No, not for Stirling.'

The old man grinned, revealing teeth brown from too much pipe. 'Aye, Seumus guessed as much. You'll be heading to fight. Looking for glory, no doubt, in the name of the King Over the Water.'

Flynt saw no reason to contradict him. 'What news from ahead then?'

'One army moves against the other, each dead set on leaving blood on the heather.' He shook his head in sad disbelief. 'Why we have such discord is beyond all understanding. There will be many a mother keening to the wind before this week is out.'

'Battle has not yet been joined?'

'No, the Earl of Mar' – Seumus spat on the ground as he spoke, as if clearing a bad taste left by the name – 'is just north of Stirling, while the Duke of Argyll' – he spat again – 'prepares to leave the castle and meet him.'

Flynt smiled. 'You have little time for the commanders.'

'Seumus McPhee has little time for those who would slaughter in the name of glory, God or king. Or clan, for that matter.'

Flynt liked this man already. 'And yet you are Highland yourself.'

'Aye, and proud of it, but too much blood has been spilled for the sake of clan. Seumus McPhee's own father, God rest his soul, fell in a power struggle between two chiefs. His brother too. So he took up this profession, where the only hammer he wields is to work the tin.' He gave them another searching look. 'If you want some advice, gentlemen, don't be taking yourselves any further. You are young men and you shouldn't throw your life away on the whims of princes who care only for the gold on their head and the silver in their treasury.'

'We won't, Seumus, you may rest assured on that,' Flynt said. 'We have other matters in hand.'

'So you did not come to fight?'

'No, we seek friends who perhaps share this road. Have you met any other travellers heading this way?'

The fact they were not bound for glory pleased the old man. 'Not many, not in this weather. A few such as Seumus McPhee who must do so.'

'We seek a woman and a man, perhaps conveyed by coach or cart such as yours. He is a powerful fellow, silent. The woman is of quality and speaks the Scots with a French flavour.'

The tinker nodded. 'Aye, Seumus saw them right enough. They are about two hours ahead of you, but not by coach, both on horseback. The woman passed the time of day, and a fine, fair lass she was.' He grew wistful. 'Aye, if Seumus had been just a few years younger…'

Flynt left him to his fantasies as he digested the information. Two hours ahead would take them past Stirling and further to the north, perhaps even Dunblane. If they could pick up the

286

pace without endangering their animals, they might just intercept them before they reached Mar's lines, wherever they were.

'And how far would you say the Highland army lies, friend?'

'They mass on the moor beyond the cathedral town. On the Allanwater at a place called Sheriffmuir, but I would not go near it.'

Flynt gave him a reassuring smile. 'We thank you, friend, and feel we have delayed you long enough. You must be eager to get on your way.'

'Aye,' said Seumus. 'Time and commerce does not favour the laggard.'

Flynt edged Horse to one side and Rab with difficulty jerked his to the other, with Blueskin and Dan following suit. As they watched the cart pass between them and sway along the track, Rab walked his horse to Flynt's side. 'Jonny, do you think she will have entered Stirling? Perhaps to strike a bargain with Argyll?'

'She will not deal with Argyll unless she has to, for he is George's man. She is mercenary but she favours France over England. No, she still expects the Fellowship to pay her price and she will follow Moncrieff.'

Rab chewed the inside of his mouth. 'So we go to Sheriffmuir?'

Flynt looked ahead through the flying ice. 'Aye. And pray we do not encounter any of Argyll's men, for we do not need to be impressed into their ranks.'

20

It wasn't Argyll's men but an advance detachment of Mar's High-land troops they encountered. They had skirted around Stirling and avoided Dunblane, for they did not know whether or not it was occupied by government troops. They had the smoke of the cathedral town to their rear when they rounded a copse of trees to find themselves facing a band of men on foot, their plaids, broadswords, and small, round leather-bound shields betraying them to be men of the north. Muskets were levelled in their direction and a cry went up for their officer. A man on horse-back cantered from their rear, but he bore no uniform nor any adornment announcing rank. He wore a smart suit of blue wool and the ubiquitous tricorn hat, while a sword draped from his midriff slapped against his riding boots as he trotted to face them.

Flynt held up his hand to show peace, just as he had done with the tinker. 'We are no enemies, sir.'

'Then who are you?' The man spoke with the not quite English accent of a Scot educated in the south. 'And why do you travel upon this road?'

'We form part of my Lord Moncrieff's household, in the borderlands,' said Flynt, the lie springing readily to his lips. 'We have come to support him in his fight for the King Over the Water.'

The officer regarded them with suspicion, his eyes alighting on Blueskin behind Flynt. 'None of you appear to me to have the look of servants.'

'I am groom to his lordship's fine stable, my friend here is bookkeeper to his accounts.' Flynt jerked his thumb to Rab, then gestured behind him to Blueskin and Dan. 'And these sturdy fellows are woodsmen. His lordship owns many fine acres of forested land that has to be tended.'

The officer seemed convinced. 'And does my Lord Moncrieff expect you?'

'He does. He sent word that we should join this great cause. It has taken us some time to reach here from the borderlands. We were almost catched this very day by a detachment of Argyll's men. We feared we would be forced to join their number.'

The officer nodded. 'Aye, Argyll knows we have them outnumbered and would seek to fatten his lines by any means. Damn the man for he is no true Scot.' He made a decision. 'We must return to our lines soon but first must complete scouting duties, so you may pass. My Lord Mar rests his forces at a place called Kinbuck on the Allanwater. You will find your master there, but you would be advised to head east first and then circle back west to avoid any of Argyll's patrols.'

Flynt thanked him profusely and they moved on, the Highland troops indifferent to their passing. Flynt studied them as they rode on. They were a mixture of young and old but all seemed fit and healthy. The cold did not trouble them for they were well used to it. He knew something of these hardy Highlanders. Some would have mustered willingly, more because it was expected of them out of duty to their clan leader, others perhaps had been forced by threat of eviction from their homes if they did not. They would fight well, he knew that, and they would die well. If there was such a thing as a good death.

It took them a full three hours, riding in the shadow of the Ochil Hills on their right while the light died around them, before they came upon the encampment. As they crossed a vast moorland plain, the sleet attacked them with such ferocity it was as though it had drawn courage from the gathering darkness. The ground beneath them was uneven and in places springy and marshy thanks to the water falling from the heavens and draining from the hills. Ahead they could see the twinkle of myriad fires and they smelled the tang of woodsmoke carried low on the air.

'As before, let me do the talking,' Flynt said. 'Especially you, Blueskin. I'm not sure how they would react if they heard your London accent.'

'They got Jacobites in England, don't they?'

'Aye, but damn few of them are up here so let's not risk any incidents. We are close to our quarry now so let me handle it, just as I did with the scouting party.'

Blueskin hawked up some phlegm and spat it into the night. 'All I wants is to hunker down beside a fire and get some heat in my bones. I'm sick of this God-rotted country and its bitter cold. I don't know how you Scotch survive in this world of dampness and ice.'

'We're a hardy breed,' said Rab. 'And seldom complain.'

In the gloom, Flynt saw Rab smile at him and wink. Behind him, Blueskin cursed fluently for a time before he fell silent.

They were brought to a halt eventually by a sentry armed with a musket. Flynt used the same lie as before – that they were employed by Lord Moncrieff and had come to support him. The sentry was young and looked weary and let them pass without further inquiry, telling them his lordship would be billeted at the centre of the camp.

'Just look for the tents,' the sentry said, 'for the officers are fond of their comforts.'

There was some bitterness to his voice and Flynt understood why. It was an unequal world in peace and in war. They guided their horses slowly around the edge of the camp, which seemed to stretch for miles. Mother Mercy had told them the customers she spoke to had stated that Mar had ten thousand men at his command and he could well believe it. Many of the men lay on the hard ground, their plaids wrapped around them, the fires they had lit emanating heat but not enough to completely ward off the November chill. They conversed with one another in low voices, predominantly in Gaelic. Most seemed sombre but now and then one would say something of wit and a laugh would shatter the brittle air. Somewhere in the darkness a young voice began to sing a sad lament. Flynt did not understand the words but he guessed at their meaning. It was a song of home, a song of longing, a song that perhaps spoke of sadness and knowledge of impending death. He had heard many Highland soldiers give voice to similar airs, sometimes accompanied by a lone piper, and had the meaning of the lyrics explained to him.

Flynt craned in the saddle to find the heart of the sprawl and found an area of lantern illumination some distance from them. That was where the Earl of Mar would be, accompanied by his commanders and advisors, among them, Flynt would hazard, Moncrieff. But was Madame de Fontaine also there, even now striking a bargain? Perhaps directly with the Jacobite commander? Or was she waiting elsewhere, keeping herself hidden and negotiating solely with the Fellowship? As was the norm from the commencement of this mission, Flynt knew little that was certain, not even what his next move would be. He did know that time was at a premium and he needed to reconnoitre. He brought Horse to a standstill and began to dismount.

'Find some ground a slight distance from the main body and pitch a camp,' he ordered, stretching his legs and back. 'Get some wood and build a fire. Root around, see what food you can beg, borrow or steal.'

'We would be warmer among the other men,' said Blueskin.

'Yes, but we may have to make a swift departure, unless you wish to be caught up in the hostilities.'

Blueskin's expression told him he did not wish that. The man fell silent again as he eased himself from his saddle.

As he also gratefully swung his leg over his horse to stand on firm ground, Rab asked, 'And what will you do?'

'Look around, see what I can learn.' He addressed Blueskin directly again. 'If anyone speaks to you make sure it is Rab who replies.' He faced his friend once more. 'Rab, keep to the story.'

'So we are to be mutes?' Blueskin said. Flynt guessed he was merely being sullen for the sake of it but it still annoyed him.

'Do as I bid, Blueskin,' Flynt said as he handed Horse's reins to Rab. 'Remember your brief from your master.'

Blueskin sneered. 'Aye, I remember. But that don't mean I has to like it, do it?'

Flynt could not argue with that. 'If you have to speak, be as taciturn as you can without arousing suspicion.'

Rab added, 'That means say little.'

'I knows what taciturn means,' snapped Blueskin. 'I ain't no ignorant oaf.'

'Perhaps not ignorant,' Rab muttered but only Flynt heard. Louder he said, 'Have a care, Jonny.'

Flynt nodded to him and left them to their tasks. He moved as easily as he could between the lounging men, neither too fast nor too slow in order to avoid drawing attention, though he was acutely aware that in his thick greatcoat, his wide hat, his riding boots, and carrying his silver cane, he struck a largely alien figure among the men in plaid. There were a few in more southern garb, townspeople who had rallied to the cause, he assumed, but none of them were seasoned fighters and they would fall easily to the slaughter, if their nerve held. He stepped around a few rude shelters, animal skins or blankets hung over sticks, and a number of military wedge tents, but most of the camp was open to the elements.

On foot he was able to catch snatches of conversation, mostly Gaelic but some in English. One word he caught was *biadth*, food, and now that he looked he realised how little was being consumed by the men. They were fatigued by their march from Perth and they were hungry. Mar had not ensured a proper supply line, a sign that he was not a good commander. Flynt thought of the scouting party they had encountered – were they foraging for food to feed a hungry army? He would wager that Argyll's men were well provisioned, and even though they were fewer in number, that would give them some advantage when the fighting began. As he walked, he shook his head. An army needs to be well fed before it can function properly. When these men faced Argyll tomorrow or the next day they would do so on an empty belly. They were strong men, brave men, but they would be all the weaker for their hunger. Ahead he saw the collection of command tents, circled by an array of lanterns and men with muskets. The sentry had spoken of the commanders with ill-concealed disdain and Flynt felt certain they were not going hungry. They would dine on beef and wine while their followers could only dream of stale bread.

He paused to study the layout of the tents. Somewhere within that small village was Moncrieff. The man he now knew to be his father, the man who had raped his mother. He was no longer shocked by the revelation but the rage still burned. All he had known of his mother was the likeness Gideon carried with him and the little he and his aunt had told him. And yet, the image of Moncrieff forcing himself upon her had leaped without invitation into his thoughts many times. He tried to understand what it must have been like for her but could not comprehend the effect such a violation would have. She had bottled it up for the nine months she had carried him, but such things cannot remain suppressed forever, so she took her final walk up to Hangman's Craig. What she was thinking, how she was feeling, Flynt would never know. In one devastating act, Moncrieff had been responsible for Flynt's creation and at the same time his mother's end.

A square tent, smaller than the others and set a little apart from the main congregation, became of interest to him, or rather the man ducking out of it and preparing a bedroll on the ground.

Gregor.

Flynt kept his distance, seemingly sauntering in an idle manner but keeping his eyes on the Russian as he worked. A light shone from within the tent and he saw Madame de Fontaine's indistinct shadow. Gregor, satisfied his evening lodgings met his needs, wandered off into the camp. Flynt watched him be sucked up by the darkness between the small fires and wondered where he was going. The latrine perhaps. In search of food. Who knew? The important thing was that this was an opportunity.

He took brisk steps to the tent flap and paused, listening in case the woman had company. Hearing no voices, he drew a pistol and stepped in.

Madame de Fontaine was lying on a low cot, blankets and a heavy animal pelt covering her to the chin. She registered very little surprise when he stepped into the dim glow of the oil lamp on the ground beside her.

'Jonas,' she said, a cool smile slipping with ease to her lips. 'How lovely to see you.'

'Madame,' he said politely. 'I wish I could say the same.'

'And with your weapon in your hand too.' She gazed at him from under her brows, her lips twitching. 'Have you come to take me up on my offer?'

Flynt did not know when Gregor would return so had no time for her flirting. 'The will, madame.'

'Ah, the will. Do you lack it? I can help with that for I am extremely proficient.'

He gave her a stern look. 'Where is the document?'

She affected disappointment. 'So very serious, it is most tedious. The document is safe.'

'You have not reached an agreement with Moncrieff?'

She frowned. 'Jonas, I really do think your seduction technique requires some work.'

Flynt grew impatient. 'Damn it, have you reached an agreement or not?'

She tutted at his temper. 'Such rage, it's quite unbecoming in a gentleman.'

'I believe I told you before, I am no gentleman, and you will realise that presently if you do not tell me what I wish to know.'

The thought did not concern her at all. 'I might enjoy that.'

Flynt sighed. He found this woman both exasperating and fascinating. He knew the coquettish manner was an act, although he was under no illusion that she was capable of using her sexuality when it suited her. 'Do you still have it?'

She smiled. 'Perhaps. Perhaps not.'

He looked around the tent. It was not large and there was only the cot on which she lay. His eye fell on saddlebags in the corner and, his pistol trained on her, he strode across the small space to rifle through them. One contained articles of a feminine nature, another a number of hemp sacks bulging with a substantial amount of silver coins. None of them carried documents. He picked one up and weighed it in his hand as he faced her again.

'You carry this much money habitually?'

'A lady abroad needs capital.'

He grunted, knowing this was the proceeds of the sale of the will. On a whim, he dropped the sack into his pocket.

She arched an eyebrow. 'You rob me now?'

'I will take it as a payment to salve the irritation I feel.'

Even though he was taking her money, she seemed in good humour. 'You do not like to lose, do you?'

'I do not.'

The loss of the money was accepted with a shrug. 'I will look upon it as a loan.'

'You may look upon it as you please.'

She gave him a wide smile. 'But there may come a day when I call in that debt.'

'You can but try, madame.'

The flap being thrown open and Gregor's burly figure filling the gap caused Flynt to whirl and level his pistol. The Russian snarled and crouched as if ready to spring but was halted by Madame de Fontaine ordering him to stay put, as though he were an attack dog. When Flynt turned back to her, he found she was sitting up in the cot, fully clothed, and aiming the small pistol he had last seen being wielded in the Mint. He was unsurprised, for he had suspected it would not be too far from her hand.

'Here we are again,' she said.

'Indeed,' he said, keeping a wary eye on Gregor. Madame de Fontaine had power over him, but he wondered if that would be enough.

'Do you think we will ever meet as friends, Jonas?'

'I find it doubtful.'

'But not impossible. I'll take that as a hopeful sign.'

'Hope is easy, reality sometimes not. You will not tell me where the will is?'

She thought about it. 'You know, Jonas, there is no reason why rivals cannot also be friends, so in the spirit of good future relations between us, your recent larceny aside, I will tell you. You saw my man Gregor here leave earlier, I trust?'

'I did.'

'Then you could not know it but you also saw the will leave my possession. A satisfactory transaction has been achieved between the parties, thanks to the financial aid of the Earl of Mar – and yes, indeed, the cash you took in a most ungentlemanly fashion formed part of the sum agreed.'

So the supposition that Moncrieff needed Mar's funds to seal the deal was correct. 'I repeat, madame, I am no gentleman.'

'And I now believe you. Gregor has delivered the document to Lord Moncrieff. Such a handsome man. He has a number of years on me but I will wager that old stallion yet has a gallop or two left in him.'

Flynt had no desire to pursue that subject.

'So, if you wish to continue with this obsession of yours,' she continued, 'you will have to do so with the will's new owner. My involvement in this affair has reached its conclusion. Now, may I suggest that you take your leave with all haste? Gregor, as you know, is not one for small talk and I can tell that he has taken it ill that he has discovered us in such intimate proximity within my bedchamber, rudimentary as it is. As you can plainly see, he still bears the marks of your last confrontation and, though he is a sweetheart, he is not a man to let bygones be bygones. I would lower your weapon to show him that you mean him, and me, no harm.'

Flynt could see the shadow of scratches around Gregor's eyes, which glared at him with considerable heat. He doubted if putting a ball in him would stop him should he charge, unless he managed a head shot. Even that might not do it. He exhaled deeply and lowered his pistol and carefully thrust it into his belt. Madame de Fontaine followed suit.

'There,' she said, a satisfied smile lightening her face and the room. 'Now we are all friends. Isn't that better?'

Flynt gave Gregor another glance but saw little amity in his gaze.

'Give it up,' the woman said, her tone suddenly devoid of her customary levity. 'The game is lost, can you not see that?'

Her face was more serious than he had ever seen it. 'We shall see,' he said.

'You will not relinquish this quest?'

He did not need to speak, she already knew what his answer would be. He tipped his hat to her. 'Safe journey, Christy,' he said.

Her face brightened. 'Ah, that is the first time you have used my Christian name! We make progress.'

He smiled and faced Gregor once again. They regarded each other for what seemed like a long moment, the Russian's eyes now deadened, though he made no move to shift from the tent's entrance, which he blocked like a troop of armoured cavalry.

'Gregor, be a dear and let our new friend Jonas go on his way.'

The man's eyes moved slowly to his mistress as if he was about to disregard her order but finally he stepped out of Flynt's path.

'I suspect this will not be the last time we meet, Jonas,' said Madame de Fontaine.

Flynt was now standing beside the big Russian and he first looked up at his now blank face and then back to the woman in the bed. 'Until next time, then, Christy.'

Smiling as he walked away, he checked over his shoulder to ensure Gregor was not following, but he was merely watching him go with that curiously neutral expression. He obeyed her every order but Flynt wondered how far that would go. Recognising there was no danger from him for now at least, he walked quickly, still smiling. She had charm, that woman. She was deadly and she was treacherous, of that he had no doubt, but he found himself warming to her. The game was lost, she had said, but he disagreed. The hand was lost but not the game. There were now only two players at the table.

21

Flynt lay on the hard ground, his head resting on his saddle, his body covered in greatcoat and blanket, the fire his companions had kindled dead and black with not even the ghost of smoke curling from the charred wood. He had watched the night sky slowly grey to reveal heavy clouds but thankfully, for the moment at least, no sleet or rain. He had lain awake most of the night, the cold eating at him along with his thoughts, listening to the sounds of the camp. Men snored but others remained awake, instinct telling them that this day would be the last some of them would see. Murmured conversations carried the twenty feet between the perimeter of the huge camp and where Rab and the others had settled beside a small stream. He thought he heard a boy calling out in sleep for his mother, already dreaming of a life's end far from home and hearth.

Flynt neared a conclusion too, although he knew not precisely of what. By day's end he would either have the will, be dead or in chains. Of those three alternative futures he favoured the first but would accept the second over the last.

On the other side of the fire he heard Blueskin fart in his sleep and then roll over. He stared at the man's back, his bulk still wrapped in his greatcoat, and wondered what the day would hold for him. If Flynt was successful in wresting the document from Moncrieff, would Blueskin do the same with him? Or at least attempt it? It was distinctly possible that Jonathan Wild had instructed him to relieve Flynt of the prize should they find it.

It had taken him some time after leaving Madame de Fontaine to weave his way through the camp to find Rab and the others and it was not until he heard Dan's fine baritone serenading them with the tale of a sailor's return home after a long time at sea that he was able to pinpoint their location with accuracy. They had been unable to source any food but they had built the fire and Blueskin was even more sullen, his complaints regarding the cold and this country increasingly bitter. Flynt ignored him, for he had some sympathy with the situation in which the Londoner had found himself. Life on the streets was hard but a man like Blueskin would have shelter and food. Here there was neither.

Once he had settled, he told them that the will was now in Moncrieff's hands and that he had considered finding his tent and taking it back but had rejected the idea. The area around the command centre was too well guarded and he suspected he would not get ten feet without catching a ball.

'So what is the plan?' Rab had asked.

Flynt had stared beyond the glow of their little fire into the darkness. 'There will be a battle here on the morrow, I suspect. I will use that confusion to somehow isolate Moncrieff.'

'And if he has already given the will to someone else, Bobbing John, say, what then?'

Flynt had been thinking on that possibility. 'Tell me, Rab, considering what you know about Moncrieff, do you think it likely he will have simply handed over this document after paying so dearly for it?'

Rab hugged his knees and considered this. 'No. He is no patriot. He will not have done this in a selfless way for country or king. He will use the will to further his own aims, perhaps even as some kind of offering should events go against the Jacobite forces. His son in London mouthing Hanoverian platitudes will only go so far to keep his father from the headsman's block if today goes ill for the cause. Possession of the will would save his neck if needed and, should fortune swing the other way, it would also strengthen his position with the Stuarts.'

'So the Fellowship is no selfless group?'

'The Fellowship is, Moncrieff is not.' In the light of the fire, Rab puffed his cheeks. 'You're gambling, Jonny.'

Flynt had clapped his friend on the back. 'That's what I do, Rab.'

As the pale light relieved the dark of night he heard the camp begin to rouse. Men coughed, spat and pissed. Dying embers were raked in an attempt to breathe new life into them. Orders were shouted from officers on horseback. Weapons rattled as they were prepared for use. Flynt hauled himself to his feet, his joints and muscles complaining not only from the cold but also the echoes of the beating he had received. He moved away from his companions and climbed a small rise to look across the moor. A fine mist hung over the land and a breeze made the chill of the air even sharper. A noise reached him from somewhere beyond the mist, muffled but growing in intensity. He cocked his head, tried to filter out the din of the camp behind him and closed his eyes as if shutting off one sense would heighten another. Yes, there it was. The faint whistle of fife, rattle of drum and clink of bridle reaching through the mist. He opened his eyes and strained to penetrate the curtain of white, seeing nothing, but the sounds told him all he needed to know. Argyll's forces were gathering somewhere out there. So it was to be today then, just as he had surmised.

He returned to their small encampment to stand over Rab, who was enshrouded in his coat and blanket as Flynt had been, and nudged him awake with the toe of his boot.

'Time to move, Rab,' he said as his friend fixed him with bleary eyes.

He heard Blueskin rouse, grumbling as ever about the cold, followed by Dan, silent as ever. Flynt realised he had heard the man utter only a handful of words since they had met, not counting those in song, and those only when pressed about his life. He liked him and wondered how he ever got in tow with a wretch like Blueskin. Lives change, though, as Flynt knew only too well, which often makes for curious associations.

'I need you all to move to the high ground there,' he said, gesturing towards a ridge of moorland that rose towards the Ochils.

Rab had risen and was stamping his feet on the earth to set the blood flowing. 'And where will *you* be?'

'I have business to attend in the camp.'

'That right?' said Blueskin, his voice still rough with sleep. His throat scraped as he dislodged a lump of phlegm and sent it flying to the ground. 'Then I reckons that I will accompany you.'

'No, what I do must be done alone.'

Blueskin's jaw jutted. 'I has my orders from Mr Wild.'

'Mr Wild be damned,' said Flynt. 'I need you, Dan and Rab out of harm's way. Do you hear that?' He jerked his thumb over his shoulder towards the sound of the government forces on the march, which was louder now. 'Battle will commence very soon and it will be bloody. I told you last night you don't want to be caught up in these hostilities, so unless you really wish to pick a side and take arms, it's best you be well away.'

Blueskin shifted uneasily as he heard the martial music floating with the wisps of mist towards them, then regarded the Jacobite soldiers preparing to form ranks, his face contemplative as he weighed his loyalty to Wild against the prospect of forming rank in a conflict for which he had little or no interest. Flynt knew which way the scales would fall. Loyalty was one thing but self-preservation was the law of the streets.

Flynt turned away as if examining the army's dispositions but the move was really designed to show he would brook no further argument. His final curt words were thrown over his shoulder. 'Now, saddle the horses, get up on that hill and await my return.'

Nothing was said behind him and he heard Blueskin dredge up another gob of slime, followed by the sound of him gathering his gear and trudging across the damp heather to where the horses were tethered.

Rab moved to Flynt's side. 'Are you certain of this, Jonny? Do you not need me to have your back?'

Flynt shook his head. 'Get to safety, Rab. I can't do this and worry about you at the same time.'

'You don't need to worry about me.'

'Yes, I do. This is part of my life, Rab, not yours.' He gave his friend a smile. 'And Cassie will never forgive me if I let anything happen to you.'

Rab said nothing for what seemed a long time but was in reality only a second or two. 'And if anything happens to *you*?'

'She will mourn but, in truth, she lost me a long time since. And I her. She is yours now, Rab, and you are hers. I mean to see you returned to her hale and hearty.'

Rab seemed on the verge of arguing further but thought better of it and turned to heft his saddle towards his horse.

Once he was satisfied the three had done as he ordered, Flynt led Horse through the camp. The mist had cleared and Argyll's lines could be seen clearly, their red uniforms standing out like a rapier wound on the southern incline of the heathland. The Jacobite forces were positioning themselves for the fight and all was a flurry of activity. To avoid being questioned about his regiment or commander, Flynt walked as if he had a purpose in order to reach the command post where he felt certain he would find Moncrieff.

He found the officers clustered around a large block of stone lying flat in the mosses and bearing the look of something of great antiquity, the fleshy features of the man he took to be the Earl of Mar holding conference with his senior advisors while the Jacobite standard fluttered above them. Moncrieff sat on a smaller lump of rock nearby, listening intently. Flynt was too far distanced to pick up their conversation but the earl seemed to be taking advice, his head nodding or shaking in response. From what Flynt could tell of the dispositions, the Jacobite force held many advantages. They occupied the slightly higher ground and outnumbered Argyll's forces by at the very least two men to one. He had noted when he arrived a shortage of food but these Highlanders were used to empty stomachs and would fight through hunger regardless. A brave strike, a confident strike, could win the day. To emerge the victor, Bobbing John would have to bob less and deliberate more.

The outcome of the battle was not his concern, though; Moncrieff was. And as he studied him, it became evident in his expression and posture that his lordship was discomfited by the situation. Men of his class could be brave – Flynt had witnessed that himself – but he suspected Moncrieff was not among their number. He bore a look in his eye that Flynt knew well. He had seen it on the battlefield, particularly in Charlie in Flanders. He had seen it on men transported by hurdle to Tyburn. It was the look of a man seeking a means of escape. In that moment, Flynt knew that Rab's understanding of Moncrieff was correct. He had joined the rising because he thought it would bring him favour with James Edward Stuart should he return to the throne, but now here he was, on the brink of battle, and he did not relish the thought. Moncrieff was a politician, a talker and schemer, and Flynt tried to delve into what the man was thinking. He had the will, he had leverage with either side no matter the outcome of this day. Why need he take to the saddle and wield a sword?

It was with some self-satisfaction that Flynt watched his lordship rise and, unnoticed by the officers who were still debating with their commander, begin to walk away. As his pace increased, so did Flynt's, leading Horse at a safe distance. Around them the Highland warriors made ready to fight, streaming to form lines facing the government troops. Against this flow moved Moncrieff and Flynt, the first unaware that the second followed in parallel, two men in black amid a torrent of plaid.

Moncrieff looked neither right nor left as he rounded the line of command tents. Flynt veered to one side to gain a clearer view and watched him untether and mount an already saddled black horse with the beaten look of an animal that had not received proper care. Flynt's lips compressed in both satisfaction and irritation. He had been correct, the gutless bastard was going to flee. He had finalised the transaction with Madame de Fontaine the night before but would not have ventured out after dark, not in this terrain. He had waited to hear what Mar had to say and, whatever it was, it was not to his liking. Time then to make himself scarce.

Flynt mounted Horse's back and urged her to follow Moncrieff, who was climbing the rise away from the camp. He glanced to the wall of red and white that was the government line. There was no frenzy there, it merely waited for the action to begin with all the discipline of seasoned troops. The Jacobite troops and horsemen were forming themselves into two lines and as he looked to the recumbent stone he saw Mar standing upon it, addressing the men around him, the words not reaching his ears but no doubt exhorting them to glory. He returned his attention to Moncrieff who had neared the crest of the rise, so he spurred Horse to pick up the pace.

Then, suddenly, all was silent, as if someone had placed a thick blanket over the land and the armies to stifle all sound. Only the breeze remained, whistling and moaning through the grass and heather. The mist might have vanished but the sleet had returned, driven by the wind's breath to bite at exposed flesh. Flynt saw that the Jacobite lines were now in place, the men motionless as they stared across the moor at the opposition. This was the point that required the most nerve, Flynt knew. Forming the line, even charging, can be easy for there is motion and intent, but this moment, the one before hostilities begin, gives a man time to think, to realise that this day may be the last he will ever see, this air the last he will ever breathe, this land the last he will ever feel underfoot.

Then, slowly, the drummers on the far side began a march and the red line moved as one. Pipers and bodhran drums struck up a counter-melody and the Jacobites also began to step across the uneven ground, walking at first but that would not last. Eventually the Highlanders would let loose with their battle cries and surge forward in a charge designed both to daunt and penetrate the opposition's line, hitting it very much like a raging bull.

Moncrieff had also paused to look back and this time had spotted him. There was distance between them, and with Flynt's face turned to the field below he would not have known who it was following his path, but now recognition dawned. He dug his heels into his mount's side and took to the gallop. Flynt swore and did the same.

Moncrieff raced along the brow of the hill, head down, body tight against his horse's neck, occasionally glancing back at Flynt, who was similarly positioned in the saddle. The sound of the hooves on the hard ground was steady, almost working in counterpoint to the drums on the field below them on the right, and the sleet flew past them as if part of the chase. The land was riven by small furrows which each steed leaped over easily. Moncrieff's animal was in poor condition, though, and lacked Horse's heart and stamina. Flynt had learned that you must take care of two things in this life, your weapons and your mount. Moncrieff held anything that served him with disdain, man or beast, so as his poor horse faltered, Flynt gained on him with ease. He galloped alongside and Moncrieff cursed, aiming a blow with his silver-headed stick which Flynt easily blocked, then wrapped his fingers around the shaft, and they each pulled at it as the horses careered across the ground. Moncrieff's terror reflected in his face as he wrestled for possession of the cane. His eyes were wide with fear and his mouth open as if screaming. He had nobody here to protect him. No servants. No pet city officials. Not even any laws. Flynt saw his mother's face then, her eyes bleeding terror, her lips parted in pain and horror. Then he pictured her stepping from the crag. One step was all it took and she was gone. What had begun in a room in Moncrieff's townhouse had led to that windswept cliff. Now it would end on a sleet-scarred moor.

If any of the combatants below had looked up they would have seen the two horsemen etched against the leaden skies as they galloped on the crest of the ridge, each struggling for custody of the stick. Flynt finally snatched it from Moncrieff's grasp and with considerable force at shoulder level swung the silver head, which he now saw was a wolf, into the man's panicked face. The solid handle cracked on his flesh like a gunshot and Moncrieff slumped to the side but retained his seat, his mount slowing. Flynt reined Horse in a few feet further on, wheeling round in time to see Moncrieff wipe away the blood from the lash across his nose and forehead, then fumble for a flintlock nestled in a bucket holder on the saddle. Flynt let Horse's reins fall, confident she would not move until he told her, and with his right hand produced Tact, levelling it before Moncrieff had even cleared the leather.

'I wouldn't,' said Flynt.

Moncrieff saw the weapon pointed at him, heard the calm, steady tone and froze. Below them a fierce collective scream rent the air and Flynt shot a glance at the battle. Argyll's cavalry had attacked Mar's left and the Highlanders, supported by their own cavalry, were hacking and slashing in a bid to keep their line steady. Moncrieff saw his chance to pluck his pistol free from the holster but Flynt was prepared for such a move and fired. The nobleman's left shoulder jerked, there was a flash of red against the black cloth, and he was plucked from the saddle, his gun flying from his hand. Flynt quickly jumped down from Horse, drew Diplomacy and crossed the few feet of frozen ground. Moncrieff's good hand reached for his weapon only inches away but stopped when Flynt loomed above him and aimed directly at his head.

'Take a telling, Moncrieff.'

Moncrieff saw sense and his hand eased back. Flynt looked back at the battle where the men fought and died amid a cacophony of musket fire and the clank of steel against steel. Flynt heard screams as they fell before musket and sword.

Moncrieff cared little for what was happening below them. 'What do you want from me?'

'I'll have the document, if you please.'

Moncrieff affected a puzzled expression. 'I told you before…'

Flynt was in no mood for that. 'No games, not now. There are men dying below, brave men, sacrificing themselves for a cause you supported because it suited you.' He raised the barrel of his pistol just slightly. 'So, the document. Now. You can hand it to me willingly or I can take it from your corpse.'

'You would do murder?'

'Why not? I have done it before and one more would scarce trouble my conscience.' He held out his free hand. 'The document.'

Although in pain, Moncrieff seemed to have found his customary lofty aspect. He did not make any move to fish the will out from wherever it currently nestled. 'And what will you do with it?'

'That need not concern you.'

Moncrieff coughed and grimaced as the action caused him agony. He craned his neck to inspect the wound on his shoulder. 'If murder comes so easily to you, why did you not kill me with that shot?'

The question caught Flynt off guard and he could not answer. Under the circumstances and at that distance he was lucky to have struck flesh at all. At least, that's what he told himself. To cover his mental confusion he looked back to the carnage. The Highlanders on the right flank had broken into a run towards the government left, their yells and the wail of their pipes rending the air. Musket fire stuttered and men fell but the Highland charge continued, swords held aloft, shields before them.

When he looked back he saw Moncrieff smiling, though his pale face was pinched and his voice was beginning to crack. 'You could not do it, could you? Why is that, I wonder?'

'I would not let it trouble you. My aim was off.'

Moncrieff's laugh was short and thin. 'I do not believe that, Jonas Flynt. I believe you have been told that my blood runs in your veins and you could not bring yourself to kill me.'

Flynt swallowed. 'It is for that very reason that I would be more than happy to end you now. For my mother's sake.'

'Ah.' Moncrieff struggled to raise himself to a sitting position, his breath laboured. 'Gideon has been telling you tales. I thought so.'

'He told me what happened.'

'No, he told you a version of what happened. Let me guess – I forced myself upon your poor, innocent mother, correct?'

Flynt did not reply.

Moncrieff winced as he shook his head. He craned downwards to inspect his wound once again, the fingers of his right hand gently probing the edge of the tattered cloth. Blood flowed easily from the hole. 'He has been peddling that lie for years now. What else did he tell you, that she was a seamstress? An innocent of whom I took advantage while her husband was away? And then later denied all?' He looked up and amusement mixed with pain in his eyes. 'Am I right?'

Flynt felt his grip tighten on the butt of his pistol. He wanted to blow a hole in the man's head. He wanted to silence him. But he could not bring himself to do it. He needed to hear this man admit his sin first. He needed to air the rage and bewilderment he had felt since leaving Edinburgh.

'Do you wish to know the truth or will you end my life believing a lie?' Moncrieff asked. 'Because Gideon Flynt is a liar, you can believe that.'

'I would not believe you if you told me the sun rose of a morning. Do you deny I am your bastard son?'

Moncrieff shrugged and flinched with the pain. 'Perhaps, perhaps not.'

'What does that mean, damn it?'

Moncrieff pressed his hand to stem the blood flowing from his wound. 'The fair Jenny Flynt was no seamstress, she was nothing but a common whore. She sold herself to any man with silver. Gideon Flynt cannot accept that, for it was his decision to be so long at sea that forced her into such privation. She was left to fend for herself.'

'You lie. She stayed with my aunt…'

'Aye, your aunt was a decent woman, a God-fearing woman, but your mother had no such scruples. Her fall from decency all but destroyed your aunt's reputation. Did I have her? Yes, I did, but so did many another. Was it rape? No, Jonas, it was a business transaction, that is all.'

Flynt's teeth gritted. 'Don't you call me by my name, you don't have the right.'

Moncrieff glanced past Flynt. 'Very well. But I speak the truth. You may be my bastard son, you may not be. Jenny was most active and, frankly, with so much seed being poured into that bowl it would be difficult to say for sure from which sack it came.'

'You're a lying bastard, Moncrieff!' Rab's voice came from behind Flynt. It did not surprise him for he had heard the horse's hooves on the hard-packed ground.

'I told you to stay safe, Rab,' Flynt said without turning.

'He's lying, you know that, don't you, Jonny?'

Flynt sneered. 'I know it, he lies with such fluency it is little wonder he is in politics.'

'Come, sir,' Moncrieff said, amending his position again to be more comfortable. 'You did not know her. She gave birth to you then died, drunk and penniless, in a wynd off the Canongate. She does not deserve your respect.'

'She killed herself out of the shame you caused.'

Moncrieff laughed again. 'Is that what Gideon told you?'

'Because it's the truth, Moncrieff,' Rab spat at him. 'Put a ball in him, Jonny, end this stream of filth. End him.'

Flynt was not prepared to put an end to Moncrieff, not yet. Perhaps it was because he needed to hear the truth. But he also had to find the will and if he killed the man and found he did not possess it, then the trail ended on this windblown ridge.

'My goodness, that woman was such a tragic figure, was she not?' Moncrieff smiled through his pain. 'Gideon has spun a fine, fanciful tale. Poor little Jenny Flynt, a good woman outraged by a noble lord then abandoned to carry the child. Finally, her mind so unbalanced by the affair, she takes her life, and many years later her son returns from abroad to seek vengeance on the brute who ravished her. God's teeth, it really is a tale worthy of Mr Shakespeare or Mr Webster. Tell me, how did Gideon tell you she ended it all? Pistol? Blade? Some kind of poison? What?'

It was Rab who answered. 'You know how she did it.'

'I do not, truly.'

Flynt knew he was playing the man's game but replied. 'She threw herself from Hangman's Craig.'

'Ah, appropriately dramatic, but sadly another fabrication for your benefit, I believe. I speak the truth, sir. I have no reason to lie.'

'You have every reason to lie, for you are under my gun.'

Another slight shift of position brought a gasp of pain. 'You will murder me or you will not. I see no profit in spinning you a yarn, unlike Gideon.'

The man seemed so certain, even calm. Flynt felt his confusion grow but he could not let it control his actions. He decided to abandon this line of questioning and return to the real reason they were here. 'The will.'

'I do not have it.'

'You purchased it.'

'I gave it to his lordship, the Earl of Mar, for use in his great cause.'

'You're lying. You lied about my mother and you're lying now.'

'As you said, you have me under your gun. It would be in my interests to give you the document if I had it, but I do not. So you must do your worst.'

Flynt looked down at the scene below. The fighting continued, the lines now fully merged with red and plaid mixed in a melee that seemed more confusion than strategy. The moorland was strewn with bodies, some moving, some not.

'You still have it,' he said with confidence. 'You did not give Madame de Fontaine your silver just to deliver it to John Erskine. You and the Fellowship have an agenda of your own...'

Moncrieff's bewilderment seemed genuine. 'You think me of the Fellowship? I am not of their number.' He looked beyond Flynt towards Rab as if turning this over in his mind. 'I see. Another lie at my expense. I should have known.' He turned his gaze back to Flynt. 'You cannot be a son of mine. You are far too gullible.'

When Rab next spoke, his voice was filled with exasperation. 'I've heard enough of your falsity, you bastard.'

What happened then, happened at speed. Flynt heard Rab's horse being spurred into motion and he took his eyes from

Moncrieff for but a moment, saw that his friend was moving forward as if to trample the man on the ground, his father's old pistol in his hand, but then another movement, Moncrieff this time, on his knees and scrambling for his weapon. So Flynt whirled, triggered without thought, without hesitation, as he knew he always would despite the man's attempts at diversion, at confusion, knowing all along that his tiny amendments to his position were merely a way of getting closer to his weapon. Moncrieff flew back, a spray of red erupting from his chest, to lie spreadeagled on the frost-bitten ground, eyes wide as if asking God what had gone wrong.

Flynt twisted to face Rab. 'In the name of Christ, Rab!'

Rab appeared stunned by what had happened and merely shook his head, his lips moving but making no sound. Flynt made a growling noise and whirled back to crouch at Moncrieff's side. The man's eyes swivelled towards him and he tried to speak but, like Rab, he could say nothing. Flynt began to paw through his pockets. One hand trembled upwards as if to prevent him but Flynt batted it away. He found a folded sheaf of papers inside Moncrieff's coat, part of it stained red, which Flynt found fitting. These papers had caused so much death.

He leaned closer to Moncrieff's ear. He knew the wound was mortal, but there was one final thing he needed him to hear. 'I should leave you to die alone, here on this worthless stretch of moorland. But I won't. Not because you don't deserve it, you do, but because I want to see the life leave you. I want to rejoice in the sight of it. I want the very last thing you see on this earth to be the son of Gideon and Jenny Flynt.'

Moncrieff's mouth opened again but all that left him was a slight hiss. His hands shook and he tried to swallow but his throat muscles ceased to be effective. His eyes seemed to plead for release but Flynt was unmoved. He returned the man's gaze with cold detachment until, finally, Moncrieff's body spasmed once then slowly relaxed as a single long exhalation carried what life was left into the cold air. Flynt remained on one knee for a moment, staring into the already slackening face of a man he had come to hate, the rage that he had fought to control rushing to the surface. It had been too easy. Moncrieff had died too easily. There should have been more pain. He should have suffered the anguish his mother must have felt all those years ago.

He roared and gripped Moncrieff by the coat, hauling the dead man to his feet, the papers in his hand crushed against the lapels. He held him for a moment, staring again into the dead eyes as the head lolled to one side.

'You were never my father,' he said and then he threw the body backwards off the edge of the ridge. He watched it bounce and roll towards the battle still raging below, finally coming to rest halfway up the rise, the sleet already shrouding his black garments. He found the man's walking stick and studied the wolf's head handle for a moment before he tossed it down the hill after its owner. This rise in the moorland was no clifftop but it would have to do.

'I told you to stay away,' Flynt said without turning to Rab.

'I saw you with him from over there.' Rab's voice was subdued. Flynt looked to where his friend had waved his hand and saw Blueskin and Dan some distance away atop another small hill. 'I thought you might have needed help.'

'I didn't and you should have stayed where I told you. Even Blueskin followed my orders.'

Rab said nothing as his eyes moved to the papers in Flynt's hand. 'Is that it? Is that the will?'

Flynt unfolded it and read the first few lines. 'Aye, this is it.'

'Then I think you must give it to me.'

Flynt should have been surprised when he saw Rab turn the pistol in his direction but he was not. He had half expected it as soon as Moncrieff denied being part of the Fellowship, for it bore the stamp of truth, unlike his version of the events surrounding his birth and the death of his mother. That did not mean he was not disappointed.

'Rab...' he began, the regret evident in the single word.

'Say nothing, Jonny.' Rab swallowed hard and held out his free hand. 'Just hand me the will.'

'You're with the Fellowship,' Flynt stated. 'Not Moncrieff.'

Rab could only nod.

'And Madame de Fontaine came to Edinburgh to give it to you.'

'That deceitful hag betrayed our trust. She decided to sell to the higher bid.'

'It is her nature.'

Rab leaned down in the saddle, his hand still outstretched. 'The will, Jonny.'

Flynt looked at the paper in his hand. 'And what will you do with it?'

'The same as that bastard Moncrieff, except it will be for the benefit of the people. That document is a weapon, Jonny, and it can be wielded against both sides in this meaningless conflict.'

'To what end?'

'To put an end to government by the rich and powerful *for* the rich and powerful.'

Flynt remembered Rab's words when he said that the Fellowship were Jacobite at heart. 'That's not the Fellowship's aim.'

'That's my aim.'

Flynt held the paper up. 'You really think this can do that? You don't even know what it contains. It may not be a bequeath to the old queen's half-brother but confirmation that she wished the throne to go to the house of Hanover after all. That could be why Moncrieff was leaving, for he knew there was no profit in this day, that the will would not assist Mar's cause.'

That Rab had not considered this was evident from his expression and he was silent for a moment while he thought on it. 'No, he was too careful not to have had sight of the document before he bought it. Think on it, Jonny, possessing that can force the wee German lairdie to listen to us, or James Edward, if that is the case. The majority of people are loyal to the idea of the throne, not necessarily who sits upon it. Let us be candid, this conflict will not go James Edward's way. Bobbing John is not the man to win this day, even I know that and I am no military man.

If that document says what we think it says, that the old queen wished her half-brother to rule, then we can compel George and his cabinet to think of the people, Jonny, not themselves, not their rich friends and patrons.'

'And if it does not say that?'

'Then we can use it against James Edward and compel him to think of the people should he ever come to power. We have been ruled for too long by selfish men. It's time for the people to rule themselves.'

Flynt felt sadness weigh upon him. 'Rab, Rab, that is the world in which we live. That is the way of it. Money creates power and power seeks money. It always was and is thus, yesterday, today, tomorrow, here, around the globe. Even when Scotland had its own parliament, the Three Estaites, and it was far from being free of self-interest.'

Rab leaned forward, his voice earnest. 'Aye, but just because it's the way it always was, does that mean it has to be the way it always is? Can we not strive to do better? Can we not at least dream of a better, fairer world?'

Flynt admitted it was an attractive dream but a dream nonetheless. Rab and his friends had not factored in human nature, which at its root Flynt believed to be mired in venality.

'This is but fantasy, Rab.'

'One man's fantasy is another man's ambition, Jonny. My ambition is to bring change peacefully, and perhaps that document can aid me. There are those in the Fellowship who would seek more violent measures and possession of that could go a long way to keep them at bay.'

Rab was using the Fellowship for his own ends while theirs remained to Flynt half in shadow, but he doubted that one peaceful man could stand in their way.

Rab jerked his head to the battlefield. 'Has there not already been enough death and blood? Have you not had your fill of it? Would you not wish to see the men who propagate such things, the kings, the statesmen, the politicians, brought to heel?'

'And this one piece of paper can do all that?'

'It's a start. Now – please – hand it to me.'

Flynt made a show of placing the document in a pocket inside his greatcoat. 'And if I don't?'

Rab blinked and swallowed hard again, as if trying to dislodge something in his gullet. 'Don't force me to choose between you and the people. Please, Jonny.'

Flynt heard the plea in Rab's voice and quickly considered his options. He had fired both pistols, he was too far away for his sword to be of any use. Moncrieff's weapon was on the ground behind him but could he reach it before Rab fired? Could he, in fact, use it even if he had it? More importantly, would his friend pull that trigger?

Flynt experienced the same weariness he had felt outside the Tolbooth. Then he had been trying to protect one friend, here another held him at gunpoint. Either way, both were lost.

'Was it you who had me beaten that night?'

Rab did not answer but Flynt could tell by the ripple of a muscle on his face he had guessed correctly.

'Why, Rab? Because you thought Cassie had feelings for me?'

'No.'

'Then why?'

'I needed you out of the way while I negotiated with that treacherous harridan de Fontaine. We had an agreement but she saw a way to profit further by approaching Moncrieff. She knew him of old, it seems, and had his measure. He outbid us.'

'Did you attack me yourself?'

Rab shook his head. 'I paid a couple of crowdies, wastrels from the gutter. They were supposed to incapacitate you long enough to let me conclude the matter but they were interrupted by your friends from London. You were lucky, Jonny, for those other voices in the Fellowship wanted you dead but I said I would take care of it.'

This news did not surprise Flynt overmuch. He was already of the opinion that any goodwill the Fellowship might harbour was not universal. Whatever their ultimate aims, they would kill when threatened. 'And you are part of this Fellowship, who would do murder with such little thought. How can this be?' When Rab refused to reply, Flynt tried another tack. 'Does Cassie know of all this?'

Rab looked horrified by the thought. 'You think she would countenance such a thing? She is – was – angered by you but she would not be part of any move to cause you harm. And her view of humanity is informed by her childhood. She does not share my opinion that mankind can be greater than it is if we could cast off the petty politicking and religious rabble-rousing. As to the Fellowship, they are a conduit to my end, no more. I use them only.' He spurred his horse a few steps forward. 'Now, please Jonny, give me that document.'

'You will have to take it from me, Rab,' Flynt said quietly.

'I do not jest, Jonny! What I'm trying to do, is important. Think on it – bringing an end to rancour and division, perhaps even bringing down borders? Is there anything more important than that?'

'Is it more important than our friendship?'

'Don't put it to the test.'

'You're already doing that.'

Gunfire and steel reverberated from the moorland below them. Injured horses squealed. Men cried out in agony. Smoke from thousands of muskets hung in the heavy air. Yet all faded into some netherworld between reality and silence as two boyhood friends stared at each other, the sleet dancing between them like memories. Flynt waited for Rab to make a move but he was motionless as he looked down on him, although the pistol in his hand did waver.

'Don't do this, Jonny.'

'I'm doing nothing, Rab. Whatever is to be done, it will be your doing.'

With hand trembling, Rab raised the muzzle. Flynt remained still, willing his old friend to pull the trigger. Perhaps it was time.

He had cheated death so often before, let him not do it here. He was tired of it all. The thieving. The killing. The truth about his parentage. And now he had been manipulated by one of the few people he had ever trusted. Just do it, Rab, he thought as he closed his eyes. Get it over with.

'Jonny, Jonny, Jonny,' Rab said and Flynt heard the sadness in his voice. He opened his eyes to see him begin to lower the weapon, his head shaking. 'I cannot do this.'

And then his back arched, the pistol dropped from his hand as his fingers spasmed, and something exploded from his chest. He stared skyward for a few moments, arms outstretched as if in supplication, then slowly tumbled from the saddle. Flynt saw Blueskin come to a halt a few feet away, smoke bleeding from the barrel of his pistol. Flynt had not heard the gunshot, it being only one among many.

'Damn you, Blueskin!' Flynt shouted as he ran to where Rab was on his back, trying to rise.

'I seen him with you in his sights,' Blueskin yelled back. 'I was told to protect you and I did.'

Flynt ignored him and kneeled beside his friend, lifting his head and setting it on his lap. Rab coughed up some blood, his eyes swimming as he gazed up at Flynt.

'I wouldn't have done it, Jonny, you know that,' he said.

Flynt stroked his hair. 'I know, Rab, I know.'

Another cough followed by an attempt at a smile. 'It's not even primed, the pistol. Even if it had been, I would have missed. I can't shoot worth a damn.'

Flynt made a soothing noise. 'Be still, Rab.'

Flecks of ice settled on his friend's upturned face and Flynt wiped them away.

'He lied, you know that, don't you?' Rab said. 'That bastard Moncrieff. He lied.'

'I know.'

'My faither told me, just before he passed. He found her, did you know? On the crags.'

'No, I didn't know.'

A shudder ran through Rab's frame. 'I don't want you to… think…'

'All is well, my friend. You must be still now.'

A gurgling sound swirled in Rab's throat. He coughed again, spraying droplets of dark blood. He struggled to look down at his wound and grimaced when he saw the oozing hole. 'Look at my good coat,' he said. 'Ruined. Cassie will kill me…'

Rab's eyes widened and sought out Flynt's face as his hands scrabbled at his forearms for purchase. His body turned rigid and a hideous choking sound emanated from his throat. Another stream of blood erupted from between his lips to coat his chin. Then, slowly, the eyes relaxed and lost focus, his grip on Flynt's arms eased, his hands fell away and he was still. Sleet landed on his open eyes but he no longer felt it.

On the battlefield life and death continued. On the hilltop, Flynt cradled a boy he had once thought brother and wept.

22

He took Rab's body back to Edinburgh.

He could not allow him to be thrown into a mass grave with the rest of the dead. Flynt retrieved Moncrieff's horse, for the poor creature deserved a better life and he would see to it. The battle still flowed as the three of them rode over the moors, Rab's body wrapped in his blanket and strapped to his saddle. It was undignified but he was beyond such cares.

Rab had told the truth, for his father's pistol was not primed. Although Blueskin had acted in line with Wild's orders, Flynt still could not bring himself to speak to him, but equally could not fully blame him for what had happened. All the man would have seen was Rab on horseback about to gun him down. He also must have seen Flynt pocket the will but he made no mention of it.

As they headed past Stirling, he wondered who had emerged the victor in the conflict, Mar or Argyll. From where he had stood on the hill it was difficult to say which army had the upper hand. If Mar won then he would control the castle, and the gateway to the south should the victory give him the confidence to push further. If Argyll won then the rising in Scotland was over. Flynt cared very little whatever the outcome. He had sympathy for the men who died, for the families who would mourn, but not the nobles and the generals and the politicians, not kings and those who would be king. In that much he agreed with Rab, but his notion of the world becoming some kind of universal brotherhood, free from the shackles of monarchs and politicians, was but a pipe dream. He wondered now if his friend had been touched by some form of madness, for there had certainly been a fervour in the way he had spoken that was almost religious. Rab had spurned his faith but perhaps found a new one and he spoke of it with all the zeal of a convert. And yet, he had said there were others within the Fellowship who perhaps thought differently. Rab wished to achieve his aims, unattainable though they might be, through negotiation, yet they seemed to favour more direct means. Flynt suspected that he had not heard the last of the Fellowship, for if they were bent on disrupting society then they would loom on Charters' horizon and, by extension, his own.

When they camped that night, Flynt kept himself apart from the two men and they left him alone. He had no wish to engage in chatter. He did appreciate Dan's singing, although the seafaring work songs had been replaced with laments of lost love and shattered dreams.

His sleep was fitful, partly because recent events replayed in his mind but also because he was primed for Blueskin to make an attempt to relieve him of the will. But the man remained curled against the cold in greatcoat and under blanket and made no such move.

–

Once in Edinburgh he told the men to remain at the White Horse Inn until he returned, when they would proceed to London. Moncrieff's mount he gave into the keeping of the stable lad who had taken such good care of Horse, telling him the steed was his now. A few coins from the pouch he had taken from Madame de Fontaine would help in the upkeep. The lad was delighted and promised to ensure the animal was brought back to full fitness. Flynt believed him. He also arranged for Rab's body to be stored there until collected. He would not offend the populace by leading a horse with a dead man draped over the saddle among them.

He walked up Canongate and the High Street for what he thought might be the final time, those memories of his boyhood keeping pace with him like spectres. Rab, Charlie and he running and laughing, ducking down wynds and into closes. Chasing other lads. Being chased. He saw them as they were and heard them as they were and not the men they had become. In his memory now they would forever be youthful, forever carefree and full of life.

He spoke to Gideon and Mercy first, telling them what had occurred. Mercy wept, a huge whooping wail erupting from her lungs. Gideon was stoic but tears welled in his eyes. When Flynt told him that Moncrieff was also dead he merely nodded once.

It was with a heavy tread that he then walked to the West Bow and entered the cobbler's shop. The door was unlocked and his steps faltered as he climbed the narrow staircase to the rooms above. He knocked on the door and waited, his heart hammering. Gideon and Mercy had been difficult enough but this next duty filled him with dread.

Cassie opened the door, perhaps expecting to see Rab, but her smile faltered when she looked beyond and saw only the staircase. Her eyes searched his face and saw everything that she did not wish to know. Her features stiffened and she turned away to sit down at the table. He had not been invited to enter so he lingered in the doorway, unsure what to do or say. The heat of the wood burning in the grate was welcome to his flesh but failed to warm his spirits.

Cassie's posture was erect as if she was holding herself steady and she kept her eyes averted. She sat with her right forearm on the tabletop, looking at something on the floor.

'Where is he?' she asked finally.

'At the White Horse. Gideon will call the wright to make the arrangements for burial.'

She blinked once, the movement dislodging a massive tear. 'He was a fool to go with you.'

'I tried to dissuade him. He had his reasons, though.'

She nodded and in that moment he knew she was well aware of those reasons. 'How did...' she began, then thought better of it. She looked at him finally.

'It was fortunes of war that took him,' he said.

It was a simple and yet complex explanation for what had occurred and he knew she needed more from him. Flynt decided he had to enter the room. He took off his hat and fished the document from his inner pocket. 'He wanted this.'

He laid the will on the tabletop. Cassie saw the bloodstain and said, 'Is this his blood?'

'No. Moncrieff's.'

Like Gideon, that news brought her some satisfaction. 'I always knew Rab's views would bring us pain, sooner or later.'

'Just as you knew I brought the shadow of death.'

'Aye. When Charlie died I thought perhaps it was lifted but when I came home and found Rab's note, telling me he had gone with you, I knew it was not. Charlie would have met his fate whether you were here or not. When I knew Rab had gone with you, I knew one of you would not return.' She looked away. 'I prayed that it be you.'

Flynt understood that but it still stung. 'Did he ever speak of the Fellowship?'

Another tear trailed down her cheek. He longed to reach out and wipe it away but he dared not. She did so herself. 'The damned Fellowship,' she said. 'They aren't what he thought.'

'Then what are they?'

'I don't know. But I know they are not the champions of the people that Rab wanted them to be. Needed them to be. They used him and they would have discarded him eventually, for these people prey on men of ideas and ideals like Rab and twist them to their own purpose. I tried to tell him but he would have none of it.'

Flynt's conscience pricked but he had to ask, 'Do you know who else fills their ranks?'

A shake of the head. Another tear. Another wipe of her hand. 'No, he would not tell me. Secrets. Men and their secrets. Men and their honour. And we are left to pick up the pieces after they are gone.' She dragged the document closer to her with a single finger and gave the writing a cursory glance. 'And all for a piece of paper and ink.'

Flynt said, 'I'll leave that with you.'

'Why?' She grasped the document in her hand, crumpled it and held it up between them. 'Isn't this what you came for? Isn't this what all this death and heartbreak has been for?'

'I want nothing more to do with that damned piece of paper. Do with it what you will. Give it to the Town Guard. Burn it. I care not. But know this, as long as that document exists it will cause further bloodshed.'

'You have read it?'

He had examined its contents by the light of the fire while Blueskin and Dan slept. It was not what Charters had feared but neither was it innocuous. The late queen had apologised to her half-brother for failing to reply to an earlier letter from him. She spoke of their father and of her enduring guilt over her part in removing him from the throne. She regretted ever questioning James's legitimacy and the lack of warmth between them. She also expressed concern that the nation would pass to a truculent, discourteous German with no interest in the wellbeing of its people. She upbraided James for refusing to bend regarding his faith, stating that if he had been a little less intractable then these isles would continue to be ruled by the House of Stuart. She urged him to reconsider his position for the sake of the nation.

The letter fell short of bequeathing the crown and sceptre to her half-brother but could prove incendiary in the hands of someone who knew how to capitalise on its contents. Moncrieff had intended to do just that, as had Rab. The Fellowship, Flynt now suspected, would have used it to create instability. Even Flynt had toyed with the notion of using it to free himself from his servitude to Colonel Charters, but realised that it may only have resulted in a pistol ball to the back of his head one dark night. He was careful but he was not immortal.

Cassie looked at the will resting on the table but did not touch it. 'And what will you tell your superior?'

'That it was all a ruse. There was no will. A letter is all, to her half-brother wishing they had been better siblings, but no promise of the throne,' he said, and there was some truth in that.

Cassie reached out to finger the corner of the papers. 'And how will you explain your empty-handed return?'

'I'll tell him it was destroyed in the heat of the battle.'

'And he will believe you?'

Flynt considered this. 'Perhaps not but there will be little he can do. It will never be mentioned again, not by me.'

Jonathan Wild might be a tougher sell but Blueskin had not seen the document's contents, so he might pull it off. He would ensure Charters gave Wild some kind of reward for his aid by pointing out how useful the man might be in the future. Charters was a man who considered the tomorrows while Flynt lived only for today. To him, tomorrow was an uncharted world while yesterday was too painful a place to revisit. He had learned that these past few days.

A footfall on the stairs made Cassie snatch up the will and thrust it into the pocket of the smock she wore.

'You must go,' she whispered. 'He should not see you.'

Flynt was bewildered. 'Who should not see me? And do you suggest I leave by the window?'

She sighed in exasperation as he turned to face whoever approached. He saw a tall, dark complexioned boy with black hair and inquiring eyes climbing the last few steps, a bundle of books under his arm.

'Jonas, this is my son,' Cassie said, wiping the moisture from her face.

Flynt held out his hand. 'I am pleased to meet you.'

The boy stared at Flynt as he took the proffered hand. His grip was firm. 'This is your namesake, Jonas,' said Cassie. 'An old friend of mine and your father's. We were all children together.'

'Pleased to meet you, sir,' said the boy. He had a pleasant voice and an easy smile. He also looked older than twelve years. When Flynt had first met Lord Moncrieff in the shop, he had without knowing seen the son in the father. Now, as he looked on Cassie's son, he saw the man in the boy. He glanced at Cassie, who was watching him warily, perhaps wondering how he would react. Then she gave him a slight nod and lowered her gaze. She had not wished him to meet the lad. She had not wished him to know.

Flynt swallowed back the realisation of the truth that had clasped him by the throat, and nodded to the books in the boy's hands. 'You are a reader?'

'Aye,' said the boy almost shamefacedly as he laid the books on the table.

'It is a good thing, to read. There is a whole world in the written word.'

'I have to read for my studies but I also like to learn of ancient places and their heroes,' said the boy.

'Greece and Rome,' said Flynt, his voice breaking slightly.

'Aye, gods and monsters, heroes and quests.' He looked around the room. 'Is Faither with you?'

In the silence that followed young Jonas looked towards Cassie, who shook her head. Flynt left the question unanswered and pulled on his hat. No matter what he now knew, he also knew he had no place here.

'I must make haste,' he said, the words barely making it past the lump forming in his throat. 'Take care of your mother, boy.'

Young Jonas frowned, sensing something amiss. 'I will, sir.'

Flynt gave Cassie a final look. A long one. She held it for a few moments then stepped to the fire, fished the document from the pocket of her apron and threw it into the flames. She watched it burn then faced Flynt again. He wanted to move to her and comfort her but he knew that was no longer possible. His coming had brought tragedy to this house and he knew it. There was nothing he could do or say that would change it now. Cassie's eyes softened and she gave him a very slight smile. He did not know what that smile meant. Perhaps she did not blame him for what had occurred. Perhaps she still harboured warm feelings. Perhaps she was relieved he was leaving. He took that smile anyway and stored it away along with what he had learned in this moment, in this room. He would revisit them in the future, on those nights when he was alone and far from home and the melancholy crept over him.

As he moved down the stairs, he heard her say just before she closed the door behind him, 'Come sit with me, Jonas, for there is something you must know...'

The door closed on the woman he loved, her son, and the past they shared. He lingered for a moment, his urge to go back into that room and take his place with the family. His family. He knew it was but a fancy, though, for he did not belong there. Perhaps once, but not now, even though he knew he was leaving something of himself in that cramped apartment above the workshop. He felt dampness on his cheek and wiped it away.

He was halfway down the stairs when he felt the weight of Madame de Fontaine's silver bump against his hip and stopped to consider. Yes, he thought, and crept back up to the door again, taking each step carefully lest the creak of a board alert Cassie. He set the pouch by the door, pausing a moment to catch the fall of a foot on the other side but heard only the dim murmur of Cassie's voice. And then, faintly, a boy's sob.

He felt his heart break further.

He left the shop quickly and silently and walked to the High Street without looking back, the ghosts of yesteryear calling to him from the wynds and closes around him.

Epilogue

The silver-topped cane lay on the desktop in front of him. Moncrieff had always been fond of that stick and its wolf-head handle. The officer who had delivered it and the other items was still dirty from battle and road.

'We discovered his lordship halfway up a rise above the field, a pistol ball in his chest, perhaps put there by a combatant from either our side or theirs.'

It may have been either government trooper or Highlander, but the man behind the desk suspected that neither had taken Moncrieff's life. Jonas Flynt had put that ball in him. 'And there was nothing else on his person?'

'Some silver, in that bag before you, sir. Those personal items, his watch, his ring, some keys. We thought perhaps you would see to it that they went to his family.'

The man flicked a finger through the trinkets. He would see to it that they would reach Moncrieff's family, damn his eyes. His personal connection to Flynt had proved damnable inconvenient and had interfered with the Fellowship's affairs, not that he knew it, of course. And now Flynt had the document he had carried, of that he was certain. Which meant it would make its way to Charters and no doubt be destroyed. No matter, that had been part of the plan.

He thanked the young officer for his discretion and instructed him to ensure that he got some rest, assuring him that he would be well rewarded. The young man left the office with a grateful smile. He was a good man. He would rise in the ranks. The Fellowship had need of men like him.

The shoemaker had been an error of judgement, not because of his position in society, for they had men and women from all walks of life in their number. They had thought they could make use of him, control him, but he was a zealot, useful in some ways but subject to impetuous behaviour. His friendship with Flynt was also an impediment, as was his love for his woman. He was too besotted by her and as such was easily influenced. His willingness to help her with the slave Nero's flight was just one example. He had been warned but he ignored it. He had been useful as a conduit to Madame de Fontaine, a pawn that could be sacrificed should she turn on them, but he was never fully informed regarding the Fellowship's aims. De Fontaine had not betrayed them, though, and had indeed proved more useful than they could have imagined. His mouth twitched at the thought of her. She was a fine piece, to be sure, and had acted true to her nature. It had been her idea to delay negotiations with Moncrieff, pushing up her price while at the same time creating a convincing duplicate of the document, watering down Queen Anne's wishes to something a little more opaque that could still be turned to his lordship's advantage. She had a fine hand for forgery, and for other things, he had no doubt. The original document she sold, as was the bargain, to the Fellowship and so reaped double reward. It was an impressive display of larceny and he applauded her enterprise.

That document was now safe in the keeping of the Fellowship. The old queen had been astonishingly cavalier with her correspondence, even though it was never despatched. Pledging the nation to her half-brother in so bold a fashion was indelicate to say the least. Had she been in her right mind she would never have written it, or at the very least destroyed it, but she kept it by her person for some time. Why she had penned such an inflammatory letter was beyond him, but she had. The Fellowship would make good use of it to bolster their power in London and beyond.

Robert Gow had wished it utilised in the cause of the common man and had believed the Fellowship shared that aim, but they did not. There were always ways to cause instability in nations and means to profit from that instability, for somewhere there would be someone who would pay. That alone was not the Fellowship's aim, however. There was profit in power and power in profit and the Fellowship sought both. They would be the men who stood in the shadows of the corridors behind the corridors of government. Faceless, anonymous, wealthy. They would influence and they would manipulate and they would, in effect, rule. Let the politicians bluster and blither, for they were transient and in their vanity and self-interest as easily manipulated as the zealots.

The man smiled, satisfied that everything had gone to plan, despite Flynt. There was little chance that he would ever have interfered with their plans in any meaningful way but he would bear watching. He was a more than capable individual and there might come a time when it would prove necessary to recruit him to the ranks of the organisation.

Or kill him.

Historical note

Although this is a work of fiction, the storyline uses real events and characters, but I have taken certain liberties with both for dramatic purposes. Jonathan Wild, Jack Sheppard, Blueskin Blake, the Duke of Shrewsbury and Edgeworth Bess all existed.

The Battle of Malplaquet was described by Sir Winston Churchill as 'the largest and bloodiest battle of the eighteenth century'. Around 200,000 men fought, leaving over 30,000 dead or wounded with no prisoners being taken. Peace was already being thrashed out between France and the British, Dutch and Austrian allies after years of war, but Louis IV was unwilling to provide troops to eject his grandson, Philip V, from the Spanish throne. That refusal led to the breakdown of talks and the resurgence of hostilities. France was in a weakened state after a series of defeats but the French general Villars was ordered to defend Mons, under threat following the fall of Tournai. They faced each other near the village of Malplaquet. In the end it was deemed an Allied victory because they held the field, but the reality was that the French retreated in good order, retained the bulk of their army and prevented a wholesale invasion of their country.

The peace talks resumed and the Treaty of Utrecht was finally thrashed out.

There was rumour of a mysterious document carried by Queen Anne but apparently destroyed after her death. There were those who thought it related to her half-brother, James Edward Stuart, and that it may have been some kind of will bequeathing him the throne.

The death of Charlie Temple is loosely based on the Porteous Riot of 1736, when the captain of the Edinburgh Town Guard was lynched following the shooting of rioters at an execution. I hope Charlie is somewhat more sympathetic than Porteous seemed to be. The Edinburgh Tolbooth, of which nothing now remains, was very much as I describe it. If you are in the city's High Street and standing near to St Giles Cathedral you will find a heart in the brickwork of the pavement – Sir Walter Scott featured the building in his Heart of Midlothian – for this was where the entrance once stood. There is an old tradition which saw locals spit on it as they passed. A series of brass plates in the roadway delineates where the tall black walls once stood.

I have not followed the details of the battle at Sheriffmuir slavishly, for my story is taking place on a fictional ridge above it. Historian and author John Prebble called it a 'revolving wheel of a battle' and when the musket smoke cleared and the blood stopped flowing neither side could claim victory. As a Jacobite ballad of the period has it:

A battle there was that I saw, man.
And we ran, and they ran,
And they ran, and we ran,
And we ran, and they ran awa, man.

On the same day, 13 November 1715, the Jacobite forces who had occupied Preston surrendered to a far superior Hanoverian army. They had manned barricades and fought in the streets the previous day but in the end their commander decided enough blood had been spilled.

On 22 December, James Francis Edward Stuart landed at Peterhead on Scotland's north-east coast, but he was too late, for the Mar rising had petered out and many warriors had already returned to glen and hillside. There had been a coronation planned for Scone but that was abandoned as Argyll's forces marched north. James agreed to a scorched earth policy to slow the government forces, then returned to the Continent in February. Mar's head did not fall on Tower Hill for he and other generals also fled the country. The rising had died but the Jacobite movement lived, and toasts continued to be made to the King Over the Water.

Author's note

This is a story that has been rattling around in my imagination for over twenty years. I first read about talk of Queen Anne's mysterious will in Hugh Douglas's book *Jacobite Spy Wars* (Sutton Publishing, 1999). The idea that there might be an adventure tale to be weaved around it took root and over the years I added details. The riot, Tolbooth and lynching set piece occurred to me when writing a non-fiction book on the history of what became known as the Heart of Midlothian. Using Sheriffmuir as a backdrop for the climactic scenes came when writing another non-fiction book about Scotland's bloody past. Jonas Flynt and the Company of Rogues was the final detail, giving me leave to incorporate Wild, Sheppard, et al.

However, I still didn't write it, concentrating on modern thrillers, unconvinced I could pull it off. It wasn't until the opening pages of my book *A Rattle of Bones* (Polygon, 2021), a chapter set in 1755, that the prospect of writing a full-length historical adventure thriller became a realistic one – and that was due to another writer. Bestselling author Denzil Meyrick read that chapter and more or less challenged me to try my hand at a full work. He was aided and abetted in this by our mutual agent Jo Bell. Still unsure that I would succeed, I set myself to writing it.

So you have them to thank or blame, depending on whether you enjoyed the book! Which I hope you did. I would like to thank them both for their encouragement. Or cajoling.

I'd also like to thank fellow authors Shona (S. G.) Maclean, Neil Broadfoot, Theresa Talbot, Gordon Brown (aka Morgan Cry), Caro Ramsay and Michael J. Malone for their feedback.

Gratitude is also due to Kit Nevile and the team at Canelo for getting Jonas out there.

Finally, in the spirit of James Bond, Jonas Flynt will return.

If you enjoyed *An Honourable Thief*, you'll love

London, 1716. Revenge is a dish
best served ice-cold…

The city is caught in the vice-like grip of a savage winter. Even
the Thames has frozen over. But for Jonas Flynt – thief, gambler,
killer – the chilling elements are the least of his worries…

Justice Geoffrey Dumont has been found dead at the base of St
Paul's cathedral, and a young male sex-worker, Sam Yates, has
been taken into custody for the murder. Yates denies all charges,
claiming he had received a message to meet the judge at the
exact time of death.

The young man is a friend of courtesan Belle St Clair, and she
asks Flynt to investigate. As Sam endures the horrors of
Newgate prison, they must do everything in their power to
uncover the truth and save an innocent life, before the bodies
begin to pile up.

But time is running out. And the gallows are beckoning…

OUT MAY 2023

Read on for an exclusive excerpt…

1

Russell Street was uncharacteristically quiet, the denizens and visitors preferring to remain indoors as close to a heat source as possible. There were a few hardy souls abroad, however: link boys carrying lanterns guided their customers through the darkened streets; some flash coves on their way to or from debauchery; Covent Garden Nuns and their lower market drabs sauntering by, one or two spotting Flynt as he waited and tarrying long enough to size him up as a possible cull, but moving on when they realised he had no interest in generating heat by dancing the goat's jig. They exchanged a few words with Lord Fairgreave's hangers-on, who showed willingness for a tumble, causing Flynt to worry that they might use his alley for a bit of against-the-wall rutting, but a terse word from his lordship put all notion of sexual gratification from their mind. The rebuffed whores moved on in search of men more eager to part with their coin.

Flynt was on the verge of giving up – despite his careful move-ments his feet were growing numb within his long boots – when he saw the Justice Dumont emerge from the tavern, his portly frame well insulated from the cold by a thick coat. He had pulled his hat tightly upon his head and was wrapping a warm muffler around his throat, but stopped when he saw Lord Fairgreave and his friends waiting for him. He glanced up and down the street and, seeing it deserted, as if some cataclysm had occurred to remove all human life but the three men before him, took a half step back towards the tavern. The action seemed involuntary for he made no move to re-enter the establishment. He stood his ground as Fairgreave crossed the street towards him.

'I would have words, little man,' Fairgreave said. Flynt was close enough, hidden in the shadows, to hear the words, but distant enough to prevent him from discerning if the judge was shocked by being thus addressed or distressed at being confronted in such a way.

Dumont's response was calm, however, with any trepidation he felt at being bearded by these men not evident. 'I would have thought you had said sufficient at the gaming tables, Lord Fairgreave.'

Flynt pushed himself from the wall, his silver cane now gripped comfortably in his right hand, while with his left he unbuttoned his coat. Attending the tables while armed was a shocking display of poor manners but that did not mean he had left his rooms in Charing Cross without his pistols. They were secreted within two special pockets sewn into the lining of his greatcoat, for Flynt never knew when it might be necessary to apply Tact and Diplomacy to a situation. He had little intention of using them this night, but life had taught him that it was always advisable to be prepared.

'I think not,' Fairgreave said. 'I think perhaps too much was said and too little done to my satisfaction.'

The judge looked from Fairgreave to his two friends. Flynt thought he could see a slight smile on his lips, as if he found this entire scene worthy of a comedy in the Drury Lane Theatre. 'You attempted to inveigle me into a duel earlier, sir, and I did not bite. I take it this is the point in our discourse where you formally challenge me, then? Where there are no witnesses?'

Fairgreave stepped ahead of his colleagues. 'I have no need to take the field of honour with a man who has so little that he would cheat at games of chance.'

Again the judge did not rise to the insult. 'You inspected the dice, you know them to be fair.'

'I know that you had more luck than any man has a right to.'

Dumont shrugged. 'That is true, I did have a decent run, and you, sir, were on the wrong end of it. But you did not tarry to see the epilogue to our little drama, for after you left I lost... and heavily.' Now Flynt was certain the judge smiled. 'Perhaps you were my lucky charm, my lord.'

Those final words angered Fairgreave even further. 'You are a cheat, sir, and, I believe, a liar. I will have your purse so that I may take back what I lost.'

Dumont held his hands out in apology. 'I regret my purse is as empty as your conscience would appear to be.'

His lordship bristled at this and drew himself to his full, not inconsiderable height. 'My conscience is untroubled by punishing a cheat and a thief, sir. Your purse, sir, that I may see for myself whether you are indeed also a liar.'

Dumont tilted his head as he considered what he knew was not a request before he signified acceptance by hitching his shoulder slightly and slipping his hand from his glove to reach into his pocket. 'I do have something here that may interest you, my lord.'

The hand reappeared with a small Queen Anne pistol. The weapon was useless at any great distance but in this instance it was a matter of inches away from Fairgreave's face. Alarmed, he took a step back.

'Before you ask, my lord,' Dumont said, 'this is indeed primed.' With one swift movement he cocked the weapon with his thumb. 'Now it is also cocked and I will not hesitate to perforate you or any of your friends if you continue in this attempt at highway robbery.'

Fairgreave tried to bluster, his eyes on the barrel of the pistol. 'Highway robbery? I am no common thief, sir, I am Lord Augustus Fairgreave and I—'

'A fine name but you remain a bully and a scoundrel. You are also a poor gamester and, what is worse, a poor loser.'

One of Fairgreave's companions leaned towards him and whispered something. Flynt strained to hear but caught nothing, although the judge evidently heard every word. 'It is true that you are three and I have but one ball in this pistol. But the question you gentlemen must consider is which of you will be in receipt of that ball?'

'You would risk the noose for a few coins?' Fairgreave said, his initial shock overcome by his natural arrogance.

'You would risk a hole in the head for the same? As for the noose, what I do would be in defence of self. What you do would be in furtherance of larceny.'

'And how would you prove that?'

The judge's pistol flicked away from Fairgreave for an instant. 'What transpires here is witnessed.'

Flynt realised with a sinking heart that the man's eyes were as sharp as his wits and he had spotted him in the shadows. Fairgreave and his friends twisted round, squinting into the dark.

'Step forward, stranger,' the judge shouted. 'Let us see you.'

Flynt sighed, for he had no option but to do as he was asked.

'Who are you, sir?' the judge asked.

'A pedestrian, like you,' Flynt replied.

Fairgreave peered at him. 'Why would a pedestrian hide in the gloom of an alleyway?'

'I was taken short,' Flynt explained, 'and had to relieve myself.'

The judge's lips twitched a little. 'I would know your name for any investigation into this matter.'

Flynt knew he could not reveal his identity. 'I think this situation can be resolved without recourse to the authorities.'

'I am the authorities, my friend.'

'Even a judge can keep some matters out of the public eye.'

The man who had whispered to Fairgreave strode towards Flynt and pushed him hard on the shoulder. 'Be off, whoever you be. This is no business of yours.'

Flynt did not like to be pushed by anyone. Ordinarily he would have pushed back but he was very much aware that his work here was intended to be covert. His orders were that he should not have direct contact with Fairgreave, and this inadvertent involvement was too direct for his liking. 'I am merely making my way home.'

The eyes of the man who had pushed him narrowed. 'You are Scotch?'

'Scottish,' corrected Flynt.

The man thought he had the upper hand and he played it. In fact he used both hands to propel Flynt backwards with a double thrust to the chest. 'Then take another route to whatever pisshouse you infest and leave us to our business, Scotchman.'

Covert be damned, Flynt thought and rapped the handle of his cane on the man's forehead. The move was swift and sharp and the man was unaware it had happened until silver made contact with flesh and bone. He blinked frequently, his mouth gaping as he stumbled back, one hand rising to the red welt already forming on his skin. Flynt had intended only to warn, not to incapacitate, but the individual was obviously not one to heed such a message. He roared in fury and lunged with arms outstretched, his hands tightened into claws as if he meant to scratch the skin from Flynt's bones. He didn't get far. Flynt sidestepped neatly and delivered a heftier blow to the back of his head. The man grunted once and pitched forward onto the road, his knees hitting the ice-hardened ground with force, his palms squelching in some particularly liquid horse droppings that had not yet frozen. At least, Flynt presumed the ordure to be horse for it was not unknown for some drunken sot to drop breeches if the street was deserted and squat where he stood. The man began to push himself upright again, curses flowing as easily as the manure had done from whatever creature left it, but Flynt had learned that once a man was down it was better he remain that way. He swung the cane a third time, feeling it crack against skull. He knew the hat and wig the man wore would soak up much of the force, protecting him from lasting damage, but the blow was of sufficient strength to lay him flat out, his face now landing in the remains of the putrid dung. Flynt inserted the toe of his boot beneath the man's chest and flipped him onto his back, for it was ignominious enough to have been bested without drowning in diarrhoea, be it equine or otherwise. He then whirled to face any further assault from

Fairgreave or his remaining companion. Neither of them had moved during the encounter but were staring at their erstwhile champion now recumbent amid the filth of the street with a mix of surprise and revulsion. Judge Dumont also watched, the hand holding the pistol now crossed over the other in front of him, his wide smile showing he had been hugely entertained by the display.

Fairgreave's attention finally shifted from his friend, who was now groaning and moving his leg as if trying to rise but lacking the strength to do so. 'Who are you, sir, that you would treat your betters in such a foul fashion?'

'Who I am is of no consequence. As to this fellow being my better, I would take issue.'

Fairgreave sneered and looked about to argue the point when Judge Dumont spoke. 'I would suggest you take your friend away from here, Lord Fairgreave. There is a sufficiency of detritus in these streets as it is.'

'Our business is not yet concluded, little man. I would have my funds returned.'

'Then you must take that up with the gentlemen to whom I subsequently lost it, for I am devoid of coin.'

'I would have proof of that,' Fairgreave said, reaching out towards the judge's pockets with intent to rifle them but stopping when the Queen Anne pistol was once more levelled in his direction.

'You forget my little friend here. And I would point out that the odds have now evened.'

Fairgreave's focus swayed between the judge and Flynt. He was a man who was unused to being denied his wishes and struggled to understand why it had occurred this night. As he deliberated, the tavern door swung open and Flynt heard a voice call out. 'Is all well, Captain?'

Flynt glanced back and saw Ned Turner with his arm around an amply proportioned Covent Garden Nun known as Drury Lane Tess. She was a buxom, good-natured woman who had clearly imbibed a surfeit of liquor, for she swayed like a thick oak in a storm as she did her best to focus upon the scene in the dark street.

'All is well, Ned, my thanks to you.'

Ned's gait hitched a little as he took in the scene, eyes moving from Fairgreave and his friend to the weapon in the judge's hand and finally to the man still sprawled on the ground. He came to a halt, Tess with her hands on his shoulder for support, her tongue already searching for an ear to probe. 'Be you certain of that?'

'A slight accident. The gentleman lost his footing and hit his head. His friends here were about to take him to seek a barber-surgeon, were you not, gentlemen?'

Fairgreave had sufficient wit left to realise that his particular game had run its course so he reluctantly gestured to his remaining friend that they should assist their wounded comrade. They hauled him to his feet, supporting him when his legs seemed unable to do so, simultaneously but unsuccessfully endeavouring to avoid the excrement smeared on his face, hands and clothes.

Fairgreave grimaced as he realised his hand had come into contact with something foul and treated the judge to a final glare. 'This does not end here. You may have the word of a gentleman on that.'

The judge slipped the pistol back into his pocket. 'Your word it may be. Whether it is that of a gentleman is debatable.'

Fairgreave's mouth opened and closed like a trout's as he sought a retort. Finding nothing, he instead helped cart his still groaning burden away. Ned Turner watched them go as he idly fondled the plumper parts of his paramour for the night, and when satisfied they had no intention of returning, gave Flynt a nod. Flynt returned the gesture with an appreciative bow, and watched as the crimp led Tess in the direction of Drury Lane.

'I thank you for your intervention,' said Dumont. 'I have no idea what would have occurred had you not been present.'

Flynt continued to regret that intervention even though it had been unavoidable, for the man's eyes were sharp as they studied him.

'That fellow called you Captain – you are a military man?'

'I was, but the rank is honorary.'

Dumont took a half step back as he considered this. 'Honorary, you say? May I ask your name? After all, I think it is only fair that I know the identity of my deliverer.'

Flynt was unwilling to part with that even now. 'I believe you had the matter well in hand without my intervention.'

He was sure the judge had detected the obfuscation but the man did not pursue. 'I remain unconvinced. I was playing a part, you must realise, for I suspect I would not have hit anything had I discharged my weapon. My marksmanship is far from adequate and my deliberate mien was merely a mask for abject terror.' He once more took Flynt's measure. 'Although I would hazard such incidents are not beyond your ken, friend.'

'I have encountered such men in the past, your honour.'

'You know I am a judge?'

Flynt jerked his thumb over his shoulder towards the Shakespear's Head. 'I was witness to at least part of your run of luck at the hazard table and heard it whispered among the gamesters you were on the bench.'

'They did, did they? It is heartening that my fame is so wide-spread. Was the person who informed you of my name a lawyer? A court officer?'

Flynt smiled as he thought of Ned Turner's profession. 'No, but he is acquainted with many guardians of the law.'

Dumont smiled back, understanding immediately. 'And those with whom they deal, I have no doubt.' He paused for a moment, then looked back towards the tavern. 'I feel some warmth is needed and also something to calm my vapours. What say, as a thank you for your service, that I buy us a brandy to fire our blood against this damnable cold?'

Flynt looked to where Fairgreave had vanished into the night, knowing well that he was unlikely to find him again. 'I would be delighted, your honour. But I thought you had lost heavily at the table?'

Dumont grinned and reached into his pocket, producing a purse fat with coin. 'Never trust a lawyer, my good captain.'